ALSO BY GLORIA CHAO

American Panda

Our Wayward Fate

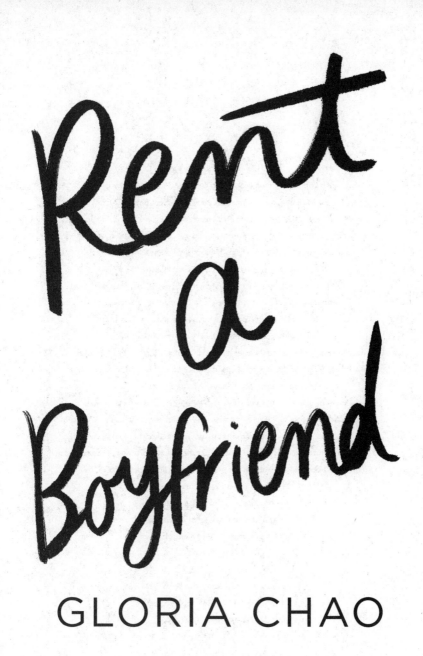

Rent a Boyfriend

GLORIA CHAO

SIMON & SCHUSTER BFYR

New York London Toronto Sydney New Delhi

An imprint of Simon & Schuster Children's Publishing Division

1230 Avenue of the Americas, New York, New York 10020

For information about special discounts for bulk purchases, please contact Simon & Schuster Special Sales at 1-866-506-1949 or business@simonandschuster.com.

The Simon & Schuster Speakers Bureau can bring authors to your live event. For more information or to book an event contact the Simon & Schuster Speakers Bureau at 1-866-248-3049 or visit our website at www.simonspeakers.com.

Jacket designed by Laura Eckes

Interior designed by Tom Daly

The text of this book was set in EB Garamond.

Manufactured in the United States of America

First Edition

2 4 6 8 10 9 7 5 3 1

Library of Congress Control Number 2020944929

ISBN 978-1-5344-6245-8 (hardcover)

ISBN 978-1-5344-6247-2 (eBook)

For Anthony, who taught me how to dream.

And for anyone who believes in love.

Author's Note

Dearest Readers,

This book is inspired by a real-life practice in some Asian countries where women hire fake boyfriends (often from classified ads, sometimes from a company) to bring home, commonly at Lunar New Year, to alleviate the pressure from family to find a husband. For this novel, I adapted this practice into a fictional diaspora version, with all details—including the company Rent for Your 'Rents—created to better fit the American setting.

I hope you enjoy reading this as much as I loved writing it!

Gloria Chao

Author's Note
about Mandarin Words

In this book, Mandarin words are spelled using the pinyin system, with the lines above the vowels indicating the pitch contour of the voice:

A straight line (ā), the first tone, is high and level, monotone.

Second tone (á) rises in pitch.

Third tone (ǎ) dips, then rises.

Fourth tone (à) starts high and drops, producing a sharp sound.

For some of the Mandarin phrases, I chose to depict the tones as the words are pronounced in conversation in my family's accent. There may be some discrepancies with other accents and dialects.

The meaning of the Mandarin words can be deduced from context—sometimes a vague idea, sometimes fully defined. The glossary included at the end is optional.

THANKSGIVING

Chloe

CHAPTER 1

MATCH.COM ON STEROIDS

November 26

Almost everyone is nervous introducing their boyfriend to their parents for the first time, but I was about to pee my sweat-soaked undies because, well, I hadn't met him yet either.

Since he already knew my life story (at least the parts that mattered), it was "highly recommended" we not meet before the "assignment" to minimize confusion. Which meant my Uber picked me up from the airport and picked him up a block away from the destination, i.e., my parents' house. Thanks, George, Toyota Camry, for earning your five-star rating by not asking us what the bejesus was going on.

As we waited on my parents' stoop and the doorbell echoed through my feng-shuied three-bedroom, three-bathroom childhood home, I couldn't bring myself to look at him. I was sure he was trained to keep the judgment out of his eyes, especially because I was the hand that was feeding him, but maybe the real problem here was that, between the two of us, he wasn't the one judging me.

My parents flung the door open and exclaimed, "Jing-Jing!" before wrapping me in hugs.

Over my father's shoulder, my gaze flicked to my "boyfriend" instinctively, to try to explain with my eyes that I had two names. But then I remembered I had only given the company (and thus him) my Chinese name, which was usually only heard between the embroidered wall scrolls of this house. My decision to list my legal but seldom-used name had been strategic in nature: to put it eloquently, I knew my parents would lap that shit up. It had to be true love if he was the first person outside our little Chinese community I'd told my real name to, right?

I'd dubbed myself Chloe in second grade after the hundredth joke about Jing-Jing sounding more like a song than a name. On a whim I'd started telling everyone to call me Chloe, after the universally loved golden retriever in my neighborhood. I think I had unconsciously hoped that there was some secret sauce in the name and that adopting it would make people like me more—which, sadly, worked. Soon it became who I was, more so than Jing-Jing. But the first and last time I had a friend over and she called me Chloe in front of my parents, my mom choked on her soy milk and my dad swallowed a tea egg whole. From then on, I kept my two worlds apart.

With the confidence of an Asian American who is used to lying to her dragon parents—the ones who named me Jing so I would shine in everything I do—I said, "Māmá, Bābá, this is Andrew." Shit. Had I remembered his name correctly? Not that it mattered: his "correct" name probably wasn't his real name anyway, so Andrew Shamdrew, po-tay-to po-tah-to, right?

My dentist parents examined now-Andrew up and down like he was a mystery specimen under their loupes. I had to hold back a laugh. In some ways, Andrew wasn't hiding anything, and in other ways, Insert Name Here was hiding everything.

"Āyí, Shūshú hǎo," he greeted my parents, calling them the polite and more-than-appropriate "Auntie" and "Uncle," which usually made me pause because the direct translation didn't make sense to

4

my Americanized ears. *You can't mix cultures that way,* my mother always scolded.

It took me a moment to notice that Andrew's perfect Mandarin had been spoken with a Taipei accent. Damn, this company was good, like Match.com on steroids, except they were matching him to my parents, not me.

Andrew smiled a healthy, toothy grin that made my parents' eyebrows shoot up in pleasant surprise. I wondered whether the company had paid for those sparkling, just-Cavitroned pearly whites.

"Aiyah, you have great oral hygiene," my dad said, which, okay, if it was that easy, why did I have to pay a make-your-nose-and-gums-bleed amount to rent Andrew today? Good aiyahs weren't easy to come by, but I guess anything teeth-related was a shortcut.

My mom's eyes darted to the UChicago crest on Andrew's zip-up sweater. That nontrivial detail had been my choice, and I still so clearly remembered checking—or I should say, clicking—the UChicago box after scrolling past Stanford, MIT, Yale, Princeton, and, of course, Harvard. I could've earned extra mooncake points (my parents would never eat brownies) for Harvard, but it had made the most sense to have "met" Andrew at school. UChicago wasn't the college my parents had wanted me to attend at first, but they had since come around after it became higher ranked than "most prestigious" Stanford down the street from us.

"Qǐng jìn. Qǐng jìn," my mother said as she ushered us in with over-the-top manners. With guests, she only had two extremes: so polite it was fake or so honest you wished she'd lie. I was grateful it was the first one. *For now,* my brain warned.

With a dip of his head, Andrew handed her the box of mooncakes he'd brought. God, was this in his training? Or had he grown up like me, in a traditional, we-stick-acupuncture-needles-in-our-faces-when-we-feel-bad household? I wondered if he also intimately knew the smell of Salonpas, the pungency of which made me simultaneously want to hurl and hug my parents—which, coincidentally, was a pretty accurate summary of my entire relationship with them.

Except . . . it didn't matter whether Andrew knew the stink of Chinese herbal medicine and how it sank its bitter claws into everything in the laundry. Because he wasn't actually my boyfriend.

My father ushered us to the dining room table, which, to my surprise, flaunted a crispy, golden-brown turkey in the middle. It was just sitting there lazily, as if there had been one every year instead of the zhàjiàng noodles, dumplings, and stir-fried hollow-heart vegetables, which now took a side seat but of course were still present—because how could you not have any Chinese food on Thanksgiving?

I briefly wondered what Andrew's Thanksgivings were like—did his family also eat Chinese food? Did he know the veggies were called kōng xīn cài?—before I snapped out of it and realized my parents were looking at us expectantly, eyes hungry but not for food.

Game. On. All I had to do was convince my parents that Andrew was the love of my life and theirs. Piece of (moon)cake, right?

Drew

CHAPTER 2

JUST ANOTHER DAY

leaned over and placed a caring hand on Jing-Jing's shoulder before pulling the chair out in a subdued manner—no flourishes. Her parents were classified by the company as Type C for affection, and those Type C eyes ate up my quiet, kind, zero-PDA gesture. (In Type A circumstances, I would have kissed her on the head or cheek; Type B, placed my hand on the small of her back; and Type C.2, I would've been a bit more theatrical with the chair pull).

Mrs. Wang nodded at me and smiled a genuine mom smile (meaning her eyes crinkled and her lips lacked any trace of judgmental pursing).

It was almost too easy.

Jing-Jing, who had been thrown off a little at first (such a newbie—I was clearly her first rental), quickly righted herself. "Andrew, you're always such a gentleman."

I'd chosen the name Andrew because it was close enough to my real name to prevent any potential mishaps but still different enough that every time it touched my ears, I remembered the part I was playing. And, of course, Andrew sounded all proper and good-boy and shit, best foot forward, all that important gobbledygook. It was funny how much of a difference an "An" could make, but trust me, that gap was huge. Those two little letters flipped a switch in my head, and as for the real me? I was so much more of a Drew, both literally and figuratively. I told my parents that if they were so hell-bent on me not being an artist, why did they name me Drew? Well, I used to tell them. We haven't spoken in years.

Hence this job. Great pay, amazing benefits including dental (which I now understood was a worthwhile investment for the company based on how Dr. and Dr. Wang gushed over my recently cleaned teeth).

I smiled at Jing-Jing, my lifted cheeks pushing into my frames, which were another subtle reminder of my role. My glasses had no prescription (unless it was a prescription for appearing smart and unthreatening to parents with Category 1 personalities), though I had added the blue-light blocker—might as well make those babies at least somewhat functional. I looked from the supposed love of my life (my second one this week) to her parents, and I softened my eyes by thinking about the new set of brushes I'd be able to buy after this commission. And, just like I was lying to all of them, I lied to myself that those brushes were the one thing missing. That they'd get me one step closer to fulfilling my dream (the real one, not the rotating ones I told clients' parents). Really, though, Successful Artist Drew was just another character I tried to play, except it was the only one I failed at.

Mr. and Mrs. Wang motioned to the food, and I dished some zhàjiàng noodles to Jing-Jing before passing the bowl to her parents. Man, it had been a while since I'd inhaled that sweet-and-spicy scent. It was the smell of our kitchen after the Chan boys—ahem, *men*, as my dad would correct me—played a sweaty, ultracompetitive game of basketball. As the aroma enveloped me, I heard his gruff, comforting, yet haunting voice in my head: *You've got to earrrn your noodles!*

I hated basketball. And now was not the time to be thinking of him, not when I had a different, fictional (read: loving) father to be telling stories about.

More plates were shuffled around, utensils clinked, and Jing-Jing shot me a nervous grin. I gave her a reassuring smile and nod; so far this was textbook. In fact, the silence was comforting, probably because of the familiarity from my childhood and from a chunk of the other jobs I'd done for Rent for Your 'Rents in the last year and a half. But as I spooned out some kōng xīn cài and the vegetable's garlicky sauce dribbled haphazardly onto my plate, there it was, at the back of my head, niggling like the goddamn parasite it was: *You and your family have so many issues because of this very silence.*

The collar of my shirt was suddenly choking me, but because touching it wasn't an option, I forced myself to think about anything else: what I was going to paint first with my new brushes, the smell of the food before me (which really was heavenly; the Wangs had gone all out), and—who was I kidding? All I could think about was how I couldn't breathe, how everything was closing in, and what the hell was I doing here?

I focused on the itch, which only made it worse. Mental note: ditch this brand and go back to Tommy Hilfiger despite the extra cost. Maybe if I told corporate how it had endangered my cover, they'd do the splurging for me.

Jing-Jing put her hand on mine, probably because she sensed my spinning from her front-row seat. How? I have no idea. Maybe she had a gift for this and should look into a position at Rent for Your 'Rents. When I glanced at her, she gave me a warm smile that extended to her eyes, and I found myself returning her grin.

Back on track.

Chloe

CHAPTER 3

ROUND 1

Wasn't he supposed to be the professional? Wasn't I paying for excellence, not nerves and awkwardness?

Or . . . was this part of it? Maybe he was playing the doting boyfriend who cared for me so much he was nervous about impressing my parents.

I tried to relax by reminding myself there was a money-back guarantee: If the operative did not achieve the mission of providing a boyfriend worthy of parental approval, as vague as that was, I could ask for a full refund. Heh, "operative," like he was James Bond, except he would be nerdy, well-mannered, and loyal—a.k.a. "guāi," as the website promised—and an Asian parent's dream. The operative's attractiveness was also assured to be high enough to promise cute babies, but not movie-star high as to invoke worries of future cheating due to endless opportunities.

Now that our plates were full of sides, my father stood over the turkey with a knife in his non-dominant hand and a fork in the dominant one. Hover right, left, above, poke the turkey.

Andrew looked to me for a moment, and I read the question in his eyes: he wasn't sure whether or not to jump in and help. To be honest, I wasn't sure either—my father liked to be the head of the house, but he also clearly had no idea what he was doing and wasn't a fan of embarrassing himself.

I smiled blankly at my supposed beloved.

"Shúshú," Andrew said, standing slowly, "you've been cooking for days, and I'd be honored if you let me do some of the work. May I serve you and Ǎyí? I probably can't carve it as well as you would have, so I hope you'll forgive any mistakes. But you deserve to rest and enjoy the evening."

Barf. It seemed way over the top to me, but my father was on the verge of humping Andrew's leg. Worth every penny, wasn't he?

As Andrew cut into the turkey and produced gorgeous, symmetrical pieces—was *that* in his training?—my father cleared his throat.

"So, Andrew, tell us about yourself."

"Yes, Jing-Jing has been strangely quiet about you!" my mother exclaimed dramatically. "You know, we were shocked to learn about your existence." Just as shocked as I had been when I'd made him up under dire circumstances two months ago.

My parents folded their hands on the table and waited expectantly.

I swallowed hard and tried to telekinetically remind Andrew what was at stake: my freedom from Hongbo Kuo. Disgusting, chauvinistic Hongbo, whom my parents wanted for me for all the wrong reasons, and who wanted me for even worse reasons. If it weren't for Hongbo, there'd be more money in my bank account and Andrew would be at some other poor girl's house this Thanksgiving weekend—and I meant "poor" in both senses of the word.

Andrew smiled easily, full of charm and, somehow, love. "Well, Jing-Jing hasn't been quiet about you! It's been such a joy hearing her childhood stories about the warm household she grew up in. I'm sure if I had known her when we were kids, I would've fallen in love the second I saw her teaching her Barbies math!"

My parents laughed heartily, filling the dining room with so much of the rare sound that, I swear, our austere photo of Yéye at the head of the table narrowed his eyes even more.

I imagined Andrew with a mental checklist, just working his way through every memory and factoid I'd uncomfortably offered up on my very extensive application—so extensive I'd even had to give them access to my contacts and social media to ensure my assigned operative didn't have a previous client who ran in any of my circles.

"Although," Andrew continued, "I guess that would've been a little strange given that I'm two years older, and when you're that young, two years feels like a lifetime."

"But not anymore," my mother added quickly with a smile.

I could practically hear her as if she'd spoken the words aloud: *Men mature slower than women, so marrying up in age is always a good idea, Jing-Jing. Especially because once you hit MENoPAUSE, the men will run right out the door—they hit pause on the marriage, that's why it's called that, I'm sure of it! So finding someone older means they'll look wrinkly too and won't flee.*

Sigh. I just . . . I can't.

For the record, Chloe does not stand for this kind of antifeminism, but right now I was Jing-Jing.

"If you're two years older, then you must be graduating this year," my mother said. "How wonderful!"

Andrew nodded. "I'm applying to medical schools right now."

"Thank goodness!" My mother slapped the table. "I just learned recently that getting into a good college isn't enough!" She turned to me. "Jing-Jing, do you remember Jeffrey Gu? He was the high school valedictorian last year and went to Stanford? Well, I heard he dropped out!"

I tilted my head side to side in a *well, sort of* gesture. "Jeff started his own company, Mămá. He left Stanford because he just received funding from a venture capitalist."

"He's a bum! He wears flip-flops and hoodies to work! And I heard he plays Ping-Pong and takes naps during the day!"

I held back a laugh. "I think Jeffrey Gu—one of *Forbes*'s latest Thirty Under Thirty tech CEOs—is just fine."

She shook her head at me. "Dropping out of college is never okay."

"Maybe it's okay if you've already raised a million dollars for your company," I mumbled. Then I noticed Andrew's tightened shoulders and realized we were getting off track.

"Anyway," I said, dragging the word out. "We were learning about Andrew, who is *not* a college dropout like Jeffrey Gu."

"No, he is not," my mother said fondly, giving Andrew all her attention. "Please, tell us about your family."

Andrew was focused on the turkey, his eyes unreadable. "Our families have a lot in common, actually," he answered as he dished a glistening cut of dark meat onto my mother's plate.

She beamed and nodded her thanks.

"My parents met in Taipei at church, got married, and then immigrated here for medical school. My older brother and I were both born and raised in Chicago, in a supportive church community."

"Chicago?" my mother interjected. "As in, they're still there?"

She'd always hated how far I was from the West Coast, and I knew the idea of having Andrew's parents nearby would please her. So of course he answered . . .

"Yes. They both work at the UChicago hospital."

Strangely, my mother's face darkened, the opposite of what I'd expected. The first time so far tonight, so overall I should be relieved, but I'd really thought I'd nailed all aspects of this.

Luckily, my father's eyes were about to pop right out of his skull. *Take that, Hongbo. Your family may be rich, but Andrew just checked the money* and *prestige boxes, sucker.* And yes, we might have been playing into the fact that my parents wished they had gone into medicine instead of dentistry after hearing too many "couldn't get into medical school?" jokes. I was not above cheap shots.

"What specialty?" My father's voice was only a smidge louder than a whisper.

"Surgery." A lauded field with a department large enough that my parents wouldn't bother learning how to google just to confirm. And my dad might have once hinted at wanting to be an oral surgeon, but he hadn't been accepted into any programs—if I was going to take a cheap shot, might as well go all out, right?

"Wow, surgeons at the University of Chicago," my father repeated, like he was trying to make the information sink in. My parents called the university by its full name, as if that somehow made it more prestigious.

"So you went to the University of Chicago because your parents guaranteed you a spot?" my mother asked Andrew with one eyebrow raised.

"I did briefly consider Harvard and Stanford, but I couldn't turn down a top biology program down the street from my family. Now, UChicago's biology may not be as good as its economics"—he nudged me with an elbow—"but not all of us can handle a major that rigorous."

Jackpot, on so many levels.

My father said, "You turned down Stanford?" at the same time my mother said, "You think economics is a good field?"

Yes, they were digs at me, but I would take the hit to remind them that UChicago was not a schlub school and that economics was not a "cop-out," "easy-A" major. Might as well get my money's worth and kill several birds, right? And the unexpected turkey on the table was a bonus dead bird.

I was smiling into my gravy, a little smug and a lot relieved, when my mother asked the last question I would've guessed. I mean, it wasn't even on the list I'd curated for Andrew, and that was the most comprehensive form I'd ever filled out, more probing than my college apps.

"What drew you to Jing-Jing?" she asked. Her eyes were dreamy, but I saw the malice beneath. How she was just waiting for him to admit he didn't know, or that, like her, he thought my smile was too wide, my hips and chest too small, my personality too anxious.

Andrew had flinched at the start of my mother's question as if the word "drew" had clued him in to what was coming next. He must have prepared for this—I mean, come on, this was the most obvious question a mother would ask, and even though I hadn't thought to put it on the list, surely the company had?

"That...," Andrew began slowly, "is a difficult question, because there are too many answers to choose from."

Barf. Please.

He turned to me and put a hand on mine briefly, so purposefully it felt timed, which it probably was. It took all my concentration not to pull away and to instead look at him as if I were gooey inside. It didn't work.

He chuckled, which startled me, and then said, "That's a perfect example right there. I love how she's so strong and independent she can't just take my compliment or enjoy when I graze her hand affectionately. So endearing, isn't it?"

My mother's raised eyebrows said *no*, but the way she was gazing at Andrew said, *Please marry my daughter.*

"But the very first thing that drew me to her? Was how her life is so neatly stacked into little boxes. I admire it, that kind of structure and discipline. I'm sure her success in life—being at UChicago and thriving—is due in no small part to this. And to you both, of course. I also love how passionate she is. I've never seen anyone fill out a mundane form with as much exuberance as her."

I almost burst out laughing. He winked at me, and a tiny frozen piece of my insides indeed melted into gooeyness.

My parents beamed at each other and at him (but not me), and we finished that restaurant-made turkey with gusto.

There was something about my parents wanting to impress Andrew that churned the guilt in my stomach. Except . . . they were the reason I was engaging in this convoluted charade. And yes, I was aware of the absurdity, in case anyone thought otherwise.

After chrysanthemum tea and pumpkin pie from a box with a hastily scratched-at price tag on top, the awkwardness notched up. To eleven.

My father cleared his throat, then gestured to the sheets stacked on the couch. "We're traditional, Andrew. We assume there's no . . ." He blushed.

"Hanky-panky," my mother supplied with a completely straight face. I wondered where she'd learned that phrase.

Andrew turned red as well, and, given the flush I felt in my cheeks, I guessed we were a pod of lobsters in that moment, minus Mom.

"Of course, Wang Āyí, Shūshú," he said, seemingly fighting the urge to take a step away from me. *You and me both, buddy.*

I bid everyone good night and made a quick exit. As I padded up the stairs to my childhood bedroom, my parents' gaze followed me, something foreign gleaming at the edges of their crow's-feet. Pride, I realized. Oh, if only they knew the truth.

I put on pajamas and brushed my teeth in a haze. When I walked by the circular mirror that I'd picked out in first grade, I cowered. I didn't want to see myself. Because what if I no longer recognized who that was?

I flopped onto the bed and squeezed my eyes shut. But the vision of my parents looking at Andrew and me with so much hope was burned into the backs of my eyelids.

How did I get here? I mean, I knew how I'd gotten here—with desperate lies that fed off one another and grew until I couldn't contain them anymore. So I'd hired a ringer: nerdy Asian James Bond. James Bong. Banh. The name is Banh. James Banh Mi, the best thing since sliced baguette with seasoned meat, cilantro, and pickled veggies.

Once I ran out of Bond puns, my mind wandered back to the web of lies I'd spun myself into.

The only way to distract myself was to focus on something equally horrifying but less painful. So I thought about every weird thing I'd said and done my entire life, like that time I met a cute guy in game theory and at the end of our conversation couldn't decide whether to say "Lovely chatting" or "See you," and I instead said, "Love you." God. Whenever that memory replayed in my head and I heard "Love you" in my sad, squeaky voice, I let out a whimper. Could I be any more pathetic?

Yes, by hiring a fake boyfriend.

I was my own worst enemy.

Eventually, around two in the morning, I threw the sheets off and went in search of some cold pumpkin pie.

Drew

CHAPTER 4

JUST ANOTHER NIGHT

I'*m helping her I'm helping her I'm helping her* . . .

Without fail, I always needed to chant those three words to fall asleep during a job. At night, alone with my thoughts, I always felt a tiny bit disgusting, maybe even a little cheap, despite the fact that I was anything but (now that I'd had dozens of perfect reviews, my prices were blush-worthy).

During the course of every assignment, there were always things that poked at my insecurities. In this case, Jing-Jing's mother speaking as if dropping out of college was the worst move ever (even if you had a million-dollar company to run) had made my college-dropout ears burn like hell. And Jing-Jing's response, though not the worst, hadn't soothed me any. Not that it was her job or anything. It just sucked. I already judged myself enough for a lifetime's worth, so did I need everyone else judging me too?

To fall asleep, I usually had to remind myself of the bolded section on the client's form, the one I always memorized. The answer to *Why do you need our services?*

I had never met the suitor Jing-Jing had written about, but now that I'd had one dinner with her, I could see her punching out her answer with forceful keystrokes, a little sideways purse to her lips. Amazing what you could learn about someone in a short time when your meal ticket depended on it. As with almost every single one of her answers, she'd gone all out, detailing how her parents and Hongbo's parents wanted them to be together for "all the wrong reasons," which revolved around their families having been friends for decades and believing their children would be a fantastic match despite them having nothing in common. Not to mention Jing-Jing's obvious disgust for him, which she had sort of tried to hide at first ("he's just not quite right for me, personally") but also not really, especially by the fourth paragraph ("I think even his mustache is evil—it twitches every time he mentions his Lamborghini, Sheila, which he named after the model who rolls around naked on top of a Lamborghini in some music video"). For the Wangs, it also didn't hurt that Hongbo's family was stupid rich due to the success of their tech company, No One Systems, which was, according to Jing-Jing, "thriving despite its founders not realizing that the period in *No. One* is important and that *No One* means something else." (I may have laughed reading that part.)

In her desperation to escape dating "one of my former bullies," Jing-Jing had lied about already having a perfect boyfriend. Her parents had agreed to give the supposed love of her life a chance— one chance—so enter Rent for Your 'Rents. Enter me. My mission (should I choose to take it, which, yes, I obviously did) was to win over the Wangs and make them feel secure enough in Jing-Jing's and my loving relationship to turn down the heir of No One Systems. Which meant that on this job, Andrew Huang had to be rich and successful, with a bright enough future to rival Hongbo's. Given how the Wangs had reacted to my parents' jobs plus my UChicago education and potential doctor future, we were right on course.

I was helping her. Providing a much-needed service. Without

Rent for Your 'Rents, what would she have done? She'd mentioned in her application that talking to her parents wasn't working, that they were convinced they knew better for her future than she did (man, did I know what that was like), so in some ways this position was honorable and not sleazy or a joke, right?

I wriggled around, trying to find that comfortable spot—you know the one, where you sink down so far it feels like you're melting. But I couldn't find it. My couch-bed was beautiful (burgundy leather, button-tufted, rolled arm), but it wasn't made for melting. Or any sort of comfort, really. Too cold to the touch, and not broken in enough to conform to my body at all. It matched the rest of this house in its clean, minimalist, not-quite-lived-in style. Sterile, like a dentist's office. The house was spacious for Palo Alto and the ridiculous pricing, but in another city it would have been on the smaller side for a family with two working dentists, I was guessing. Perhaps that explained the modernist approach to the interior design—an attempt to make it grander than the size and layout inherently were.

All in all, it wasn't the best or worst couch I'd slept on for a job. The jackpot was getting a king-size bed to myself, which had happened twice, and the range for other jobs had included bunking with a younger sibling, an air mattress on the floor, and even a sleeping bag in the dog's room (Denny was very friendly and cuddled me as I slept).

As I tossed and turned that night, I told myself it was because I was missing my Froot Loops pillow, the little one with the faded Toucan Sam that I liked to hug when I slept. The one my little brother, Jordan, had given me so long ago you could barely make out Sam's eyes now. I hadn't seen Jordie since my falling-out with my parents, and the most we caught up these days was exchanging **Are you okay?** and **I'm fine** texts once at the start of every month (a.k.a. the most he felt he could do without ruining his relationship with our parents too). Jordie was currently three months into his freshman year at Berkeley (the golden sheep to my black), and three quarters of the time I was glad I had dropped out of college so that he could afford to go now and do more with it, like study computer science instead of art history.

Maybe some late-night pie would help me sleep. Except, that was a creepy thing to do in a stranger's house. Even if I were her boyfriend, or maybe especially if I were her boyfriend, I wouldn't want to make myself too at home and overstep the imaginary boundary. Or perhaps I was oversensitive because of my first client, Michelle. Less than an hour into the job, I'd used the fancy soaps in the bathroom, only to be screamed at by Michelle's mother. Apparently, those "display-only" soaps (which, in my defense, had been located closer to the sink than the regular soap) had been in her family for fucking generations, as if that were a thing. Not that I'd know—the only family heirloom we Chans passed down was insecurity and an inability to communicate. Michelle was my only client who'd asked for a refund, but those damn soaps haunted me at night when I couldn't sleep, especially on jobs.

To get my mind off midnight pie, I started counting jumping sheep wearing different pajamas (the wilder the better, all designed by me, of course). And finally, *finally*, I started drifting off.

Then I heard footsteps.

Chloe

CHAPTER 5

MIDNIGHT MOONCAKES

Andrew's tall frame was smooshed on the couch, his back to me and his face buried between the cushions. It must be terrible to sleep in so many strangers' homes, feeling vulnerable, assuming a different identity. Unless the person I'd seen tonight was just him? Doubtful. At least he was well compensated for his discomfort?

Despite having grown up in this house, I stepped right smack-dab in the middle of the creaky step, the one that had been squeaky since I could remember and was identifiable by its crooked wood. I was so totally off my game here, even though the definition of "home" told me I should feel otherwise. My eyes darted over to the couch as I inched closer to the kitchen. Given Andrew's too-steady, too-quiet breathing, he must be awake. Whether it was my fault or not, I wasn't sure. I briefly considered abandoning my mission altogether, but . . . pie. Instead I tried to hurry past him.

I'd cleared the living room, my back now to him, when I heard, "Couldn't sleep either?" from behind me.

I pasted on a smile and turned to face him. After a couple of awkward seconds with me rocking back and forth heel to toe, I uncharacteristically admitted, "Most people can't wait to get home and sleep in their childhood bed, but it makes me a ball of—"

"Shénjīng," he finished for me. The Mandarin surprised me, enough to make my head pop back—*and your double chin appear,* my mother said in my head.

"Uh, yeah." *Except I wouldn't have said it in Chinese.*

"I picked up on your nerves during dinner," he said in a low voice as he stood and followed me to the kitchen. While I turned on the light and took a quick survey of our options, he continued, "Is it because I'm here and you're worried about how it's going? Because I can tell you from experience you can let some of that anxiousness go."

"Thanks," I said, even though my unease in this house had been present since way before I'd paid him into my life.

I grabbed the pie and some paper plates. But right before I dished it out, I pointed to him, then the pie, and raised my eyebrows to ask if that was what he wanted. His eyes widened in surprise before he caught himself and nodded at me.

My gaze focused on my busy hands as I asked, "Are you not used to people asking what you want? Because your job is all about pleasing others?" I briefly wondered what his family was like and what they thought of his Rent for Your 'Rents position.

"It's a rarity because of the line of work, yeah, but I assume most of the world is like that too?"

I shrugged. "People are selfish."

The silence between us filled with unspoken experiences, but the agreement was palpable.

My tongue savored each bite, rolling it around to mimic all the thoughts rolling around my mind.

"Don't you want to ask me more questions? Like why I did this?" I asked.

"I already know why." He was staring down at his pie.

"Well, you know what I chose to tell you, on paper." *And I may not have told you everything, because I just couldn't bring myself to.* "You can't fully understand from just a few words, can you?"

He shrugged. "You're pretty good with them."

"You flatter me—is that a reflex?"

He laughed, one short exhale. "No? Maybe? I don't know anymore."

"It's been that long, huh?"

"Yeah, I guess, and it feels even longer than it's actually been because I have to, uh, really immerse myself." He fumbled a bit, scratched his neck, and I backed off.

The little tics that manifested now almost made him look like a completely different person. One without glasses. When he shifted in his seat, I couldn't help myself.

"How do you do it?" I asked. "Turn off a part of your brain? Is it like a performance? Is it something you can train yourself to do?"

He sucked on his bottom lip. Eventually he said, "It's one of my rules that I don't really talk about this with my clients. Nothing about the company or training, and nothing about my personal life." His slight frown hinted at some kerfuffle from the past.

"Sorry. I wasn't trying to pry—I mostly wanted to know because I often wish I could turn off part of my brain. Just . . . constant worrying about stuff I know I shouldn't be worrying about, but knowing that it's not worth my time doesn't seem to do anything."

His eyes flicked toward my parents' bedroom. "Uh, I think you have a right to be worried about stuff. Stressed, even."

I laughed—loudly—and, having surprised myself, I had to muffle the noise so my parents wouldn't hear. Or maybe it would be good if they heard?

"Were they what you expected?" I asked even though I really wanted to ask, *How do they compare with the other parents you've met on jobs?* which would then seamlessly transition into *What are the*

*other girls like? Am I different? What's wrong with me? Can I talk to
one of them so I feel less alone?*

He smiled. "Yes. You're not my first, you know." He coughed.
"Sorry, I actually didn't mean for it to come out that way. I just
meant a lot of the client parents have similarities. Not completely,
of course, but I've seen enough to be able to make some conclusions
based on certain things I see." He gestured to the cabinets surrounding us. "Given how your parents boxed up the leftovers, I'm guessing
one of these is dedicated to recycled ziplocks and washed-out marga-
rine tubs."

I pulled out the drawer with the free plastic utensils, chopsticks,
and soy sauces from past deliveries, then opened the door to our cab-
inet dedicated to crinkled but "perfectly good" recycled foil and plastic grocery bags. We laughed together, and the guilt from poking fun
at my parents was quickly overshadowed by my wonderment that
someone else *understood*.

"And this clearly wasn't your first Thanksgiving with Chinese
food and turkey," I added. "Did a past mistake teach you that eating more Chinese food than turkey equals two mooncake points or
whatever?"

He laughed. "Mooncake points? I love that!"

I hadn't meant to let him in on that joke of mine, but now that he
approved, I wondered what other jokes he might laugh at.

"Speaking of . . . ," he said, then stood and retrieved the box of
mooncakes he'd brought. In front of me, he opened it and raised an
eyebrow exactly as I had with the pie. "This is the good stuff too,
trust me," he said.

We each snatched one, took a bite, and groaned. I'd never met a
mooncake I didn't like, but this was by far the best I'd ever had.

"You haven't eaten a mooncake until you've had one of these,"
he said.

"For real." I took three more bites in rapid succession. "How'd you find these? Does the company have, like, taste tests for this stuff?" I let out a short laugh. "Mooncake taster—what an awesome job. I'd apply in a heartbeat."

He gave me a tight smile.

"Sorry," I said when I realized I was asking him about the company not five minutes after he'd told me his no-company-talk rule.

"All good," he said with a shrug. Then he finished off his mooncake in two big bites, bidding me a muffled good night before he'd even swallowed.

Drew

Yes, we have taste tests. Because a mooncake can buy your way in. It's infinite mooncake points, if you will.

I kept that joke to myself even though I was pretty sure it would have killed.

Chloe

CHAPTER 6

FRANKENBĀO

November 27

We didn't do breakfast in this family. Which explained why, the morning after Thanksgiving, the dining table was covered in very, um, inventive breakfast food—Frankenstein's version of it, with pieces put together from different cultures to form one monstrous mess. *You can't mix cultures that way,* I always wanted to throw back at my mother, but she wouldn't get it. For the record, I think fusion food can be fabulous, but my mother is more concerned with presentation than taste, so giving her a buffet of ingredients to play with is similar to handing the kitchen over to my cousin's daughter, whose specialty is cheese-and-red-bean pancakes because "the yellow and red are so pretty together."

Andrew bit into a scrambled egg, ketchup, and Kraft Single sandwich on pan-fried raisin bread drizzled in ginger honey. How he didn't spit it out immediately was beyond my taste buds and certainly made me feel better about his backbreaking price.

He swallowed his sweet-and-salty lump with a grin. "Thank you for making me feel like part of the family so quickly, Wang Ăyí, Shúshú."

Ha. My parents were faking as much as he was. And nowhere near as well. I poked my misshapen ball of fried dough and cheese wrapped in a white fluffy bāo.

As Frankenbāo neared my reluctant mouth, our doorbell rang.

Saved by the bell. I dropped the monster, which, for the record, smelled exactly how I expected it would: not Chinatown sidewalk garbage on a hot day, but not edible, either.

Andrew, my father, and I all stood in hopes of using the doorbell to delay more bites, but my father held up a palm to insist he have the honor.

Andrew coughed a few times into his napkin, having stood too fast.

"Did you choke on a raisin?" I asked, rubbing his back like I guessed a good girlfriend would. I lowered my voice. "Because that's a perfectly normal thing to find in your scrambled egg–honey sandwich."

He let out a sudden cough-laugh, which made me jump.

"Hmm? Some inside joke?" my mother asked.

I nodded. Andrew and I shared a smile, but mine promptly fell when my father reentered the kitchen with a visitor in tow.

"Look who so kindly decided to drop by, Jing-Jing!" exclaimed my dad—now Vanna White—as he waved his hands up and down the visitor's body to present him to the table. My father's face was lit up like a Chinese New Year lantern, his previous hump-adjacent excitement over Andrew now forgotten.

My mother ran over and shoved an empty chair between Andrew and me.

For Hongbo.

Drew

This was most certainly Hongbo.

Slightly raised chin and half-concealed, half-on-display smug expression? He might as well have been wearing a name tag.

"Hey-o, boys and girls!" Hongbo said too loudly, followed by a chuckle.

Despite the obvious fact that I was here with Jing-Jing, like *with* with her, Hongbo marched right up to us and stuck a bouquet of bloodred roses under her nose.

"Roses for my rose," he said, nudging her with the plastic wrapping in an effort to force her to accept. "You look . . . rosy . . . as always."

He couldn't even sell the compliment, choking on the words as they came out. Amateur. He should've just pretended he was talking to his beloved Sheila, to which Jing-Jing had devoted an entire paragraph on her form. And, sadly, Hongbo didn't know Jing-Jing well enough to know her hatred of flowers, especially roses. *They're cliché, a waste of money, and a half-assed effort from someone who barely knows you,* she had written. Nailed that square on the head, hadn't she?

Jing-Jing sat there, frozen, her eyes downcast, so Hongbo threw the bouquet on the table, smashing my sandwich in the process. As classy as the Lamborghini T-shirt beneath his freshly pressed blazer. Yikes.

Hongbo was holding back whatever was on his mind, and not very well; his teeth were clenched so tight his jawline fluttered like a hummingbird.

What the hell was going on here? Hongbo obviously had no interest in Jing-Jing (I'd seen better liars kicked out of Rent for Your 'Rents on day one), yet something was driving this pathetic courting (if it could even be called that). Why bother, when this was all their parents' idea? He should be on our side, not theirs.

"Thank you so much for the flowers, Hongbo," Jing-Jing said, her voice small. This was not the girl from the application who had angrily typed (in the sixth paragraph) about the *misogynistic, philandering, sorry ass of a human* who was necessitating my paycheck.

"They're lovely," she continued, "but I can't accept them. It would be rude to my—"

Before she could finish, her mother rushed over and scooped up the roses. "Aiyah, you shouldn't have, Hongbo. So generous you are, just like your parents. Such fee-lan-therapists."

With disgust, Hongbo corrected her: "Philanthropists."

Mrs. Wang flushed all shades of red but recovered quickly. "I just heard about your parents' latest donation to the church, which was larger than any other donation ever given, a record they also previously held. Amazing! They've donated so much that everything should be named after them, but they're so humble and always refuse the recognition."

Right. Jing-Jing had mentioned in her application that the church was the pillar of their community, and Hongbo's family, as the biggest financial supporters, were like gods (but second to the real God, of course).

"Number One donors and Number One bachelor here," Mrs. Wang finished with enthusiasm.

Mr. Wang clapped Hongbo on the back. "We just invested a large chunk of our savings into Number One stocks. Do us proud, yes?"

Jing-Jing's raised eyebrows told me this was unexpected.

Even though all the attention was on him, Hongbo wasn't even pretending to listen. He was staring at me.

Realizing she wouldn't get anything out of Hongbo until she addressed the five-foot-eleven (hopefully great-at-art) elephant in the room, Mrs. Wang gestured to me and said, "Hongbo, that's Jing-Jing's friend. Anthony. I mean, Arthur? Adam."

Rent for Your 'Rents would have booted her on day one too.

"You know his name, Mǎmá," Jing-Jing said, still quiet. Then, a little louder, she told Hongbo, "My boyfriend's name is Andrew."

I smiled, trying to encourage her to be herself a little more.

Hongbo looked me up and down, then laughed until his eyes

grew watery. "I'm not intimidated by this pretty boy."

I kept my face neutral, not reacting.

"Well, if you're intimidated by just his looks, you should probably leave before he actually says anything," Jing-Jing said, shocking me. I quickly stifled my laugh.

Hongbo's eyes darted to my UChicago T-shirt. "Pfft. You think I'm intimidated by that safety school? I didn't even apply there."

"Because your parents had already paid your way into Stanford with Kuo Hall," Jing-Jing muttered, which I already knew.

Hongbo looked to Jing-Jing's mother, then father. "You know, my parents only blessed this union because of Jing-Jing's virginal reputation, but maybe that's not the case anymore. Maybe I should tell them to look elsewhere."

What the fuck? Had he seriously just said "virginal reputation"? I scooted closer to Jing-Jing, wanting to protect her not because of any role I was playing, but because this was all sorts of disgusting and no one should have to deal with it.

"No!" Mrs. Wang yelled, waving her hands frantically. "Anthony is just a friend; no hanky-panky happened. Jing-Jing is still considering your proposal, okay?"

Holy shit, this guy proposed to her? The fact that Jing-Jing had left that detail off her form threw me for a second. Was I supposed to pretend I already knew? Was I supposed to stay out of it since she, for some reason (or maybe I should say for obvious reasons), hadn't wanted me to know?

Gently, Mrs. Wang reminded Hongbo, "You so kindly gave us until New Year's, remember?"

"Only because she's so clearly lost her mind and needs time to find it!" Hongbo spat.

Really, an ultimatum? Come on, man.

"Girls beg for a chance to be considered by me!" Hongbo thundered.

"Aiyah, you know our innocent Jing-Jing," Mrs. Wang said as if her daughter weren't sitting right next to her. "She's so young and pure, and she doesn't know how to handle interest from the most eligible bachelor, the heir of the mighty Number One Systems! She just needs a little time to wrap her head around marriage, that's all."

"For the second and final time, the answer is no," Jing-Jing declared, grabbing my hand. "I'm with Andrew."

My training kicked in and I stood, the quickness of my movement pushing my chair back.

"I think it's time you headed out, Hongbo," I said as I continued to squeeze Jing-Jing's hand, presenting a united front (which I probably would've done even without the mission because, just, ew).

"Excuse me, but this is our house," Mr. Wang piped up.

Crap. I knew her parents were pro Jing-Jing & Hongbo, but their Category 1 personalities were also supposed to respond positively to a protective significant other.

As I faltered, unsure which way to play this, Jing-Jing also stood.

"Hongbo, please leave. You're not welcome here, at least not by me."

He shook his head at her. "Like I said, UChicago is a safety school, which explains why you have no brains, girl. I don't need this shit." He turned to me. "Be careful, dude, because she might be a lesbian since she said no to *this*." He gestured dramatically to himself, chin up, chest out.

How did he manage to be worse than the monster Jing-Jing had described?

Hongbo stomped off.

Mr. and Mrs. Wang trailed after him, yelling "Hongbo! Please! Jing-Jing doesn't mean it!"

I turned to Jing-Jing, whose fists were clenched. She slowly sat back down.

"Sorry," she said, her voice and eyes faraway. "I . . . He . . . It's—"

"You don't have to say any more," I interrupted.

We shared a sad smile. I hovered a hesitant hand over hers, unsure if she wanted comfort from me, Drew, while her parents were nowhere in sight. She reached up and grabbed it, and we sat in a quiet that would have been comfortable if not for the bang-your-head-against-the-wall words floating down the hall.

Tell your parents Jing-Jing is as virginal as they think.

Anthony's just a friend, we swear.

Jing-Jing's too innocent to know what's good for her, that's all!

"Do you want to get out of here?" I asked.

She didn't say anything. Just shot up out of her chair and led the way out the back door.

Chloe

CHAPTER 7

NON-FRANKENBĀO

As I stepped into our poorly-cared-for backyard—the previous owner's plastic pink flamingo looked like it had died three deaths with its deep-rooted brown smudges, toppled form, and gaping hole—I heard the front door open and slam shut. Then raised voices filled the air.

Andrew and I hurried through the once-white gate, through the neighbor's backyard, and onto the street.

Once we were a couple doors down—in the opposite direction Hongbo would be heading—I paused. Were we just going for a stroll or did we need a destination? And given that we were in my neighborhood, were we supposed to act like a couple to keep up the charade? Did we want to stay away for a bit so I could catch my breath, or should we use this very expensive time to let Andrew work his operative magic?

Even though it had been my plan—an uncharacteristically shoddy one brought on by emotions after my mother had told me I should be jumping at the chance to be with dreamboat Hongbo, who had "magically" set his sights on plain ol' me thanks to his parents' attraction to my golden vagina—all I could think about now was how I shouldn't need Andrew. How my no should have been enough. But it never was, not with my parents. When I'd tried to show them Hongbo's true puke-green colors, they had tsked and slapped me on the wrist for not recognizing how ol' Dreamboat was so dutiful to his parents he was willing to propose to their top choice regardless of his feelings, as if his motivations were driven by filial piety and honor, not access to his parents' bank accounts.

I jumped when Andrew's fingertips grazed my arm, and my previously tense muscles relaxed a smidge. I hadn't even realized how clenched I'd been.

"I can't believe my parents are pushing me to marry someone for money," I whispered. "And not just someone, but the worst person I know."

I closed my eyes and saw Hongbo from different points of my past: begging for a dog at age ten, then locking her in the laundry room as punishment for stealing the spotlight; peeing on the sandcastle that I'd spent hours on when I was six and he was twelve; telling the Asian community when I was in high school that I was such a prude I must've been born with a shriveled vagina.

"I'm really sorry, Jing-Jing," Andrew said, standing completely still beside me, waiting to see what I needed. Because I'd paid him for that. Everything in my life was fake: my parents, my suitor and his proposal, the boy beside me who was pretending to care.

I fought back tears. "I don't want to talk about it anymore."

"How about we go get some edible breakfast?" he suggested. "I know an awesome place around here." When I still wasn't convinced, he added, "They have a breakfast banh mi with fried egg and chili sauce. And, like, fifty ways to order matcha."

My James Banh Mi was offering to take me to banh mi. Normally, I'd have laughed, but in this moment I gave an unenthusiastic nod—it was the most I could manage when my mind felt like congee.

We argued over who would call the Uber, and I finally caved when he—the real him, I could tell—said kindly, "I'm off the clock right now, okay? Not hired Andrew—just a friend."

"Okay," I finally answered.

We said hello to Paul, 4.8 stars, known to be a good conversationalist, and piled into the back seat.

"Have you ever seen this much mayhem"—I gestured back toward the house—"on the job before?"

Andrew offered a sympathetic smile, but I couldn't read what was going on beneath his piercing gaze.

"Never mind," I said quickly. "I don't want to know." Not to mention, I was breaking his rule again.

Quietly he said, "It's never easy for the client."

Paul glanced at me in the rearview mirror.

We rode in silence despite Paul's exceptional conversational skills.

The cozy café had photos of menu items on the wall and a golden plastic cat by the register waving its arm to bring in good luck. The familiarity soothed me.

"Do you want to share the banh mi?" Andrew asked as we stood in line.

I found BANH MI OP LA on the wall in big block text, then looked at the tiny sandwich pictured beside it. "What? No way. I want my own."

"Sorry, force of habit," he replied quickly. When I tilted my head to ask for more details, he hesitated before explaining, "When I'm on the job, I try to eat as little as I can when the parents aren't present so I can stuff myself to the brim in front of them."

"Ah. Especially if they cooked, right?"

He nodded, then said with a grin, "For mooncake points. You know how it is."

"I do." *I really do.*

Maybe he was bending his sharing rule because he'd meant it earlier when he said he was just a friend right now. Or maybe my Hongbo situation was so pathetic that these were pity details and consolation jokes.

He added, "If you don't eat enough, you get in trouble, and two seconds later they turn around and tell you you're too fat, right? You just can't win! With . . . anything." His gaze shot to the floor, but only for a second before it returned to me. "I mean, I'm sorry about your situation. Seems like you're between a shítóu and a hard place, no?"

The Mandarin kept throwing me off. Why would he use it when he didn't need to? I'd understand if it was a word that didn't have an English equivalent, but, come on, "rock"? I had relayed to Andrew my mom's frequent complaints of *Why can't you embrace where you come from?*, so was this part of the job and he was Method operative-ing, staying in character even though it was just us? Or was he actually that in tune with his Chinese side?

"Do you want me to stop using Mandarin around you?" Andrew asked.

Damn, had he always been this perceptive, or did he learn it on the job?

"Nah, it's cool." Maybe I'd pick up the habit and get my mom off my back for a minute. But probably not. Especially when I didn't really *want* to start melding my two sides.

I pointed to the banh mi picture. "Let's get two. If you don't fin-ish all of yours, I'll have the rest."

He smiled at me, genuinely, and I wondered for a second what he would say if I let him in. If I told him the mess of thoughts I never shared with anyone because I was too scared how they would respond.

But I didn't have a chance, because he was already ordering for us.

We sat across from each other in a four-person booth.

"What do you like about economics?" Andrew asked as he fiddled with his straw.

I stirred my matcha latte to make sure there were no undissolved pieces at the bottom. "I didn't give you enough information in my application? This isn't a real date; you don't have to bother."

He choked on his iced matcha. "Sorry, I was just curious," he said a little sheepishly. "Forget I asked."

I sighed. *The more he knows, the better our mission will go,* I reminded myself, though I much preferred typing out my answers to telling him face-to-face.

"I like thinking about how the world works and trying to find ways to make it better. When I interned at a genetics lab in high school and realized you could answer hard questions and think about problems for a living, I knew that's what I wanted to do. Finding the right subject took a little time and a lot of reading and taking different classes, but . . ." I shrugged. "When I knew, I knew." *I just wish everything else in life were as easy.*

He nodded, and his faint smile and hooded eyes told me he understood what I was talking about. He had a dream, and I was pretty sure it wasn't doing this. But instead of asking—I didn't want to push his friend side too far—I just nodded back at him. It made sense why our interaction was so one-sided, but it was beginning to feel more like an interrogation than a conversation.

"Thanks for talking up economics to them," I said.

He looked at me like he couldn't wrap his head around my parents having a problem with that, but luckily, he kept those thoughts to himself. Though he did say, "You feel a lot of pressure from them, huh? That must be hard. I'm sorry."

I shrugged.

"So they named you Jing as in . . ." He broke off and wrote the character in the air with perfect stroke order. Quite elegantly, I might add, forming each of the three "sun" characters that comprised "Jing" like he was painting.

"Yes, that's me. Three suns. Shiny, bright, and so successful others can't open their eyes."

"Yikes."

"I know."

He pressed his lips together, hesitating, before saying, "Is that . . . why you always seem to be someone else? The shiny person you think your parents want?"

I wanted a fake boyfriend, not a deep dive into all the things I wasn't ready to face. I shrugged again, hoping he'd get the hint.

He leaned closer to me. "For the record, I like the version of you from the application, the one who stands up to gross Lamborghini-loving douchebags, not the one who feels like she has to be nice and smile for the world just because they said so."

You're the only one.

Our banh mis arrived and we dug in. Fried egg + crispy baguette + chili sauce = delicious enough to make me momentarily forget Hongbo, my parents, and Frankenbāo.

I had devoured mine, the yolk running every which way, and had just grabbed a piece of Andrew's when the flurry of texts arrived from my mother.

Jing-Jing where are you?
Jing-Jing don't be ridiculous.
Jing-Jing come home.
I need to talk to you right now!

I tried not to look at my phone each time it buzzed, but I couldn't not read her messages either, like she had some spell on me—which, I guess, would actually make me feel better if it were true, because then I'd have an excuse for my masochistic behavior.

"We should go soon," I said, licking the yolk dribbling down the side of my hand.

He nodded. "When you're ready."

Then we would never leave.

Even though I felt safe here, even though leaving was the last thing I wanted to do, I shoved the rest of the banh mi in my mouth and stood.

Chloe

CHAPTER 8
BÀI TUŌ

My mother dragged me into the den the second I arrived home without even a hello to Andrew, who was not that far away and could probably hear us.

"Tiān āh, Jing-Jing! Bài tuō!"

I ignored her wailing as best as I could. She wasn't really saying anything—just exasperated mutterings sprinkled with drama.

By her third "bài tuō," Jing-Jing was sent back to the box I kept her in when I was outside this house. "Aiyah, Mămá, bài tuō yourself!"

She crossed her arms. "That Chinglish phrase doesn't make any sense."

"Just like you." Her eyes glinted ominously. "I meant your logic, not your language," I added quickly. Why was I always taking such care of her ego when she never returned the favor?

"How could you treat Hongbo like that, Jing-Jing? You might've ruined your chances!"

"His family just wants me because of my reputation," I argued. "A reputation I didn't ask for."

"You're the purest of them all!" she exclaimed, which both made me want to laugh and cry. It was one of her favorite things to say to me. "You should be honored! Don't you know who he is, who his family is? Did I raise a fool? Beggars shouldn't be choosing."

My fists clenched and I shoved down my urge to throw some English mutterings her way. "I'm not a beggar—I have Andrew."

She raised one eyebrow. Then the other.

"And unlike Hongbo, Andrew *sees* me. Didn't you hear what he said about how he loves my organization, my neuroses that you claim aren't attractive?"

Her lips pursed to one side. "That's just one thing."

"One thing you claimed was a problem. It's not a problem for him—it's a plus." And there it was: the fracture in her wall, visible from the fact that she was now chewing on her upper lip even though it would remove some lipstick. I had to barge through and topple the walls now, freeing her—and subsequently me—from Hongbo's hold. "It's just one thing, but Hongbo doesn't even *know* that about me, let alone have an opinion on it. He doesn't know anything about me."

"But you went on that date—"

"No, you tricked me into going on that date."

She made a disapproving *tsk*. "I tricked you because you were too naive to see the golden opportunity in front of you. What's that English saying? Something about a golden duck laying money nuggets?"

"Yup," I said, even though Aesop was turning in his grave.

"You let that gold duck run away without even reaching a hand out to catch it!"

I sighed.

A mix of sadness and anger clouded my mother's eyes.

"Hongbo didn't learn a single thing about me that night," I told her. Again. "He brought me to a strip club!"

"Boys will be boys."

"Andrew doesn't go to strip clubs."

"How do you know?"

"Because he's not a disgusting douchebag."

She shook her head. "All boys do that. Some just hide it better than others."

"So Bǎbá goes to the strip club?"

"I'm sure he does, but as long as he provides for our family, I don't need to know about it."

Jesus.

I tried another tactic. "Don't you see the way Andrew looks at me? How much he cares?" I was paying a hefty sum for those professional glances.

"You still have a young person's view on relationships. Sometimes financial stability is more important than other things, which can fade."

"Well, Andrew's family is well-off too. I've seen their house." Man, was I desperate.

"They can't be as well-off as the Kuos—their company went public."

"If you would stop kissing Hongbo's trust-fund ass for one second, you'd realize what a huge mistake you're making discounting Andrew. His parents have family money too, in addition to their surgeon salaries." *This is all part of the plan, to get Hongbo out of the picture,* I told myself. But I was still ashamed of what I'd resorted to, playing into my mother's shallow standards and acting as if family money were an essential part of a relationship.

I hated who I became with my parents.

My mother turned my words over in her head, frowning as she deliberated.

Finally she nodded. "Good for you, Jing-Jing. I hope you can keep him interested. Won't be an easy task if he's as eligible as you say."

She whisked into the next room, and through the doors I heard a muffled "Andrew, would you like to join us for a game of mahjong?"

Which I—and thus Andrew—knew translated to *I'm going to interrogate you using the ruse of a friendly game.* Phase two had begun: my mother was starting to give him a chance. I was so relieved I almost started crying, but I had some tiles to shuffle.

Drew

CHAPTER 9

PÒNG!

fter Jing-Jing and I declined lunch with a strategically timed "The delicious breakfast filled us up—we couldn't possibly eat another bite!" the Wangs brought out a collapsible square table. (Was it specifically bought for mahjong?)

We settled in, shuffled, and stacked the tiles in silence. Five minutes later, we'd each had a few turns, there was a growing discard pile of directional tiles in the center, and it was *still* deathly quiet. Like this was the World Series of Mahjong, golden bracelets at stake. Jing-Jing had warned me via application that it would be intense and her mother would try to learn things about me from my strategy, but I wasn't completely sure what that meant. So I stayed on guard (on the inside, while acting relaxed on the outside).

"Who taught you to play?" Mrs. Wang asked me, breaking the silence but not looking up from the tiles.

It was part of my training—rounds and rounds against other operatives so we could become good enough to impress Category 1–3 parents, and to throw games for Category 5–7s. "My wàipó," I answered, because Category 1a hearts melted at the thought of grandmas passing knowledge (especially Chinese culture–related knowledge) down to their grandsons. "She was tough to beat," I added with a chuckle. "I have so many wonderful memories of playing with her."

My real wàipó was stone cold and hated my love of art because it reminded her of her penniless husband. *Huàidàn*, she used to call me. Rotten egg. Which was better than what she used to call my paintings (*lèsè*, for "garbage").

I discarded a red *middle* tile. "And she used it to teach me lessons about critical thinking, planning two steps ahead, stuff like that."

"Oh?" Mrs. Wang raised an eyebrow.

Maybe I was flying too close to the sun, drawing too many parallels to her. "But mostly she just wanted to spend time with me doing what she loved. We'd play with my older brother and one of his friends," I added, hoping for a distraction and another mooncake point. (That term still made me smile so much.)

She clicked her fingernails on the table. "Ah, you have an older brother. I'm surprised he didn't come up sooner."

He had (I'd mentioned him yesterday). I was sure of it because I'd been waiting for the usual questions to come, but Mr. and Mrs. Wang had been too focused on my parents. Instead of pointing that out (and contradicting Mrs. Wang unnecessarily), I just told them about my fake brother: "His name is Peter and he's a computer scientist at IBM." Big enough company that it wouldn't invite potential truth-revealing conflicts, and a cushy, money-making job to ensure that he wouldn't become a financial burden and would be able to support my parents as dictated by firstborn-son expectations (which I knew from Jing-Jing's form was something the Wangs worried about).

Both her parents nodded. Sometimes I wondered—if my words were too perfectly curated, would they seem too good to be true? So far, that hadn't been a problem on any of my jobs, but what if several instances plus time led one of the parents to figure out the truth down the road? Well, I guess I wouldn't know if that happened. I had no idea what the clients did after my time with them. (Was there a horrific breakup? Did they continue telling their parents we were together but I was otherwise occupied?) But that wasn't my prerogative, so much so that it was a company rule. *Not your prerogative, Operative.*

I dropped a *seven* bamboo tile.

Mrs. Wang raised her eyebrows. "Either you have a fabulous hand or you don't know what you're doing."

Or I just don't have any other bamboo tiles and it doesn't make sense to hold on to it.

Jing-Jing rolled her eyes. "That's not a Nash equilibrium," she mumbled.

"What's that?" her mother said.

"Nothing," Jing-Jing said even quieter.

"No, go ahead and tell me. I'd love to know what you think I'm missing when I've been playing mahjong for twice as long as you've been alive."

A switch flipped in Jing-Jing. "It doesn't matter how long you've been playing when game theory says—"

"That's enough," Mr. Wang said, a pained tilt to his lips.

This was way worse than silence.

My inclination had been to win (if I could) in order to prove to the Wangs I was smart enough to match their incredibly intelligent daughter (which I wasn't, but I needed *some* way to trick them into thinking that, and mahjong was a good one). However, her father definitely had an ego, and so did her mother (especially with mahjong, it seemed), so there was some risk with that too.

I paid attention to what they were discarding: useless directionals and other non-suit tiles, plus numbered tiles from the two ends. They were playing it safe, not wanting to help anyone else, or worse, "drop the bomb" and discard the winning tile (leaving them to fork over some dough—or plastic chips, in our case).

After a few more circles around the table, I was pretty sure both Mr. and Mrs. Wang were making their hands worse by only discarding the safer tiles.

Okay. I decided to focus on maximizing my chances of winning, even if it meant taking risks. Especially because that was how Jing-Jing was playing, and there was something romantic and poetic about our united front, even in mahjong strategy, right?

After another "risky" discard on my end, Jing-Jing beamed at me, already catching on to my plan.

And she didn't even have mahjong training with Master Liu. (There aren't actual mahjong masters, to my knowledge—he just insisted we operatives call him that.)

I smiled back at her, and for a moment it felt like it was us against the world. Er, well, us against her parents, who were indeed formidable foes.

"Pòng!" I exclaimed, grabbing the *one* circle tile Mrs. Wang had just dropped and melding it with the other two in my hand. If she wanted to drop the numbers on the ends, I'd take advantage of that. This must be that equilibrium thing Jing-Jing was talking about.

Jing-Jing and I continued to "pòng" and "chī" her parents' tiles, but at the expense of dropping risky pieces, which they picked up. And with each declaration of "Pòng!" or "Chī!" it felt as though a one-against-all game had become team versus team.

No one said anything as I declared, "Hú," and pushed my winning hand onto the table to reveal my tiles.

Mrs. Wang sniffed at me. "You're reckless."

"But it worked," Jing-Jing said with a laugh. She was gradually becoming more like the girl from the application, the one with oomph and humor and a sparkle hinting at the three suns' worth of light beneath. I stared at her with a lopsided grin before catching myself and wiping it off, only to realize that, wait, I was *supposed* to be looking at her like that.

Christ, I had to pull myself together.

Eight minimal-talking games later, I had won four, Jing-Jing three, and Mrs. Wang one.

"You're ganging up on us," Mr. Wang joked with a deep chuckle. "Is the secret that you're working together but your mother refuses to help me?" He turned to his wife. "Come on, Lǎo Pó, help me out here."

I knew that Chinese husbands sometimes called their wives "old woman" in Mandarin in the same way someone might say in English "ball and chain" or "little woman" or even "honey" (as I'd heard one man claim, "It's endearing!"), but it still jarred me when I heard it. (And I could tell Jing-Jing didn't like it but was more used to it.)

Mr. Wang tapped the table in front of his old woman. "Drop something tasty for me to eat, hmm?" he joked, referencing how he could only "chī" or "eat" a tile to form a run from the player before him, a.k.a. his wife.

"Tiles are about as tasty as anything else around here," Jing-Jing whispered to herself, but I heard and laughed. Her eyes widened in surprise, but then she joined in, loud and hearty.

I winked at her and she graced me with a cheek-to-cheek smile.

Mrs. Wang used her clear plastic tile holder to push her latest losing hand facedown on the table. "Okay, I've had enough. Andrew, you certainly are reckless, but I guess you know enough to use it to your advantage."

Jing-Jing pulled her face down in shock, then mouthed *miracle* to me as she tipped her head and thumb in her mother's direction, exaggerating so her mother would see.

Mrs. Wang swatted her daughter's hand down. "I'm a very nice person," she said gruffly, on purpose, before letting out a short, one-syllable "Ha!" Then, to my shock, she asked, "Are leftovers okay for dinner, Andrew?"

She strode to the kitchen and I hurried after her, calling out, "Yes, of course! Let me come help."

Was my victory not limited to mahjong? Fifty mooncake points!

Chloe

Had Andrew just won my mother over a smidge, and through *mahjong*? How many mooncake points did that impossible feat equal?

Dinner was a strange meal of Thanksgiving sides plus a turkey soup my mother had made from the otherwise useless bones. But the strangest part was how Andrew stole the show and became the center of the family.

As he filled the otherwise silence with stories about playing basketball with his father, moon-gazing with his mother, and indulging in Sichuan food at the holidays—all fake, I presumed—my parents ate up his charm along with the leftovers.

When he discussed his family's deep involvement in their church and mentioned bringing me with him to Sunday services, my mother's eyes bugged out of her head.

"Why didn't you tell me sooner?" she gushed. "Aiyah, what good news!"

I couldn't stop beaming as I dreamed of a life without the Kuo family sniffing around my twenty-four-karat vagina.

After dinner, I started to wash the dishes, but Andrew approached me and said, "Go spend time with your parents; I got this."

He jumped in, grabbing a dirty fork and scrubbing it in the worst way possible—petting it with the sponge as though it were a timid dog.

"How did they not teach you proper technique?" I asked in a joking tone. Wasn't impressing parents with dish scrubbing, like, day two?

He laughed, low and rumbly and sincere, as if it was just for me.

"They did," he whispered back. "Part three of orientation." Then he continued flailing the sponge at the fork with exaggerated wrist waves. "But it's just too easy to make you squirm," he teased.

I snapped the dish towel in his direction, spraying him with a few droplets. He yelped, dropped the fork, and grabbed the dish soap, aiming the nozzle at me.

"Truce!" I yelled, throwing my hands up in surrender.

He aimed toward the ceiling and squeezed, scattering a few bubbles in the air before putting the bottle down with a chuckle. "You don't have anything to worry about; I would never."

"I would." I made a sudden lunge for the dish soap.

He flinched, and then when he saw I was just joking around, we both laughed.

Without thinking, I poked him in his side. Genuinely. Flirting. His smile was wide as he started to lean toward me—maybe to poke me back?—but then everything changed in the same moment: the playfulness melted off his face, and his body recoiled. Then he cleared his throat and exited the kitchen, leaving a chilly trail behind him.

What had I been thinking? We had a few fake moments and suddenly I was poking him for real even though I'd never poked anyone else before? Pathetic. Almost as pathetic as someone trying to flirt by poking.

I cringed so much a tiny groan escaped my lips. Then I heard movement from the corner. When I turned, I saw that my mother was watching from the other doorway, arms crossed and a single eyebrow raised. Our eyes met and she ticked her chin in my direction, then left. I had no idea how to read that. Or how long she'd been standing there.

Leaving the rest of the dishes unwashed, I returned to the dining room to join the after-dinner chrysanthemum tea. My parents were chatting easily with Andrew, and I slipped into my place at the table.

But something had changed with him, with the poke, and it

hadn't reverted back yet. I laughed in the right places and smiled when Andrew grinned at me, but unlike before, the spaces between were now empty. My parents didn't seem to notice, perhaps because the spaces with them were always empty and they couldn't see the difference. Still, though, I worried they'd notice at some point. And besides, I had paid through the nose and gums—I deserved a better performance.

I decided to talk to Andrew later, when my parents were asleep, to make sure we were still on the same page. And so he would know that the weird moment by the kitchen sink had just been part of my act, a clear failure, and to be forgotten. Forever.

Drew

CHAPTER 10

LINE

ater that night, lying in my makeshift bed, my face toward the cushions, I heard footsteps. They halted by the couch. Waiting, assessing. I tried to breathe as if I were asleep, but I sounded gaspy with a side of sleep apnea. Was it better or worse for her to know I was faking?

When Jing-Jing had poked me, I'd had the urge to poke her back, which should *not* have been my first thought. Her parents hadn't even been watching! And had they been (and I should have assumed as much, as per Rule 26—never drop character while the parents are under the same roof as you), I should have been thinking about how the Wangs' Type C classification prescribed a hand graze or bright smile in return, *not* flirting with her as I would in front of Type A parents or, yikes, on a date.

To be completely frank (and Drew), I might not have been in operative mode for a chunk of that last interaction (which, what the hell, had never been an issue before).

Why did she throw me off my game? Why was it not about formulas and trained responses when she was around?

Had her poke been real? Her expression had shifted from playful to embarrassed (maybe even ashamed?) when I'd brushed her off. But it didn't matter what she'd been thinking or possibly feeling. *That* couldn't happen. It was too messy. Which was why I had swung the other way and acted so cold.

Rule 5 of the Rent for Your 'Rents Operative Handbook (a rule I had memorized but never thought twice about until today): Always know the line between the job and reality.

The mission, her future, and my livelihood (and thus my artist dreams) were on the line, pun intended.

Find the goddamn line, Drew, and dig it into the dirt until you never lose it again.

I continued with the wheezes until she tiptoed away toward the kitchen. I counted sheep (one dressed in glow-in-the-dark pajamas, one in a giraffe onesie, and three sheep masquerading as a clump of cotton balls) until I truly fell asleep, no midnight mooncakes in my stomach.

Chloe

CHAPTER 11

HOOK, LINE, SINKER

November 28

accidentally slept in the next day, having stayed up too late wondering why Andrew had pretended to be asleep when I came downstairs around midnight. Had I done something worse than I'd realized and upset him? Was he scared I was into the fake him and was now distancing himself to set me straight? Had he . . . felt something for real too? I quickly convinced myself it was a hard no to that last one, given how unlikely it was.

Also, did he really think he was fooling anyone with that laughable heavy breathing?

When I padded to the kitchen early afternoon, only my mother was present, eating congee at the table. Honestly, I so dreaded time with why-don't-you-wear-more-makeup Māmá Wang that I would have preferred it to be the "love you" guy from game theory sitting there.

"Where's Andrew?" I asked, sliding by her to put the electric kettle on for some green tea.

"A few patients called with emergencies and Bǎbá decided to handle them with Andrew's help so we could have some girl time."

My hand slipped and I missed plugging the kettle into the outlet. "What? No!"

I hadn't paid all this money for Andrew to sit around suctioning my dad's pulpotomies. And if he was going to spend the day with anyone, it should have been my mom, not my dad, because turn Mămá Neck, and Head-of-the-Wangs Băbá would be swayed too, I'm just saying.

My mother waved a hand at me. "Oh, stop worrying. It's just a little male-bonding time."

"Yeah, and maybe they'll hit up a strip club after."

My mother snort-laughed, and in my surprise I laughed with her.

"You've always been my funny girl," she said, her tone softer now.

My nose and eyes burned. She was so awful with other people around that I often forgot she was sometimes different when it was just us—extra emphasis on the *sometimes*. Was she playing the part with company or with me?

"So sometimes I'm funny, and other times those same jokes are disrespectful?"

She swatted the air. "You're disrespectful when you challenge me, joke or no joke. Why do you always have to do that? You know I just want the best for you."

"Yes, wanting the best for me with your great priorities, like how my future husband needs to have money and a double eyelid, which you've been telling me since I was, like, five."

"Andrew has both of those," my mother said with a smile. "I can already picture your cute babies. *With* eyelid folds."

"Could you be more shallow if you tried?" *And did you have to go from zero to sixty billion in one second?* I'd been desperate for her to just accept him, and now we were already talking babies?

My mother threw down her napkin. "Do you want your kids to be made fun of? To face more racism than they're already going to? Having a fold in their eyelid will help them blend in a little more."

That was *not* what I'd been expecting. But why was I so surprised? Whenever I was ready to tell her off or stop caring, she always found a way to give me a piece of her. Was it manipulation or sincere? Did it matter? Because each time, I fucking bit the hook and sank myself. Sometimes I wondered whether things would be different if I had another person to lean on, or at least more friends, but that probably wouldn't change much; she would always be my mother, and somehow that bond held more weight than anything else.

My mother put down her spoon and joined me by the kitchen island, making my tea for me the way I hated: by taking already steeped-for-hours tea and adding lukewarm water to it. She was always scared of me burning my mouth and didn't care that it was undrinkable.

"Aren't you the one who always tells me mouth tissue turns over in just a few days?" I asked softly. "Is burning your palate really all that bad?"

"Is wanting your daughter to be most comfortable all that bad? I leave this on the counter when you're home," she told me, pointing to the bitter mother tea.

I stopped resisting and, as usual, took the cup and thanked her.

"You know, Jing-Jing," she said, gesturing for me to join her at the table, which I did. "I'm starting to feel like I have nothing left to teach you. You stopped needing me so long ago. Mahjong felt like the last thing I could offer, but you don't even need me for that."

Isn't that a good thing? I couldn't help wondering.

She tapped her fingers on her own non-bitter cup of tea. "I kept thinking you and Andrew were still in the honeysweetie phase—or, no, I mean, you know what I mean—"

"Honeymoon," I said quietly, feeling bad even though she had asked.

"Yes, honeymoon phase. It almost felt like an act until I saw you two yesterday at the sink. I don't know what was going on, but it was the first time anything felt real. I was going to warn you that the honeymoon phase is too early to know what the future holds, but maybe you two are past it."

Well, shit. She was way more perceptive than I gave her credit for. My pits were starting to sweat thinking about how all of this could blow up in my face if she saw just a little too much. Honestly, I hadn't thought about it before because I felt like my parents hardly noticed anything with me, but in reality, they just noticed what they wanted to, and the problem seemed to be that we deemed different things important. But if I shared my mother's belief that incoming pimples were devastating and "priority number one," then yeah, she was the most perceptive person in the world, noticing my undergrounders before I was even aware of them.

"I know you're smart, Jing-Jing. But you've barely had any boyfriends, so maybe I can teach you one last thing: All relationships have problems. It's how you solve them that matters." She laughed, one short exhale. "And I've had experience with that!"

She clapped her hands twice. "Okay! Since the boys are away, hurry and eat so I can take you out for a facial and some new clothes!"

My mind knew she was being generous, that it would be nice to do something together and that this was her way of showing me love, but I also couldn't ignore that it was always *her* thing, it was usually about my appearance, and I was just so tired.

"Can't wait, Mǎmá."

Drew

CHAPTER 12

DR. HUANG

Human mouths are frigging disgusting. This was most certainly not in my training. (I'd have to tell corporate to add a Don't Upchuck after Contacting Human Fluids course.)

"You okay, Fangli?" Jing-Jing's dad asked through his mask.

The middle-aged patient gave him a thumbs-up, unable to do more.

I'm not okay! my brain screamed, but luckily my face mask covered a lot. It would also catch my vomit, right?

In my year and a half at Rent for Your 'Rents, I had been covered in spit, yes (when Michelle's mother yelled at me about the soaps and a spray accompanied every third consonant), had worn a mask, yes (at Grace's house, because her nǎinai was a hundred and we all had to cover up so she wouldn't get sick), but no, I'd never been covered in spit while wearing a mask that suddenly felt too thin. All while holding *tools* in a stranger's mouth.

"To the right, Andrew," Jing-Jing's father said sternly, and I tried not to look at the puddle of spit as I directed the thick white suction tube toward it.

Shit, and I was supposed to be a promising medical student. This might be the closest I'd ever get to having my cover blown.

Keep yourself together and the bile down! I yelled at myself. Fangli was the last patient today, but I hadn't gotten better with experience. Somehow worse, it seemed.

I tried to pretend Fangli's mouth was just a canvas, and our goal was to create some art. Oh God, and now look, some blood—I mean, red paint—to use.

"We hit pulp!" Mr. Wang declared triumphantly. "That means we're into the part of the tooth that houses the nerve, so we'll put medication in to alleviate poor Fangli's pain, and we'll do the root canal—"

"Ooot cawnaw?" Fangli said, her mouth still open because of the bite block.

He patted her assuredly and amended, "We'll do the *painless* root canal on Monday. So this is actually the start of the root canal procedure, but because today's just an emergency visit, we'll stop here and use a temporary filling over the medication. Name of the game today is no pain, right, Fangli?"

She nodded ever so slightly, which to me felt dangerous given how many power tools were in her mouth. Sheesh.

Since the mask limited my reaction options, I tried to show with my eyes how fascinated and not gross I found all this gobbledygook.

"You like art, Andrew?" Mr. Wang asked, mixing the medication on his tray.

Ha. Life can be funny sometimes. "I suppose."

"Well, dentistry is like medicine, but it requires proficiency with art and your hands, even more so than most doctors." He cleared his throat. "But, er, of course your parents know that, being surgeons and all."

"Uh-huh." I moved the suction around, trying to tell myself it was just water, perfectly normal and not bacteria-filled.

Note to self: When possible, lean toward playing the future archi-tect, computer scientist, lawyer, or CEO—any profession where it's okay to look as nauseous as I feel in a medical setting.

Thirty minutes and too many hand washes later (I hoped Mr. Wang wouldn't notice how much less soap he had now), I threw my borrowed white coat into the hamper and took a seat in the Wang Dental Palace waiting room (I was *not* sitting in any of those disgust-ing operatories, even after I saw how much disinfectant was used).

"Andrew?" I heard from down the hallway.

Even though I wanted to call out *What now?* and stay where I was, I forced myself to get up and make my way to him. Instead of walking right in, I peeked around the door to his office, hoping it'd be quick. "Yes, Shǔshú?"

He gestured to the chair in front of his desk as he swiveled away from his computer and toward me. I loped in and sat with my ankles crossed (relaxed but respectful). I sincerely hoped he couldn't hear my beating heart from where he sat.

"Andrew, I—" Then he cut himself off and started over. "Look, you're a good kid. But Jing-Jing's my only child. Her mother and I are very protective of her—her mother more so than me—and when it comes to Jing-Jing, I defer to my wife because she knows our daughter best." *Does she?* "And look at what her nurturing has done so far! Jing-Jing is living up to her name!"

He cleared his throat by coughing into his fist. "I don't know what Jing-Jing's told you about . . . other suitors, but you have to understand that we just know certain families well. And we haven't met yours—hadn't even met *you* until two days ago! I'm sure you've noticed I'm older than my wife"—I hadn't, and Jing-Jing hadn't mentioned it either—"and so for me, at this point in my life, I just want to make sure she'll be okay."

"I understand," I forced myself to say.

He gave me a curt dip of the chin. "Good. So . . . I know yesterday may have been a bit awkward for you"—*a bit?*—"but if you care for Jing-Jing, then you should want her to consider *all* her options. We don't want her to miss out on something great, you understand?"

Something great? Was he serious?

I was about to nod (what the hell else could I do?), but then I heard *Hey-o, boys and girls,* and my belly flamed. The idea of someone like Jing-Jing having to deal with *that . . .*

I sat up even straighter. "Shǔshú, I hear you, but I'm completely confident that Jing-Jing shouldn't be considering Hongbo." I dared to say his name even though Mr. Wang weirdly hadn't. "I'm not sure I'm the best for her—I'll certainly try to be good enough—but she deserves so much better than that spoiled jerk who knows nothing about her despite them growing up together. I don't care how much money he has; Jing-Jing deserves respect and someone who truly sees and cares for her. That, at the very least, I can do."

Mr. Wang's head slid back in shock, but he had an approving frown on his face that implied he'd underestimated me. I hadn't been thinking about types and categories when that came out, but of course Category 1 Mr. Wang would love how I was defending Jing-Jing and talking her up.

He nodded once, twice, thinking, and then he leaned forward. "Well, answer me this, Andrew: Have you ever shadowed your parents?"

I didn't know where he was going with this, and thus I didn't know what my answer should be. To stall, I tilted my head to the side, throwing him a questioning look.

"It's just that," he continued, "I was surprised at how hard a time you had today." *Shit.* "I don't know if you're cut out for medicine." *Shit shit shit.*

I hung my head slightly; acting defeated was all I could come up with in the moment, my mind churning much too fast with too many maybes and what-ifs and *Type C* this, *Category 1* that.

He then said, "I understand if you want to follow in your parents' footsteps to make them proud, but . . . not all careers are good matches for everyone."

Well, that was extremely progressive of him, and surprising, given everything else. Maybe it was different when it wasn't his own kid?

"So, Andrew, my question to you is this: If not medicine, then what? You have to understand—yes, I'm concerned about you, but my daughter comes first, and if you can't support her as a doctor, what will you do?"

Man, had this roller coaster turned multiple times in the past couple of minutes. But at least I was caught up now.

I confidently answered, "Jing-Jing doesn't need anyone to support her, not with her abilities. But as for me, I'm loving—and excelling in—my biology classes, so even if it turns out surgery isn't my thing, I still think I'd make a wonderful generalist or researcher or teacher."

Mr. Wang crossed his arms in doubt. Ignoring the first part of what I'd said, he replied, "Generalist? I'm skeptical. Researcher or teacher? Do you think you would make enough money with that?"

Was this guy serious? Jeez. "Yes, I think that would provide a generous salary to live a relaxed life on." *You pretentious dick.* "I also believe that college majors don't determine your entire future, and with a degree from a place like the University of Chicago, I'm not worried." *Oof.* That one had been a little hard for college-dropout Drew to get out, even as Andrew.

"Well, maybe you would be worried if you knew a little more about how the world works." He turned back to his computer.

I took the hint and stood. "Thanks for letting me tag along today, Shūshú. I learned a lot." *Like how you're kind of an ass.*

He nodded absentmindedly. "Thanks for the help and for saving me from having to call my assistant in. If you do stay on this path, you'll need a gentler touch with the suction, though, eh?"

Given that I had barely touched the patient out of disgust, I was pretty sure he was talking down to me to make me feel small.

"Should we grab some food?" I suggested. "Maybe ask Jing-Jing and Wang Ǎyí to join us?"

He checked his watch. "It's late; I'm sure the girls have eaten." What about me? He'd whisked me out the door before I could grab something. "Why don't you text Jing-Jing and see where they are?"

<Drew>
Help
I mean, where are you?
We just finished up here

<Chloe>
You need to help ME
My mother and I are bra shopping
And we have very different priorities
Let's just say I want comfortable and she . . . does not care about that
TMI?

"They're bra shopping," I told Mr. Wang.

His face flushed bright red. "Okay. We'll just go home. Tell her to . . . uh, actually, no. Just stop texting her."

As I trailed him out of the office, I discreetly texted:

<Drew>
Nothing's TMI with me
We're heading back
Need me to fake an emergency of some sort?

<Chloe>

No because I'm my own knight in shining armor

See you soon, Dr. Huang

I'd forgotten she didn't know my actual last name. I shoved the phone back in my pocket.

Chloe

CHAPTER 13

FREE WILLY

"How about this one?" My mother held up a sheer, lacy black bra with a matching thong that screamed both *UTI* and *yeast infection*.

"Remember how just a couple of years ago you wouldn't let me date?" I said, pushing her hand and its uncomfortable contents away. "I prefer that to this, please."

"Just to be clear, there still shouldn't be hanky-panky. But if your bra strap or underwear . . . strap ever peeks out, it should be something like this, not the boring skin-colored ones with holes you insist on wearing."

My mother wanted me to have a sexy whale tail.

"Mǎmá, I wear the same bras I got from Taiwan years ago because they're all that fit me. I don't conform to any of these"—I waved my hands around me—"body shapes. My rib cage is too big and my boobs too small, so . . ." I shrugged.

My phone buzzed. Thank God.

I found a nearby seat and took a breather from Mǎmá Free Willy.

I thought she'd still be off replenishing her embarrass-Jing-Jing ammo when I heard, "What are you smiling about?"

I looked up from texting Andrew to see my mother standing before me, a sly curve to her lips, an actual corset in her hand. Who made those nowadays?

"Nothing," I said, sending off my last text. "We should go soon."

"Why? We haven't found anything yet because you're so stubborn. You haven't even tried anything on!" She thrust the pink corset at me.

Time to end this. Like I'd just told Andrew, I was my own knight in shining armor. I gestured to my phone. "Bǎbá says he misses you." She glared at me. "Just kidding. He said through Andrew that he wanted to know what was for dinner—are you cooking?"

"Tiān āh! I don't know!" She hooked the corset on the nearest rack. "We have to figure out dinner! Will you help me?"

Even though I had known this was coming, I felt terrible for exploiting a sad, sexist part of her life. She was an equal partner in Wang Dental Palace, yet it had always been her job to have food ready on the table and take care of anything involving me.

I put a hand on her shoulder. "Let's order takeout. We can bring it home."

She opened her mouth, but I filled in the words for her. "From a Chinese place, for Bǎbá, and on our way home so it doesn't take too long."

She nodded, rewarded me with a small smile, then hurried to the register.

"I don't want anything!" I called after her.

She pulled three extra-large granny panties out of the store's mesh shopping bag. "I need new underwear; some of us don't like holes!"

I thought about asking why she wore underwear three times her size—she weighed about a hundred pounds—but I decided I didn't want to know. Would her beauty standards change for me once I got married, or was there just some weird double standard between her and me I didn't understand? Like, did she believe I had so many other flaws I had to make up for it in ways she didn't have to worry about?

I swatted the corset on my way out. Even the smelly mall corridor adjacent to the busiest bathroom was better than this.

Drew

CHAPTER 14

QUIZ

The car ride from the dental office back to the house was silent, as expected. Only a few more hours, then a sleep, then this job would come to a close.

Then Jing-Jing would be a memory.

I found myself wondering what her plan was in regard to me (Andrew) after this, but, *not your prerogative.* Either I'd get rebooked in the future or I'd never have to think about her or the Wangs again. I laughed to myself that, just like Dr. Wang, I took notes on my jobs too, except mine were to keep things straight in case of rebookings.

After Mr. Wang and I arrived home, I was hoping to have a moment to catch my breath, but he took a seat on the couch—the one space in this house that could be considered temporarily mine—and it was no accident.

Now what?

I thought he might pat the cushion beside him, but he folded his hands in his lap instead, as if waiting to see what I'd do.

So, with a half-hearted smile, I settled in next to him, my left ankle on my knee and my right arm resting across the back of the couch—relaxed, poised, in command.

"You think you know my Jing-Jing?" he asked, his words suspicious but his demeanor cool.

"Of course I do." *Probably better than you . . . though I guess I cheated.*

The all-too-familiar glint in his eye alerted me it was quiz time. Not my first.

"So you know her favorite food?" he asked.

Kimchi nachos from that Korean fusion place near campus, tied with hot pot. "Her mother's dumplings."

"Movie?"

"*The Butterfly Lovers,*" I answered, when it was actually *Monsters, Inc.*

It went on for a bit (and yes, most of the questions had two answers).

"None of these things are important," I finally said after enough time had passed to show that I knew the answers and was saying this because I meant it, not as a way out. "Even a stranger who saw these facts on paper could parrot them back."

Treading in dangerous waters here, but I knew it would pay off.

"So how do I know you're more than a stranger who has memorized these facts?" he asked.

"Because I see her. How she's nervous being home, having me here, and how much she wants to please you. I can't prove it, but I think it's obvious even to you that I know her better than Hongbo does—both superficially and in the deeper ways that matter."

The door opened (perfect timing), so I nodded at Mr. Wang, then hurried to greet Jing-Jing and her mother.

"Hey," I said, helping Jing-Jing with the delicious-smelling bags in her hands. She smiled her thanks.

I hurried to deposit the bags so I could help Mrs. Wang with hers. And as soon as her hands were free, they were on her hips.

"Eh! Did you see that, Lǎo Gōng?" she yelled to her old man. "That's a proper gentleman!"

Mr. Wang stayed where he was. "When Andrew's my age, he'll stay seated too." He clutched his back dramatically, then chuckled.

When her mother left the kitchen to ask Mr. Wang about the appointments, Jing-Jing raised her eyebrows in my direction, and with a tilt of her head she asked me how things had gone today with her father.

I didn't want her to know how close I'd gotten to blowing it (I was normally a much better operative than this, I swear), so I focused on the conversation after Fangli's part–root canal.

"I didn't know your dad was older than your mom."

She unknotted the plastic bags carefully (so they could be reused). "Why did he tell you that?"

"He was trying to explain *why Hongbo*. He said that at this point in his life he wanted to make sure you would be okay."

She stopped unpacking the food. "That doesn't sound like him."

I shrugged, then reached over to take over food duty. "He seemed really concerned about my earning potential—it seems consistent with your theories about why they love Hongbo."

She nodded absentmindedly, and for the first time I couldn't read what was turning her brain gears.

I took a guess and said, "Don't worry. I think I managed to move us a step or two closer to our goal today." When I stretched past her to put the largest box on the emptier part of the counter, my arm grazed hers.

She stared at her elbow where our skin had touched. "Are we past whatever weirdness that was last night?" she asked quietly, still looking down.

"I wasn't being weird," I lied. But somehow my acting skills were less effective with her (maybe because she knew I'd been acting this whole time).

She brought one of the Styrofoam boxes to her face, sniffed, then hovered it in front of my nose. Soup dumplings. Heavenly.

"Look," she said, "I was just playing my part last night, and since I don't have training like you, I have to rely on trial and error. Sorry if it was too strong. But whatever that was after—can you pull it together? My parents notice more than they let on, especially when it comes to us. They want Hongbo so bad they're looking for things."

Obviously I knew that. It was just that after the poke and all those swarming thoughts, I'd been so flustered that the best I could do was pretend she wasn't there. But since my job clearly depended on me being more doting than not, well, I had a free pass, right? That was more important in the moment than some arbitrary line. Besides, I of course knew where the line was at all times. This was part of it, getting a little swept up, even if it had never happened before.

Right?

"You have nothing to worry about," I lied.

Chloe

CHAPTER 15

THE LAST HURRAH

With the takeout placed in the center of the table, we settled in and my parents gestured to Andrew to start—a good sign. "We" had an early morning flight tomorrow, so this was kind of the last hurrah.

Andrew grabbed the nearest box and served both my mother, who was sitting on his left, and me, on his right, before serving himself and passing the box along.

My mom harrumphed at my dad, who laughed and served her some garlic green beans—a first.

My mother winked at Andrew, and my heart sank at how this was all so real and so fake. At the start of this, I never could've guessed a successful outcome would make me feel so many contrasting emotions.

Remember Hongbo . . . and suddenly, I could hear his half-assed proposal, feel his unwelcome hand on my arm, and see the fucking ring box I had thrown under my bed after he wouldn't take it back.

Thinking of non-Dreamboat always succeeded in pushing away my guilt about lying, at least temporarily. Too bad anger took its place.

My father reached for the soup dumplings, but a shaky hand knocked over his tiny dish of black vinegar. All three of us hurried to help, and instead of sitting back and enjoying his position as the head of the household, my father leaned down too, his face flushed with embarrassment. In the process, his shirt rode up, revealing a deep purple bruise on his lower back in the shape of a perfect circle.

"Bā," I said, alarmed. "Are you okay? How'd you get that bruise?" I wanted to reach out and pull his shirt aside for a better look, but I obviously didn't.

My father groaned as he sat back up. "It's nothing." He hastily yanked his shirt down, unintentionally exposing a matching bruise on his upper back, just below his neck.

"Oh my God!" This time I did reach out, but he pulled away.

My mother stood, leaving Andrew to finish wiping up the mess on the floor. "Aiyah, Jing-Jing, it's just cupping. How do you know so little about your own culture?" The problem wasn't how much I knew—it was that my opinion on it differed from hers.

"Bǎbá's never done that before." *And he's acting so shady right now.* Case in point, he turned back to the table, ignoring all of us and uncharacteristically straightening the plate and chopsticks in front of him.

My mother tsked. "What, so he can never do it just because he's never done it before?"

"Are you feeling okay?" I asked him, because that was the only thing I could think of. He had never been opposed to the practice, but he hadn't been a patient before, and had even previously laughed with me when I'd made jokes comparing it to bloodletting—which, coincidentally, had been done together with cupping once upon a time. "You know there's no scientific evidence that it does any good but there *is* evidence of negative side effects, right?"

My father sighed. "Please, Jing-Jing. Can we have a nice meal before you leave tomorrow and for once not make it about the latest study you've read?"

"Yes, and respect your culture a little more," my mother added with a sniff.

Since that argument never ended in my favor, my mother's comment shut me up and put me back in my seat.

By now the floor was clean—thanks to Andrew, which neither of my parents acknowledged—and we were all back at the table, a vinegar-scented discomfort enveloping us.

"Thank you for hosting me these few days," Andrew said in an attempt to dispel the heavy air. "It's been such a pleasure, Wang Ǎyí, Shúshú, and you've been much too kind to me. Such gracious hosts."

"Aiyah, Andrew, it was our pleasure," my mother said, blushing. Blushing! Her! "So you will join us for Christmas, right?"

He looked at me, hesitant, and I jumped in. "He wishes he could, but he can't. His parents expect him to be home, especially since he spent Thanksgiving here—"

"Andrew, we insist," my mother said, glaring at me.

"Uh . . ." Andrew looked from my mother to me.

"Jing-Jing, a word?" my mother said, ticking her head toward the bathroom.

Unngghhhh. I reluctantly followed her, glancing at Andrew one last time to try to read his face, which seemed to say, *Sorry, wouldn't want to be in your shoes.* (At least it didn't say, *$$$!*)

My mother rudely closed the door behind us. "Jing-Jing, you have to bring him back for Christmas. I can't decide what I think of him after just three days!"

"You decided with Hongbo in like a minute."

She slapped the air. "I did not! We've known him *and* his family for decades! You haven't even introduced me to Andrew's parents yet—how can I know if he's good or not without knowing where he comes from?"

Did Rent for Your 'Rents also provide fake in-laws? Damn, this hole was starting to feel deep. And I was getting pretty tired from digging.

"Men can only pretend for so long," my mother continued. "You need more time with him to see his true character. You've barely been together; the minimum is two years, Jing-Jing! Two years before a man can stop acting and show you what's beneath." Oh man, so much irony there. "But we don't have that kind of time with Hongbo's proposal hanging over us!"

"Mǎmá, *I've* met his parents. Don't you trust me? And he already told his family he'd be there for Christmas—it was part of the reason why they didn't object when he came here this weekend! You have to respect their—"

"Either Andrew comes or Hongbo comes."

I couldn't stand her sometimes. Oftentimes. "Well, maybe I'll just go spend Christmas with Andrew's family."

Her eyes flared. "Don't threaten me. And don't miss time with us for something as petty as this. We're getting old, Jing-Jing, especially your father." Her tone dipped with the last three words, so subtle no one else would notice, but I was hyperattuned to her.

I thought of what my father had said to Andrew, the cupping, even the change in his financial plan from *Mutual funds are the only safe bet* to investing in No One Systems for the first time. *A large chunk of our savings,* he'd said to Hongbo.

"Is Bǎbá sick?" I asked.

The shock in my mother's eyes seemed to be less from the idea and more from the fact that I was asking. But it quickly shifted and she tsked. "He's just old. If you were more xiàoshùn toward me and Bǎbá, you wouldn't ask me something like that."

She was changing the subject on purpose. Bringing up filial piety because she knew what that did to me. Slapped me into submission even though I already felt like I always put their feelings, their wants first, above mine.

"Please tell me if Bǎbá is sick."

She ignored me. "Show us how xiàoshùn you are and bring Andrew home for Christmas, okay? We want to see both of you. Most important, though? I need to get to know him better, before Hongbo's proposal deadline."

She swept out of the bathroom.

There was something wrong with my dad. How serious, I wasn't sure, but they wouldn't keep it from me if it was simply a cold. I had to find a way to get to the bottom of it. Which was just one more problem to add to the pile. Because I didn't have enough money to afford Andrew again next month. But I didn't really have a choice, did I?

Drew

Mrs. Wang returned to the table first, smiling at me. "It's settled, Andrew. You'll join us for Christmas. If your parents want to, they're welcome to come here for the holiday—your brother, too. Then you'll all be together and they can't be upset."

I was caught off guard for a second (a rarity) but managed to pull it together. "That's so generous of you. I will of course let them know. I'm afraid they tend to host all the extended family for the holidays since our house is the most centrally located and the largest"—her eyes gleamed, and I felt a little gross—"so they likely won't be able to come, but I'm sure they will be so appreciative of the invitation."

I *really* hoped Mrs. Wang was not ballsy (rude?) enough to invite herself and Mr. Wang over to "my" house for the holidays instead.

Also, mental note: bring the Wangs something from "my parents" if Jing-Jing rebooks me.

"Ah! Too bad. Maybe we can find another time to meet them."

Did Jing-Jing have enough money to rent some in-laws?

"Excuse me, I'm going to check on Jing-Jing," I said, putting my napkin down and walking to the closed bathroom door.

"She might be going to the bathroom!" Mrs. Wang called out to me. "Number one, of course, but still."

I rapped my knuckles lightly, just a couple times. "Jing-Jing? Are you okay?"

The door opened so quickly it startled me, and before I'd even realized what was happening, she brushed past me and returned to the table.

"I'm fine," she said brusquely as she whizzed by.

Throughout dinner, as the Wangs asked me more about my parents and brother, Jing-Jing's plastic smile slowly faded. At one point I tried to brush her hand with mine, but she pulled away. Not wanting to push it, I gave her space, but a knot slowly formed in my throat.

Jing-Jing didn't eat much, which was out of the ordinary. I missed her enthusiastic bites that, since Mrs. Wang was always scrutinizing her, felt like subtle F-Us to her mother and maybe even the rest of society (not to be dramatic).

I tried several times to loop her into the conversation (even finding a way to bring up her favorite economics professor), but she was as listless as the two-day-old pie on the counter.

After dinner, she excused herself to bed, claiming she had a headache. And unlike before, when I could tell she was constantly thinking about how to use every second of this weekend to accomplish our mission, she didn't seem to care that her already-paid-for time was going to waste.

I thought about going after her, trying to be a friend again, but . . . *not your prerogative, Operative.*

Chloe

CHAPTER 16

PRETENDING

I hugged my dad extra tight when saying good night—did he notice? Did my mother?

My father was eleven years older than my mother, which had never felt that significant, but then again, it still wasn't, because sickness didn't discriminate. I tried to step further and further back into my memories, one visit home at a time, trying to pinpoint when their words or actions had first started to change.

But then I realized we didn't talk much. Didn't do much. It was just stifling silence all the time, the constant urge to shove food, water, anything in my mouth just for something to fucking *do*. Andrew's presence had shifted that, which should have made me feel better about the money I'd spent, but for some reason it only irked me. Why did it take this actor to improve our family dynamic, and was it even real given that he wasn't? Were we all pretending, putting on a better face to fool everyone around us, even our family? I guess I'd been doing that my whole life, with Jing-Jing. Did anyone else go by two names and feel like that separated who they were? Did Andrew's other clients?

I considered getting a midnight snack—I hadn't eaten enough at dinner, and I was starving—but instead of going downstairs for mooncakes, I scrounged in my room until I found three very expired granola bars from my high school days, stashed in my drawers for whenever Frankenbāo appeared.

They tasted as shitty as I felt.

Drew

She didn't come downstairs that night.

Chloe

CHAPTER 17

OFF THE CLOCK

November 29

As I said good-bye to my parents early Sunday morning, I blinked rapidly to hold back tears.

This trip had been more emotional than I'd anticipated—which was saying something, since I had anticipated PMS-level roller coasters. It wasn't just about my father's possible-but-definite illness, but everything. Part of me even wished I could have a few more hours with my parents, but I'd picked the earliest flight out to avoid going to church and seeing Hongbo. And because I couldn't afford to rent Andrew another day.

Andrew shook hands with my father, then hugged my mother.

"Safe travels," my mom called out, waving her hand up and down so frantically it looked like she was trying to fly with one arm.

"Are you trying to be the golden duck, Mămá?" I joked. To my delight, she laughed and flapped harder.

"If I'm a golden duck, I'm twenty-four karats!" she called back.

My chest hurt as I piled into the Uber with Jorge, 4.9 stars.

"Are you okay?" Andrew asked as I stared after my parents, too many thoughts fighting for center stage in my brain.

I ignored him as I continued to stare, worrying about my parents' health, worrying about what I was supposed to do next, wondering when everything had become so messy.

"Remember when you were young," I said, still gazing out the window even though my parents were out of view, "and things seemed so easy yet so hard? I wish we'd known then to enjoy it while it lasted."

"Or maybe things would hurt more now if you'd enjoyed it then," Andrew said quietly. Then he quickly changed the subject by asking me again if I was okay.

"You're off the clock," I replied. "You don't have to bother."

I could feel him shaking his head even though I couldn't see him.

"C'mon, Jing-Jing."

It's Chloe, I wanted to tell him, but instead I said, "That's not even my name, at least not outside my church community. Just like how I'm guessing you aren't Andrew outside these jobs." I turned to face him. "I don't really know how I got here. I feel like I blinked and then—*poof*—I'm caught in the middle of a ridiculous web of lies I created, and now I'm going to have to spend the next month finding the money to hire you again. I thought this was going to be a one-time thing."

But my plan was obviously poorly thought out and on fire.

It was silent in the car. Even Jorge the driver seemed to have stopped breathing.

"I'm sorry. I was trying to help, not . . . " Andrew paused, but I didn't want to hear what he had to say next.

"Where do you want to be dropped off?" I asked.

"Here's fine," he said, voice robotic.

Because he doesn't want me to know where he lives. The company had run extensive background checks on both of us for each other's safety, but one could never be too safe.

"Thanks, Andrew. Or whoever you are." I stuck my hand out and he took it. I held on a second longer than I needed to. "Really, though. Thank you. You did me a solid, and I really am just . . . so grateful. I'll, uh, see you at Christmas if I can get the money together."

He nodded at me, then exited the car swiftly. His bag was already in hand; he must not have put it in the trunk because he knew he'd be making a quick escape.

I slumped in my seat as Jorge pulled off. He handed me a travel pack of tissues and said nothing.

I gave out two five-star ratings that day.

Drew

Not your prerogative, Operative.

AFTER
THANKSGIVING

Chloe

CHAPTER 18

BETTER SKIN

Whenever I left California and landed in Chicago, it felt like I shed my old skin and put on a more comfortable, better fitting one.

My steps were already more confident as I swiped into my dorm and made my way to my single.

I waved shyly to my floormate, Summer, who was, as usual, surrounded by a group of friends. She'd invited me out with them a few times to parties, but since I don't drink, I'd said no and they'd soon stopped asking.

High school had sucked and I couldn't wait to get to college, but I wish I'd been more prepared for how important alcohol would be. I was immediately declared a party pooper by the couple of groups I had tried to be a part of. Maybe if the drinkers had also been missing the gene to metabolize alcohol and zoomed past buzzed straight to raging hangover, they'd understand, but to them, I was just no fun. I thought I was plenty of fun even without alcohol—and didn't drunk people find everyone fun?—but apparently drinking was an all-or-nothing kind of activity.

I had "friends," as in people with whom I worked on problem sets and had dinner, but no one I was close enough to tell about Andrew. Maybe if I'd had someone, I wouldn't have gone through with the rental, so I couldn't decide whether I was grateful or sad for that.

My closest friend in high school, Genevieve, was a friend of circumstance, in that we started hanging out because my parents approved of her. That girl could give Rent for Your 'Rents operatives a run for their money. In front of my parents, she was shy, obedient, and studious, one of my only classmates to win them over. But when they weren't around, she was do-any-dare, seek-all-thrills wild. Sometimes I wondered what she saw in me, but based on her taste in romantic relationships, I think she liked the challenge my parents posed. A different kind of chase. When she went to UCLA and I went to Chicago, we fell out of touch, though knowing her, she would be happy to hear from me. But she wasn't really a tell-me-your-feelings, ride-or-die kind of friend. And she would *not* have understood—her parents were the opposite of mine.

I threw my luggage in the corner of my dorm room, telling myself I'd unpack when I didn't feel like death. Then I took the fastest shower in history and flopped on my twin bed like a dead fish. Even though I felt like I'd just pulled an all-nighter, even though my single felt like home and every poster, knickknack, and crack held both comfort and a story, I tossed and turned most of the night.

Now that I was alone, now that the mission and navigating my parents weren't at the forefront of my mind, dangerous questions started to form. Had Andrew meant it when he said he liked my organization, my passion, the real me? *I like the version of you from the application,* he'd said.

I repeated that sentence in my mind several times. I'd always been too scared to show my true, bright-red, fiery colors to anyone, since my previous environment punished me for them, but . . . he'd seen Chloe on his own and had even figured out that Jing-Jing existed as the shiny front that other people wanted, not me. And apparently not him. The same guy who was somehow more in tune with my feelings than maybe I was. Who had laughed over my mooncake points, Frankenbāo, and tile-eating jokes—which, for the record, had felt real. And he'd seen the puke green of Hongbo immediately, defending me while also somehow recognizing that I could defend myself, too.

You're just attracted to the attentiveness you paid for, the part he's playing, the rational part of my brain told me. *It's the same as being attracted to a character in a movie—a.k.a. not real, not pursuable. He's trained to be whoever he needs to be, lies flowing from his lips like honey, lies told so well everyone devours them easily.*

Yet sometimes I'd felt like I could see the real him underneath, the one with tics and good vision and a love for banh mis.

I wanted to know his story—his real one—and ask him his thoughts on my mess, my parents, my decisions. He seemed to understand what it was like to have parents like mine. To have that pressure, that need to please them even though you were hurting yourself to do it.

But the real him was off-limits. Partly because of his rule and partly because he had clearly rejected me when I'd poked him, but mostly because that would be like adding accelerant to this on-fire mess of a plan.

I tried to distract myself from these too-complicated, no-solution issues. And, of course, my masochistic mind wandered to the time in second grade when I'd farted during a schoolwide moment of silence.

When I finally did fall asleep, my subconscious combined the two, forcing me to dream-live through farting in front of Andrew and my parents at the Thanksgiving table.

Upon waking the next morning, I felt just as drained as yesterday, but at least this weekend and Andrew felt like the past. What magic sleep had, even fart-filled sleep.

Drew

CHAPTER 19

FOOL

November 30

After each job, especially holiday ones, I felt drained. Social situations are rough for anyone, but as an operative, I was pretending to be someone else 24/7, even worrying about accidentally talking in my sleep and ruining my cover. (My boy James Bond deserves a pay raise.)

Non-holidays were less busy, for obvious reasons, so I was going to have a lighter load until Christmas (and whether Jing-Jing—er, whoever she was—hired me or not, I told myself it didn't matter). I still had jobs in between, but they were usually one-evening dinners, a Saturday get-together, or a church visit plus brunch, which were all more forgiving than a multiday holiday immersion.

Chinese New Year was by far the busiest (and most lucrative) holiday, the one around which Rent for Your 'Rents originated. The practice of bringing home a fake boyfriend for Lunar New Year was more common in China, with women going to the classifieds to find actors for hire. Our founder, known to everyone as just Mr. J, saw a need in the Asian-heavy California communities and started with just a few operatives—himself, his brother, and a close friend. Six years later, we had approximately a hundred operatives in several locations. I'd even recruited a couple of artist buddies, though we were a small subset (the majority being aspiring actors, of course, who made up almost all of the LA branch).

My East Palo Alto apartment was "cozy and quaint"—officially, since my super had said it twenty times during the initial tour. It wasn't much (nine hundred square feet and overrun by some pretty scrappy ants), but it had become home, both because it was mine and because of my roommate, Jason, who was a fellow artist and operative. (We'd met through friends of a friend of a friend; then I'd recruited him to Rent for Your 'Rents.) Talking art with him and boosting each other's creative energies was as wonderful as game nights with him and his boyfriend, Marshall. I was the Splendor champ; Jason, Takenoko; and Marshall, Ticket to Ride.

Living with another operative was a blessing and a G-D curse. Having a buddy to commiserate with was priceless and kept me stable, but he also noticed *everything*. Like yesterday, when I'd walked in the door fresh off the Wang job, Jason had immediately sensed I was off and wouldn't let it go until I feigned diarrhea. ("Mom's cooking, you know how it is," I had said, and he'd nodded.) I'd spent the bathroom time trying to pull myself together, chanting *not your prerogative* waaay too many times. He'd let it go, but this morning, in the kitchen, as I heated water for green tea in a half-awake stupor, he side-eyed me once or twice and asked how my bowels were doing. I rubbed my lower abdomen and made a couple of faces. And I definitely did *not* tell him that I was this tired because I had lain awake last night thinking about whatever-her-name-was.

Why her? Why was I so captivated by her type-A tendencies (an opposites-attract thing?), her perceptiveness (I mean, it was annoying when Jason saw through me), her part-selfless yet fierce personality (wasn't that completely contradictory?). Maybe because all of that, together, added up to the most intelligent, driven, passionate, caring, yet strong person I'd ever met. It also didn't hurt that she made me laugh (mooncake points to her!). The monologues I had given her parents weren't just from training, but also because I felt like I knew her and truly believed she deserved all I mentioned and more.

My defenses dropped when Jason left me alone to start his morning routine. Even though we didn't have to (and in a perfect world I'd stay up all night painting), Jason and I tried to keep a "normal" schedule so the transitions during jobs were easier.

I was setting the oven timer for a three-minute steep when my Rent for Your 'Rents app dinged. Well, more accurately, it went *ba-boop-boop*, alerting me with its unique notification of a potential job.

"Yours or mine?" Jason called out from the bathroom, where he was washing his face with the door open. His phone was charging in the kitchen beside me.

"Mine!"

I checked the timing of the job: to start in a week (less prep time than average, meaning this could be a desperate and possibly volatile situation). Then I skimmed through the small block of information we receive to gauge our preliminary interest.

The parents were Type A (ugh, it was extra draining for me to be affectionate) and Category 3, which rarely matched to me (Type C, Category 1, like the Wangs was my area of expertise). I continued scrolling to see what in this client's file had made me the ideal operative for her.

Ah, her parents were native Taiwanese and preferred the daughter be with someone who could speak Mandarin *and* Taiwanese. My Taiwanese wasn't great, but I'd taken a few classes, and it was a skill few operatives had.

I kept reading, and, oh boy. My heart started to hurt. Because under the *why* she had written: *I'm not ready to come out to my family yet, but they're starting to wonder why I've never had a boyfriend.*

"Well?" Jason said to me as he took a seat at the counter, a.k.a. our dining table.

"It's a tough one," I said quietly.

"Oh no," he said, catching on. "What do you want to do?"

"Don't I have to take it? How can I not? If she's not ready, she's not ready, right? Or . . . am I just making everything worse for her?" I chewed on a fingernail. "WWJD?"

"Jesus? Well, I don't think you want to ask that," Jason tried to joke, even though he already knew the *J* referred to him. "I don't know, bud—there's an argument either way. What about the rest of the info? Have you clicked interested yet?"

I shook my head. "This is still the preliminary stuff."

He nodded. "You in enough to know more?"

"Not yet. You know I don't like to get more info unless I'm pretty sure."

He pursed his lips to one side. "I get that, but how can you decide if you don't have all the facts? And it's not like you know any identifying information at stage two." We didn't receive that until the job was booked, confirmed on both ends, and paid for.

Jason and I had already had this discussion several times before. I was too tired right now.

"I'll decide later," I said, setting a reminder on my phone. Right before I closed out of the app, I saw that Jing-Jing had rated me five stars.

I retreated to my room with my green tea.

When I'd moved in a year and a half ago, I'd lofted my bed so I could maximize my work space, which was small enough that it forced me to be organized and methodical. (I hadn't decided yet if that was good or bad for my creativity.)

The moon was usually my muse, and I was working on a paper treatment that created the texture of the moon's surface (and maybe one day, Cháng'é willing, would be the thing to make me famous). But today, without thinking, I painted a silhouette that dissolved into a galaxy in which he didn't belong.

Art flowed through me, compelling me to create, but so far my creations were only for my eyes. Even after all this time, I hadn't been able to share my paintings with anyone, not even Jason, not really. (I made myself show him only when I desperately needed feedback, and that was as painful as dragging a knife across my skin.)

Once my parents had cut me off for dropping out of college to pursue art, I'd halted at the bridge connecting us, terrified to stomp on the last, already-splintered wooden plank. Terrified to *actually* go for it. Because if I tried to make it, if I shared my art with someone, then that would make it real, and it would be harder to go back. My parents had been the ones to break the other planks, but I still had control over that last one.

Worse, what if I failed? What if I shared only to learn that I sucked at this and I'd thrown away my family for nothing? I had already fought and lost; I couldn't lose again with the one thing I had left.

That's why I can't stop thinking about her, I realized. Jing-Jing and I had a connection, not because of how her parents were with her (I'd seen that on every job), but because of how she was with them. She cared but was also fighting for what she wanted—a life without Hongbo.

I was thinking about her just because of my own messed-up shit. Nothing else.

I tilted my head and examined the painted silhouette from all angles. My art didn't feel complete without a moon. So at the top I added a half-moon crying over the broken silhouette, unable to put the pieces back together.

And then, like the fool I was, I texted her. Maybe because I had hope that she would understand me when no one else did, not even myself. Maybe because every time her face scrunched with worry and that little dimple appeared on her forehead, I felt a need to fix it, and that dimple had been front and center the last time I'd seen her.

Maybe I just couldn't help it, prerogative or no prerogative.

November 30, 1:23 p.m. PST

<Drew>

Thanks for the five stars

Hope you're ok

December 1, 11:41 a.m. PST

<Drew>

Sorry

You don't have to respond if you don't want

I know this is weird

Erm, I'm making it weird

I shouldn't have texted

Sorry

Um, take care

Drew

CHAPTER 20

HEAD BANGING

December 3

t was for the best that she didn't respond. For her sake, for mine, even for her parents, who would most definitely not approve of Jing-Jing fraternizing with a starving artist side-hustling as a professional fake boyfriend. Though it didn't keep me from banging my head against the wall as I checked my phone every five minutes for a few days until it finally sank through my thick skull that nothing was coming except more ba-boop-boops.

Regret. Embarrassment. More head banging on the wall. I painted sad, blue, dripping moons.

Soon, as always (given enough time), with each brushstroke came the memories.

Drew, why you pick a career with no future? The best you can wish for is getting paid to draw silly distorted doodles of tourists at the beach.

Why can't you be more like your younger brother? You're supposed to be the role model for him, not the other way around.

If we'd known you would just throw away everything we've given you, we wouldn't have given you so much.

Every swirl of paint reminded me how my parents were right—I was a failure. At school, at the very passion I had given up so much for, at everything except pretending to be someone else—a better, more put-together fake person that, ironically, they would have been proud of.

I painted red, angry, fiery moons fueled by memories. Moons that no one would see except for me.

Chloe

CHAPTER 21

A TEXT A DAY

December 13

was considering removing text messaging from my phone. Or blocking my mother's number. Because in the past week and a half, she had sent a flurry of nauseating texts, one a day to keep the joy away.

December 3
Don't forget! No hanky panky!

December 4
Hongbo is very sad without you. His parents have never seen him so sad before.

December 5
Hongbo is worried Andrew is bad for you. He has a sixth sense about these things.

December 6
Did you know Hongbo is also a skilled martial artist? He

has a black belt! He was so good he jumped all levels and got it in just one year! The first person to ever do that!

December 7
The Kuos are sending gifts to us every day. Their chef's homemade sauces, the best peaches shipped from overseas, the rarest teas from Taiwan.

December 8
They gave us No One stocks today!

December 9
The Kuos are spoiling us. We are getting a taste of what it will be like when you and Hongbo are married. Maybe you can give him another chance? Can you at least keep your options open? It won't kill you to send him a nice message. Hello. How are you. I'm thinking about you. Do it for me!

December 10
Kuo Ayi has been fighting off the other Bible study mothers. Remember Penny? Her two permanent front teeth came in first out of all you kids? Well Penny's mother tried to talk up Penny to Kuo Ayi today and Kuo Ayi shut her down immediately! Because of you! Don't you feel honored?

December 11
Oh and don't worry. Hongbo's parents do not know about Andrew. That's why we were sure to tell Hongbo Andrew is just a friend. You know me. I'm always thinking five steps ahead!

December 12

Jing-Jing. Please.

December 13

Can you please say something back so I don't feel like I'm talking to the Great Wall? Or a duck. A golden duck heehee. And so I know you're alive? And so I know if you're considering Hongbo like I asked you to?

I'd been in brainstorming mode, trying to find an alternative solution for Christmas—some magical hidden option—but with these texts, I knew I had no choice but to hire Andrew again and keep up the lies, no matter the cost. Because if my mother was this bad now, thousands of miles away, what would it be like under the same roof with the impending proposal deadline and no Andrew? So I would have to scrounge up money I didn't have, all of which *should* have been going toward tuition. My parents were dentists, but they lived and worked in Palo Alto, where the cost of living was *not* for the faint of heart. They were only able to contribute a small amount of tuition money each year, so I was on track to be paying back student loans for a long time—now even longer, thanks to Andrew's exorbitant but necessary fee.

I opened the Rent for Your 'Rents app and rebooked Andrew—quickly, so I couldn't second-guess my decision. And as soon as the booking fee went through, the anger at my parents for putting me in this position consumed me as much as the guilt over what I'd let this become.

I had successfully ignored Andrew's texts up until now, but . . . he was the only one who knew what was going on. And, after lying awake night after night, spiraling into the abyss, I needed a lifeline like Hongbo needed manners.

December 14, 2:31 a.m. CST

\<Chloe\>

Is there something wrong with me?
How is my relationship with my parents so messed up that I'm renting a fake boyfriend AGAIN?

\<Drew\>

There's more than one person in a relationship

I didn't expect you to be up
Sorry if I woke you
I don't even know why I texted in the first place

Because I've seen it firsthand

Yeah

I'm here. You're not alone, in that sense, but also in the sense that our company has no shortage of clients. I've already had 2 jobs since Thanksgiving

What are the other clients like?
No personal info of course because HIPAA or whatever code you all have

There are underlying similarities but it's still pretty diverse
Some clients aren't ready to come out to their parents, some don't want to get married at all, some have significant others the parents wouldn't approve of

Yeah

All that makes sense

And some people do it to try to get rid of a disgusting suitor who isn't actually into them

I'm disappointed in the damselness of that

You are no damsel

I'm not but Jing-Jing sometimes is

Brief pause.

She's really not

But I think the underlying thing you're circling is that you don't feel like yourself with them

And you always deserve to be yourself

Another pause.

I thought this was just going to be a couple jokes or some good ol' Hongbo-bashing

I'm not ready for real talk 😰

This can be whatever you want

I know I just rebooked you but you're not on the clock right now

You don't have to say things like that

102

I know

This can still be whatever you want

If you were me, would you have hired you?

After a minute:

Still there?

Yeah sorry

Was thinking

In my life I've always been myself with my family and someone else with everyone else

But being myself with my parents was what made me lose them, so even though it wasn't what I did, I at least understand why you hired me

Maybe that's the better strategy, who knows

Another pause.

I go back and forth all the time because some jobs are harder than others (I had a tough one recently), and I can't tell if I'm helping or hurting

So there's just no right answer?
If you pretend, you feel awful
If you're honest, you feel awful

I'm sorry

Do you get texts like these from all your clients?

You're my first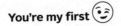

> Ha
> That's embarrassing
> And nice perfectly timed banter there
> From your training?

We're trained to impress the parents, not the client
I don't think your mom or dad would be particularly
charmed by bad innuendos

A second later:

> Do you ever lie awake at night, worrying about everything in a downward spiral that goes so deep you think about embarrassing things from your past because even that's better?
> And you just keep going and going until you whimper out loud, only to realize no one is there to hear or care?
> Because I don't
> It was hypothetical

Hypothetically, I don't do the embarrassing past thing,
but yeah when I can't sleep I stress about stuff
Doesn't everyone?
I have a hard time sleeping on jobs especially

> What do you do when you can't fall asleep on a job?

Midnight mooncakes help

Well more the company than the mooncakes

Seriously though? I remind myself why I'm there. Why the client needed to hire me

It doesn't always work unfortunately

And in those cases . . .

I might count sheep

Dressed in wild pajamas 🙈

Omg

I did not see that coming

It's as shocking as it is adorable

What kind of embarrassing stuff do you think about?

Right before I texted you, I was remembering how in high school I told the football star, Jerry (I'll never forget his name), that I was impressed by how he lived up to the name of his position

I thought he played defensive line and I was trying to thank him for backing me up to a teacher who wrongly thought I'd been cheating, but turns out . . .

He was the freaking tight end 🙈

Oh no

You inadvertently told Jerry you like his ass?

In front of like everyone

Why do you think about stuff like that when you can't sleep?

Because it's better than thinking about my parents and this sticky web I've spun myself into

It's not that bad. It'll turn out ok

Yeah? How do you know?
Do your clients follow up with you after the fact?

No
But maybe that means all is well?

You're not helping

Well in my experience, clients hire me because they love their family and they're trying to make it work. Even though it's not ideal, it's not the worst place to start from

I'll try to think about that to fall asleep
And maybe some sheep
Good night

Good night, sleep loose
If you can

Sleep loose? I love that!
You sleep loose too

December 15, 1:26 a.m. CST

<Chloe>

What kind of pajamas?

I just keep thinking of red, orange, yellow, green

Maybe a stripe or polka dot here or there

But that's it and it's not helping

I'm guessing it's not working because I'm not thinking of the right pajamas?

<Drew>

They can be anything!

Pj's with little mooncakes on them . . .

One that turns the sheep into a giant mooncake . . .

One with a fake sheepdog attached to its butt trying to nudge it inside a fence . . .

A sheep with antigravity boots . . .

The sky's the limit! Because we don't want the poor antigravity sheep to float past the atmosphere. That's dangerous!

Chang'e would have to catch him and send him back down

Omg

You might have missed your calling as a sheep pajama designer

Or a children's book writer

I've still got time

You just need to find an illustrator

I have someone in mind for that and the actual pajama making

Though I need an engineer for the antigravity stuff

I'll try to find an aerospace class
Maybe online since UChicago doesn't
offer it
Good night
Sleep loose

You too

<Chloe>
The best I came up with was a sheep in a tuxedo
But that's just a different piece of clothing

<Drew>
It's creative though

I'll leave the designing to you

So am I your non-booty booty call?
Erm text

Sorry I couldn't sleep again
Are we breaking like a million company rules right now?
We weren't even supposed to talk before the assignment

Ehh what do they know?
They just have a dedicated analytics team to scrutinize every piece of data we get
Maybe we're actually helping by getting to know each other even better

We're talking about sheep pajamas

Well if your parents ask me what your favorite sheep pajama is, I'll now know to answer tuxedo

That's not my favorite
It's just the one I came up with
My fave is your mooncake one tied
with the antigravity boots

**Well good thing we straightened that out by texting,
right?**

Haha right
Sleep loose

You too

December 17, 12:23 a.m. CST

\<Chloe\>

I'm sorry about your parents

I should've said that a few days ago when you told me about them

\<Drew\>

Rereading our texts? Has that replaced thinking about embarrassing things?

And don't worry I haven't been rereading our texts either 😉

No I haven't been doing that

Oh

Me neither

☝ **that previous text had no subtext between the lines**

My apology is part of the spiral

I replay all my previous interactions at night searching for where I went wrong

But with you (unlike with Jerry), I can correct it

I didn't say anything that night because I was so worried about crossing a line since you don't like to talk about stuff, but I should have at least said sorry

I didn't mean for it to come across like I didn't care when really, I was just making sure to respect your rule to keep the role and real you separate

Though I did want to know more
I mean, only if you want to tell me
Which you don't
So you shouldn't
Maybe I should stop texting you in the middle of the night when my filter's asleep before me

Sleepiness, alcohol's sneakier sibling

Are you old enough to drink? 😉

I'm 21

So you *are* older than me by 2 years!
That wasn't a lie to my mom
😂 😂 😂
Why is that so hilarious?

Because it's after midnight (for you)

Alcohol's sneakier sibling strikes again

Thanks for the kind words about my family
I haven't talked about them to anyone in a long time

I get that
It's too hard, especially when other people don't understand

Yep
I hear "good riddance" a lot but it's not like I chose this

Is it hard for you to spend holidays on the job, away from family?

One could argue that's why this job is perfect for me
It gives me somewhere to go

Is there anything I can do to make it easier for you during the upcoming job? Like any traditions you want to do?

Wait didn't you say your family eats Sichuan food around the holidays? Well if that was a true story

It's true
But um . . .

What?

Sorry, as lovely as that sounds and as kind as it is that you remembered, it goes against one of my rules

?

Pause.

You have to tell me!

I try to stay away from intestinally unfriendly foods while on the job, just in case 🙈

No shit

Correction: No gas

Shit's ok though

Okay

No Sichuan food

Or escolar or beans or ghost peppers

Much appreciated

Chloe

CHAPTER 22

BA-BOOP-BOOP

December 17

My password-protected Rent for Your 'Rents app—which showed up on my phone screen as HOMEWORK PLANNER, one of five stealth shields offered—went *ba-boop-boop*, reminding me that the payment (minus the already-paid booking fee) for Andrew's upcoming rental was due in four days.

I had to get my shit together. Finals had ended and though I was three days into the paid research-assistant gig I had recently nabbed with my favorite professor, the paperwork and thus payment hadn't gone through yet. And, more importantly, with the help of that trusty *ba-boop-boop*, I had been reminded of how complicated my texting with Andrew was. Mostly because my feelings had gotten more involved than I would've preferred, and now was the time to untangle that mess so it didn't affect the very important, life-altering mission ahead of us.

No more texts, not with the boy beneath the role.

Drew

Her loving my sheep pajamas (and even trying to come up with some of her own), telling me about Jerry's tight ass . . . it made me forget my rules for the first time.

But then she didn't text for the next four days.

December 21, 1:45 p.m. CST

<Chloe>

Payment should have just gone through

<Drew>

I know, my app just pinged

Actually it went ba-boop-boop

Annnd confirmed on my end

I'm looking forward to seeing you

Good

You're already in character

Drew

CHAPTER 23

ELIZA SCHUYLER

December 21

"Why do you seem so nervous?" Jason asked me.

I was ironing clothes for a date tonight (as in a date date, not a job) and for my upcoming week with the Wangs, which would start in two days.

"I'm not nervous," I said calmly, using my training to sell it (I looked him in the eye, breathed not too fast or slow or loud, and continued spraying water and ironing as if I weren't fazed). Really, though, my stomach was knotted tighter than one of my grandfather's red Zhōngguó jié wall hangings. Because I was losing it.

On December 15, after our second night of texts, I'd painted something for Jing-Jing. A sheep dressed as a mooncake with anti-gravity boots, floating past a moon. I'd hidden it under my bed.

Then yesterday, after rereading her application, I'd ordered jasmine oolong tea, her favorite, because I wanted to know what it tasted like. And I ordered it from her favorite tea store. (Insert monkey-covering-eyes emoji here.)

Jason examined me head to toe again. "I've never seen you so worked up over a date before."

I said nothing, scared to give him any clues as to what was really going on.

But it didn't matter, because the five-star operative figured it out.

"Oh, it's the upcoming job, not the date." Pause. "This is the same client as Thanksgiving, right? You were weird then, too. Was she an Inspector Gadget?" (That was our nickname for clients who think they're helping but actually make the operative's job harder, either by mixing up facts or by bringing up details that haven't been agreed upon.)

I shook my head.

"Was she a Katherine Heigl?" (Bad actress. My last client before Jing-Jing, Kristen, had been one of these. She had actually tried to rebook me this Christmas, but I'd given Jing-Jing priority—because of the Katherine Heigl bit, nothing else, I swear. And I did feel horrible for not being able to help Kristen out, though I offered to try for another time in January.)

I shook my head again.

"Were the parents Sherlocks?" Another head shake.

I looked up to find Jason staring at me, eyes wide and boring into mine, while one hand covered his mouth in shock.

"What?" I retorted, mustering all my acting skills to play innocent. But he'd received the same training as me.

"You didn't!" he gasped.

I wondered how his boyfriend, Marshall, could stand him always figuring stuff out. (Though, since I liked when Jing-Jing did it, I already knew the answer.)

"What about—" Jason started, but I couldn't hear *prerogative, Operative* one more time; it had been continually running through my head the past month. (Did it bother anyone else that the two words only sort of rhymed?)

"You got it all wrong," I lied. "She's a category all unto herself. A . . ." My brain flashed through possible traits to latch on to. (I could've made something up out of the blue, but it was quicker and safer to base it in truth.) "She's an Eliza Schuyler—too selfless." *And yet so very strong.* "Made it harder, you know?"

Jason raised one eyebrow at me. "Mm-hmm. We all know you have a crush on Eliza Schuyler."

A garbled scoff made its way out my nose. "She was alive hundreds of years ago; that's not a thing."

"Fine, you have a crush on the version Lin-Manuel brought to life." He started shaking his head. "Oh man, please stop this before it's too late. Wait, what about your date tonight?"

I said nothing, hoping he wouldn't figure out that I'd been texting with my client, and that Jing-Jing's last text had jarred me into making the date. *You're already in character,* she'd said, when I wasn't, not at all. I'd completely lost the line between job and reality, so in desperation I'd opened up the first dating app I spotted on my phone and swiped right until I made a match.

"Don't shit where you cat," Jason warned.

"I would never." I turned off the iron to let it cool on the kitchen counter (a.k.a. our ironing board) and retreated to my room to finish getting ready. And I definitely did not tell him that it already tasted kind of poopy in my mouth.

Voicemails from Chloe's mother

December 19

Wéi? Jing-Jing? Wéi, is anyone there? Oh. It's voicemail. Jing-Jing? It's your mǎmá. Look, I've been thinking, and I just can't live with myself taking Andrew away from his family another holiday. Maybe he shouldn't come here, so he can be a good son, of course, no other reason. What do you think? Tell him not to come. Okay, Jing-Jing? For everyone's sake.

    [silence]

    Eh? How do you turn this thing

December 20

Ah, there's the beep. Jing-Jing? It's Mǎmá again. Why haven't you text message me or called me back? I know you're upset about some of the things I said, but I taught you better than to ignore your poor mǎmá who is just looking out for you. And Andrew. I'm looking out for him and his poor mǎmá who will surely want to see him over the holiday. Win-win, right? I mean, not a win for us. Lose for us, of course. But we will make the sacrifice for him and his family's sake.

    Okay? Please. If you don't call me back, I'll assume you just did what I asked!

December 21

Oh, clever. You call me when you know I'm working. Well, fine.

    I *am* thinking about Andrew and his parents. Maybe I'm also thinking about us and Hongbo, but above everything, I'm thinking about *you*, Jing-Jing! It's always you!

But fine, yes, I don't want Andrew to come because I want you to focus on Hongbo. He likes you so much, Jing-Jing, and so do his parents. You don't know what it's been like for me this month! Not just the gifts, but they've been having us over for dinner constantly. And I've seen your future, Jing-Jing, and it's so bright! They're talking about everything they'll give you and Hongbo as their only heirs. Describing all the future vacations we'll take together—all of us! To Taipei, to Kaohsiung—don't you want to see where I grew up?—to Europe, Australia, Beijing. Remember when you were little—oh, so little—and we used to watch those videos about the Forbidden City and Great Wall, and you'd beg me to take you there? What happened to that girl, so eager to see where she came from? Well, now you can! You can get back the curiosity for your culture that you used to have!

The Kuos are so excited to have you as their daughter-in-law, and to have Bǎbá and me as family by extension. You know how rare it is for them to be so forward, and rare for you, Jing-Jing, to have this kind of attention. And from the Kuos—the *Kuos*! I didn't even *dream* of this for you because it was so unlikely! Andrew is a nice boy, but don't miss out on this golden duck of an opportunity. We've known Hongbo his *whole* life, and Andrew just a short time. It's nothing about Andrew personally. You understand.

Think about it. Please. I'm your mǎmá, Jing-Jing. I know you. Just trust me.

Chloe

CHAPTER 24
ARMOR
December 22

Packing for a visit home was more complicated than texting fake boyfriends late at night. Most of my go-to clothes were too loungewear for applying-makeup-is-the-same-as-being-polite Mǎmá Wang, and I had so outgrown the clothes that remained that they now pointed giant neon arrows at my not-completely-flat stomach. Might as well just draw a bull's-eye there for my mother to throw mean jabs at. There was no winning here, so I packed the loosest of my mother-approved wear and called it a day.

I already had a feeling I would need armor for this visit. Thanksgiving had been a joke compared to what was likely coming, with the impending deadline and my mother's change in attitude, which was apparently still developing given the voicemails she was leaving me. She'd switched over from text about three days ago, probably because I had been sending her one-word replies.

I zipped up my suitcase and, with a sigh, resisted the urge to reread certain non-Mǎmá texts—which I had been doing despite my lie to Andrew. I reminded myself of the main objective this Christmas break: Get. Rid. Of. Hongbo. That was it. Anything else only got in the way.

Voicemail from Chloe's mother

December 22

Eh, Jing-Jing. Wéi? [long sigh] Why didn't you call me back before you got on the plane? You haven't boarded yet. Why aren't you picking up now?

I guess I can understand why you couldn't uninvite Andrew. But . . . don't put all your duck eggs in one place, okay? At least see Hongbo this break. Keep thinking about the proposal. Who wouldn't want to wear that huge ring? Did you know it's twenty-four-karat gold? The Kuos know what's best! Andrew hasn't even proposed yet. Don't lose a sure thing for a maybe.

Think about it, okay? For me, your poor mǎmá who is constantly worrying about you so much her blood pressure is high. Don't send me to the grave early!

CHRISTMAS AND NEW YEAR

Drew

CHAPTER 25

CHRISTMAS COOKIES

December 23

I was outside, sort of behind a tree, waiting for the Uber with Jing-Jing in it to pick me up. It was routine, but my hands were clammy.

I fidgeted with my UChicago scarf (the only emblem I was sporting today) and cringed, remembering that this was the very dagger that had killed my dinner date two nights ago. Okay, that was dramatic, and obviously my actual date the human didn't die, but the abstract idea of that date had met a fiery end.

After a dinner of pad see ew, yellow curry, and crab Rangoon, she had asked to come over so I could draw a caricature of her (twenty-five miles away, my mother was having herself a good laugh). Caricatures I had no problem showing others, so I said fine (meanwhile thinking, *As long as she doesn't ask to see any of my real work*, which was hidden away in boxes). But I didn't have to worry about any of that because, not one minute after she entered my room, she noticed my UChicago scarf on the floor, then the Harvard sweatshirt peeking out of my closet, and she'd marched right up to the closet door and flung it open to see STANFORD, MIT, BERKELEY, UCLA on the sleeves of hung-up shirts.

"What the fuck?" she had asked, but I'd said nothing. Just stood back and watched as she pawed through, pausing on each one just long enough to verify that it was, indeed, yep, another school.

I'd tried to lie about having family ties to all those colleges, but given that those clothes made up the majority of my closet (the company paid for them, okay?), she fled. I yelled sorry after her, then felt weird about the rush of relief that came over me.

Honestly, we'd said about ten words to each other at dinner (three of which had been "I like art"), and she'd been on her phone a lot. I was pretty sure I even saw her swiping right and left with a suspicious rhythm, which, fine, yes, we weren't hitting it off, but she couldn't wait until I wasn't in front of her face?

The date had not only been a Mentos-in-Coke explosion, but it had also massively backfired, making me think about Jing-Jing and our easy conversation *more*.

I took the scarf off and angrily stuffed it in my bag.

When the little car on the Uber app approached my spot, I picked up the poinsettia at my feet and emerged onto the street.

"Hey," Jing-Jing said with a small, nervous smile when I opened the door.

I climbed in and tried not to give her a sappy grin.

"Hey," I said, all the extras dying on my tongue: *I'm so happy to see you. You look nice. I've been painting sheep in weird outfits for you, but you'll never know because that's just strange.*

"Are you ready?" she asked.

"Of course. Are you?"

She shrugged, then chewed her bottom lip. "My mom may have taken a step back, so . . . just be prepared. Okay, that's an understatement. She definitely took twenty steps back. Hongbo's parents have been wooing her."

I—Drew—was about to respond and reassure her when the Uber driver interrupted. "Why did I pick you up there? You could've walked to the destination."

That happened maybe one out of five times.

But we were already pulling up to the now-familiar three-bedroom, three-bathroom gray house with its bright red door. Jing-Jing and I exited the car without answering his question.

Right before she rang the doorbell, I raised an arm to block her path, taking care not to make physical contact.

She flinched anyway, sending a pang and, more importantly, a reminder, through me.

"Yes?" she asked, her voice soft but her body tense.

I reluctantly let my training take over, flipping the Andrew switch.

I smiled at her in the way that was supposed to relax the client (corporate made us practice in the mirror, then with each other). "Hey. This will go great. It's not unusual for the parents to have taken a step back with time, no matter how well the first job went. And regardless, we'll have some fun." I gestured to her face. "Your current expression might make your parents think you're just constipated, but it also might make them think we're going through a rough patch, which isn't the best way to start this off."

She laughed, just as I'd hoped, then pressed the doorbell with an upward tilt to her lips. "What if I'm also constipated?"

"Then I'll run out and get you some prunes."

She shook her head. "No need. My mom stocks up from Costco, exactly for this purpose."

"Some things transcend oceans and culture, right? Prunes must really work."

We were both laughing—genuinely—when the door opened.

Chloe

My parents hugged me, and then my mother hugged Andrew stiffly while my father stuck an unenthusiastic hand out.

Once inside, Andrew handed them the poinsettia he'd brought, which my mother placed in front of the fireplace beside the still-full box containing the unassembled artificial tree.

My father cleared his throat. "We are so sorry to do this, but we were called into the office with a couple of last-minute emergencies. You know how it is before the holidays: the pain threshold changes and patients call when they normally wouldn't have."

Damn it. That was hard-earned paid-for time we were losing.

"Maybe they can come with us?" my mother suggested.

My dad glanced at Andrew—and not that subtly—before saying, "I already called Patricia to come in and assist. It'll be quicker that way."

What was that about? I mouthed to Andrew. He bit his lip and looked away guiltily.

Once my parents were out the door, I started wondering how this empty stretch could best serve our mission, but Andrew already had a plan.

He rubbed his hands together. "It's time."

"For what?"

His hands burst apart as he said excitedly, "Christmas cookies!"

I blinked at him.

His hands dropped to his sides. "Are you not a fan of baking Christmas cookies?"

I shrugged. "I've never made them before."

"Well, let's remedy that and give you some data so you can decide where you stand."

"No milk, no baking powder, and ten-year-old vanilla extract," Andrew said, drumming his fingers on the counter after he'd scoured every nook and cranny of the kitchen. "The milk one is really the wrench."

I grabbed his arm. "Holy crap, does this explain Frankenbāo?"

His mouth dropped open. "Maybe. Partially. I also have been wondering—yes, I've spent way too much time thinking about it—

if there's something related to the fact that sweet and savory seem to go together more in Chinese cuisine, and maybe that's part of your mom's inspiration?"

I pointed a finger at him because he was onto something. "Oh my God. She hates American sausages because they're 'just salty,' and she loves the Chinese ones that have a little sweetness to them. Oh! And! She used to tell me about these sausages she'd go to Tainan to get, with sugar in the middle."

He snapped, then pointed at me, saying one word per gesture. "Mystery. Solved."

"You put the Drew in Nancy Drew, An*drew*," I joked.

He gave me such a strange, unreadable look I opened the fridge for something to do. "We have coffee creamer," I announced after poking through.

"Your parents drink coffee?" He came over to peer into the fridge with me.

"Uh, my mom . . . drinks that as is."

Andrew gagged.

"Yeah, I know."

"She *really* likes sweet stuff, then."

"Yeah, maybe it's not so much a Chinese thing as a 'my mom' thing."

"Well, her sweet tooth may have saved our cookie mission." He grabbed the carton. "Let's do it."

We also had to substitute giant noodle-soup bowls for mixing bowls, but after getting past those fairly big hiccups, we were finally measuring and sifting and stirring.

While I was beating the eggs with chopsticks, Andrew moseyed over to preheat the oven. I yelled, waving my hands for a second before shutting it off.

"Wha—" he started, but I opened the oven door and hastily pulled out pots and pans and extra dishrags.

"How did you of all people not know this was a possibility? This one I know isn't just us—I have other Asian friends who use their oven for storage."

He hit his forehead with a palm. "Yeah, okay, I'm embarrassed I didn't realize that."

He helped me clear it out, then set the oven to 375 degrees.

We finished mixing and spooned out the batter in silence, the only sound being the beep of the oven when it was ready. We whisked around the kitchen, focused on our tasks, but the limited space made his arm brush against mine as he discarded dirty dishes in the sink, and my butt bump into his side as I leaned down to open the oven door.

He stuck the cookies in, I shut the oven door, and we set the timer together, me punching in eight minutes and him hitting the start button when I was done.

We both paused, then turned toward each other, our faces millimeters apart.

"Hi," he said.

"Hi." His eyes were laser focused on mine, and though I felt an urge to look away, I also couldn't.

"Are you doing okay with, you know, everything?" he asked with so much compassion I melted a little. "I know this month hasn't been the easiest."

I nodded. "Um, thanks for all your support. You went way above and beyond the job description."

He looked away, his forehead furrowed in thought—in uncertainty, I realized. Then the worry lines disappeared, replaced with resolve. "I didn't do it because of the job," he told me, his voice unwavering.

I didn't say anything because I couldn't.

His face softened. "And just so you know, I wasn't in character before, when we were texting." His voice was hushed, almost inaudible.

But I heard. How could I not, when I was so completely focused on him, his lips moving, his chest rising and falling?

"I already knew that." Now my chest was rising and falling so rapidly it became my focus.

He looked like he wanted to lean in, but he held back, letting me lead.

"I can't stop thinking about you," he said. "And it's messing with my focus on this job. On everything. It's why I didn't think about how there was probably stuff stored in the oven, why I've been sweating through this shirt worrying about whether I can keep it together this week, why I've reread your texts so many times I can probably recite them back to you from memory."

Without thinking, I replied, "Me too." To all of it.

And suddenly it felt like the dam within was bursting, and I couldn't hold everything in anymore. The desire for him to lean down toward me until our breath mingled was winning, pushing out all the other thoughts that no longer felt so important. How much could it hurt the mission if we did kiss just this once? In that moment, with his glistening lips not far from mine, with the scent of sugar and holiday warmth emanating from his tall, lean body, I couldn't think of a single reason why this would be a problem.

I glanced at his mouth, then back up at his eyes. "If we give in to what we're feeling, it would only help sell the story, right?" I whispered, my voice sounding as choppy as I felt.

"Mm-hmm," he murmured.

My mother burst in, and we jumped apart guiltily even though, what the hell, we were doing exactly what we were supposed to be doing. Except not. Oh my God, why had I spun such a complicated web?

"Oh!" my mother exclaimed, her face turning red. "I hurried home because I felt bad we were losing time together. I, uh, hunh."

The oven timer went off, and the shock on her face grew. "You used the oven?"

Andrew hurried over, used a rag to take the cookies out, then stuck a chopstick through the thickest one to make sure they were done. "No dough residue—came out great!" he said with way too much enthusiasm.

He transferred a few cookies onto a plate, and the three of us dug in even though they were way too hot; we just needed to fill our mouths so we wouldn't have to talk about the weirdness in the air, even though *there shouldn't be any weirdness*. I'd been caught almost kissing my supposed boyfriend, so why did everything feel so wrong?

The answer: For my mother, because Andrew wasn't Hongbo. For Andrew and me, because our situation was an Escher drawing come to life. Now that the spell was broken—thanks, Mǎmá—my turned-on-again brain understood how close I'd been to letting momentary pleasure threaten the mission. What if we went down that road and messed up his cover in front of my parents? Because I couldn't get to know the real him without risking what we were trying to accomplish.

I would *not* let my feelings get in the way again. Eyes on my douchebag-free prize.

I took a bite of cookie, then immediately spit it into the sink. "Oh my God, way too sweet," I said with a cringe.

"Blech, yeah," Andrew agreed, swallowing his but with half a cup of water. "Guess the creamer was too much."

"These are fantastic!" my mother exclaimed, her eyes bugging out. "Good job, you two."

Andrew and I burst into laughter that was heightened by both the inside part of the joke and the tension bubble bursting.

"What?" my mother asked, taking another cookie. We just kept laughing. "What *is* it?"

Chloe

CHAPTER 26
THE PRICE OF PEARS

As my mom disappeared to freshen up post-work, I couldn't meet Andrew's gaze. I cleaned the kitchen like my life depended on it. For once, I was relieved when my mother returned.

"So, Andrew," my mother said, trying to sneak another cookie off the pan without us noticing. "I heard about your shadowing . . . fun at the dental office last time. Have you given any more thought to my lǎo gōng's wise advice?"

I looked at him questioningly, but despite what he'd said earlier about being distracted, he was ready.

"Of course, but I'm not worried," he said easily. "It was my first time, and I've already made plans to shadow my parents in a few surgeries over spring break."

My mother raised an eyebrow, unconvinced. But our house rumbled as the garage door opened and she hurried away to greet my father.

"What happened when you shadowed?" I asked.

His gaze dropped in embarrassment. "Um, it was the closest I've ever come to losing my cover. Dentistry is disgusting!" He winced, then joked, "Are you going to drop my rating down to four stars?"

I laughed. "Hey, I hear you. There's a reason I'm not following in their footsteps, which they're disappointed about. They're still pushing me to apply to dental school, 'just to see.'" I mimicked my mother's voice: "'It'd be perfect, Jing-Jing! The economics classes will help you run the business—you'd be unstoppable! How easy would your life be, inheriting Wang Dental Palace and all our hard-earned patients?'"

Andrew lowered his voice and said, "Well, I followed in my grandpa's footsteps, and it's what caused the rift between my parents and me."

My mind filled with questions. *What did your grandfather do? What happened to him? What happened with your parents? Do you regret your decision? Are you okay? What . . . do you think of my situation based on your experiences?*

But then I remembered: If I didn't get rid of Hongbo now, the outcome was so bad I couldn't even think about it.

Eyes on the douchebag-free prize. Even if it gutted me. "Sorry, but I think you were right before. We need to stick to your rule. To prevent confusion."

The shock that flashed in his eyes quickly turned to understanding, but I still loathed myself.

"Of course. I'm so sorry," he said just as my parents shuffled in with plastic bags of food.

Andrew and I set the table with utensils and plates as my parents laid the takeout boxes in the middle.

We all leaned forward and removed the lids to reveal stir-fried chicken, scallops, duck, and fried rice from the Chinese café next to my parents' office.

"Thank you so much for this feast!" Andrew said enthusiastically to my parents.

"Thank you for joining us for the holidays," my mother said, half-assed, with zero enthusiasm.

Silence descended.

As we dug into the food, the quiet stretched on, and as it grew, so did my stress. Before Andrew, being home—"home," really, with air quotes—had been this, all the time. It hadn't happened over Thanksgiving because Andrew had been a novelty then and my parents a smidge more open-minded, but tonight the silence wrapped its claws around my neck and squeezed until I couldn't breathe.

Then my instincts kicked in, and I had an overwhelming urge to just scarf down all the food in front of me, partly so I could escape to my room sooner, but also because I needed something—anything— to do so it wouldn't be *this* suffocating.

My other option was to talk, telling whatever boring story I could think of just to fill the air with meaningless drivel that my parents could nod their heads to absentmindedly without actually listening. But that was painful in another way. And drawing attention to myself sometimes led to worse outcomes, like my mother complaining about my "muffin belly roll," "turkey chin," or "inflamed skin."

I shifted in my seat, adjusting my clothes so that my shirt was puffed out and my waistband above my stomach. I also held my chin a little higher. But there was nothing I could do about my skin.

I hated myself in this house. I hated what my priorities became, what I worried about, the things I said and, more so, didn't say. I used to think it was the house itself, but now I realized how obtuse that logic was; it was obviously because of my parents, me, and our relationship, not a stationary thing. But still, I found myself wishing we could go out to a restaurant, to at least have some background hubbub. Rent for Your 'Rents encouraged home meals when possible, though, to prevent potential run-ins with past clients.

"You look beautiful tonight," Andrew said, shocking me out of my thoughts.

"What?" I said before I remembered myself. "I mean, thank you."

My mother's eyes were about to pop out of her head.

"You really do," he said, softer this time, and I could tell he didn't have to reach far to look at me like I was the hoisin sauce to his duck. It made my heart both soar and sink.

"Thank you," I repeated, trying to match his tone but my voice coming out squeaky.

My mom narrowed her eyes at us, and even though there was no way in hell she could figure out what was *really* going on here, I started to sweat down under.

Instinctively, to distract them, I said, "My quarter went really well."

When my father's eyebrows lifted, I revised it to "My semester," because they still hadn't figured out that UChicago was on a quarter system, even though I had tried to explain it multiple times.

"All As?" my mother asked, not looking up from her food.

"Yes." I had worked my ass off to do it, too.

My father nodded at me.

I knew this was how it always went—I had to offer my good news unprompted, and they didn't know how to be nice, normal humans about it—but even after nineteen years of practice, disappointment still shot through me. Suddenly my achievement felt less triumphant.

Was this their plan? To make me ask more of myself because nothing was ever enough? Probably not—they were likely just incapable of reacting any other way.

And then, as always, it got worse.

"I was a straight-A student at Táidà, *and* I was shūjuàn jiǎng," my father bragged, not looking up from his plate. As if I had any clue what that last thing was.

Andrew's knee jerked and bumped into mine. I glanced at him, and though he had a smile on his face, his masseter muscle was clenched, making his jawline and temple flex.

"That's great, Bā," I said robotically, my questioning eyes not leaving Andrew.

"I was also number seven in my dental school cl—"

Andrew abruptly stood, grabbing his water in the process and raising it. "Jing-Jing, I am in awe of you. What an amazing achievement, getting all As." He lifted the glass in a sharp movement, some liquid splashing over the side. He ignored it. "Gōngxǐ."

Everyone sat frozen, including me.

"You interrupted my dad" were the words that chose to come out of my lips. Mainly because I couldn't say, *Get your shit together and focus on the mission!* Unless this was part of it?

Andrew turned to my father. "I'm sorry, Shǔshú. I just felt like we hadn't appreciated Jing-Jing's accomplishment enough."

Andrew sat back down. This time the silence was so thick with tension everyone else stopped breathing too.

We all inhaled our food, trying to speed up our escape from this squirmy, claustrophobic atmosphere.

I guess I should amend: all of us but Andrew, who was on the clock despite how he had acted ten minutes ago.

"Did you have a successful month?" he asked my parents. "I'm sure it's busy with patients wanting to use up their insurance, flexible spending, et cetera, before the year end."

My parents grunted, and I think my dad said, "Uh-huh, busy," between shoveling salt-and-pepper scallops into his mouth.

Which said a lot, because I knew he loved discussing dental insurance and telling everyone it was a scam—information that, yes, I had relayed to Andrew on my application. Probably why he was bringing it up now.

It wasn't going great, but I still gave Andrew points for effort because he didn't let up for the rest of the meal. And when I was still chewing the last of the roasted duck, he left the table to retrieve a bag from the living room.

"These are from my parents," he prefaced before setting down a giant sack of pears. Seriously, giant as in I wasn't sure how he fit that *and* all his clothes in his suitcase.

"You couldn't have grabbed them sooner?" I quietly joked to him, feeling a surge of hope.

Except my parents were staring at the fruit, my dad's lips pursed and my mom's eyes tight.

Instead of saying thank you, my mother asked, "Do your parents grow them or something? I wouldn't think pears thrive in Chicago."

"We special-order these," Andrew said. "I know one of the hardest things for my parents when they immigrated here was adjusting to the food, and Asian pears were one of the many items they missed." He gestured to the sack. "These are from Korea."

"So . . . they bought them especially for us?" my mother said slowly, a crease forming on her head—a bad and rare sign from don't-give-yourself-wrinkles Mămá Wang.

"They're probably expensive and so hard to find," I added before giving my mother a pleading look. "What a thoughtful gift."

"No thank you," my father said, finally speaking up.

Jesus. "What? Why? Because of earlier?"

My parents shook their heads but didn't elaborate.

"What is it?" I asked, shocking even myself. I was sick of being in the dark.

My mother sighed, then explained, "Giving pears is an insult. 'Lí'"—*pear*—"sounds like 'lí' as in 'fēnlí,' to separate. We can only assume they're wishing separation of us from a loved one." Her voice began to rise. "Maybe they mean Jing-Jing . . . maybe they want to cause our separation. They're staking their claim on the two of you in the future, wanting you to stay in Chicago instead of coming back to California!" She slapped the table. "Is this true? Is that what's happening? Because then it's war! I was afraid of this when I found out they live in Chicago!"

Holy cannoli.

Andrew sputtered, probably because he wasn't used to a blunder like this in his well-researched world. "I promise that's not why they gifted these. They always send pears to their closest and most cherished friends. These are imported; they're quite pricey. I swear these are given to you with respect. And appreciation for you hosting me."

My father stood. "It's hard to believe they wouldn't know the meaning of this, given their background." He eyed the pears one last time. "And don't split one between you two—you'd be dooming your relationship here and now. *Fēnlí*: 'separate,' or 'split a pear,'" he explained.

"Or maybe you *should* split one," my mother spat.

They both left the table. It was silent between me and Andrew as they trudged up the stairs, then slammed the bedroom door.

Goddamn it. I couldn't look at Andrew or the pears.

Drew

CHAPTER 27

O CHRISTMAS TREE

As soon as her parents had shut the bedroom door, Jing-Jing said, "Why'd you have to get them the freaking pears?" She was pretending to joke but I could tell she was part serious.

With a forced laugh I said, "That wasn't on purpose." Obviously. Though I was really frigging embarrassed about the mistake. Rent for Your 'Rents did a shit ton of research, but there were so many nuances in each diaspora family's interpretation of culture that these kerfuffles did happen every so often. "Maybe you helped a future client whose parents are also superstitious about pears?" I offered, knowing that would ease some of her frustration.

"That helps." She rubbed her temples. "I guess it's just as much my fault too. I've never heard my parents talk about pears before, but now I'm realizing that I've never seen them share one—though before I would've just assumed they each wanted their own."

"It's nobody's *fault*," I said. Her comment was in character for her (Eliza Schuyler), but I still wasn't used to how quick she was to blame herself. "It was pears, not a sack of dog poo. Or a stack of Harry Potter books."

That got her to laugh. She'd told me on her application that because the Kuos had declared Harry Potter evil (witchcraft, ahh!), everyone in their community was banned from owning or reading them. Jing-Jing had anyway, borrowing from the library and reading under the covers while sweating through her pajamas worrying she'd be caught. (And I found that detail and the fact that she'd mentioned it not adorable at all.)

But her laugh was short-lived, and she returned to rubbing her temples. (Did she need some ibuprofen?) Then, suddenly, she dropped her hands and looked at me so sternly my shoulders hunched. "You need to pull yourself together, refocus on the job—it's like you've forgotten why you're here."

"The pears were an accident," I said, even though I knew this wasn't about that.

"You know what I'm talking about." Her voice was wavering, like she wanted to increase the volume but couldn't on account of her parents upstairs. "Why'd you have to interrupt my dad?"

"Because you deserve to be treated better."

She shook her head at me. "That's not your concern."

"Someone needs to stand up for you since you aren't doing it yourself, even though you can and do otherwise."

"Don't."

The word was a warning. A start of a sentence but also the punctuation at the end of this topic of conversation.

She sighed. "Look, what happened in the kitchen earlier, with the cookies . . ." She took a breath. "That was a mistake. It can't happen again, and it can't affect what we're trying to do here."

Oof. My chest hurt.

What if I can't help defending you, wanting you to have more?

As if she read my mind (she probably read it on my face), she reached a hand toward me (but no contact) and said, "You help me the most by getting rid of Hongbo."

I nodded. That I could do. I'd find my way back, focus on the assignment so that, like always, my decisions would be made by recalling information, analyzing the situation, and executing. Formulaic, not driven by emotion, yeesh.

She stood. "Come on, let's go set up the Christmas tree. Maybe if we make this place more festive it'll change the mood."

"Don't you want to do that with your parents?"

"They hate it—I usually do it alone."

I know what that's like.

Jing-Jing pushed away from the table and I followed her to the den.

She opened the box and dumped the contents on the floor. Fake branches, ornaments in ziplock bags, free-floating tinsel, and one massive ball of lights fell out.

"Yikes." How late were we planning on staying up?

She forced a short laugh. "I know, sorry."

We constructed the tree in silence, with Jing-Jing untangling shit as I stuck fake branches into the plastic trunk.

The bedroom door opened slowly and creakily, like the sneaking culprit was trying to mask the sound.

We shared a hopeful look.

And then, as if a switch flipped, she grabbed a paper lantern (the kind my family also used to make out of construction paper, glue, and scissors) and threw it at me. Catching on, I laughed and declared, "Oh, it is so on."

But before I could retaliate, she hurled, like, twenty things at me (all soft, but still, quite the onslaught).

Between the laughter, we flung tinsel and streamers and felt ornaments at each other, some of it landing on the tree but most of it hitting our targets.

When we were short of breath, our fight turned even more playful, with Jing-Jing using the fake snow to give us fluffy beards, and us first linking plastic candy canes to see who could make the longest chain, then dueling with them.

It had become real for me. I thought maybe it was real for her, too, especially because her mom (or dad) had likely retreated back into the bedroom two play fights ago. But . . . *not your fucking prerogative, Operative.*

You help me the most by getting rid of Hongbo, I repeated in my head, which centered me.

"I think we're good," Jing-Jing whispered, and we put down our candy-cane weapons to assess the aftermath. A gorgeous, shining tree stood tall and confident before us. Just kidding. It was a kid's tantrum come to life in plastic-fir form, a Charlie Brown tree missing half its branches, with only the bottom third decorated haphazardly as if . . . well, as if it was the casualty of people fighting near it.

"Should we start over?" I asked.

"Nah, it's late. We'll do it tomorrow."

I nodded. Then, feeling awkward (even though I was trained not to), I wiped my hands on my pants. Then scratched my brow.

Jing-Jing was standing there watching me, her eyes taking in every fidget.

When I forced my hands down by my sides, she smiled, threw the last of the tinsel in my hair, said a quick good night, and bounded up the steps two at a time.

"Sleep loose," I whispered to no one.

That night, every time I tried to focus on pajama-clad sheep, Jing-Jing would appear—playing with the sheep, hopping over the fence with one, dancing with another. Always at a distance.

Chloe

As I lay in bed, I tried—so hard, I swear—to think about *anything* else. Sheep. Game theory. My parents. Other strategies to finally kick Hongbo out of my life. But no matter what I was trying to force to the front of my mind, Andrew would pop in, a flash of lips or laughter or tousled hair.

The faux flirting—or whatever you want to call our Christmas-tree giggle fest—had been real for me. Not at first, especially because of the big speech I'd just given him, but, well, I'm human. And I knew it had been real for him—the fidgety, not-Andrew side.

Was my solution to the Hongbo problem also going to be my downfall?

Chloe

CHAPTER 28

LUMINOUS

December 24

woke up exhausted after a night of tossing and turning. Determined not to repeat the pretend-but-real flirting of last night, I joined my parents in the kitchen and asked if they wanted to decorate the tree with me.

"Why would we? That's for kids," my mother said with a yawn over eggs. We were having them sunny-side up with tiánmiàn paste on the side, a sweet-and-savory breakfast that was far better than a reanimated Frankenbāo.

"Right. Of course." I tried not to let my emotions show.

I dished myself an egg and wondered if I'd be able to sneak in making a cup of green tea without my mom pulling out the mother tea, which, lo and behold, was on the counter. Maybe I could get Andrew to do it for me.

Speaking of, where was he? These were prime winning-the-'rents-over hours, especially before I was awake. Had he gotten overzealous with pajama designing last night and stayed up too late? Damn, did I want to tell him that joke, but it would only make everything harder.

"Besides, isn't it already done?" my father added.

I hurried to the den, scurrying past the couch with a recumbent Andrew, who got up and followed me wordlessly.

A gorgeous—I mean, it was freaking luminous—tree stood before me, perfectly frosted and decorated with familiar ornaments that evoked too many childhood memories to count. But there were also new touches: crisply folded origami cranes and stars, flowers assembled from cut construction paper, little 3-D paper mooncakes with googly eyes and tiny smiles, and . . . a few sheep. One dressed as a mooncake, another with a sheepdog on its butt, and one with the cutest little antigravity boots, floating near a half-moon.

"Oh my God, I can't believe you did this," I said, still staring forward even though he was behind me. I couldn't look away.

I touched the three sheep individually, purposefully, so he would know I'd seen them. But I wasn't sure if I should do more than that.

I finally turned to him. "Did you stay up all night doing this? Why?"

He shrugged. "Because you thought it could help."

"It's stunning," I said, gesturing to the whole tree. "It's like something you'd see in a model home or a Christmas issue of *Architectural Digest*. Or it's the work of . . . an artist," I realized.

I stepped closer to the tree and fingered one of the mooncake faces. "You're so talented."

His cheeks flushed. "I was just playing around."

"Well, then, that's all the more impressive."

An electrically charged moment passed between us, and, shockingly—pun intended—he ended it first.

He cleared his throat and took a step away from me. "I was just trying to turn the mood—the bad one I created, sorry," he said without meeting my gaze. Then he leaned toward me and whispered, "It's what any good operative would've done."

His breath on my ear made me shiver. "Right. Of course. Thank you." Even though I had asked him to distance himself, to stick to his rule, his words etched a painful crack in my glass heart.

He quickly changed the subject. "Do you want a pear for breakfast?"

"Sure. Only if we each get one." Then I sputtered, "Just because I want my own. No other reason."

"Of course."

Drew

Thank goodness, because I didn't want to split a pear because of the other reason. But I respected her wishes and kept that to myself.

Drew

CHAPTER 29

GOLDEN OPPORTUNITY

Jing-Jing and I ate our own eggs and own pears, no splitting. The latter was super delish, with so much juice and that unique crunchy texture my parents always raved about (yes, the pear gift was something my real parents did). Mr. and Mrs. Wang hovered silently (and awkwardly) as Jing-Jing and I ate the traitorous fruit, only a pinched look from him and a forced nasal exhale from her. I considered conjuring up an apology email from my parents (which would've been almost no work on my part and expertly done by the company—they already had email addresses set up for my "parents"), but I followed my well-trained gut and gave them room to breathe.

When I'd first sat down, Jing-Jing had tilted her head at me, then at her parents, but I gave her a *trust me* nod even though I didn't feel as confident as usual. She'd nodded back at me, but the worry didn't leave her eyes.

Not ten minutes later, her parents stood and excused themselves.

"Make sure you clean up before the party this afternoon," Mrs. Wang said sternly, mostly to her daughter.

"We're going to that?" Jing-Jing asked, completely surprised, and her mother answered, "Of course," with a wave of her hand.

When it was just us, Jing-Jing said, "So, uh, apparently we're going to the annual Christmas Eve party for our little community. The entire congregation usually shows up, even the not-so-religious ones, for the food, of course." She paused. "And it's at Hongbo's parents' house."

"Oh," I said, the shape of my mouth and eyes matching the sound that had just come out.

"Yeah."

"Is this a good or bad thing?"

Jing-Jing tapped her fingers on the table. "I just assumed we wouldn't be going since my parents wouldn't want everyone to see us together, but maybe this is their tactic to get me and Hongbo together for a longer stretch of time, where it's harder for me to run? *Except*," she said with emphasis, raising her right index finger, "we'll use it to our advantage."

"My thoughts exactly. Get ready for your entire community to know how in love we are."

She grasped her cup and tilted her head toward me. "Do you have any specific tactics in mind? I just . . . I feel like this is it. The golden opportunity, you know? We have to reach out and"—she grabbed at the air and formed a fist—"clinch this whole thing."

"Why don't we take a walk?" I suggested, ticking my chin up toward her parents' bedroom.

She nodded.

We gobbled up the rest of our (edible, phew) breakfasts, she slipped a sweatshirt over her striped cotton T-shirt, and we went for a scheming walk around the neighborhood.

Chloe

CHAPTER 30

PRIME STRIP

As we left the house and started wandering aimlessly, Andrew suggested, "Maybe we can attack this from *both* sides, not just your parents'. Maybe the Kuos have a weak spot we can hit."

"Yes, brilliant."

He looked at me expectantly, waiting for more info, but I just nodded, over and over and over again. Stalling. Because in order to figure out a plan, he had to know all the nauseating details, including what I'd left off the application. On purpose. I was about to relive some truly awful moments I'd been trying to forget since they happened. But for the sake of the mission, I sucked in a breath and spat the story out.

Three months earlier, my life had been pure bliss—no thoughts of Hongbo, and certainly none of him and me together. Using this to her advantage, my mother had tricked me into going on a date with anti-Dreamboat. And on that horrible, life-altering night, I'd started the evening thinking I would be tutoring him for the GMAT in exchange for money.

Before I'd left, my mother had fussed over my outfit and makeup, but to her credit, it hadn't been more than usual. Hongbo picked me up, and then, weirdly, drove me to his parents' house.

"Just wait here a sec" is what he should've said before leaving me in the car in his parents' driveway.

Fifteen minutes in, I was *this* close to using my phone to mail-order him a durian. (No, that's not a real thing. But it will be, once I raise enough money to start my totally legal revenge business.)

At twenty minutes, I strode through the mansion's white columns and past the unlocked front door to find Hongbo throwing a tantrum, stomping foot and all, in the foyer in front of his mother.

"Everything okay in here?" I asked.

"Aiyah, Jing-Jing, you were in the car? Wǒ de lǎo tiān yé!" his mother exclaimed. "Hongbo, how could you? I thought you were picking her up later! Why didn't you at least invite her inside?"

He shrugged, then used his mother's complaint against her. "Let's not keep her waiting longer; just give me what I asked for."

His mother sighed. "You just received your allowance last week, and that should be plenty. Don't you think three thousand dollars is a big ask? Even if it is for dear, sweet Jing-Jing," she said, smiling at me so wide her eyes crinkled.

Holy baloney, was he planning on paying me three thousand dollars? We hadn't discussed the fee in detail other than my mother promising he would "shower me with money." But I hadn't dreamed *that* big. Big enough to make a sizable dent in my student loans. I tried to keep a gigantic grin from spreading across my face.

Meanwhile, Hongbo's tantrum continued.

"Don't you think this is a worthy cause, Mother?" His eyes narrowed. "Don't make me remind you what's at stake."

With this threat, Mrs. Kuo frantically took her phone out and pressed, typed, and swiped—presumably transferring money. Then, with way too much enthusiasm, she said, "Okay, you kids have fun."

Because I was too entranced by the flashing money signs, I failed to see the red flags: Hongbo had needed to beg for money; Mrs. Kuo's behavior toward me had changed from previous indifference to hungry interest; Hongbo's massive ego would never allow him to be tutored by someone six years younger than him; and Hongbo's Gudetama ass would never want to attend business school when he already had blood rights to No One Systems.

But in that moment I had practically skipped back outside and into the BMW. "Where's Sheila?" I asked, trying to be friendlier.

"In the shop."

Which was less appealing, someone who drove a Lamborghini or someone who lied about having one? But I forced a smile in response.

Then the next red flag was accompanied by alarm bells: Hongbo zoomed past the library.

"Hey," I blurted, pointing back toward where my mother had said we'd be studying. "Aren't we . . . Where are we going?"

"Prime Strip," he answered, devoid of emotion.

I wasn't happy about prolonging my time with him, but for three thousand dollars, fine.

"I like steak," I told him, like a nincompoop.

He laughed. At me, not with me. "See? This is why I need you," he chuckled.

"I don't get it."

"Exactly."

We pulled into the parking lot. Of Prime *Strip*. As in neon boobs jiggling and a chalkboard out front advertising EXTRA FREAKY FRIDAY DEAL! TWO DANCERS FOR THE PRICE OF ONE!

"What the . . . ," I started, but trailed off because I couldn't think of any explanation for this.

"They have good steak, too, I promise," he teased as he pulled the parking brake up.

"I'm not going in there."

He sniggered, feeding off my discomfort.

"Seriously, why are we here, Hongbo?"

He shrugged. "When I agreed to this date"—*what the fuck?*—"I was scared you'd think it was real since it's probably your first, so, I dunno, I thought it'd be a good idea, and funny, to bring you here."

"Date?" I repeated in shock.

He scowled at me. "What's wrong with you? Yeah, date. The one our parents set us up on."

And, just like that, I was the fool, triple-pointed hat and everything.

I replayed my conversation with my mother.

Me: Just so you know, I was able to put a chunk toward tuition last quarter—I mean, semester—with my tutoring.

Mom: That reminds me, Hongbo requested you personally.

Me: For tutoring? What, for the GMAT or something?

Mom: Why don't you see him Friday?

Me: [inaudible grunting]

Mom: His treat. Bài tuō le, Jing-Jing.

Me: No need to get dramatic. [pause] I'm not in.

Mom: He'll shower you with money. I already told him you would do it. What's so bad about spending a few hours with him at the library on Friday?

Goddamn it. That crafty badger.

The math tips and vocab word lists in my purse were laughing at me. The previous red flags I'd unconsciously ignored now came screaming to the forefront at full speed, mocking me and telling me I deserved Prime Strip for letting myself get bamboozled by money.

"Take. Me. Home," I said evenly through my teeth.

Hongbo rolled his eyes.

When he didn't start the engine, I exited the car, slamming the door as hard as I could.

He jumped out of the driver's side. "Hey! Easy on the door!" He hurried over and blocked my way. "What's wrong with you? Just come in, eat some steak, watch the show—you could learn a thing or two. Here, I'll even be a gentleman and let you use this." He pulled out a filled-out punch card that said FREE NACHOS AFTER 10 LAP DANCES. "Or maybe we'll share. I earned this, after all."

I pulled my phone out to call an Uber and he threw a palm up. Worried he was reaching out to take my phone, I tucked it into my armpit.

But, worse, he was reaching up to point at my head as he said, "You have a screw loose up there? Girls would give up their first-borns for a chance to be with me! Not that I'm sterile or anything—I have supersperm—it's just a metaphor. Do you know what a meta-phor is? Because I do. Obviously."

"Oh my God, I know what a metaphor is!" I burst out.

"Well, good, because I'm asking you to be with me metaphorically and only metaphorically. Because I'm not, like, attracted to you or anything. Blech—you have the sex appeal of a cactus."

I was so overwhelmed and angry and disgusted I didn't bother ask-ing what being with someone "metaphorically" meant, and I instead tried to fully convey how not interested I was. "I would rather have sex with a cactus than be with you."

He narrowed his eyes with resentment even though he'd *just said the same thing to me*. Then he shook his head. "You idiot, it's a busi-ness transaction: you do me a favor, I do you a favor."

"How in the hell would you be doing me a favor?"

"By pretending to date me, you'd get to live a little more."

"What, like free nachos while someone's ass waves in my face?"

He rolled his eyes. "No, I meant more like"—he gestured to his car—"stuff like this. *And*, if you play your cards right and we get married, you'd get a piece of the fortune."

If I had been drinking water, I'd have spat it out dramatically, like in a movie. But since I wasn't and my mouth was completely dry, I choked on my own tongue and, surprise, Hongbo didn't notice, continuing, "It's all pretend. You're obviously allowed to do whatever with whoever, if you even want that"—his eyes flicked to my private parts as he snickered, and I could hear him all over again telling everyone about my shriveled vagina—"and I obviously would live the same life as now. Who knows? Maybe you'll even be lucky enough to get a piece of me too, though you're not my type, and guessing by this"—he gestured vaguely at my genitals with a circle of his hand—"you don't have the experience to make up for the rest of it."

I'd never kicked anyone in the balls before, but that didn't mean I wouldn't be good at it or that I shouldn't.

I had to swallow some bile. "Why the fuck would I want anything to do with you, let alone a fake relationship?" I pulled my phone out again. "I'm leaving. Please don't ever contact me again."

This time he did swipe for my phone, but I dodged him.

"Look," he said, a little desperate. "My parents want us to be together, okay? Because, you know, you're like the community virgin or whatever."

I was sort of aware that I had that reputation, but I hadn't known it was so official. Why would it be, when it was nobody's business but my own? The ironic part was that their so-called community virgin was and had always been open to romantic relationships, including the physical parts, but had just never found anyone who made her stomach flip or whatnot. Maybe because the community's flagship bachelor was worse boyfriend material than a cactus.

I shook my head over and over and over. "All of this is . . ." I circled a hand, not able to find the words for how absurd this was. "We're so far off the deep end we're not even in the pool anymore."

"See? You're perfect for this. 'We're not even in the pool anymore,'" he mimicked. "Who fucking talks like that?"

Finally my eyes and voice turned as murderous as I felt. "Stay the hell away from me."

I retreated to the other side of the parking lot to wait for my Uber, and he left me alone.

But not for long.

One week later and one day before my escape halfway across the country, I was focused on more important things: Were two hats, three scarves, and fifty hand warmers enough for the upcoming winter? Better make it sixty.

The doorbell rang and I assumed it was a family friend stopping by with a home-cooked dish, but . . .

"Jing-Jing!" My mother's shrill but singsongy tone told me exactly who it was.

I threw the additional hand warmers into my suitcase and fought off the urge to scream.

Only nineteen hours and forty-two minutes before you're outta here, I reminded myself as I reluctantly dragged my ass downstairs.

My parents were fawning over him, complimenting his Nike high-tops, asking about his parents and their company. "Aiyah, your family is so impressive. Number One Systems is number one all right!"

As soon as my foot touched the hardwood of the first floor, Hongbo . . .

Excuse me, I was gagging in the corner.

Hongbo fucking *pulled out a ring box.*

My mother gasped so hard she dissolved into coughs.

He shoved the box toward me. When I recoiled, he opened it, as if the size of the stone would sway me. The fucking Hope diamond wouldn't have done it, let alone the square-cut canary one picked out by his mother.

"No," I said, trying to fight back tears. How had it devolved into this, and so quickly? "Please leave," I begged, simultaneously trying not to hurl something at him or hurl, period.

"Shut up!" my mother yelled at me as she grabbed the box. "We humbly accept, Hongbo."

I ran. I didn't know what else to do.

"How dare you, Jing-Jing!" Hongbo shouted. "Can you get that stick out of your ass for one second and smarten up before it's too late?"

"He'll provide for you; your life will be so easy," my mother called after me. "And we've known his family for so long—what more could you ask for?"

"You've never had a serious boyfriend—how can you know what you want?" my father added.

I had never felt so utterly, completely alone.

I ended my recounting there since it naturally picked up with where Andrew came in, though in reality a piece was still missing. But it was a piece I couldn't bring myself to share with him because it was embarrassing and horrible and made me feel like a piece of shit on the sidewalk. And thus I had left it off the application, too. He didn't need to know; none of our potential plans were affected by this final nail in the coffin—just my ego and self-worth.

When I finished relaying the hellish details to Andrew, it felt like a weight had been lifted. A nacho-and-lap-dance-loving, Lamborghini-faking weight.

Around the Prime Strip part of the story, Andrew and I had taken up residence on a bench in Cottontail Park, where, sadly, I had never seen a single cotton-tailed friend.

"Holy shit," Andrew uttered. It was the first thing he'd said, having been silent the entirety of my recollection except for a few reactionary noises here and there.

"You can say that again."

"Holy shit." He paused. "First, I'm so sorry. That is just, well, fucking appalling. I can't think of a word that summarizes it well enough, and I can't even fathom what it must've been like for you. I'm sorry."

We sat quietly for a moment as the horror sank into his face, then morphed into confusion. Probably because there were things that didn't add up.

"Why is Hongbo so supportive of this?" he asked.

"I've thought about this. A lot. Too much." *It keeps me up at night, in fact.* "Hongbo doesn't want me, but I suspect he wants the life and inheritance that comes with following his parents' commands."

"Fuck."

I nodded. "Fuck me for being the apple of his parents' goddamn eyes."

"And for the grossest of reasons."

"Well . . ." A light bulb slowly brightened in my head. "Maybe we can use that. Take my reputation down a notch."

"You shouldn't have to do that."

"I'm not talking about anything disastrous. We'll have fun with it. Like, 'Hey, Kuo Ǎyí, did you know I've smoked a cigarette before?'"

"A *marijuana* cigarette," Andrew added, and we both laughed. "Not the easiest to bring up in conversation, though."

I shrugged. "If it's awkward, it's awkward."

"It still bothers me that you're the one suffering for the sake of others. And you're the only one who hasn't done anything wrong."

"I lied to my parents."

He sighed. "For a good reason, unlike everyone else."

"You don't have to protect me," I said, when in reality I craved it. I was tired of standing my ground on my own.

"I know," he said, and I could tell he was thinking, *But I want to,* which only made it hurt more.

"Well, maybe the best plan is to just show everyone how in love we are," I said. "Convince the community we're a solid item so the Kuos back off." Maybe my original plan was the best strategy after all.

Andrew nodded. "That's what I'm trained for. Get ready for

some impromptu slow dancing, lots of hand grazes, maybe even some finger-food feeding if we're feeling really cheesy." A mischievous glint appeared in the corner of his eye. "We'll take it into the desert."

"Huh?"

The right side of his mouth quirked up. "You know, your joke. We'll take it so far off the deep end we'll be out of the pool, into the car, and miles inland where there's no water in sight."

I burst out laughing.

"For the record, I liked that line," he said. He nudged my shoulder with his. I flinched when we made contact, and he scooted away an inch. "I'm sorry."

Not as sorry as I was.

I put my hand out, palm down. "One, two, three—fuck you, Hongbo!" I chanted. And even though we were far from a foolproof plan, Andrew put his palm on mine and we pressed down, then threw our hands and worries into the air.

Drew

CHAPTER 31

SHARKY SEA

was as ready as I could be for the Christmas Eve party to end all parties: freshly showered, deodorized, shaved, and suited up (just a regular suit, not a superhero suit, unfortunately). Most importantly, I had also received an all clear from corporate about the party. As soon as Jing-Jing and I had returned from our walk, I'd sent Rent for Your 'Rents an alert with the party details, and they had combed through their database and the internet for potential conflicts with any previous clients of mine. The chances were already low because, before I had even been assigned to her, Jing-Jing had listed her communities and family friends and contacts for the algorithm to take into consideration. But I liked to take every precaution, meaning, if the all clear hadn't come through, Rent for Your 'Rents would have tried to contact the other client, or I would have found a way out of the party.

I was sitting on the couch, fighting my urge to twiddle my thumbs, when Jing-Jing descended the stairs in a flowy, scarlet, knee-length cocktail dress. Three pink peonies were splashed across the top half, above where the skirt flared out, and two adorable Chinese knot closures joined the two sides of the slanted collar. And, this had *never* happened before, I promise (and I'd never *wanted* it to happen), but it felt like she was coming toward me in slow motion.

I had somehow stood as she came downstairs, but I didn't remember moving any muscles.

"Wow." I cleared my throat. "I mean, wow," I said in exactly the same hoarse, embarrassing way.

Everything sped up again and she smiled at me as she approached.

"You clean up nice," she said, gesturing to my maroon button-up shirt, navy suit, and forest-green pocket square. (Maroon was a UChicago color and, with the forest green, also checked the Christmas-colors box.)

Then she leaned over and whispered, "Good performance."

Performance? Right. Jing-Jing subtly tilted her head toward her mother, whom I now saw for the first time, peeking at us from around the corner, her eyes wide and lit up like that time at Thanksgiving when I'd complimented how strong and independent Jing-Jing was.

But the light in Mrs. Wang's eyes didn't last long. When we arrived at the *obscene* mansion by the man-made lake (there were fucking columns out front and *two* spewing fountains), we were engulfed by other guests as soon as we entered. And suddenly I didn't exist, to the point where Mrs. Wang did everything she could to create physical distance between me and the rest of them.

A middle-aged man with salt-and-pepper hair and broad shoulders placed a hand on Mr. Wang's shoulders. "How are you feeling?" he asked, his volume low as if it were a secret.

"Dr. Lin, hello!" Mr. Wang answered nervously, shaking hands with him longer than normal societal standards would dictate.

At the same time, a woman ran up to Mrs. Wang and, in lieu of a greeting, rambled, "Aiyah, I heard your Jing-Jing is studying economics at UChicago! I wish my Charlie would major in something that practical, but he just *had* to become an MD-PhD, which, giǎ xiáng, is a *nine*-year program—though I think he's on track to do it in six, giving me gray hairs worrying about how hard he's working!"

Mr. and Mrs. Wang threw their coats and scarves on top of me to slow me down. As I tried to untangle myself, the chatter around me increased as more guests swarmed the Wangs.

"Oh! Hey," I heard Jing-Jing say.

A voice I didn't recognize said "Hey" back in a mocking way. (How could anyone make fun of the word "hey"?)

I'd just freed my head from Mr. Wang's scarf when Mrs. Wang threw Jing-Jing's outerwear at me too.

"How are you, Lisa?" Jing-Jing said with a forced smile. (I couldn't see her, but I knew from her tone what her facial expression was.)

"Oh, you know, there's a lot of pressure on me in law school, but it's Harvard so I can't complain, right?"

Oh, gross.

A boy piped up, "The pressure probably comes from your older sister having three master's degrees and now getting a PhD, right?"

"Well, everyone in our family has at least two master's, so that's not a big deal, but yeah, the PhD is prestigious."

"And I'm going to be a Rhodes scholar!" another girl blurted as if she couldn't hold on to the information a second longer without bursting.

How the eff had Jing-Jing survived high school with people like this? My childhood Asian community had been nothing but supportive, lifting one another up because no one else would help us.

I finally escaped the choke hold of the outerwear and passed everything to the (very confused) maid, but the Wangs were nowhere in sight. Lisa took one look at my UChicago scarf and she and her minions turned their backs to me (what would they have done if they knew my real background?). Then the faux bragger, who had zero interest in finding out who the Wangs' coat servant was, turned to one of the overt braggers to tell them how positively dreadful it was that poor Charlie was working so hard he wouldn't be having kids anytime soon.

Part of me wanted to stick around and watch faux bragger vs. overt bragger, buuut I was already sure all outcomes would annoy me.

I calmly handed the maid my scarf, but I slipped out of my dress shoes and placed them near the other shoes myself so the maid wouldn't have to touch something my feet had. Then I moseyed into the sharky sea as if I had all the time and calm in the world, like I was so sure of my relationship with Jing-Jing that I didn't need to rush after her (or own her, like Hongbo surely would).

The foyer was massive, with ceilings taller than my apartment building (okay, maybe not, but it felt like that because it was so cavernous). On the right side of the hall, two curved staircases from opposite sides met in the middle, melting into one grand, oversize staircase. To the left, the library or den or whatever you call that usually empty, meant-to-impress room was teeming with people. And even more chatter was coming from beyond the *indoor* columns (can't believe I had to specify that).

So Jing-Jing was saying no to all this. For just a small piece, I would have faked a relationship with Hongbo (clearly—I'd done it for a lot less).

My green socks with red polka dots glided over the polished marble floor. I looked for Jing-Jing while reminding myself to give off cool and comfortable vibes by keeping my spine straight, shoulders down, lips tilted slightly, head at the perfect angle (not too high and arrogant, but not low as if trying to hide).

My outer appearance remained relaxed, but inside, I was on guard just in case. It was super unlikely I'd run into another client (especially given the all clear), but bolting was the best defense for face-to-face run-ins, where deniability was difficult (which was our strategy otherwise, and why we changed last names between jobs and avoided photos).

I passed between the indoor columns, then traversed a hallway nook with great acoustics where two women dressed in Tang dynasty clothes were playing the pípa and èrhú (gorgeously, I might add—

the music, not the women . . . well, also the women, maybe; I wasn't looking). Then I passed an enormous room (ballroom?) where guests were chatting and snacking on egg rolls and chāshāo bāos and turnip sī bǐngs served by staff in red and green qípáos. Eventually, I found Jing-Jing in the very back, in the kitchen, which was vast but not meant for company, as evidenced by the lack of Christmas decorations. In fact, it was devoid of anything save for a plastic bag tied to one of the drawer handles, which made me happy: even crazy rich Asians still recycled plastic bags in a distinctly Asian way.

They were still a few yards from me, but I could see that Jing-Jing was surrounded by her parents and the Kuos, with Hongbo hovering slightly outside the circle, looking uncomfortable. Jing-Jing's head was nonstop nodding like a bobblehead, and a polite smile graced her face, but I knew from the tightness in her eyes that she was trying to escape.

Hongbo was dressed in a shiny silver silk suit (nice *s* alliteration there—I'm sure that was what he was going for). Every time his slippery suit brushed against Jing-Jing's elbow (he was pacing now), she flinched.

When Hongbo saw me, his head perked up, and then he sidled over to put his arm around Jing-Jing. As predicted, both sets of parents urged them on with their hungry, disgusting eyes.

I'd never felt so desperate to book it across an overwaxed floor in socks. Except I knew she didn't actually need me. Which she proved half a second later when she grabbed Hongbo's hand and turned it sideways. He pulled his arm back and tried to shake it off, but he was the one who was shook.

Good.

As I (finally) neared her, I heard Jing-Jing say calmly to Hongbo, "Please don't touch me."

A shadow crossed the parents' faces at the same moment Hongbo stalked off.

And headed straight for me. I instinctively backed up, not wanting whatever was coming to happen in front of the parents since it was a wild card.

Hongbo followed, catching up to me in a mostly empty hallway I'd turned down.

"*You're* the reason she hasn't said yes," he said, his eyes narrowed in frustration. He pressed a finger to my chest, one push per sentence. "*You're* the obstacle here. You're the thorn in my ass I have to remove." The spot hurt where his index finger had dug in.

"That's not true at all," I answered quickly. "Even if I weren't in the picture, it wouldn't change how she felt about you." I wished there were a way to fully show him that, but I couldn't tell him the truth of how I knew Jing-Jing's counterfactual (which was really her factual).

"You need to break up with her," Hongbo declared like the spoiled, privileged ass he was, so used to demanding things of others, even strangers. A diaspora version of Little Emperor syndrome at its finest.

"Do I get a say in this?" a voice said from behind us. A voice that made my knees a little weak.

I turned to watch Jing-Jing approach, her steps confident and an exasperated but take-no-shit look on her face.

Chloe

"Why do you even care this much? Is it just about the money?" I asked Hongbo. An image of him begging his mother for three thousand dollars popped into my head. "Are your parents threatening to cut you off if I don't marry you or something?"

He scoffed, a spit-spraying *pfft*. "You think they would do that? Even your vagina isn't shriveled enough for that."

Andrew's fists clenched, but he let me lead.

"Well, if it's not the money, then what? You clearly don't have feelings for me."

Hongbo cringed. "Ew. No shit."

"We're missing something," I said, half thinking out loud, half to Andrew. Definitely not to Hongbo, but he responded anyway.

"Maybe if you'd gone to Stanford like me, you'd have figured it out."

I snapped my fingers. "You must have done something! And it must've been really horrible, even for you."

Hongbo wore his usual smug expression, but I saw the hint of panic in the lines around his eyes. So I kept ruminating, because if he and his parents were hiding something, maybe we could use it against them once we figured out what it was. "Well, given that you wanted me for my reputation—" I started, but before I could finish, he turned to leave.

Time for drastic measures. Even if I guessed it, he wouldn't admit it, so I had to change tactics. And what was Hongbo's biggest downfall? His behemoth, blown-out-of-proportion ego.

I hurried around him so he'd have to face me. "Maybe you're going along with all this because you're having a really hard time finding a girlfriend and need Mommy and Daddy to do it for you. Why would you need to marry me, someone you supposedly can't stand—though maybe you're lying about that, too—if you could get anyone else? Maybe you're all talk and no game. If someone as 'inexperienced' as me doesn't even want you, maybe no one else does either. Maybe you talk about all your 'exploits' to cover up that you've had none." Then I used his own prejudices against him: "Maybe you're still a virgin."

"I am *not* a virgin," he said with a laugh.

I shrugged. "That's what you *say*. You brag about Prime Strip and supersperm because you have no idea what you're talking about."

Throughout my volleys, he had slowly been steaming, a kettle about to boil, and with that last comment he exploded. "I've had so much sex it would blow your shriveled mind!" Hongbo yelled at me. "And I do have supersperm! I got someone pregnant! She's due on New Year's!"

168

My mouth dropped open. So did Andrew's. And Hongbo's.

"That's not true," he backtracked. But he knew it was too late. "You can't tell anyone. No one would believe you. I'll—I'll hunt you both down if this gets out. I know people!"

I was still processing. "Your parents wanted me to be with you to, what, fix your reputation with mine? As proof that you've changed? To distract people with engagement news so they don't notice the baby news?" He didn't answer. "And that's why you were cut off, as punishment," I realized. "So this *is* about the money for you."

A hopeful look crossed Hongbo's face. "Well, now that you know, maybe you can help an old friend out?"

I gave him my own *pfft*—a spit-spraying one.

Andrew spoke to just me. "You should tell your parents about this. Then it'll be over; they'll stop pressuring you."

Hongbo scoffed. "What makes you think they don't already know?"

My vision blurred. He was lying. He had to be. He was trying to get back at me. Trying to make me angry.

But then his next words rang in my ears. "Your mom told us they'd be honored to help. 'Jing-Jing is the purest of them all!'" he finished, mimicking my mother's voice saying the catchphrase she only used with me in private—well, I guess, not anymore.

Bloodred shame and red-hot anger exploded into existence simultaneously. The lava coursing through my veins was so overwhelming that my mind blanked for a moment. But when I came to, I knew exactly who to take everything out on.

Chloe

CHAPTER 32

SHATTERED

stormed right up to my parents, who were hovering behind the Kuos near the entrance of the ballroom like sad, desperate puppies waiting for their owners to give them attention again.

"You knew this was because of an unwanted pregnancy and you *supported* it?" I asked as soon as they were within earshot.

"Shh," my mother hissed, glancing around to make sure no one had heard. Everyone was pretending to look elsewhere, but I could tell from their collective leaning in that they hadn't made out my words and were now trying to.

God, I hated this community.

I lowered my voice to stick it to the eavesdroppers, even though another part of me wanted them to hear, as punishment for my parents. And the Kuos. "Tell me it's not true."

My parents led me away, into a less-crowded foyer that housed a row of towering porcelain vases. "Why does that matter?" my father asked.

"You've got to be kidding me."

My mother put her hands on her hips. "Well, really, Jing-Jing, what did you expect? Why else would Hongbo—would the Kuos, the *Kuos*—want you?"

If my mother had reached into my chest and dug her nails into my heart, would that hurt less than right now?

She continued, "We're just being honest. Realistic. Because we love you. We tell you the truth when no one else will."

The truth. There were no truths here anymore. Except for the fact that my own mother believed my sole redeeming quality was my untouched vagina.

I didn't know how long I stood there, on the precipice, so angry and hurt and sad that nothing came out, not even a tear. I just knew that when I started to come back to my body, my parents had stopped talking. And Andrew was hovering beside me worriedly. And then, in my peripheral vision, I saw Hongbo and his parents separate themselves from some clingy guests to join us.

Blurred remarks were exchanged, barely audible in my haze. But I snapped to when I heard Mrs. Kuo snarl, "Who is this?" while glaring at Andrew, who was standing very close to me.

"A classmate," my mother answered calmly.

"This is my boyfriend, Andrew," a voice—my voice—said.

"Kuo Āyí, Shūshú, nice to meet you," Andrew said politely, shooting them his professional-charmer smile and then bowing his head slightly.

"What's the meaning of this?" Mr. Kuo growled to my parents, whose faces were flushed. "We've been telling everyone that Hongbo and Jing-Jing are together. You realize how this looks?"

"How long has this been going on?" Mrs. Kuo asked my parents.

Much too long. I've been ignoring my own happiness as long as I can remember.

"They've been friends for a few months—just friends," my mother answered frantically. "I mean classmates! They're classmates! Studying together. In groups!"

Loudly, my father added, "There's nothing going on here. Really."

The Kuos shot them doubtful frowns.

A beat passed where they stared each other down.

Hongbo broke the silence. "I told you none of this was my fault. I did everything you asked."

"Be quiet!" his father reprimanded.

Hongbo ignored him. "Maybe we should call this off. Since, you know, she probably isn't as pure as we thought."

Mrs. Kuo sniffed disdainfully. "That's a great point."

Andrew looked ready to tear this place down. He kept looking at me, waiting for a signal, but I was too angry, too overwhelmed, and still processing from ten steps ago, because how could my parents have *known* and *still pressured me*?

"Jing-Jing's pure, I promise. The purest!" my mother piped up. Of course.

Mr. Kuo coughed once, on purpose. "I'm uncomfortable. We should call this off."

And my mother panicked. "Jing-Jing accepts your proposal, Hongbo!" she declared, yelling it to everyone in the vicinity. "We came here tonight just to share this good news with you all!"

The guests who were hovering in the background pretending not to eavesdrop gave up the charade and broke into applause. People started yelling congratulations, a champagne bottle popped nearby, and a small group started approaching us to celebrate.

No! my mind screamed. *No! No! No!*

Everything was happening too fast. I couldn't think.

Hongbo was coming over to me. The Kuos, wary just moments ago, were suddenly accepting handshakes and exclaiming how wonderful it was that Hongbo would be settling down with a girl so innocent she didn't realize the male friend she'd brought to the party was actually interested in her. Someone pulled Andrew away from me and too many hands were clapping me on the back, touching my arm, invading my space.

My parents didn't see me as human. Didn't care how I felt, what I wanted, how much I was suffering to try to make them happy.

If I allowed this engagement to happen, that would be it. I'd be letting them win and consigning myself to a future where I'd slowly fade into nothing. It was already happening. And my parents didn't even notice. I could feel my spirit dying, slowly choking on the lies, the pain, the sacrifices.

I felt comforting fingers encircle my wrist briefly before they were pulled away again.

For the record, I like the version of you from the application, the one who stands up to gross Lamborghini-loving douchebags, not the one who feels like she has to be nice and smile for the world just because they said so.

Inside, a momentary burst of strength shouted at me to snap out of it. To fucking fix it before it was too late.

So I did.

"I'm pregnant," I announced, shattering my virginal reputation just as someone in the room dropped and shattered a glass— probably a crystal Waterford champagne flute or whatever the fanciest one was.

The *entire* room froze. Completely. Not a single muscle twitched.

"She's just kidding!" my mother said with a laugh, throwing her head back in exaggeration, but not before her eyes met mine with a question in them.

Mrs. Kuo's gaze dropped to my stomach, which, as always, did have a little protrusion because, well, I'm human, but obviously it was not a full-blown preggers belly.

"It's still early," I said, letting my fiery red shine bright. I considered adding that it wasn't Hongbo's, but then I realized it didn't matter whose it was. Maybe it would be better if people *did* think it was Hongbo's, just to punish the Kuos more.

My mother started waving her arms. "She's not pregnant! Tiān āh, you have to believe me!" She grabbed my elbow and shook it frantically. "Tell them, Jing-Jing! The truth!"

I pressed my palm to my abdomen. Andrew, who had been staring at me in shock a second ago, pulled it together and came over to put his hands on my shoulders, a united front.

My father looked like he was about to pass out. My mother's head turned in a circle, looking from one person to another, and, realizing that they believed me, she lost it.

"I'm going to go get a pregnancy test right now and prove it to you all! Come on, Jing-Jing." She started pushing me toward the front door, but I held my ground.

"How will I know it's actually Jing-Jing's pee on the stick?" Hongbo's mother exclaimed to mine, also clearly having lost it. "*You* could pee on it or something—we wouldn't know!"

"She'll do it in front of you, okay?" my mother screeched.

"That still doesn't prove she's a virgin," Mrs. Kuo fired back.

"We'll have a gynecologist confirm her hymee—hymen?—is still intact. Isn't Tsai An here?" My mother's head turned frantically, searching for Dr. Tsai in the crowd.

"Everyone shut the hell up!" I yelled, the words erupting from my lips. "No one is looking at my private parts. Jesus! What is wrong with all of you? Does no one else see how fucked up this all is?"

The older generation gasped when I swore, but I charged on, a wild bull finally loose in the China house. "I'm not an object, I'm not anyone's property, and I'm just done with all this. I don't care what any of you think of me anymore—for the first time, and much too long overdue."

"It's off," Hongbo's mother said icily to mine. "Hongbo is too good for your Jing-Jing."

Andrew and I laughed, but everyone else remained frozen in place.

"Do you really want me to comment on that?" I asked. "On how we all got here?" I would spill their secret with *pleasure*.

Mid-laugh, I felt a rush of wind, heard a loud thud, and felt Andrew's warmth disappear.

People around us shrieked. Everything felt slow and fuzzy and my head buzzed and swirled, dizziness overtaking me. Arms and other limbs surrounded me. I fell to the floor. It wasn't until I blinked a few times that I put two and two together: Hongbo had thrown a punch at Andrew.

I was shrieking his name before I'd fully processed everything. At the Kuos' instructions, servants grabbed Andrew and the rest of my family and deposited us on the lawn. The front door opened and closed and someone threw a bag of frozen wontons at us, which Andrew scooped up and placed over his eye.

I tried to ask if he was okay, but my mother was screaming at me.

"Jing-Jing, how could you?! Our miànzi! Tiān āh! What were you thinking?!"

My dad clutched his chest, and my mother rushed over to him.

"Are you guys okay?" I asked, staying by Andrew but also worried about my dad now.

"I'm fine," Andrew said quickly.

"No one cares!" my mother yelled.

"Lǎo Pó, I don't feel well," my father said, his voice shaky.

"Bā, are you sick? Is something wrong?" I hurried to his side.

"Let's get him home," my mother said softly, and the fact that she stopped yelling and completely focused on my father confirmed my worst fears: he was sick.

But now wasn't the time to ask questions.

At home, my mother settled my father in bed, and I tried to make Andrew comfortable on the couch as he sprawled out, an ice pack wrapped in a paper towel against his eye. He kept insisting he was fine, but I felt awful.

I sat on the edge of the cushion near his waist.

"Are you okay?" I asked him for the eleventy-fifth time. "I'm so sorry this happened."

"I'm not. You were brilliant!" He let out a mini whoop, then grimaced in pain.

The consequences of what I'd done were still sinking in, slowly, in waves. "My parents are going to be so pissed at me." I'd escaped their wrath thus far only because of my father's health, which sent a different wave of panic through me. "And I got you punched in the face," I added apologetically, reaching a hesitant hand up to hover near his injury.

"So many firsts with you," he joked. "Seriously, though, you were inspiring tonight. Going after what you want, fighting—it was fucking amazing."

Then why didn't it feel amazing?

"I know I told everyone I don't care what they think, but . . ." I couldn't quite find the words. It wasn't the actual lie that bothered me but the fact that I'd had to lie at all. And that I needed to use prejudices I despised to manipulate the situation. "I just hate that it's always judgment with that group, you know?"

"I get it. It's especially unfair that you had to take the hit when you were the victim, but that's who you are. You could've thrown the Kuos under the bus or torn into everyone there, but you sacrificed yourself."

"I'm not the only one who took the hit," I said quietly, the guilt shifting front and center.

"You took the path of less destruction."

Maybe I wanted to hurt my parents in the moment too, I thought with shame.

"I hope it was worth it? Now that Hongbo's gone?"

What.

Holy Mother of God.

Hongbo was gone.

I'd been so focused on the guilt, the worry, the adrenaline still coursing through my veins, that this very crucial piece of information hadn't fully registered yet.

But I'd done it. I successfully burned the Kuo bridge down with a spectacular show of fireworks set to the background music of Tang dynasty performers.

"We did it. Hongbo's out," I said, because I needed to hear it. Because for one freaking second I wanted to focus on that and not on how I'd also burned down my reputation and my relationship with my parents—which now, in the aftermath's rubble, felt like a much bigger deal than it had at the time of the explosion.

Andrew looked at me expectantly, waiting to see what I would do next.

Except I didn't quite know. I'd been so obsessed with the virus infecting my life that I'd forgotten how to function without it.

"I'm thrilled for you. You deserve to be happy, Jing-Jing."

I hesitated. "It's Chloe," I told him. Finally.

"Chloe." He said my name slowly, like his tongue and mouth were trying on the new syllables and sounds.

"And you are . . . ?" I asked because it felt uneven otherwise. "I mean, only if you want to tell me."

He beamed. "I'm Drew. Drew Chan. Nice to meet you."

"That's, like, the same name as Andrew!"

He chuckled. "Not to me."

I gave him a *come on* look, and we laughed together, partly because it was funny, partly because I didn't know how else to react to this momentous step, and mostly because I had too many emotions fighting for attention and this was a form of release.

My mother's voice cut both of us off immediately. "How can you two be laughing at a time like this?"

I turned my torso toward her, instinctively inching my butt farther from Drew out of guilt.

"Can we talk?" she asked, not meeting my eye. Without waiting for my answer, she made her way upstairs.

Drew squeezed my knee, and I told myself I wasn't facing my mother alone. Many firsts, indeed.

CHAPTER 33

MIÀNZI

We were sitting in my bedroom, which felt too sterile and too not mine to bring me any comfort. I was curled up on my wooden desk chair and my mother was sitting on my bed, back straight, hands folded in her lap, completely prim and proper.

"Is Bā okay?"

"He's just old," she lied, brushing it off with her words and a careless hand wave.

"Please," I whispered, trying to convey with my voice how much I needed to know.

"That shouldn't be your main concern right now." How could it not be? "You should be taking a good hard look at yourself and your recent behavior. What happened to you?"

"I'm not pregnant, Māmá." It was all I could think to say.

"But you told everyone you were," she shot back, as if it were the same thing.

The words carved my heart out. Made me regret down to my empty chest cavity that I hadn't done the very thing that had made me feel empowered, proud, and free back at the mansion.

She continued, "How could you do this to us after I worked so hard to do the impossible and get you in with the most desirable bachelor?"

"How could you go along with this after you knew their motivation?" *Why else would they want you?* I heard her say in my head, and I wanted to crawl into a hole.

My mother rolled her eyes. "Aiyah, boys will be boys—just be glad he got that out of his system *before* you. Who doesn't make mistakes? At least the Kuos are rich enough to make that baby go away." *My God.* "The DUIs will be harder, but they have good connections."

"DUIs?" Jesus, what else was there?

She barreled on. "Jing-Jing, you hurt not just yourself but Bǎbá and me tonight. Don't you know that because of your outburst, our family has no liǎn now? Do you know what that means, to have no face? How are we supposed to be a part of the community after what you did? We're ostriched, Jing-Jing!"

"Ostracized," I said quietly.

"No, ostriched! So shamed we have to stick our heads in the sand! We're the embarrassment of the town! You clearly don't understand how deep miànzi goes. Even though it's the same words, it's not like what you Americans say about 'saving face.' It's many layers beyond that. It's how our community functions—"

"How can you say I don't understand?" I interrupted. Especially when she had shoved miànzi down my throat to the point where it took *an engagement to Hongbo* to make me stand up to it. "I grew up in this community too. Maybe it's not as . . . intense for me as it is for you and Bǎbá, but I feel those same pressures." So much so that miànzi had dictated my life for nineteen years.

My mother shook her head. "If you understand it like you say, you wouldn't have thrown our reputation in the toilet for no reason. Jing-Jing, do you remember the story about the emperor who overthrew a kingdom with the help of two generals? Then he worried about the generals killing and overthrowing him, so his solution was to give one general three awards and the other two. The one who received fewer was so ashamed—had no face—that he killed the three-award general. Then the emperor ordered the two-award general to be executed as punishment for committing murder, which, ta-da, secured his throne. See how important miànzi is?"

"See how *dangerous* it is?" I threw back. How was that story supposed to be enlightening? "And do *you* remember the story about Moses getting the tablets and one of the commandments being no murder?"

She made a spitting noise at me; I couldn't be sure whether it was because I'd insulted her by joking she didn't know the Ten Commandments, or because of how I'd interpreted her emperor story.

"Well, do you remember the phrase, 'pō chūqù de shuǐ'?" she retorted. "Well, that's you! Once you ruin your reputation, you become poured-out water I can't take back."

I'd rather be poured-out water than Hongbo's girlfriend.

I wasn't getting through. And I didn't have much fight left.

I wanted to reach into my chest and hand her my heart so she could finally understand what made me tick. Maybe then she would also see how each of her words perpetuated the crack she and my father had put there months ago.

But since that wasn't an option, I turned and grabbed the Band-Aid that was dangling in front of me. It wouldn't solve the situation long-term, but had I *really* expected anything to change? Wasn't that part of the reason I'd brought in Andrew to begin with? "Well, now that I'm a pariah in the community, you better be nice to Andrew. You made such a scene I'm not sure if he'll stay around."

"*You* made the scene, Jing-Jing, not me!"

"Well, regardless, Hongbo's out. Andrew's your last hope." And I stopped there, not able to say the other words that had popped into my head—words my mother had said to me three months ago after I'd told her I didn't want Hongbo, words I hadn't been able to tell Drew this morning. *You won't be able to find someone else. Who will want you, with your flat chest, plain face, and worrying personality?* She'd certainly proved today just how deep this fear extended, so why not use it against her even if it did strike me through the heart?

Her face registered first surprise, then horror as she realized I was right. And then, slowly, the horror morphed into panic. So much panic.

I tried to ignore that her stricken face only emphasized how unlovable she truly believed me to be. Pushing aside the pain, I drove the nail in as deep as it could go. "And Andrew is everything you've ever wanted: he comes from a great family, he has so many opportunities ahead of him, and he's incredibly kind—even you must see that. He's the first person to like me for me," I said, that last sentence completely true and warming my insides. And even though she didn't care about the following things, I kept going, mostly for me. "He's thoughtful, and creative, and so intelligent—more perceptive than anyone I've ever met." Then my final blow. "Maybe you ruined it with him by continually trying to kick him out the door since he arrived."

She shook her head. "No. No, no, no, no," she repeated in time with her head shakes. "I can't have ruined it."

"Well, then, you'll drop Hongbo for good?" She nodded, so I took it and ran, hoping to cover my bases for when Andrew wouldn't be coming around in the future. "And you'll be nice to him, never making him give up another holiday with his family because you're still evaluating him? In fact, he's so upset about this he may not visit for a while."

My mother kept nodding her head. "Yes, yes, whatever it takes."

And even though it had gone my way and she had agreed to things I hadn't even dared dream, my heart sank into my pelvic floor.

Because the bottom line of all this was: my mother didn't think anyone else could want me, and her only goal in life was to marry me off to the shiniest bidder.

"I'm still angry at you for what you did," she said.

Right back at you. But unlike her, I didn't express my feelings aloud.

And then, worse, she said, "But I'm so glad you're not pregnant, Jing-Jing. And I'm even more glad that, in all the lies, Andrew is real."

Like I said, it was a Band-Aid. But, my God, had we taken a gigantic step forward.

Drew

CHAPTER 34

UTERUS IN

While Chloe was upstairs talking to her mother, I paced the living room so many times I left a giant oval in the carpet.

I used to pretend I was a balls-in kind of guy, chasing after my art dream. But in real life, I'd been floating in purgatory for years, refusing to break that final tie to my parents.

Chloe had gone for it. Balls (uterus?) in, pregnancy gun blazing. She was continually going after what she wanted—first by hiring me, then by finding another solution when that wasn't working.

When I'd told her earlier on the couch that she'd been inspiring, I'd meant it. In the aftermath of her declaration, I was rethinking my life decisions, wondering why I hadn't at least done *something* to get my art out there. Before, it had seemed bet-everything-on-red scary, but now it felt reckless *not* to have tried.

As I shuffled my feet to erase the oval path, I vowed to do better. To at least try. Baby steps were okay, but I didn't want to be treading water anymore, not when there was no one coming to rescue me. Like Chloe, I needed to be my own knight in shining armor.

Chloe

CHAPTER 35

WONTONS

When my mother and I came downstairs, Drew had made dinner for us.

"Aiyah, Andrew!" my mother yelled at full volume. "You are the nicest person in the world." Then she gave me a pointed look that seemed to say, *See? I can do what you asked.*

It was so much I had to stifle a laugh. As I said before, she had two extremes. And I guess this—so polite it was fake—was technically better than so honest you wished she'd lie.

I pointed to the closest bowl of wonton soup. "Are these . . . ?" I trailed off, not wanting to bring up Hongbo in front of my mother. But Drew knew that I was asking if these were the very wontons that had been thrown at him earlier.

"Why waste them?" he said with a shrug and a smirk.

This time I failed to stifle my laugh, but my mother was too busy preparing a tray to notice.

"Jing-Jing, will you bring dinner up to Bǎbá?" she asked. "Don't worry, I'll continue to be nice to Andrew."

Even though I knew this was a ploy to get me to talk to my father,

185

even though I was dreading it for multiple reasons—seeing him sick, not getting answers to my questions, accepting the consequences of the grenade I'd set off at the party—I steeled my shoulders and ripped the Band-Aid off.

I rap-rap-rapped on my parents' bedroom door with my elbow, my hands grasping the tray of soup tightly so it wouldn't spill as I knocked.

"Jìn lái," my father's voice said through the door. And since he used the less polite "come in" rather than "qǐng jìn" for "please enter," I knew I was in for a salty chat.

"I brought you dinner." I placed the tray on the empty side of the bed, then sat beside it with care.

"Bā . . . ," I started, then stopped, not because I was scared of him, but because I was scared to know. "Are you okay? I mean, are you sick? With more than just a cold?"

"I'm not as young as I once was, that's all," he said with a smile. But it was hollow. "I just get more run-down than I used to."

"You can tell me the truth," I said. "I want to be here for you."

He held a hand up, silencing me. "I don't want to talk about it anymore. If I say I'm fine, I'm fine." He took a few sips of soup; then his eyes grew wide when he put everything together. "These are from earlier?" he asked, pointing at the wontons.

I nodded and he chuckled. Hope surged in my chest.

But then he said, "Aiyah, Jing-Jing, what were you thinking, saying that at the party?"

My voice was barely above a whisper. "I wanted to choose my own future."

"Who wasn't letting you choose? We were only making sure you saw all your choices."

"You didn't tell me vital information." I left it at that. Unlike with my mother, I couldn't fully express my anger. My relationship with my father was too uncomfortable. Too fragile.

And he didn't pick up on the emotions beneath my words, saying carelessly, "We did what we felt was necessary for you to end up with the best option. We know more than you, Jing-Jing. We're older. We have life experiences. Haven't we taught you to respect your elders?"

Sometimes it felt like talking to a skipping record—outdated, repetitive, and unable to change. I tried the same tactic that had worked on my mother. "Well, the Hongbo ship has sailed. Can you give Andrew a chance now?"

But my father shook his head. "I can't reward your terrible behavior by giving you what you want."

"So, what, you're not going to be nice to your own houseguest?"

"He's not who he says he is."

No way. He couldn't know . . . could he?

"He's squeamish!" my father exclaimed, as if he were dropping the mic. "He's not going into medicine like his parents—he's going to have to find something else. He could barely keep his breakfast down when he was assisting me."

I wanted to laugh until my knees gave out. But I managed to hold it back to just a few chortles.

"What's so funny?" my dad finally asked after chortle number five.

"Andrew still has plenty of other well-paying job options."

"Not as high-paying as doctor. Why not give yourself the optimal start? A fighting chance? The best of relationships can't survive when money is an issue."

"And relationships aren't worth having if they're with the wrong person," I said quietly.

"You're still young; only fools believe in love."

I tried not to dwell on what that implied about his relationship with my mother.

"Love can grow," he continued, "but only if you have life's necessities to support the roots."

My voice was still small. "I think you're wrong."

He turned away from me and stared at the empty white wall. "Sometimes I don't think I know you."

You don't.

"Please tell me if you're sick," I begged.

He didn't answer, and his eyes didn't leave the wall to meet mine as I eventually left, out of options. My heart couldn't take any more.

Drew

CHAPTER 36

FALLEN

Chloe was silent at dinner, pushing her wontons around list-lessly.

Perhaps it was because of how we'd obtained them. Or, more likely, because of how the talk with her father (which I knew from experience could be hella scary) had gone.

I knew she was going through a lot (like, more than most people by this age), and I wasn't sure how to best support her. Did she want space? Did she want me to help somehow? As Andrew or Drew?

"These are actually really good," I said, biting into a fourth wonton. I'd made them earlier as a joke, but it turned out the Kuos had access to some top-notch frozen Chinese food.

"Thank you for making them," Mrs. Wang said for the third time.

And again I nodded, even though her thanks felt over the top; all I'd done was boil some water and plop these bad boys in.

Mrs. Wang had been perfectly pleasant to me while Chloe was upstairs talking to her father, but it had been mostly quiet, with the only words exchanged revolving around how the wontons looked and smelled.

"And thank you for getting them in the first place," Chloe said, a hint of a smile on her face, finally.

I hovered a palm over her knee, unsure what she needed right now. My hand (and heart) warmed when she reached up and interlaced her fingers through mine. I squeezed, hoping the small gesture could say some of the things I wasn't saying out loud: *I got you. It'll be okay. I'm on your side.*

"Are . . . are you okay?" Mrs. Wang asked me, not looking up from her soup. "Your eye, I mean." She slurped loudly.

"Yes, thank you."

This wasn't a nineties sitcom (obviously—we were all Asian here), but it did feel like Hongbo was no longer a wedge between us. Awkwardness remained in the wake, but, wonder of wonders, Chloe and I had accomplished what I'd come here to do. Perhaps she and her parents could emerge from these ashes stronger.

"Really, these are fantastic," Mrs. Wang gushed. "I can't believe you made these from scratch, and so quickly."

Annnd I realized she didn't know where they'd come from. Made sense. She'd barely looked at me when everything happened, only coming around after her one-on-one chat with her daughter.

"Hongbo helped with the recipe," Chloe deadpanned.

"They're a pain to make, but it's worth it," I added, and Chloe bit her lip to keep from smiling.

Mrs. Wang didn't seem to be listening. She just stared into her bowl. A minute later she said quietly, "I'm going to check on Bǎbá."

As soon as she left, Chloe whispered, "I think my dad's sick. Like, *sick* sick. Will you help me figure out what's wrong? Because he won't tell me."

That surprised me. "Of course."

She pushed her bowl away. "My mother is either upset about that, or that plus what I did to them tonight. I was so proud at first, but now I just feel like a sack of shit, even if it did work. And even if they did kind of deserve it."

I squeezed her hand again. There was really nothing else to say, because when people saw the world this differently, there was no winning, no happy ending, no way to feel good.

"They only care about what everyone else thinks," she said sadly.

I nodded. "The dreaded miànzi."

"Exactly. Did you grow up in a similar Asian community?"

"I know all about miànzi because of my parents, but . . ." I hesitated, not sure if now was the right time to tell her this. But since she had asked . . . "My Asian community was a little different. The kind that brings food over when a neighbor loses their job, takes care of the kids when so-and-so's grandma is sick—not this Hunger Games version you seem to have, where you're all trying to murder each other with Rhodes scholarships and doctorates."

Whereas you don't even have a college degree, my parents' voices reminded me. But I couldn't share that with her, not now. Maybe not ever. After seeing her community (and remembering the Thanksgiving conversation about Jeffrey *Forbes* 30 Under 30), I felt even more insecure about my lack of higher education, which I previously hadn't thought possible.

Pushing aside those thoughts, I finished, "Most of the Asians I know came from nothing, like my family, so we had to band together, especially since no one else helped us."

"You'd think that'd be the way to go," Chloe said, "but my experience has always been that there's only room for one Asian, so you have to step on the other one to get a leg up. I guess they're both survival tactics, though I wish my experience had been like yours. No wonder you're more at peace with your Chinese side than I am—you know, sprinkling Mandarin on everything like it's sriracha."

I laughed at her metaphor (and yes, sriracha deserved to be on *everything*), but most importantly, I was touched that she'd noticed.

"Chinese culture does often bleed into what I say and do. It certainly influences my art." I paused, remembering my rule and her request. When she'd asked me my real name, was that all she wanted to know? Or was the door open to more? "Sorry. Do you want me to—"

"I'm not sure what I want."

We both fell silent.

She sighed. "I feel what you feel—you know I do. How can I not? But . . ." She looked at me with sad eyes. "How can it be real? I barely know you. I know Andrew." I started shaking my head, but she pressed on. "Of course I fell for the perfect-on-purpose package. This probably happens with a bunch of your clients—falling for your curated persona that's not really you."

"You've fallen for me?" My heart sprouted wings and flew around the room.

She threw her hands in the air. "No, not for *you*—aren't you listening?"

"But that *was* me." I'd never felt so desperate to convey something to someone. "In the moments that mattered: eating mooncakes in the middle of the night, the Christmas cookies, all those texts"—*texts that I've memorized*—"that was me. Drew. The artist."

"How can I know that? You've literally been trained to become different people, and to charm others."

I laughed. Couldn't help it. "Correction—to charm *parents*, remember? Trust me, this power does not extend to my romantic life. Or at least it hasn't before." Nerdy, guāi, empathetic boys were not known for being swarmed by girls, strangely.

"Okay, well, you know everything about me—which is weird—and I know mostly lies about you."

"Well," I said slowly, "do you want to get to know me—the real me—better? We'd be starting from an unconventional place, but it's not square one. More like square five-point-two."

She looked down at her hands.

I examined mine, too, focusing on the paintbrush callus on the side of my right middle finger. We sat in silence for a minute (an awkward one—a first for us), and I fought the urge to twiddle my thumbs. Or maybe I shouldn't fight it, to show her what Drew was like. Except she already knew about my fidgeting, I remembered (her eyes had followed my movements that night in the kitchen right before she'd asked me how to turn off part of her brain, and then again after our Christmas-ornament fight).

She opened her mouth, then closed it. My head shot up. Then I had to force myself to wait patiently.

Eventually she said, "Sometimes I can't tell if there's actually something here or if it's just because you know so much about me that you know how to . . . I don't want to say 'manipulate,' but you know what I mean. You know the right buttons to push for me. Because of the application."

I nodded to show my understanding. "Does it help you to know that in the year and a half I've been doing this, it has *never* been like this, not even close?"

"Yes, but . . . I don't know, something's holding me back."

After a hesitant beat I said, "Your parents?"

Chloe

It's always my parents.

Every time, without fail, they came first.

Drew's serious eyes met mine, boring into them to make sure I heard what was coming next. "Chloe, I'm not saying this in reference to you getting to know me, but in general. It's okay for you to try to be happy. You fighting for a life without Hongbo? Admirable and necessary. In fact, it's making me rethink some of my own decisions. Maybe today can be a start, not an exception."

"It's not that simple. How my parents feel affects me, too."
Though it's decreasing the more they show me they don't care about my happiness.

"I understand," he said.

The only person who had ever cared about how I felt was right in front of me, and I was pushing him away.

Why was I fighting this so damn hard? He was asking me to *get to know him*. It should have been a no-brainer.

But . . . if we moved forward, we would be on borrowed time, with the prospect of my parents finding out—either from us or, horrors, on their own—looming over us. Could we even be happy under those circumstances?

Then I thought about the counterfactual scenario where I let Drew go without trying. Would I be okay with that? With not knowing him or where this could possibly go?

Abso-fucking-lutely not.

That would be letting my parents win. Again.

Drew was right; I'd been pushing him away for my parents' sake, not mine. Fear of their disapproval, fear of how to untangle the fact that they already knew him as Andrew.

I wanted to stop making decisions out of fear.

"One thing I gotta know," I said, and he tensed slightly. "Were the imaginary sheep real?"

He threw his head back and laughed. "Yes. Well, no. They were imaginary. But yeah, I do the pajama thing when I can't sleep."

We snort-laughed together. I could feel molecules shifting, and when we shared a smile, it now felt as if there were a red thread attached to the both of us, lifting the corners of our lips in tandem, for the same reasons.

"Okay," I said with confidence. "Thanks for being patient. If you're still willing, can you tell me about your parents? About following in your grandfather's footsteps?"

Drew

CHAPTER 37

HOLY HELL

Where to start?

I dove into the murky waters of my memories. No oxygen tank, no floaties.

"My family—and when I say 'family,' I mean my parents, my wàipó, who lived with us, and my younger brother, Jordan, who's a freshman at Berkeley—always had practical values. You know, work hard in school so you can get a good, reliable job doing something really boring in a cubicle somewhere, dreaming of the day you'll earn enough to do what you actually love. Which was a life I had been preparing for—and sometimes even now I think maybe that *was* the way to go . . ." I exhaled. "But then I took some art electives in high school to pad my college apps, and, unsurprising spoiler, I loved it. For years I kept thinking there was something there for me, especially with painting, but I was too scared to say anything. Junior year, when I finally worked up the nerve to suggest to my parents that maybe I would want to apply to colleges with art programs, they flipped their shit."

I mimicked each family member's voice.

My father's, gruff and authoritative: "'Art is for people who have no other choice in life, no other skills.'"

My mother's, hoarse and stern: "'I thought I'd raised a fighter, not someone who has so given up on life they decide to paint.'"

My high-pitched, nasal wàipó: "'I always knew you were just like my worthless husband. He died penniless and alone—just like you will!'"

"Jesus," said Chloe.

"I didn't even know that was why my wàigōng hadn't been in our lives growing up." I regretted not having known him, especially since my creative genes apparently came from him.

"What about Jordan?" she asked.

"He was so young at the time—still in junior high—and I didn't want him to get caught in the middle."

"But he got caught anyway."

I nodded. "I had to let him go too. He needed my parents still."

"Oh, Drew. I'm sorry."

She rested her head on my shoulder, and I leaned on her, physically and emotionally.

We stayed like that for too long (my neck started to cramp) yet not long enough. But I couldn't bring myself to break it up first, so we came apart only after she started to stir.

"If you're willing," she said, "I'd love to see your work sometime."

I hesitated out of instinct (and maybe still out of fear). *Even if you say yes now, it doesn't mean you have to,* I rationalized. *What a perfect baby step,* said another part of my brain. *She'll hate it,* said the awful you-know-who part.

"That'd be nice," I said, my voice cracking. Those words in themselves were a step forward. I said them and didn't die. But even more of a step? I felt panic, yes, but there was also some excitement there. Hope.

It was all too new and overwhelming, so I covered it up by gesturing to the bowls on the table and making a joke. "The wontons might be as cold as when we first got them."

She laughed. We packed up the leftovers and started on the dishes.

"Ready to witness my exceptional dish-washing technique?" I grabbed a fork and held it in the air.

She handed me the sponge and after a few flourishes (C.2–style) and even a jazz hand, I proceeded to pat the fork exactly as I had back at Thanksgiving.

She burst into laughter. "Very funny," she said sarcastically.

"Yes, obviously, since you're laughing right now."

She shoved my arm lightly, and I realized too late that she was pushing me out of the way so she could grab the dish soap. In one swift movement, it was in her hands and aimed at me.

"Aha!" she declared playfully.

Unlike at Thanksgiving, this time I didn't hesitate and lunged for her, grabbing her around the waist and ducking behind her so I was shielded from the weapon.

Between laughs, she squirted a few bubbles in the air before giving up and putting down the soap.

When I poked her side, her face lit up. Then her gaze dipped to my lips.

God help me.

With my arms still wrapped around her waist, she turned to face me. Her nose was millimeters from mine.

Our eyes met and it felt like we had an entire conversation without words.

She closed the tiny distance between us.

Our lips became one. Our breath became one.

It was too good. A perfect fit. Effortless yet passionate, another conversation without words.

Worried she would think this was because of my job and not

us, I pulled back and said, "Just for the record, in case you were wondering, I don't have any training in kissing—"

She pressed her forehead to mine. "Me either. But I don't think we need it."

She sucked my bottom lip into her mouth.

Holy hell.

"Right you are," I said, my bottom lip still between her teeth.

She threw her head back and laughed. Then our untrained lips found their way back to each other.

Amazing with a capital *A*.

We broke apart with huge grins on our faces. I bit my lower lip, suddenly feeling a little shy, and I struggled to find something to say.

"Thank you" came out of my mouth, and then my cheeks felt hot.

With a sly grin she returned my thank-you, and we both chuckled.

Then we looked down at the sink. She groaned out loud. I groaned inwardly.

"Soap 'em and soak?" I suggested.

She nodded, looking as if everything from today was catching up to her. "I'm pooped. I may not even make it upstairs."

I hurried to soak the dishes, then turned my back to her and bent my knees. "Your midnight chariot awaits, m'lady," I joked. "To your evening chambers, I presume?"

She made a delighted noise, then hopped on my back.

And then she fell right off. Because her father had just come downstairs.

Chloe

The second my father came in, I just let go. Without thinking.

Because Drew was clutching my legs tightly, I toppled backward and hit the floor with a thud.

"Fuck, are you okay?" Drew burst out. He was so concerned, he

198

didn't even notice he'd just sworn, which was probably breaking Rule 53 or whatever—which he likely wasn't thinking about since he hadn't been Andrew for the last hour.

He released my legs and dropped to the floor beside me.

Once he knew I was okay, embarrassment crossed his face. "Sorry, Shūshú, I didn't mean to swear. I was concerned."

My father just continued staring blankly at us, like he had floated out of his body and neither he nor his ghost could figure out what the hell we were doing.

"I just wanted some water," he said. Then he turned abruptly and left without getting any.

"Did that just happen?" I said after my dad was gone.

Drew gathered me in his arms gently. "Are you sure you're okay? Do you need some frozen wontons?"

I shook my head, more dazed from my instinctive reaction to my dad than the physical impact.

"At least he didn't walk in a little sooner," I joked. "What would I have done then? Flung myself through the window?"

Drew laughed, then hugged me closer.

When I went upstairs, a glass of water in hand, my parents' bedroom door was locked. I knocked, but exaggerated snores came from the other side. I considered leaving the glass on the floor but worried someone would trip over it, so I retreated to my room, drinking the water myself to calm down.

That night, I couldn't stop licking my lips, touching them with my fingertips. Drew was still there in the heightened sensitivity. In the tingle that seemed to travel through my entire body.

I wanted to tiptoe downstairs and slip beneath his covers, but the threat of my father walking in on us kept me firmly in my own bed. Who could've guessed the *no hanky-panky* rule would ever be an issue for me?

Chloe

CHAPTER 38
NONWHITE CHRISTMAS
December 25

Christmas in the Wang household was never a white Christmas—and when I say "white," I don't mean snow—but this year was especially cold (again, nothing to do with the weather).

It was early afternoon, but my father was still asleep—was he okay?—so my mother, my not-real-but-not-completely-fake boyfriend, and I were sitting in front of the luminous tree on throw pillows scattered across the floor. I wasn't sure I'd ever get over those little sheep ornaments, my favorite of which was the antigravity-boots one, which I'd named Cháng'é. Even though I was pretty sure Drew would approve—his text from a couple of weeks ago had inspired the name—I was too embarrassed to tell him. Maybe because the Chinese still felt weird to me? Or maybe because it was just so dorky.

The three of us—quite the odd trio—were exchanging gifts, the stress of which was making my mother's leg jiggle uncharacteristically. *Ladies sit still, Jing-Jing,* she always liked to say.

"Sorry this is it," she apologized to Drew. "We don't do much for Christmas. In fact, I never celebrated it growing up, and we started doing the tree just for Jing-Jing, when she was a child. But come back at Chinese New Year and we'll show you how we party."

"*Mǎmá,*" I warned.

"Or . . . I guess if you celebrate with your family, that makes sense, since you joined us now and Thanksgiving. Though if I'd known we'd have to choose, I'd of course have picked Chinese New Year."

"I have exams then, anyway," I told her, which was true, though I usually still found a weekend to come home so we could eat Chinese food until we burst.

My mother huffed. "It's so ridiculous—in Taiwan, we get weeks off for Chinese New Year."

She handed Drew a soft gift wrapped in old Chinese newspapers. He was so cute, his eyes lighting up in spite of the sloppy wrapping.

He tore through the paper, leaving strips of half-destroyed Mandarin characters strewn on the floor, to reveal a Stanford Medical School sweatshirt. "It's lovely—thank you so much!" he said with sincere enthusiasm just as I burst out laughing.

"Not a very subtle hint," I said to my mother.

Drew pulled the sweatshirt on. Except he couldn't quite fit his long torso into the too-tight fabric. He paused when he got stuck, not quite sure what to do. I had to stifle a giggle as I yanked it off him. Then I saw it was a women's medium.

"You got this for me?" I blurted to my mother.

"No," she said while also shaking her head, the double insistence displaying her guilt.

"You didn't get him anything?" I said.

"I got him that!"

"When did you buy this?"

"Aiyah, I don't remember. But it's for Andrew," she asserted. "You should be thrilled, Jing-Jing! It shows how much I support this relationship, wanting you two to be close to home in the future." Then, beneath her breath, she mumbled, "Just be happy it isn't pink."

My jaw dropped and I turned to her, but she had already moved on, telling Drew, "If you don't like it, I'll mail you something else, okay? Just give me your address."

"It's fine, Mămá," I said quickly just as Drew responded, "I love this. Thank you."

To change the topic, I handed my mother her gift, a spark of excitement stirring inside before my defense mechanisms kicked in and extinguished it. *She might hate it. Depends on her mood, which doesn't bode well for me.* That pessimistic gatekeeper was honed from experience, and it knew better than my silly, hopeful side.

Turned out, both sides were right—or wrong, depending on whether you're a glass-half-full or glass-half-empty kind of person.

My mother tore into the red-glitter wrapping paper I'd specially chosen in an attempt to meld customs (red is both a Christmas color and the Chinese celebratory color). When she saw the mahogany Chinese-and-English Bible with gold-foil trim—the gold extending to where her Chinese and English names were engraved—she gasped in delight, her hand flying up to daintily cover her open mouth, which, ugh, reminded me how many times she had instructed me to do the same whenever I gasped, yawned, or laughed.

"Do you like it?" I fished.

She didn't answer, and as she stared, her face, shoulders, spirit gradually slumped.

"It's gorgeous," Drew jumped in.

We shared a look, and I gave him a small shrug, not knowing what my mother was thinking.

"It's trimmed with gold because you're the golden duck," I said as lightheartedly as I could. "Everyone else in Bible study wants to catch you because you fly so high." It was a lot, but I was that desperate.

She didn't laugh. Or smile. She only continued to stare.

"Thank you," she said finally—quietly, with no exuberance at all.

I tried not to sound as defeated as I felt when I said, "If it's the color or the design"—I gestured to the embellishments around the edge—"we can see if they'll let us exchange it."

She shook her head. "No, it's not that."

I waited, not sure if she was actually going to tell me.

"Kuo Ǎyí called this morning and told me not to come to Bible study anymore."

And then I wished she hadn't told me.

The Bible study group—held at the Kuo mansion once a week, on Thursday afternoons—was my mother's version of women's tea, brunch, book club, or whatever else it was that middle-aged women did. It was so important to her that she worked on Saturdays so she could have Thursday afternoons free.

She'd been going for as long as I could remember, bringing me when I was young to play with the other toddlers while the maids watched us. It had been my first introduction to the sharky community, not to mention Hongbo, and my Thursdays as a child were spent listening to other kids practice violin while I defended my marker drawings from getting eaten by Hongbo. Apparently, he had figured out at a young age that having marker ink near your face felt good, but he hadn't fully connected the dots to his nose yet.

My mother had tried to get me to join Bible study when I turned eighteen, and on that Thursday afternoon before I'd left for UChicago, I had never been more grateful to be attending school halfway across the country.

First, all the women had pawed at my hair, then pinched my sides and told me I'd better watch the freshman fifteen, to which my mother nodded. Then we'd gossiped for thirty minutes about the latest community scandal: Jessica's mother was absent today because she was staking out the high school to see if her daughter was dating behind her back.

Each whisper had been worse than the last.

I bet she'll find Jessica with someone and *smoking.*

I'd put my money on Jessica suddenly needing to go visit the grand-parents in about eight months. Or being absent out of the blue for— how long does it take to recover from an abortion?

Unless she's with another girl, which is what I'd bet on—haven't you seen her latest outfits?

I had been ashamed that I hadn't said anything, and even more ashamed that my mother was regularly a part of this.

But I had rationalized it away with the fact that my mother hadn't been as complicit, adding the more benign smoking comment and not encouraging the homophobic one.

Mrs. Kuo had then read one Bible passage as everyone *mm-hmm*ed and *amen*ed, and after a very shallow, five-minute discussion of what it meant—"God is good"—the maids served expensive oolong tea from the highest mountain in Taiwan and flakey turnip-strip cakes.

The turnip cakes had been the only good part—you can't get those most places because they're too labor-intensive, and Mrs. Kuo's chef had been selected solely for her ability to make them as delicious as at a fancy restaurant on the top floor of a Taiwan department store.

Bible study was terrible and ridiculous, but it was my mother's version of cosmopolitans with Carrie, Samantha, and Miranda, and I had taken it away from her.

With one last look at the gold-trimmed Bible, my mother whispered, "Please excuse me," to Drew and me, then retreated to her bedroom.

I couldn't look at Drew; it hurt too much to be reminded of everything I'd done.

To distract myself, I shook the gift from my mother, the rectangular eight-by-five-by-four box making only a few muffled shifting noises, tissue paper rubbing back and forth against cardboard.

I unwrapped it, the skiing-penguins wrapping paper making a satisfying rip to fill the quiet.

"She usually gets me a new dress or makeup or jewelry," I blabbered, even though he already knew those details from the application.

I froze when I opened the box and saw what was buried beneath crumpled Chinese newspaper. "Oh my God," I whispered, my hand actually flying to cover my mouth for once.

It was a slip of paper, so easily destroyed or lost, but it held the weight of the world.

"She wrapped it that way as a joke?" Drew said with a laugh, not close enough to see what I was holding. "I didn't realize she was so funny."

I hugged the tuition check to my chest. The amount was enough that I wouldn't need student loans the next academic year.

The massive wave of guilt hit me head-on.

"I lied to my parents about my college applications," I whispered, referencing a secret I had never told anyone before. "I had to get away from here—it was my only option."

The tears spilled over my cheeks and splashed onto my thighs. I hugged the check closer, keeping it safe from the moisture, but simultaneously feeling like it was searing into my skin, burning me as punishment for what I'd done.

Drew put a hand on my knee, and the sudden contact made me flinch.

"I don't deserve your sympathy," I said, not meeting his eye. I looked down at the gift from my mom, wondering if she would've given it to me had she known the truth. "I never applied to Stanford," I admitted. "I lied and told my parents I was rejected. I couldn't go there. Even if they didn't make me live at home—an unlikely scenario—they would've shown up every week, unannounced, and I just . . . I couldn't."

"Hey," he said gently. "You were protecting yourself. Making the best decision for you isn't something you ever have to apologize for."

"If they knew, they'd be so angry. And hurt."

"They wouldn't understand, and they wouldn't think about it from your perspective because not many people are like you, Chloe."

He was staring at me so intently I couldn't look away. Surprisingly, I didn't want to, because in his fervor, I saw his admiration for me, and maybe it was finally starting to reflect back.

"I used to think I was weak for feeling so much," I said. "The whole community, my parents, my classmates—they all but told me so every day. It's why I hid my real self from them, why Jing-Jing exists."

"And yet you held on to who you are despite that."

"You make it sound like I've known who I am all along, but I still don't know. What kind of confident, strong-willed person would find herself in this mess?" I gestured to him—Drew and Andrew—in a vague circle.

"Someone who cares more about her parents' feelings than her own."

I sighed.

Then I noticed he was trying not to look at the check, and it dawned on me that I hadn't told him what it was.

"It's tuition money—a whole year's worth." I put it on my lap and smoothed it out, over and over. "I can't even imagine how many extra hours she had to work for this." I looked up at him. "This money feels tainted."

"It's not. If anything, you earned that by always putting them first."

"I still lied."

He tilted his head at me and his voice lowered, heavy with experience. "It's never that straightforward, lies being wrong and truth being right. Or at least that's what I tell myself before every job."

"Does it get easier?"

"Some days."

I stored the check in a safe place to deposit as soon as possible. The guilt clawed my stomach lining raw.

I knocked on my parents' bedroom door quietly. After my third rap, my mother flung the door open and said, *"Shh!"* much louder than my gentle knocking.

"He's sleeping!" she hissed, jerking her head toward the bed.

She stepped into the hallway and closed the door behind her.

Then she folded her arms across her chest. "What is it?"

"Thank you so much for the gift. I can't even . . . I appreciate it so—"

"It was nothing," she said, waving a hand.

Why couldn't either of us communicate?

"No really, it means—" I tried again, but she cut me off.

"It's fine."

Silence.

"Is that all?" she asked.

I shook my head. "I'm sorry about what happened. With Hongbo's parents, with Bible study, everything. I . . . I didn't mean for you to get hurt." *Although you hurt me more,* I didn't say.

She pursed her lips to the side and said nothing.

"Please, Mǎmá."

She sighed. "Give us some space, okay? You threw a bomb at us. Maybe . . . maybe you and Andrew should do your own thing tonight. Somewhere else. Okay? Chinese restaurants will be open—on me and Bǎbá."

But I only see you a few times a year.

But it's Christmas.

But it was self-defense for me. Like always.

Aren't I the victim here, not you?

"Okay," I said instead.

She started to leave, but then she stopped and turned back to me. "At least you have Andrew. If you didn't, you'd be in a lot more trouble. You better hang on to him, okay? Make this all worth it by showing me you were right about him, that he'll be rich and successful and by your side. Do you think there's a ring coming?"

"My God, Mămá. I haven't even graduated college yet."

"Yes, but when they have money, you have to lock them down sooner. You don't have to get married tomorrow, but getting the ring is good."

"What aren't you telling me?" I blurted. "How serious is Băbá's whatever-it-is? Should I be taking some time off school to spend at home?"

"Don't be ridiculous. If the University of Chicago is as good as you say it is, you wouldn't make such stupid conclusions."

"Please. Just tell me if there's something," I begged. If they were trying to spare me from stressing, not knowing was much worse, because my mind had already spiraled to the darkest conclusions. But I couldn't tell her that—she hated how I worried, told me it was my least attractive feature.

Instead of answering my question, she said, "Bring a jacket when you go out tonight." Then she slipped back into the bedroom.

Drew

CHAPTER 39

FOR REALS

But it's Christmas was the first thought I had when Chloe relayed that her parents didn't want to see us the rest of the day. For obvious reasons, I kept it to myself.

"I'm sorry," I said. "What would you like to do? What do you need?"

"What are my options?" she said with a (very) forced laugh.

"Well, we could wait a little and see if they change their minds. Or we could just plan something and hope they'll join us? What do you guys usually do?"

She shrugged. "Not much. Just dinner at home, maybe a game—you've already had a full tour of a Wang holiday. Our whole lives revolve around food and when and what our next meal is."

That I related to. "So I'm guessing there's food in the fridge we could make if you want," I suggested. But, seeing the pain on her face, I kept going in the hopes that I could smooth the dimple on her forehead. "Or if you need a break—which would be more than okay and quite frankly, very understandable—I'd love to take you out."

209

The pain (and dimple) disappeared, replaced by a spark of excitement. "For real?"

"For reals."

She beamed at me.

Man, did I want to sweep her off her feet.

"Let's plan to get going in an hour," I told her, checking my watch.

I had some arranging to do.

Chloe

CHAPTER 40

FISH BALLS

Okay, I was really excited.

Since I wasn't sure what we'd be doing, I showered, then dressed for cute comfort: baggy but semi-flattering boatneck red sweater plus stretchy black pants. I planned to pair the outfit with my purple knee-length puffy jacket and gray padded boots.

So that took twenty minutes. I swiped on some mascara but left it at that since I wasn't my mother's daughter: any more makeup and I'd be dealing with smudge city later from accidentally rubbing my eyes.

Thirty-five minutes to go. And I was *not* someone who should be left alone with her thoughts.

I sat down at my desk and doodled, trying to draw a sheep in a tuxedo pajama, but, um, it ended up looking like a donkey stuffed into a Twinkie with filling spilling out the sides. I tried drawing another sheep with antigravity boots above Mr. Twinkie. She fared a little better, but not by much. She was sheep-adjacent at least, but also part donkey.

I slipped Frankensheep into my pocket anyway, because why not, but I folded the paper six times because it was truly that bad.

I still had thirty minutes until we left. Yes, that was how fast—I mean, bad—that drawing was. My thoughts wandered to all the places I hated: the stickiness of the situation I'd inadvertently created; the shame, guilt, and disgust at what I'd done to my parents and what they'd done to me; and all the secrets we were *still* keeping.

I needed to know what was going on with my father. By the time I stood and made my way downstairs to find Drew, I'd come up with a plan about as risky and desperate as my rent-a-boyfriend one. And it was a good thing I had that horrible sheep drawing as a bargaining chip, because I would need Drew's help. Again.

When I reached the living room, I paused, wanting to run back upstairs.

"I didn't know you were dressing up," I said, embarrassed by my casual outfit. Drew had paired an ivory shirt and red tie with the navy suit from yesterday, which still had a little grass stain on the sleeve.

Before I could turn around, Drew peeled off the jacket and yanked the tie over his head with such speed he got slightly caught. It was so adorable I couldn't help a small chuckle.

"Ready?" he asked, throwing the jacket and tie on the couch and grabbing his more casual dark gray coat from the rack by the door.

"Yeah." I looked up toward my parents' bedroom. "Apparently, they're not coming out until we leave, so . . ."

His sympathetic eyes met mine. "I'm sorry."

"No, I'm sorry. I don't want to talk about them the whole time. I don't even want to *think* about them. I've been doing that my whole life, and this is my night off."

"Whatever you wish," he said, and even though I used to hear his training behind those kinds of words, I now smiled.

"Whatever *you* wish."

His face lit up, and it briefly made me sad that it took so little. That he was so walked-on and forgotten that words, which could be empty, could make him shine so bright.

Mine will not be empty, I promised both him and myself.

As we took our seats for hot pot, I was especially glad I hadn't dressed up.

I closed my eyes and inhaled the familiar, savory scent. "Oh man, good choice. One of my favorites." Which of course he knew.

I left out that hot pot reminded me of my parents, and that it somehow felt blasphemous to enjoy it without them, though we usually did hot pot at home with our little portable tabletop cooker.

Drew smiled. "Dinner is straightforward—I know you love hot pot and this is one of my favorite places—but I'm hoping dessert will be more memorable. Shit, and I don't mean that in a sleazy way."

"I know." I laughed. "In some ways, you're the perfect one to charm the parents, huh? So innocent you don't even realize those innuendos until after."

He chuckled with me, but when our laughs subsided, an uneasy quiet set in. Maybe because we both realized this was a real date, and it was kind of weird.

Except that what he was really thinking was even weirder. "Sorry . . . I just remembered that your parents like to do hot pot—actually, didn't you guys used to have it at Thanksgiving? We didn't this year, though, huh. Should we not have come here? I didn't think of it until—"

"You know so much," I interrupted. "It's like you've read my diary or something."

"Oh God, that's creepy. I'm so sorry."

I sighed. "It's not your fault. Obviously. It's just . . . a little awkward, I guess."

He leaned toward me. "What would help?"

I thought about it. "The more I get to know you, the better it will be. It just feels a little . . . uneven right now." I let out a forced laugh. "Too bad you don't have an application I can just read, right?"

But even as I said it, I knew that the parts that were missing were not the important things. I might not know his favorite color or book or anything else they might ask on *The Newlywed Game*, but I knew his character. His pain. His dreams. His gigantic bleeding heart.

Not knowing how to say all that out loud, I focused on the menu.

Drew

After she made the joke about the application, I had an inner tug-of-war.

I actually had one I could show her: my Rent for Your 'Rents operative application, with questions as probing as the ones she'd answered. I could give her exactly what she wanted, and it would put us on even footing.

But (and this was a huge, Sir-Mix-a-Lot-size *but*) then she would know I dropped out of college. I assumed she already suspected it since it hadn't come up, but the fact that she hadn't asked both comforted and bothered me. Was it not coming up because it was no big deal? Or because it was a Big Deal with capital letters? Maybe she didn't want to know because it would change things. How could it not, when she was surrounded by people who pinned worth on degrees?

Maybe it's okay if you've already raised a million dollars for your company, she had said in response to her mother's *Dropping out of college is never okay.* Maybe she'd been defending Jeffrey and didn't think a college education was necessary. Or maybe she thought that dropping out was only okay if you had a major company to run.

I wanted to give her the benefit of the doubt, but I'd seen her community. If I hadn't moved past my shame yet (and I'd had years!), how was she going to react?

But I also didn't want to be with someone who didn't know *me*. I was able to be somebody else daily, but not with the people I cared about, regardless of the cost.

As Chloe checked off boxes to order our dinner, I discreetly pulled my phone just far enough out of my pocket to send Marshall one more text message. He was helping me set up dessert since Jason was on a job, and I had spent most of my planning hour figuring out details with him.

Okay. Balls in.

Fish balls too. Because Chloe finished looking over the menu and slid it between us.

"Let's get at least two orders of lamb—it's amazing," I said, my mouth already watering.

She grinned. "Glad your usual rules are out the window tonight."

"This lamb is worth any intestinal issues that may arise, which, for the record, is just as bad on a date as it is on a job."

"Well, I'm eating it too," she pointed out.

"Maybe we should get three servings."

After we passed our order to the waiter, I basked in Chloe's smile, the smell of broth in the air, the fact that I was, for once, spending Christmas with someone I cared about.

"Merry Christmas," I said, raising my cup of tea.

"Merry Christmas," she said, her smile tinged with sadness.

"I wish I could take your pain away," I said as we clinked cups.

"Actually . . . I have an idea," she started. "A way to maybe find out what's going on with my dad."

"I'm already in."

She'd barely explained anything before I confirmed that I was still in, adding, "Doctor's office tomorrow, no sweat. We're already pros at cons."

"Great pun!" she complimented me, and we chuckled together.

By the time Chloe had obtained the doctor's phone number from her mother and left a message to make an appointment, our uncooked food had arrived.

"Does your family use gōng kuài too?" she asked, picking up the spare chopsticks she'd asked the server for.

"Nah, we just use our own chopsticks to pick up the raw meat, and then we sterilize the tips in the boiling water for a couple seconds."

She shuddered. "I need these for peace of mind." She picked up a slice of lamb, cooked it for five seconds in the bubbling part of the broth, then dropped it on my plate. "Isn't it weird that we're paying to cook our own food?"

"Not any weirder than Korean barbecue," I said in a strange voice because I'd (sigh) taken a bite of the still-boiling lamb and was chewing with my mouth open to let the steam out. Hot hot hot but yum yum yum. I took a swig of ice water. "At least with hot pot you get to finish your meal by drinking the broth you've created."

She cooked a second slice of lamb for herself, blowing on it before popping it in her mouth.

She groaned. "Okay, you were right: the lamb is fantastic. Are three orders enough?"

"We can always get more. But here, try this." I lāo-ed her a fish ball with the gold netted scooper. "It's the best I've ever had."

"I'm not really a fan of fish balls," she confessed.

"This one has a meatball inside. And this"—I plucked her a different fish ball with a pointed top like a gnome's hat—"is filled with fish roe."

She went for the fish-roe one, biting in way too fast. "Oh my God. So freaking good. Even worth burning my palate for."

"I know, right?"

With the meatball one, she took the time to dip it in shāchá sauce before chomping down. After another groan she concluded, "Okay, I take back what I said; I guess I just never met the right fish ball before." She paused. "It's different when it's right, isn't it?"

"Totally."

She couldn't meet my gaze, but I found that even more endearing. I was seemingly the first person she'd felt this way about. And, well, she was my first too.

Drew

CHAPTER 41

BETWEEN A SHÍTÓU AND A HARD PLACE

"I ate waaaay too much," I said. We had gotten a fourth order of lamb, because, duh.

She groaned. "Me too. But it was worth it."

"I should've left more room," I complained as I slurped up the last of my glass noodles. "But I can't not eat these—they're my favorite part of hot pot." They soaked up the aromatic soup and summed up the meal in one perfect, flavorful bite.

The check came, and we fought like good children of Chinese immigrants—meaning we tussled, but, unlike our parents, we kept it verbal, no one caused harm to others while rushing their credit card to the server first, and no one had called the restaurant in advance to prepay.

"Is this just instinct?" I asked as we both threw cards on top of the receipt. I grabbed hers and pushed it back into her hand. She started to resist, but then we dissolved into giggles as a play fight broke out (one that mimicked our candy-cane duel from the other night).

After a minute she paused, and the card went limp in her hand. "You know, sometimes I have these weird, vaguely Asian instincts

I can't explain. Like when I'm at a buffet, I have to eat until I'm so stuffed I can't move—"

"And you have to eat the most expensive dishes, right?" I added.

"Steak or sashimi all the way," she said with a laugh. "And I overthink every purchase and don't buy things I need because of my urge to—"

"Shěng qián," I supplied.

She nodded. "Yup. Saving money trumps everything else. Well, almost everything." She poked my card with hers again. "Everything except fighting for the check and renting boyfriends, apparently."

I pushed her card away. "Well, give in to your shěng qián instincts for dinner. Besides, look." I flipped the check over so she could see how cheap it had been (yay, holes in the wall!). "And," I added, "I feel so guilty I'm on the clock right now. I've been meaning to tell you—I want to return a chunk of the money you're paying."

She refused (of course, pointing out that I still had to be Andrew in front of her parents), and after a few back-and-forths (both verbally and play jabbing with our cards) she relented on the check, but only if I would agree to stop bringing up the rental payment in the future. Which, to be honest, brought some relief. I hated constantly thinking about how I rented myself out for a living (especially now, with our dynamic shifted).

We inched our way into our coats and out of the restaurant, groaning every now and then.

"I know I'm moving as slow as a sloth right now," she said as we neared the door, "but really, I'm so excited to see what's coming next."

Thank goodness I'd eaten so much it was distracting me from the nerves that were trying to take over.

"I really hope you like it."

Because if you don't, it could destroy me. Not really, but sorta. Am I too dramatic?

I led Chloe up to the spacious but rundown roof-deck of my cozy and quaint apartment building.

Marshall was finishing up stringing lights around the perimeter. I introduced them, and Marshall pulled Chloe into a hug.

"You must be really special," he told her, and I coughed.

"All right," I said, my voice wavering with embarrassment. Then, sincerely, I added, "Thanks, buddy. You really outdid yourself here."

We clapped hands and patted each other's backs.

"Hey, anytime, man. Thanks for never complaining that I practically live in your place without paying rent."

I grinned at Marshall, glad he was here instead of Jason because he left it at that.

I hurried to take over the last of the setup.

Right before he took off, Marshall leaned over and whispered, "They're really good. Really fucking out-of-this-world good."

I had to hold back a sob.

After Marshall scooted out, I flipped the light switch.

Chloe's face glowed when she saw the towel-covered chairs set up around the perimeter. Some of my paintings fit under their towel cover, but others were so large the bottoms peeked out. It wasn't a glamorous art gallery, but it might as well have been, given how nervous I felt.

I turned to Chloe and took a deep breath.

"I haven't been able to show others my work before today."

I paused, unable to say more because suddenly I wasn't a hundred percent sure I wanted to do this. Marshall's comment had been encouraging, but Chloe's opinion meant so much to me it felt like bet-everything-on-red to show her.

"Your family never saw?" she asked. "Before the rift?"

I shook my head. "My parents refused to look. They disapproved before they'd even seen, and once their mind was made up, they didn't want to know more. I didn't want to involve Jordan in that mess so I hid everything I made. One person did see, but not because I showed her: my wàipó would snoop around my room, looking for what I'd last created just so she could tell me it was lèsè, like me and my wàigōng."

Chloe gasped, then pulled me into a hug.

Long-buried emotions seeped back in, but in her arms I could tell her about it. All of it. Everything from how I was scared to break that last wooden plank on the bridge to my parents, to how I worried I wasn't good enough, to how she had inspired me to try harder.

She listened to every word, holding me close for some parts, and stroking my back, my hair, my arm for others.

I'd never felt so supported. Fittingly, her first words were "I'm in awe that you pushed forward even though you've never had anyone on your side."

Tears welled in my eyes. "It's no big deal."

"It *is* a big deal." She pulled away and cupped my cheek with her hand. "It's really brave of you."

I sighed. "It never felt like the brave choice. I saw myself as the coward who took the easy road by choosing what made me happy."

She stroked my cheek with her thumb. "Is that really how you see it?"

I hesitated. *You failed*, I heard my parents tell me in my head. *How could you not do what all your other classmates could? They finished college and got jobs—real ones with a future and money.*

"There's always a closed door when you switch paths, and that's all I could see," I told her, simplifying it because that was all I could manage.

"Have you ever considered how many people want to take the other road and pursue their passions, but are too scared to?"

"Or maybe they're just smarter than me."

"Drew . . ."

And I leaned forward and kissed her, because hearing my name from her lips, in her sweet voice, did things to me, and I felt safe and cared for—two things I hadn't felt in a long time.

"Drew, you are so smart."

And the tears spilled over. How had she known that was my biggest hang-up?

"You know why you're such a good operative?" she asked.

"Because of the training?"

She tilted her head and peered at me. "You think Hongbo could get enough training to make him even a smidge like you?" I laughed. "You're a great operative because of how empathetic you are, naturally, and because you're so damn quick. Your brain is constantly working faster than others, and you notice things and process them and sort through so much data"—she had no idea just how much data—"before others have even blinked."

I didn't know how to tell her what her words meant to me.

"And before you say they taught you those skills," she continued, "you can't train something like that. Drew . . . *you're so damn smart.*" Her eyes bored into mine, willing me to see what she saw.

"I dropped out of college," I told her, finally revealing the weight that was perpetually dragging me down. Even though my application was printed out and waiting for her on the other side of the roof, I couldn't hold it in anymore. And this was better, it coming directly from me, out loud, even though saying the words hurt like a fresh wound.

"Really?" Her expression wasn't my worst nightmare, but it wasn't comforting, either. She looked . . . shocked but not shocked. And confused.

Fuck.

"Does it matter?" I asked, more harshly than I meant (or maybe not—maybe I meant it).

"No! I mean, yes! I mean . . ." She trailed off.

I waited with a semblance of patience (somehow), while my insides twisted and maybe even died a little.

"Sorry," she said. "I don't want to say the wrong thing."

This was a Huge Fucking Deal in my own head, but she wasn't supposed to think so too. She was supposed to assure me it didn't matter. That society got it wrong, not me. That she despised how her parents and community equated education with human worth.

She wasn't supposed to be choosing her words carefully and needing extra time to process the information like I'd just told her I hated puppies.

Chloe

I had kind of assumed he was in school for art and doing Rent for Your 'Rents on the side to support himself, especially with his parents out of the picture. But I had also been acutely aware that he hadn't offered that information readily, and what that implied.

I felt shock. Confusion. And so much shame.

Because it did surprise me. It caught me off guard and I didn't know how to react. My whole life, I had run from my community's ideals, but apparently I hadn't run fast enough and they had already sunk their toxic claws into me.

I took a breath. "I'm sorry. I'm just surprised because I meant it— you're so smart."

He frowned. "Not all smart people get degrees, and not all people with degrees are smart, as hard as that might be for you and your community to accept."

I couldn't let Drew know what was going on in my head. The value I'd assigned to college education was ingrained in me, not how I *wanted* to feel. Not how I *truly* felt, deep down. Right?

I refused to drag him into this shit. *My* shit.

"I'm just sad that it might've been something you wanted but weren't given the opportunity," I said carefully. Truthfully.

He sighed. "At the time I wanted it because it felt like . . . like I

222

would be dooming my future if I didn't, because that's what society tells us. But then we didn't have the money and I was scared of all the loans that would accrue, and given that there was something else I loved and wanted to do more . . ."

"Did you want to go to art school?"

A shadow crossed his face. "Why, because everyone needs higher education?"

I mentally kicked myself. Hard. Why did I keep making things worse? He was trying to show me who he really was, trying to take a huge step and share his work with me like I'd asked, and I was turning it into a minefield.

"No, of course not. I'm sorry," I said, because that was safest.

He squeezed his eyes shut briefly. When he opened them, his face relaxed a hair, and he answered my previous question. "Art school had crossed my mind, but I never considered it seriously. I didn't have the time or resources. My parents kicked me out, and my greatest concern was figuring out how to feed myself and get a roof over my head."

I thought about telling him he could dream, and if he wanted to have those art opportunities, he should, but it would also sound like I was telling him he needed more education.

I was stuck between a shítóu and a hard place.

So I focused on the reason we were here: the amazing step he was about to take if he was still willing.

"I am in awe of you, Drew Chan," I said. Then I tilted my head in the direction of the nearest towel-covered chair. "Do you still want to?"

I held my hand out, palm up.

Drew

CHAPTER 42

CHÁNG'É

took her hand. And told myself to put that conversation behind us. She had reacted . . . okay . . . and, well, okay.

Part of me wanted to wait to show her my work because this moment felt tainted now, but I also didn't know if I'd be able to do it later. The confidence I'd felt earlier when I'd texted Marshall seemed like a dream. One I might never have again.

But she was already leading me to the first painting. My palm pooled with so much sweat I worried she'd slip out.

"Here we have a light blue terry cloth, much too old and probably should've been thrown out years ago," I joked, gesturing to the embarrassing towel covering the first painting. I wiped my sweaty hands on it because, why not try to own the nervousness? And then I whipped it off with a flourish (Type C.2–style) to reveal a full moon in hues of blue, purple, and red, partly hidden behind dark clouds but managing to shine through even at the covered parts. Tree branches peeked out from the bottom, reaching for the light at first but then withering and giving up.

She gasped. I may have breathed a sigh of relief. And maybe melted a little.

Marshall had affixed the paper to the chair back with putty. It was the first time I'd ever seen my paintings purposefully displayed, and this less-than-classy presentation on a splintering chair felt very me. Raw, down-to-earth, and a little broken.

Chloe was staring intently, her head flitting around with sharp hummingbird movements to take in all the details. Her smile grew so wide I could see most of her beautiful, very white teeth (which was my favorite smile of hers).

Because I'm me, I jabbered to fill the silence. (Why couldn't I just let her xīnshǎng in peace?) "So, have you ever written or painted with máobǐ?"

"In Chinese school," she answered. I could tell from her expression that she hated it—the máobǐ, not my painting (phew).

"Well, I use máobǐ and rice paper. At first it was because my parents had it lying around, but then I got really attached to the combination, especially after I started playing with the paper to get different textures." I pointed to the painting in a spot where it was especially three-dimensional. "I want the moon to feel completely present, to be the focal point even though it's not the largest object on the page, you know? So I scrape, fold, and crinkle the paper until it creates—"

"Magic," Chloe finished with a whisper.

She pulled her phone out and shined the flashlight directly on the moon for a better view. Then she examined every fiber of that paper (it felt like), murmuring here, whispering "oh" and "wow" there, and almost seeming to forget I was present.

I felt like I was about to soar up into the sky like Cháng'é.

Chloe looked from the moon to me. "Did you actually used to go moon-gazing with your mother? Or was that just part of your cover story?"

My heart skipped a beat. Not only had she remembered that detail from Thanksgiving, but . . . *that was exactly why I painted moons.*

I held it together and said, "No, that was real." A thousand percent, knife-to-the-heart real. I glanced at my painting and the spindly, lonely branches reaching for the moon. "My mom used to take me for a walk every evening when I was little. She'd give me a red-bean Popsicle, we'd circle the neighborhood waving to everyone, and then we'd sit on the lawn atop a ratty blanket, watching the moon come up as the last of my Popsicle turned my hands and the blanket sticky."

There were too many emotions starting to bubble up (ones I'd bottled for a reason), and I didn't want to face them right now. I couldn't. So I went to the next chair and pulled off the towel (with less of a flourish than last time).

"Spoiler: they're all moons," I told her.

As Chloe xīnshǎng-ed with all her admiration displayed on her face, I hovered in the background (stealthily, if I do say so myself) while remaining on high alert so I wouldn't miss a single sound or extra pause.

Chloe

He was hovering behind me like an awkward, adorable weirdo.

I took my time with each painting, not because he seemed to need me to, but because they really were that breathtaking. I wanted to know each brushstroke and paper crease, and as I stared into the beauty, I tried to imagine him creating these masterpieces. What did he think about? How did he know what to do next?

In my economics classes, there was right and wrong, a definitive solution and an objective path. Clear-cut steps. But with this, while there were obviously better paths than others—my moons would come out looking like blocks of cheese—I couldn't wrap my head around the creative subjectivity of it.

"I'd love to watch you work," I said quietly, when actually I meant, *I wish I could see into your mind.*

He blushed. "You're just being kind."

I shook my head. "No, I want to see these come to life before me. I can't believe you start with blank space and turn it into this. Art."

His face shone brighter than his moons.

I tried to find a way to convey how blown away I was. To be honest, I'd never really understood art before, but I had also never truly looked.

"They make me feel hopeful," I realized. "They remind me that there's beauty and greatness out there, even in the darkness, and that I need to look for it." I turned from the painting to him. "I feel like I finally see what you see." It was that same perspective that had helped him follow his dream, helped him show his parents who he was. Maybe if I looked at his creations long enough, I could be transported there too.

So I continued to the next past-its-prime towel. And I sucked in a breath when I saw what lay beneath. "It's Moon Rabbit," I whispered as my eyes traced the outline of a rabbit pounding a mortar with a pestle to make the elixir of life for Cháng'é. Just like in real life, Moon Rabbit's shape was made up by the peaks and valleys of the moon's surface. I looked up at him. "You really do let Chinese culture influence your work."

"I've always seen the rabbit in the moon ever since my mother told me the story when I was a child." He pointed to a woman's silhouette beside the rabbit, partly ensconced in clouds but clear once I focused on that portion of the painting. Her hair was half up in two tall loops and half flowing behind her back. I could almost see the wind rippling through the ribbons on her dress.

"Cháng'é," I said, then reached into my pocket and clutched the drawing I'd done of Cháng'é the sheep and Mr. Twinkie. With a grin I told him, "I named the sheep with antigravity boots Cháng'é."

He stared at me with wide eyes, then walked over to the last painting. With a flick of the wrist, he pulled the towel off.

I gasped. Very loudly. I was lucky I didn't swallow a bug. I looked from one Cháng'é to the next, the latter being a sheep dressed as a mooncake with antigravity boots, floating past a gorgeous, textured moon. A short laugh escaped my lips. "It's perfect."

The fact that we'd drawn the same thing for each other was adorable, unsurprising, and a reminder that we were indeed starting from square 5.2 as he'd said yesterday.

I sheepishly—pun intended—handed him my drawing. "Yours is much better than mine."

Instead of laughing like I thought he would, he smiled. "I can't believe you thought to do this. You have to sign it for me."

I glanced at the bottom right corner of his nearest painting and saw that he had signed it in both English and Mandarin, the latter hand-drawn but resembling a printed name seal with its square outline, crisp Chinese characters, and red ink.

Before, I would have just signed *Chloe Wang*, but I did both, just to try it on. And when I formed each sun character in my Chinese name, I couldn't help thinking how fitting it was that I was three suns and he painted moons.

He held my horrible drawing to his heart, and I was maximally embarrassed—why had I shown that to him? Especially after I'd seen what he was capable of?

He gestured to his sheep Cháng'é. "I painted it for you," he said shyly.

I had given him Frankensheep and he was shy to give me this work of art he'd created specifically for me?

I didn't know what to say. None of my words felt enough. "This is the most beautiful and personal present I've ever received. I'm going to cherish this." I wanted to hug sheep Cháng'é to my chest, but obviously I couldn't without crumpling her.

"Drew," I said, then paused, because I needed him to know that I truly and completely meant these next words. "I believe that one day the world will thank you for the sacrifice you made to paint these."

He looked away, then back at me, blinking quickly. I reached a hand up and caught the tear that had escaped.

"I'm—I'm speechless," he said, his voice barely above a whisper. He closed the distance between us, stopping when our faces were inches apart.

My stomach was somersaulting—or was it filling with butterflies? Or just struggling to digest all that hot pot? No, definitely a romantic thing. I felt a . . . hunger for him.

"Thank you for sharing your work with me," I said, hoping he knew I was trying to acknowledge the huge step he'd taken without making it *too* big of a deal. "And thank you for my very own original Drew Chan. You're quite the charmer, you know that? I'm glad there isn't a Rent for You company, or else you'd be out there using this charm to woo girls, not their parents."

He leaned down and touched his forehead to mine. "My charm is very specifically catered to you, I think."

"That it is," I murmured.

We kissed—soft, slow, and sweet as pure honey. The inner hunger grew. He tasted a little like the gum he'd chewed after dinner, but more like *him*—this indescribable sweetness enhanced by his pheromones. His mouth gently pressed against mine, and then his tongue parted my lips and caressed me with just enough pressure to ignite all my nerve endings. His movements were soft and slow, tender, but I needed more and dove in, throwing self-consciousness to the wind and following my heart for once. I couldn't kiss him hard enough, inhale him enough, or taste him enough.

I stopped thinking about what I looked like or whether I was doing anything that could be considered weird and just sank into the moment. And when I say *sank*, I mean the opposite, because as I kissed him, my left leg wrapped around his side, and then he grasped my thighs, and before I knew it, I was in the air, straddling him, pushing my body against his with so much fervor I had no idea how he didn't fall over.

Then he did stumble, and we chuckled as we tumbled forward, but he caught me in his arms.

Everything felt so easy and safe that my brain somehow turned off, finally not worrying about what my parents were doing in that moment, how I was going to untangle this web, what was wrong with my father. Because all that could wait. Like I said earlier, this was my night off, and right now, I deserved to be happy.

Chloe

CHAPTER 43

ANSWERS

We kissed in every nook and cranny—against surfaces, on the floor, in an extra chair that held no painting. After an hour or two—I lost track of time—we came up for air. I didn't know about Drew, but I'd worked off enough lamb and fish balls to make room for whatever literal dessert was coming.

Drew led me to a table on the far side of the roof with lit candles, slices of chocolate cake, and a pile of papers, which he gestured to first.

"Earlier, when you said you wished I had an application you could just read . . ." He picked up the stack. "Well, your wish is my command."

"What?" It took my brain a second to register what he'd just said. "How?"

"This . . . is *my* application. To be an operative." He handed me the packet, then tugged on his shirt collar. "I want you to have it. So we can be on square fifty together."

Oh my God. I didn't have any words for a second.

"We didn't exactly have a meet-cute—" I started.

"Meet-purpose?" he suggested.

"More like a meet-weird."

We laughed.

"But this?" I placed an appreciative hand on the papers. "This takes the mooncake."

His shoulders relaxed and he grinned so wide I could see his first molars. He helped me with my folding chair—and good thing, because his application already had my full attention, and without him, my butt might have ended up missing the seat.

I skimmed, reading too fast because it all felt so urgent and overdue, but then I missed so much I had to go back and reread anyway.

"Your answers are, like, a sixth of the length of mine," I teased, sneaking a bite of chocolate cake. Yum. Thick and dark, the way I preferred my chocolate. Just as I'd told him in my application.

He poured hot water from a travel thermos into my teacup, which was already loaded with a teabag. When the steam curls reached my nose and I smelled the familiar aroma of jasmine and oolong, I let out an embarrassing noise resembling *aww*.

He beamed. "All your favorites."

I'd soon have that power too. Maybe not for his favorite kind of tea and dessert—I doubted Rent for Your 'Rents cared about those details—but I'd know other, more important facts. And the more surface-level ones, I could ask.

Q: Why do you want to do this?
A: To help people. And I'd be good at it. I think.

I laughed. "You're so honest, even adding the 'I think' at the end."

"My answers may have been more stream-of-consciousness than advised for a job application, but it was the only way I could go through with it—type quickly and send before I changed my mind."

I squeezed his hand.

Q: What's your relationship with your family like?
A: Currently nonexistent. We don't talk because I told them the truth about what I want in life (to be an artist), and they didn't approve. In fact, I wonder if that would make me a better operative. I can understand what the clients are going through in a unique, personal way. I know how to support them.

How my heart hurt. I knew he didn't feel this clinical about his relationship with his parents, but to see it that way on paper was still jarring.

Q: Will you be able to do holiday jobs?
A: For the foreseeable future, yep. No conflict at all. In fact, maybe it's even a plus. Holidays alone are no fun. Not recommended.

Check all you are willing to do for a job:
☑ Pretend to have a political allegiance different from your own
☑ Pretend to have religious views different from your own
☑ Learn a new skill, with lessons provided by Rent for Your 'Rents (please check all that apply):

- ☑ Sports
    - ☑ Golf
    - ☑ Basketball
    - ☑ Football
    - ☑ Soccer
    - ☑ Frisbee

- ☑ Dance

- ☑ Instrument
    - ☑ Violin
    - ☑ Piano
    - ☑ Èrhú
    - ☑ Dulcimer
    - ☑ Pípa
    - ☑ Guitar

- ☑ Games
    - ☑ Mahjong
    - ☑ Bridge
    - ☑ Chess
    - ☑ Chinese chess
    - ☑ Go

- ☑ Chinese calligraphy
- ☑ Chinese painting
- ☑ Chinese history
- ☑ Chinese philosophers

- ☑ Language, spoken
    - ☑ Mandarin
    - ☑ Taiwanese
    - ☑ Cantonese

- ☑ Language, written
    - ☑ Traditional characters
    - ☑ Simplified characters

- ☑ Cooking

- ☑ Learn new subjects for possible majors/careers/etc.
    - ☑ Science-related
    - ☑ Math-related
    - ☑ Sociology
    - ☑ Political science
    - ☑ Economics
    - ☑ Business
    - ☑ Health care
    - ☑ Entrepreneurship
    - ☑ Law
    - ☑ Tech

I paused and looked up when he started speaking.

"I signed up for every class I could take, especially the art ones. Chinese painting didn't teach me anything I didn't already know from playing around, but it was during that class that I first started experimenting with the paper."

"When you talk about the company, you seem really appreciative."

He sighed. "You know, I *am* grateful—it fed me all this time while giving me access to valuable resources I wouldn't have had otherwise. But it's also this strange dichotomy, where the good doesn't get rid of the associated shame I sometimes feel."

"Because you're lying?" I guessed.

"Maybe. Except some lies are born out of love."

Yup.

I asked, "Do you ever think about going home and saying you're now an engineer or doctor or philosopher or something, then using your training to faux prove it?"

Hesitation. "Not anymore. I used to."

"But . . . ," I urged.

More hesitation. "I don't know how to be someone else with them, even if it means I get to have them back."

Silence.

"But that doesn't mean it's the right choice for everyone," he added, obviously for my sake. "My situation certainly isn't something to strive for."

"How come you can be someone else with everyone but not with your family?" It was the exact opposite for me.

He ran a hand through his hair. "It's not like I planned it this way. I knew they wouldn't be happy, but I didn't think they'd reject me. Maybe that messed me up a bit."

"I'm sorry. Do you regret your decision?"

Immediately he shook his head. "Question? Yes. Regret? No, not anymore."

I looked back down at the application. Drew was no longer the lost boy who had filled it out, but he also wasn't quite whole yet.

"Thank you for sharing this with me," I said, hugging the papers. "I now have a better appreciation for what the clients go through—I feel like I'm standing in front of you naked!"

We laughed, then finished our cake while perusing more of his application. And all our resulting inside jokes were the icing on top.

Drew

CHAPTER 44

CLOSING IN

At two in the morning, when we stumbled through the front door of Chloe's parents' house, the air was filled with hope and joy. My arm was wrapped around her shoulder and hers around my waist, and our cuddling felt as natural as our laughs. But then we bumped (almost literally, but not fully) into Mrs. Wang, standing in the middle of the living room, hands on her hips.

Chloe quickly hid the sheep Cháng'é painting behind her back, then passed it to me roughly. I took it tenderly, the slight rip in the corner (my thumb couldn't stop rubbing it) mirroring the rip in my heart.

Her mother didn't seem to care what it was. "Where've you been?" she asked, the iciness of her voice freezing any residual warmth in the air.

Shockingly, Chloe matched her mother's stance. "You were the one who asked me to leave. On Christmas."

Mrs. Wang's fists slid down in shock and her eyes went wide for a second before they narrowed in frustration. "Are you drunk? What's wrong with you?" She turned to me and pointed an accusatory finger. "You're a bad influence on her."

Chloe pushed her mother's finger down. "I'm not drunk; I'm

happy, Mămá. He's a *good* influence on me. He makes me feel more like myself."

Normally, I'd be sucking up to the parent, but as Chloe's sort-of-boyfriend-but-also-hired-gun, I was a chicken running around with its head cut off.

Quietly I said, "She was really hurt you didn't want to spend Christmas with her."

Mrs. Wang scoffed, then eyed her daughter up and down. "She doesn't look hurt to me. Quite the opposite."

Chloe retorted, "I can be hurt by you and still have a good time with my boyfriend."

My heart soared for a moment before I remembered that the word didn't necessarily mean anything given the circumstances.

Mrs. Wang seemed ready to lob another attack, but then she hesitated and stood there mulling things over before turning to me and forcing an unconvincing smile. "Well, I'm glad you could be there for her, Andrew." That name flipped the switch, and my head felt even more muddled. "Hope you whisked her off her feet, maybe opened your wallet to show your appreciation for what she—and we—have sacrificed for your relationship."

"He doesn't need to spend money to show me he cares," Chloe said boldly.

Mrs. Wang looked like she'd been slapped. "Are you saying you don't appreciate the gift I broke myself to scrimp together for you?"

"No! Of course not!" Chloe's face was aghast. "I didn't mean . . . I just . . . No, I'm so appreciative." She took a breath. "Can we take a step back and not do this when we're all so tired? Can we maybe spend tomorrow together?"

"Doesn't Andrew have a doctor's appointment?" Mrs. Wang asked.

Chloe's face fell. "Oh, right." She looked at me with frantic eyes. "Well, maybe we can cancel that, especially if—"

Mrs. Wang turned and started up the stairs. "You should go with

Andrew. Don't lose this one too, and be left with no one."

Chloe's face was sad but her fists were clenched as she watched her mother disappear from view. "Because the only thing that makes me worth anything is who I'm with," she whispered, hauntingly devoid of emotion.

She took the painting back from me and, seeing the tear (both in the corner and in me), her face drained of color.

"I'm so sorry," she whispered. "I'm a monster."

"It's no big deal," I lied.

She shook her head frantically, so fast it matched my sped-up heart-beat. "No," she said. "I'm . . . I can't . . ."

"It's okay," I whispered.

Then I pecked her on the cheek quickly (and maybe without much heart) and retreated to the uncomfortable, definitely-starting-to-smell couch.

I needed a second. I knew it hadn't been on purpose and that the rip had been a result of unrelated messiness, but that was also exactly why I was bothered.

She and I were built out of lies. Were we strong enough to survive?

Chloe

I hated myself.

But I didn't know what else to do. The walls were closing in and there was only one path forward: keep up the lies.

I knew all the consequences were chasing me down, but I needed to keep running running running without looking back to see what was about to bite me in the ass. If I slowed even for a second, it would all fall apart. I would lose everything.

I thought about Jerry, about sheep, about the "love you" game-theory guy, in an attempt to keep away the worst thought haunting me: *Maybe I'm going to lose everything anyway.*

Chloe

CHAPTER 45

DR. LIN

December 26

"Thank you for doing this," I said to Drew, who was sitting across from me, atop the examination table.

We were visiting my community's choice primary-care doctor on the pretense of Drew needing his eye checked. Upon arrival at the office, we had filled out a medical-history form—were Drew's answers accurate?—before being ushered to a room by the receptionist, who I of course knew from church.

I glanced at Drew's legs tapping against the side of the table. "I know this is a little demeaning. Okay, a lot demeaning."

It couldn't be fun for him to be playing up the altercation, but wasn't it also good to get his eye checked out? It would certainly bring me a little peace of mind.

"Happy to do it for you," he told me, though his refusal to meet my gaze indicated that he was indeed a little humiliated, which made his gesture even more amazing. *Except, in a way, you're paying him to do it,* a nagging voice said in my head.

Dr. Lin walked in with a dramatic flourish. "Ah, Jing-Jing, nǐ hǎo," he said, grabbing my hand.

"Shūshú hǎo," I answered, dipping my head slightly. Force of habit. "This is my boyfriend, Andrew. Thanks for seeing us."

Dr. Lin shook Drew's hand. "Andrew, nice to finally meet you. Well, officially. I saw you at the party but didn't have a chance to introduce myself before everything."

We all forced tight smiles. Except Dr. Lin's wasn't all that tight. Or forced. Maybe it was even a little hungry?

"And please, no need to thank me. I'm here for you. Both of you," he said, pulling his squat, round doctor's stool over and taking a seat. "Would you like me to check the baby?" He gestured to my belly.

And this was exactly why Drew needed to be the patient today, not me. Even if my appointment had been for something not baby-related, Dr. Lin would've given me an ultrasound, and that was just too messy. Not a good path to our goal of learning about my father's health.

"How long has it been?" Dr. Lin continued. "Prenatal vitamins on the regimen, Jing-Jing? Do you have a birth plan?"

Even though a normal doctor would have asked these questions—or at least, I presumed they would have—I knew from the underlying glint in his eyes that he was digging for gossip and just wanted to know the whole story.

"Just Andrew's eye for today, please," I said, calmly but boldly, trying to take charge.

He cleared his throat. "You know that kissing doesn't lead to pregnancy, right, Jing-Jing?"

"What?" I said just as Drew seemed to choke on his own saliva.

Dr. Lin scooted a little closer. "Someone suggested to me that maybe you missed a period and didn't know that can happen without being pregnant."

"Are you kidding me right now? Whoever told you that was probably trying to embarrass me!"

I wanted to run right out of there, but I told myself to hang on, that we had a mission, and that it was okay. At least Drew was on my side—though, truthfully, I might have preferred he not be here for this.

"I just want to make sure you know everything," Dr. Lin said calmly. "I know parents in our community aren't always great with sex education, so I've gotten used to being the one to, you know. Talk about all that."

And what a fine job you're doing, I thought sarcastically.

Luckily, Drew piped up. "I think we're good on that. Can we move on?"

Dr. Lin seemed to have forgotten Drew was there. But the words must have sunk in because he said, "I'm sorry. I overstepped. That's a danger of treating patients you know well. I apologize."

And here was my chance. "That's okay. It must be hard. Is it especially difficult when your patients are very sick? And you have to tell them, treat them, inform their families?" His eyes met mine, but he didn't say anything. "Was it hard to tell my dad?"

He let out a breath. "Oh, he changed his mind and told you. It wasn't as hard to tell him since his news wasn't all that bad, as you know, but it's obviously still awful. But being able to help is the silver lining. I'm glad we caught it early."

"Me too," said a tiny voice, which, yes, was mine, but I was now functioning on autopilot as my mind worked to process everything.

He was such a terrible doctor. I guess I could accept how much he had overstepped with me earlier given that it was this very trait that was allowing me entry into my father's condition, but I also couldn't stop thinking about how my parents needed to see someone more professional. Maybe he was at least good at diagnosing and treating, I tried to reason.

I had to fight my urge to demand he tell me more, or to pull the fire alarm and steal a look at my dad's files. But I stayed still because I knew Dr. Lin, and the info dump was coming; he loved to hear himself talk, especially as the expert.

"Your father's prostate cancer is slow-growing, so even though it's of course scary, his prognosis is good. If you need to talk to anyone, I can give you some names, but as long as you're prepared for what's to come, you'll all get through this. Together."

Except we weren't together. And I didn't know what was to come. I didn't fucking know anything.

"I'm glad he told you," Dr. Lin continued. "It's not usually our way, and I used to think that was the right way too, but I've seen how for some families, especially ones that grow up here, that can be traumatizing." He sighed. "I don't know what the right answer is. Do you?" I was shocked he was asking me, but then he laughed, signaling it was rhetorical and, somehow, a joke. "Have you ever thought about how hard it is for your parents to try to meld traditions from two cultures, Jing-Jing?" *They never try all that hard.* "Your generation will never understand ours."

And you all will never understand us, especially not with that attitude.

I sat quietly in my seat, my hands folded in my lap, half tuning out Dr. Lin while trying to process the new information about my dad. Except what was I supposed to do with it? Just like everything else, I wasn't supposed to know, and we were all using our overflowing supply of secrets to build walls between us.

What would happen when one came to light? When should I reveal my truth, or that I knew my father's?

Dr. Lin shined a light in and out of Drew's eye, then asked him to follow his finger. He pressed down on the surrounding soft tissue, checking Drew's reaction for pain.

"Nothing to worry about. Just take some ibuprofen for any discomfort." He clapped Drew on the back. "Lucky you, huh? I heard Hongbo could've been a ranked boxer, but he chose to run the family business instead."

I still said nothing, because I couldn't.

"Thanks, Dr. Lin," Drew said, hopping down from the table.

"Thanks," I echoed, only so that he wouldn't put together that he'd just broken HIPAA. And then I remembered that Dr. Lin was giving us a courtesy visit, as a friend, since we obviously couldn't use Drew's health insurance—which I had explained to Dr. Lin as Drew wanting to save face and keep the punch from Hongbo off his medical record.

"Thanks for everything," I added sincerely. "And for helping my father so much." I had to force back tears.

"Just doing my job," he responded nonchalantly.

Drew piped up. "And, uh, I think Wang Shūshú is still having a hard time with everything going on—"

"Especially with me knowing," I interrupted, jumping in when I caught on to Drew's goal of preventing Dr. Lin from telling my dad about our conversation. "It's not the usual way, as you said, so I think it'd be best for his recovery if you, you know—"

"I get it," Dr. Lin said with a nod. "It's good he's in such denial. Many Chinese people believe that the knowledge of the sickness is what gets you, even more than the actual disease. Don't worry; I know how to best deal with that."

He applied hand sanitizer, then gave me one more smile. "Your parents love you, Jing-Jing. Maybe try to remember that before making your public declarations in such a dramatic way? Your father's been through enough." He stood. "Next time you're in town, we should check your blood pressure. And do a full workup on the baby."

I was tempted to tell him the truth, but that suddenly felt of no importance.

As soon as the door shut behind Dr. Lin, I asked Drew, "He doesn't know what just actually happened, right?"

"Does it matter?"

"Yes, I need to know how likely it is that my parents will find out

I know." I was spinning. Focusing on weird, less important things because I couldn't face what I'd just found out. What I'd just *tricked* Dr. Lin into telling me.

Drew gently sat me down on the examination table next to him. "Let's try to process the information first before we get ahead of ourselves. But most likely, no, he doesn't know."

I took a deep breath and he joined me, matching my tempo. "I'm so tired," I whispered when my heart had slowed a hair, though I could still hear the beats in my head.

"I know," he whispered back, cradling my torso and hugging me to him. "I'm sorry about everything."

We rocked back and forth to the rhythm of my heartbeat. Drew didn't comment when my tears splashed against his chest, and I let them fall fall fall until nothing was left.

Drew

CHAPTER 46

THREE SUNS

nce we left Dr. Lin's office, Chloe wasn't ready to see her parents yet. We stopped for boba tea, but she didn't really touch hers except to stir the fat straw around.

"I should go," I said, even though it went against everything I wanted.

Chloe looked up from her taro milk bubble tea. "Go where?" she asked, her eyes not quite there.

"Home." I had to force the words out. "To give you time with your parents."

"You can't leave now!" she burst out before I finished my sentence. Then her voice grew as small as her hunched body looked. "You're the only one on my side."

"I'll be on your side even if I'm not there physically. I'm just a phone call away."

"Except you're not," she said, a little frantic. "If you leave, then my parents will think you're back in Chicago, and you won't be able to pop back in. I mean, yeah, we could talk on the phone, but . . ." She trailed off.

I wasn't sure if she was thinking about how we'd never done that before or how it wasn't enough. Regardless, I was too many steps ahead of her. "Forget what I said. What do you need right now?"

She grabbed my right hand with her left, and we sat in silence, sipping our tea and chewing our honey-soaked tapioca pearls.

Thirty minutes later she said, "Okay."

Okay . . . you're ready to go home? You want to tell your parents you know? You want me to hug you and never let go?

I waited patiently.

She sucked up the last dregs of tea noisily, the purple liquid sputtering and flailing at the bottom of the cup. "You're right, I think. I need some time with my parents."

Even though her sentence had started with "you're right," even though I was proud of her for figuring out what she needed, even though it was what I already knew, my heart sank.

But now was not the time to be selfish. "Okay," I said, giving her my trained *you've got this* smile.

I grabbed her now-empty cup and was about to stand and track down a trash can, but she stopped me by grabbing my free hand. My knees bent and lowered me back to my seat.

"I hope you know what you mean to me," she said, slightly shy, her eyes darting away periodically. "I . . . I really don't want you to leave, but . . ." I nodded at her to show I understood. "I don't know where your head's at with us, now and going forward, but for me, I want to see where it can go. I know it's messy with all the history, not to mention the distance, but—"

"I feel the same way," I interrupted. Then, with a genuine, untrained, Drew smile, I said, "I think we owe it to Cháng'é."

She laughed. "The sheep or the goddess?"

"I don't care, as long as it means this doesn't end."

Her lips tasted like taro and sunshine—three suns' worth.

Chloe

CHAPTER 47

FALLING FALLING FALLING

"I'm so sorry to hear your grandmother's sick," my mother told Drew over dinner. We'd just informed my parents he was leaving tomorrow. "Please give us your address so we can send a care package."

"I got it, Mā," I said quickly. "I'll give her something from all of us."

"How lucky you are to have grown up with your grandma," my mother said. "Cherish her while you can."

Drew looked at me with sympathetic eyes, and I knew he was remembering from my application that my grandparents had died before I was born: one at sea (the fisherman grandpa), two in an automobile accident (my dad's parents), and one from leukemia (my mom's mom, right before I was born).

I returned the sympathy and hoped he knew it was for his grandma's comments about his art, for the estranged grandfather he'd never met for the worst reasons, and, as I had recently learned from his operative application, for the grandparents he lost to lung cancer and heart disease when he was young.

"This is the same grandma who taught you mahjong?" my mother continued, and I knew she was being kind—finally—but for some reason, I was on the edge of my seat. Knowing the truth behind the lies was making me antsy, though for Drew this was just another day.

Stop sweating, I told myself even though, obviously, I had no control over that, not really.

My father hadn't said a word, and I was trying not to stare at him as if I could somehow see the cancer cells now that I knew they existed.

"Would you have told me Grandma had leukemia if I'd been alive then?" I asked, my eyes on my father as I slowly chewed the steamed fish in my mouth.

But my parents ignored me. My mother tried to change the topic by saying, "Andrew, earlier today I noticed the Christmas-tree ornaments you brought. How kě'ài! Where did you get them?"

"He made them," I said without missing a beat. "I named the one with antigravity boots Cháng'é."

Her eyes went wide at my first statement, but even wider at the second.

"Maybe he's a good influence on you after all," my mother said, then turned to Drew. "Thanks for reminding my daughter where she comes from. I'm always telling her she needs to embrace her roots more."

"He *is* a good influence on me, but not because he reminds me I come from a toxic community that judges how I look, study, breathe."

"Jing-Jing!" my mother chastised. She cleared her throat, trying to clear my words from the table. "Well, I love that you have a *healthy* relationship with your culture, Andrew. Using it to inspire your little crafts—how wonderful!"

I was tired of playing my part, and seeing all of them play theirs was making me sick.

"He's a talented artist," I said.

Drew placed a hand on my knee under the table, but I ignored it.

My mother smiled at Drew, a little forced. "Well, that'll serve you well in medicine—or dentistry, perhaps?—if you can get over the germy parts, of course."

"Or that would serve him well as an artist," I said with a shrug.

"Jing-Jing," Drew said, gentle, as if asking me whether I was okay, but hearing that name come out of his soft, familiar lips frustrated me.

"What?" I said, a little more harshly than I'd meant to.

He leaned in close, much too close, and even though he was probably trying to get a private moment to ask what the hell was going on, his scent overwhelmed me. I'd fallen off his back simply because of my father's presence not that long ago, but in this moment, with my parents' and my lies infecting the air, our relationship, my brain, I gave in to my urges and pecked Drew on the lips.

His head snapped back in shock, and though I understood he was just surprised, it also felt like rejection. My parents pretended not to see.

Drew leaned back in, but not as close this time. "Are you okay? Do you want to go get some air?"

How could I be okay when I'd just found out my father had cancer? And I couldn't even *talk* about it! How could they not tell me? How could we ever be normal—whatever that was—in each other's presence again?

I felt myself crumbling. The room around me was crumbling too.

I turned to Drew, my eyes pleading, not sure what I needed but convinced he knew how to fix this.

"I think I should head home tonight," he announced quietly to the table, his eyes downcast.

"No! Why?" flew out of my mouth.

My mother tsked at me. "If he wants to be by his grandmother's side sooner, that's noble."

Drew gave me a look that seemed to say, *You need time with them, and I'm in the way.*

I shook my head at him. I had no fucking clue what I needed except to not be alone. And yes, if he left, I had my parents, but I would *feel* alone, which said a lot, and was precisely why I needed him *here*.

He gave me that *you've got this* smile that used to make me feel confident, but in this situation made me panic. I was flailing, no ground beneath me and nothing to hold on to.

"Are you sure you can get a flight out tonight?" my father asked, the first and only sign that he knew Drew was a human and in our presence.

Drew nodded. "My cousin works for United. Don't worry about me." Then he stood. "Thank you, Wang Āyí, Shūshú, for your hospitality."

My father sniffed loudly, wiping his nose with his napkin, and my mother nodded with a tight-lipped smile.

"Safe travels," my father said.

"Best wishes to your grandmother and family," my mother said.

I followed Drew out of the kitchen in a stupor.

My parents were completely silent and obviously eavesdropping as Drew packed up the rest of his things and rolled his bag to the front door. So we were silent too, and I waited until we were outside before blurting, "Don't go. I need you here."

"I'll stay if that's really what you want, but I'm in the way," he said gently, caressing the side of my face with his hand. "I may not be able to pop back in, but I'm still here for you. You can call or text anytime."

I managed a nod. "I thought you'd *want* me to tell them about you. Your art."

"Not like this." Then, with pained eyes, he surprised me by saying, "I think when you tell them—not just about me, but more so about your dad's cancer—it should be when you're sure, calm, and ready. If you want to tell them now, okay, it's your choice, but . . ." His gaze dropped. "When I talked to my parents, it was in a ball of emotion, and sometimes I wonder if that's why it spiraled out of

251

control. This is obviously not the same thing, but I don't want you to be chewed up by regret."

"Okay," I said, with little emotion. I was too spent.

"Okay," he said, equally devoid of sentiment. Maybe he was in operative mode, assessing my situation and churning through data.

But then he leaned down and scooped me into the air, which, ironically, grounded me.

"It'll be okay," he whispered next to my ear.

"How do you know?"

"Because you're that strong."

In one swift movement, he put me down, pressed his lips to mine firmly but quickly, and then rolled his way down the driveway. He didn't have to leave my side yet—he hadn't even called an Uber—but I let him go because I didn't want him to see my face. Because the tears were falling falling falling. And no one was there to catch them this time.

Drew

I wanted to hold her close. Dry her tears. Shield her from everything that caused her stress and pain.

It took all my nerve to keep walking down her driveway and not run back. I hoped I was right that her confusion was because of my presence, not in spite of.

I'm helping her I'm helping her I'm helping her . . .

Then why did it feel like the opposite? Why did it seem like all the options now and in the future led to misery for everyone involved?

They're not happy even with Andrew, said a voice in my head, one that sounded like a mash-up of my mother's and father's voices. *Good luck impressing them as Drew. Maybe that's why you ran, not because you're trying to help her.*

By the time I looked back, Chloe was gone.

Chloe

CHAPTER 48

HOURGLASS

"What *was* that?" my mother asked when I returned to the table.

Had she actually noticed my spiraling? Sometimes I forgot that when she wanted to, she could see me.

"He was trying to get back to his sick grandmother, and you were so selfish to want him to stay," she clarified.

Oh.

I said nothing.

"Thank you for staying behind, Jing-Jing," my father said. "I'm glad we'll have a little more time together."

Please just tell me.

But he didn't. And I also didn't spill what I knew, because I was a hot mess of emotions right now, and I trusted Drew. Or maybe I was just a coward who couldn't stand how my parents already looked at me, even without knowing I'd invaded their privacy earlier today.

"So kind, caring about his family like that," my mother muttered into her rice. Then she looked up at me. "I'm glad you found a nice boy with such a promising future. Certainly makes me worry less."

"Me too," my father said—mostly to his bowl, but still.

"Yeah, me three," I answered. *He just may not have the exact "promising future" you were hoping for.*

In the silence that followed, I could hear the sand passing through the hourglass, counting down the time I had left before the consequences bit me in my tired ass.

December 26, 10:32 p.m. PST

<Chloe>

Why'd you have to go?

<Drew>

I'm sorry

I thought it was for the best

Pause.

Do you want me to come back?

I could say I missed my flight

Another pause.

I don't know

Longest pause.

Yes and no

Maybe I just need to have a good night's sleep and I'll feel better in the morning

I'm so tired but can't seem to fall asleep

I've already counted so many Chang'e sheep, but . . . nothing

A little help?

Hmm

How about a sheep being chased by a piece of stinky tofu?

Poor guy!

The sheep or the tofu?
Because the tofu just wants to be friends

And then there's Tiger Balm sheep, who carries it on him
and uses it to cure everything
He's currently trying to wipe some on Stinky Tofu to help
him smell like spicy menthol instead of feet

Does Tiger Balm sheep resemble an old Chinese dad in an undershirt, sitting on a white turned-over bucket, cooling himself with a circular fan?

 Of course

I'm glad you got that one
Wasn't sure you would

I've been around the Chinese block once or twice
I used to work at our local Chinese grocery store

And I already knew that because of your application
😄
This is fun

Another falling asleep tip . . .
I have a xiao zhentou I hug

A little pillow? How little?

Perfect cuddle size. And it has Toucan Sam on it
I used to love Froot Loops as a kid because they're
colorful (I've always been more artist than food critic), and
the pillow was a present from Jordan
I may love where the pillow came from more than the
pillow itself . . .
But I'll get you your own xiao zhentou

Then I guess mine would need to
be string cheese themed
Either have a picture on it or be shaped
like one
Ooh maybe peelable?

Long pause.

I miss you

I . . . may have been typing that and
deleting it and typing it again
Thanks for saying it first

I may have been typing and deleting something else
Three words

Chang'e. Has. Diarrhea.

You should keep her out of your rotation for the rest of the night

She ate too much Sichuan food

Maybe that's why you didn't fall asleep earlier

You're ridiculous

Sleep loose

And Chloe?

It'll be ok

Someway somehow pieces will fall

And even though it doesn't feel like it, you will have some control over parts of it

It's just too fresh for you to see all that right now

Okay

Thanks

Chloe

CHAPTER 49

WANG DENTAL PALACE

December 27

hated spit and pus and blood, not to mention the screeching noises and scent of sterilization, but I went with my parents to the office the next day. Sunday. I wasn't sure if the Kuos had blacklisted us from all church activities or if we were hiding our faces because we had "no face," but either way, I needed to rack up mooncake points. Lots of them.

And yet, once I was in the back room of Wang Dental Palace preparing to pour Mrs. Lee's impression, I regretted my decision to come here today.

I gloved and goggled up, sprayed down her impression with *way* too much CaviCide disinfectant, then prepared the yellow stone mixture. My parents would be so disappointed to learn I'd forgotten the composition of the stone—calcium something?—but they should just be grateful I wasn't gagging like I had the first time.

I turned on the . . . vibrating machine—almost called it a vibrator, but no—and pressed the impression tray to it, my hand and the rest of me shaking with each rapid pulse. It made me feel numb, maybe a little invincible in a weird way, like time had slowed but I was still

259

at full speed, Flash-style. Even though it was gross that I was holding a saliva-covered object that was a negative rendering of someone's teeth, I did kind of like pressing the thick stone mixture to the impression with my spatula and seeing the vibrations turn it to flowing liquid. Watching molecules shift before your eyes—*that* was the kind of science I could get on board with, though fewer bodily fluids would be great, please.

As I hit my rhythm scooping and oozing the stone into the impression's nooks and crannies, I pictured using this method to create a 3-D Cháng'é.

Suddenly I stood up straighter. This really was just art, I realized. I knew my parents had been saying that forever, but now I actually understood.

A laugh escaped my lips as I remembered how Drew hadn't even gotten this far on his day here. I pictured him cringing over the patient's mouth. Poor guy, just like poor Mr. Stinky Tofu.

And with that I forgot that I was going to confront my parents later today, and I hummed to the vibrating machine, also forgetting that I was holding something that had been in the dirtiest part of another human being.

The day started and ended with emergency visits, and in between, my parents caught up on records and billing while I helped them with their lab backlog. When the last patient left, I helped my mother CaviCide the operatory. *Spray, wipe, spray, let sit.* I'd been doing this since I was a preteen.

"You finished the Essix retainer for Lee Ǎyí?" my mother asked.

I nodded. "Why do you make so many of those as temporary mouth guards when a real mouth guard is so much better for the teeth?"

She sighed. "Not everyone can afford a mouth guard, even if I only charge them the lab fee and not for my time. Insurance doesn't cover it. So I make them a free Essix. It's not as sturdy as a traditional mouth guard, but it helps them in the short term."

"Why don't you charge them? It's a lot of work for me," I joked, even though I kind of enjoyed softening the plastic with heat and then using suction to hug it to the stone mold of the patient's teeth. But between pouring the mold, letting it dry, and making the retainer, it was hours of work.

"We're a community," she said quietly, and I knew she was thinking about her Bible study and what I'd done to her place in said community.

"I'm sorry," I said again, which, of course I was sorry, but also, why was I always the one apologizing?

"Thank you for your help today," my mother said, then left.

I was so frozen I heard her enter the office she shared with my father, then flop into her desk chair.

After a few minutes of listening to them click-clack at their respective keyboards—my mother a distinctive *click pause pause click clack pause* and my dad a slow but steady *click click click clack*—I took a deep breath, coughing when the CaviCide burned my nose. Then I strode over and into their office with confidence.

Except I didn't. That was just the plan. In reality, I crept up to their door like the Cowardly Lion and hovered outside trying to gather my nonexistent courage. Which, yes, was embarrassing, but also led me to overhear this:

Dad: "Do you think Andrew will be able to take care of Jing-Jing when I'm gone?"

Mom: "Aiyah, don't talk like that. You'll be okay."

Pause.

Dad: "I want to make sure, just in case."

Mom: "I know, I know, you don't think I want the same? Hongbo was my idea, remember?"

Another pause.

Mom: "Do you think you'd feel better if you told her?"

Dad, immediately: "Of course not. Why worry her for no reason? We're protecting her. What will her knowing accomplish, except hurting her focus? Her grades? Her future?"

Mom: "She's strong."

Dad: "Yes, but why even put her through that?"

Longest pause.

Dad: "And . . . maybe telling her will make it too real for me. I can't handle that right now."

Even though I couldn't see them, I pictured my mother nodding at him, not looking up from her computer, and my father's eyes also never leaving his screen.

I ran my feet over the couple of tears that had fallen to the floor, then slunk my way back to the tiny lab I was supposedly tidying up. Except all I did was lean against the counter and squeeze my eyes shut, counting my breaths because I didn't feel in control of anything anymore.

My parents and I had too many lies between us. How would we find our way back from all this? And . . . was I running out of time?

In a messed-up way, I understood where my father was coming from. Yes, dysfunction—and a whole lot of it—was at the root of our lies, but so was love. If we didn't care, we wouldn't bother. I would've just given up on our relationship because of the Hongbo mess instead of going to the extremes of hiring Andrew . . . yet hiring him was also so ridiculous I sometimes couldn't look at myself. But when you feel as desperate as I had, the absurdity slowly distorts until, eventually, the previously absurd path becomes the only way out, then a good idea. Obviously, if I could wave a magic wand and make it so my parents and I could understand each other, I would. *Expecto Perspectivito!* But life was, maybe both unfortunately and fortunately, not a Harry Potter book, and I say fortunately because I'm pretty sure I'd be a muggle. Or a squib.

Girls like me don't get to be the hero, just the weird sidekick.

I had no idea how much time passed before my mother came to get me.

"What's wrong with you?" she asked, half gentle, half accusing.

I rubbed my nose. "The CaviCide got to me."

She shrugged. "You get used to it. Ready to go?"

"Yup," I said with way too much enthusiasm. She didn't notice. Or maybe she did and we were all playing our parts. Maybe Andrew was the most real out of all of us.

December 27, 5:08 p.m. PST

<Chloe>

I don't want to talk about it, but I decided not to tell them I know. I just want to spend time with my dad.

<Drew>

Ok

Okay it's the right call?
Or okay you support me either way?

Just . . . ok, it's whatever you need.

Tell me what you're thinking
Please

I want to help you but I don't know how

I don't know either
I don't know what I need
I wish there weren't so many lies

Me too

I wish I could see you

Me too

Drew

CHAPTER 50

FULL ROM-COM

was in the kitchen making chicken congee for dinner when Jason came home from his Christmas job.

"Dude," he said in greeting.

"Dude, no," I threw back immediately. I was not ready for this. I quickly checked the rice cooker, then retreated to my room. But Jason followed behind like a pet. An annoying one who wanted the details, not one who'd missed me (well, maybe he'd missed me a little, I'd like to think, seeing as I'd missed him).

"You went full rom-com on her?" he asked.

"Hardly," I said dismissively. "No boom boxes were involved, no chasing through an airport, no declarations of love. I just showed her my paintings."

"Exactly."

"So?"

"So!" He threw his hands in the air and I couldn't help a laugh. "So this is such a big deal!" He ran up to me and grabbed me, jumping up and down. Complete, utter shock on my end. "I'm happy for you!"

"You're not going to lecture me about shitting where I eat?" I struggled to say between jumps.

He put me down. "Well, yeah, that too, but also, yay! I'm bummed I missed her."

I wanted to tell him, *No worries, she'll be around soon*, but then I realized I had no clue when that would be. I wondered if his operative senses were tingling as I skirted this and said, "You'd like her."

"Anyone who can get you to stop being so weird about your paintings? I fucking *love* her."

I laughed. "I'm not that bad, am I?"

He gave me a sideways look like, *Are you kidding me?*

I nudged him with an elbow. "I'm just joking; I know I'm the worst. But . . . maybe not anymore."

His face lit up. "Yeah?"

I shrugged. "Yeah. I'm looking into a few programs, some contests. Just to see what it's like, in case it's something I want. Maybe I'm a little excited too." I shrugged again even though my heart was racing.

"Yeah you are," Jason said with a smirk. "Proud of you."

"Thanks, buddy." I looked away so I could keep it together.

Chloe

CHAPTER 51

BY THE SEAT OF MY PANTS

December 27–29

I naively hoped the next few days would revert back to what 'rents time had been before Andrew, but there were too many emotions in the way.

"Do you want to play mahjong?" I had asked my parents the first night it was just us, but my mother had simply huffed, "We don't have a fourth," even though my entire life thus far had been us playing a three-person version with some tiles removed. Somehow Drew's one-time addition had shifted that—though, really, I knew that wasn't it. She was still mad at me.

The next day I asked if she wanted to go shopping—I was so desperate I might've even tried on some whale tails to make her smile—but she had said there wasn't enough time, all the good inventory had been bought up for Christmas, her favorite salesperson was on vacation, and her farmers' calendar dictated she be frugal today. *So many reasons,* I had responded, and she hadn't laughed.

I tried not to, but I also hovered around my father. I brought him water and snacks like a sad dog that knows something is wrong but can't say what. Then I would get scared I was making it too obvious that I knew about the cancer, so I'd keep my distance for the next hour. I was like a frantic Ping-Pong ball, and between that and my spiraling thoughts at night, I felt more unmoored than I had in a long time.

I tried to focus my energy on other things: planning out my coursework for the rest of my college years, reading ahead for my upcoming quarter, putting so much extra time into my research-assistant gig I worried the professor would think I had no life.

And I plotted how to lighten at least one of the weights between my parents and me. Because I couldn't live with myself otherwise.

Five days after ridding myself of the Kuos—though it felt more like a lifetime, to be honest—I reentered the belly of the beast. I pulled up to the gross white columns, the mere sight of the pillars making me want to hurl chunks. This was not going to be fun. But it was still better than many of the alternatives, like coming here to visit my fiancé, or waiting in a not-quite-Lamborghini for a visit to Prime Strip.

I saw the part of the grass that Drew and my family had been dumped on post-party and I suddenly wanted to laugh. There wasn't anything to demarcate the specific spot, but I knew the exact location regardless. The amount of adrenaline that had been coursing through me at the time made me remember precisely how far we had been from the door, from the koi pond, and from the out-of-bloom peonies, which triangulated to one specific spot.

This can't go worse than that night, I told myself.

After a few deep breaths—ironically, they were similar to Lamaze techniques I'd once seen on TV—I exited the car and made my way up the steps in one swift breath, rapping on the door before I'd processed all the moves I'd just made.

Mrs. Kuo opened the door, and relief rushed through me, since she was the one I'd come to see. I was braced, ready in case she slammed the door, but she let it hang, neither shutting me out nor letting me in.

"What do you want, Jing-Jing?" she asked in a tired tone.

"Kuo Āyí, I came to apologize." When she didn't respond, I added, "Please."

She hesitated, looked around the foyer—I had no idea what for—then sighed. Still without opening the door further, she turned and walked into the study on the left, which had floor-to-ceiling bookcases filled with wǔxiá novels, Chinese scholarly texts, and biographies of tech moguls.

I followed her and settled into the closest antique chair—square, dark brown wood, and carved with Chinese characters.

I waited a beat, instinct telling me she was going to offer me tea or snacks, but she widened her eyes to ask me, *Well?* and then added a waving hand when I still hadn't spoken a second later.

"I'm sorry for how everything devolved that day," I said. "I'm sorry I embarrassed you, and I'm sorry I ruined your party." Those things I did mean. Mostly. Though, honestly, it *was* hard to separate those feelings from my anger at what she and her family had done.

The next part, on the other hand, I not only didn't mean, but in order to get it out without gagging, I had to channel every tip Drew had given me last night when I'd texted him my plan. *Memorize the words and repeat them beforehand until they have no meaning. That way, when you say them, you don't even have to be present. If that doesn't work, pretend it's a joke and you're deadpanning right now. And if that still doesn't work, take a few breaths and remind yourself you can barf later.*

"I knew I wasn't good enough for Hongbo," I said evenly. "So I lied and told everyone I was pregnant for his sake, and yours, and Kuo Shǔshú's."

Mrs. Kuo's face widened with surprise, her eyebrows and mouth stretching to increase the length of her face. But otherwise she was completely still, trying to give the semblance of control.

"And why would you sacrifice everything—your family's miànzi—for Hongbo? For us?" she asked.

"Because nothing else was working, and I think a failed marriage is more shameful than a moment of embarrassment."

"That doesn't add up," she accused. "Obviously pregnancy outside of wedlock is much worse."

"I panicked. I didn't know what else to do." Jesus, was I flying by the seat of my pants.

"All lies. Why are you really here?"

More like drowning by the seat of my pants.

She pointed an accusatory finger at me. "You're trying to make me lift the ban on your parents. Why do you even care when you were the one to throw them in the gutter in the first place?" She gestured to her house. "You had the chance to give them everything, to elevate them to float among gods, but instead you threw it all in the trash."

Did she really just call herself a god? My God.

"Like I said, it escalated too fast and I panicked. It's not true; I'm not pregnant." Scared that my not-knocked-up self would get roped back into the previous arrangement, I quickly added, "But, like I said before, I'm not good enough for Hongbo."

"Obviously not, especially after all this. It doesn't matter what you say now; everyone thinks you're pregnant. You can't take that back—it's like pouring out water."

That was my new most-hated phrase.

"Please, this had nothing to do with my parents." Apparently I was resorting to begging now. "My mother is devastated she's no longer allowed at Bible study. I came here, with no face, to apologize to you and beg for forgiveness. Can you please not punish my parents for something I did of my own volition?"

She was already shaking her head before I'd finished. "There's no such thing. Your parents raised you; they are responsible for your actions."

"For how long? I'm an adult!"

"Forever!" she declared, her voice booming.

"So then you're responsible for Hongbo impregnating that girl, and for his DUIs?"

"How do you know about that?" Her eyes grew so wide I could see white above and below her pupil. "Your parents couldn't have told you," she murmured. "They would never disobey one of my requests. . . ."

"Hongbo told me." *Sort of.*

She tried to play it cool by barely reacting to what I'd said, but I noticed her jaw tightening. Then her eyes scrutinized me, narrow and prying as if she was trying to read me, but before I had a moment to think, she blurted, "Of course your parents are welcome at Bible study. I shouldn't have gotten so worked up about what happened at the party. Just a little spilled tea in the past."

She stood and smoothed out her dress, waiting for me to stand as well.

I was still recovering from the whiplash when she shoved me outside with a final "I'll let your mother know myself!" before slamming the door behind me.

I stood for a moment on the front steps, replaying her expressions, and I realized she had been trying to figure out if I had it in me to betray their secrets.

I almost started laughing.

If I didn't say a word, it wasn't officially blackmail, right?

Chloe

CHAPTER 52

MOVING FORWARD

My parents were already home from work when I returned from the Kuos. I went into the kitchen and tried to be as nonchalant as I could by pretending I was a Rent for Your 'Rents operative.

"Where were you?" my mother asked, one eyebrow raised.

"Out." I opened the refrigerator.

My mother followed me over. "Well, the strangest thing just happened—Kuo Ǎyí called and said she's looking forward to seeing me at the next Bible study." She grabbed the fridge door and opened it further so she could pop her head next to mine briefly. "Jing-Jing, do you know anything about this?"

"That's great, Mā," I said, not looking up from my rummaging. "I'm glad this is all over with."

When I shut the refrigerator door, she was standing next to me, her eyes shiny.

"Did you do this?" she asked.

"Yes," I whispered, hoping she wouldn't ask me for details.

"That . . . is . . . appreciated," she said slowly, the in-between pauses punctuating that there was more she didn't know how to say.

She pulled me into a hug. It stunned me so much I dropped the leftover (non-Franken-) bāo in my hand.

Was this actually happening?

She squeezed me, and I wrapped my arms around her tiny body.

But as soon as I allowed myself to enjoy it, she pulled away and wiped her eyes.

"I'm glad we can finally move forward," she said. "I'm ready to accept Andrew with open arms—him, his family, and his family money." She laughed, signaling it was a joke, but I had to force my chuckle out. Because I knew it was only part joke; she did actually care about all three of those things, and not in that order. "Well, I'm ready to accept him as long as you're not really pregnant," she added with another laugh.

As my mother bounded out of the kitchen, she bragged, "I can't wait to show all those other women my new Bible! It'll prove how much my daughter loves me, more than their daughters love them!"

I suddenly wasn't hungry anymore.

<Chloe>

The ban on my parents is lifted! I did it!

<Drew>

I knew you would!

I'm ready for my Operative Certificate now

You've always been ready

Is there a Chicago branch?

Yep
They have to come here for a lot of their training since it's smaller and there's less demand, but it exists

Long pause. Both type and delete multiple unsent texts.

So is there actually an Operative Certificate?

No but I can have one for you the next time I see you

Well we better make that soon then, huh?

Yeah we better

Okay

Ok

I don't want to take time away from your parents, especially your dad, but . . .

Is there actually a way I can see you before you leave?

(I couldn't tell if that was banter earlier or real . . .)

Another long pause.

How about New Year's Eve after my parents go to sleep? Around 9?

I'm going to have to figure some stuff out

As you know

But yeah

Let's do it

It's a date

Wear something you can dance in

Oh man

Do you have dance training?

This could be embarrassing for me . . .

A minute later:

Okay you definitely have dance training. I remember you saying you were open to dance classes on your application

Maybe we should do something else

I promise it'll be fun

No judgment

One laugh out of you and you have to do one of my game theory problem sets
Actually you probably have training in that too

😂 I promise you're worrying about nothing
I'll pick you up down the street at that park at 9:10, silly

Okay but be prepared because I have access to YouTube, which was teaching randos to do things before Rent for Your 'Rents existed

I'm shaking

Me too
My hips and shoulders
In preparation

How'd you guess my favorite moves?

Chloe

CHAPTER 53

THE TALK

December 30–31

The next two days with my parents were . . . lighter. Not as light as dòuhuā—my mother's favorite melt-on-your-tongue, silky, sweet tofu dessert—but maybe more like almond Jell-O? Secret-filled awkwardness still sliced through our interactions, but now there were a few *actual* laughs instead of forced ones. We also broke out the mahjong set—and at my mother's suggestion, no less.

New Year's Eve afternoon, my father was napping upstairs—which tugged at my heartstrings, but I made myself be "normal" about it—and I was on the couch sipping bitter tea, definitely not trying to get a whiff of Drew from the cushions or anything.

My mother sat down next to me, a steaming mug of not-bitter tea in her hands.

"Do you get to have the mother tea because you're the mother?" I joked. She looked at me blankly, so I explained, "The mother tea, the one that eventually becomes the bitter one you leave on the counter to make mine with."

She shook her head. "Of course I make you your own. No need to share germs."

"I was making a joke, calling it the mother tea because it births the teas I drink. You know, like how sourdough is made from a mother dough that has spores growing in it."

She made a disgusted face. "Yuck, who would want to eat spores?"

"What do you think stinky tofu is?"

She laughed, loud and hearty, and the sound cracked a smile across my face. "Okay, you got me, Jing-Jing. I was being hip—hippo—"

"Hypocritical," I supplied.

"Yes, that, by judging what's not familiar to me, just like what the Americans always do with our best things."

My smile extended to my eyes.

"You know," she said, "sometimes I forget how lucky I am."

I held my breath, but it wasn't about me.

"Bǎbá and I have been lucky to find this community, to live in America *and* hold on to our culture. It's a luxury. Maybe . . . maybe I haven't always thought about what it must be like for you, being in that environment but also growing up in America. It can't be easy."

My mouth filled with saliva from . . . nervousness? Anticipation? Whatever it was, I swallowed and kept waiting for more.

But then she said, "Jing-Jing, my parents never talked to me about the sex, so I didn't talk to you about it, but maybe we should."

The alarms in my head went off like there was a fire and tornado and flood around the corner.

"The sex is when a man puts his penis—"

"Oh my God!" I yelled. "I know that! Can we not?"

My mother grabbed my forearm before I could cover my ears. "Jing-Jing, listen to me. I've seen a few of those—what are they called? Sitcoms. They say this is important. That I need to talk to you about these things, even if it makes me uncomfortable."

Every wish I'd sent up to the heavens for more sitcom-like parents came back and bit me in the ass at the same time. *I take it back!*

278

"There's a reason Christians like us believe it's an act for mar-riage," my mother continued. "It's very emotional, and it should be saved for your husband."

"I know all this." Whatever to make it stop, even if I didn't agree with her. My head was in my hands.

"Well, maybe you don't know that it doesn't feel good for women. I'm telling you from experience: don't give in to the temptation because it's not worth it. Then you'll be thrown-out water, and all for what? A bad time."

I considered telling her it was supposed to feel good for women too, but the idea of talking to my mother about her orgasms made me want to throw up.

"You're not doing the sex with Andrew, are you?" she asked.

"No." *Not yet.* "Not that it's any of your business."

I stood, ready to escape.

She grabbed my hand. "I just . . . I want to protect you, okay? If he's a good person, he won't mind waiting. Relationships don't have to be about the sex."

I looked back at her and said, this time sincerely, "I know, okay? You don't have to worry."

She let go. I was about to leave when she sighed and said, "I had the sex before marriage and it almost ruined me."

I froze. Completely, even my breathing.

Her words from earlier repeated in my head: *I'm telling you from experience: don't give in to the temptation because it's not worth it.*

Oh. *Oh.* I thought she had meant that she knew from experience it didn't feel good, but she had been trying to tell me something else.

When I sat down next to her again, she had tears in her eyes. Her gaze locked on mine, pleading for me to listen.

"Nobody wanted me after that. I didn't tell anyone, but he did, bragging, and it got around the community I grew up in." Her next words were so quiet I struggled to make them out even after leaning all the way in. "The only one who wanted to marry me didn't know—and still doesn't know—what happened."

"Oh, Mǎmá." I put my hand on hers.

I wanted to tell her that the people at fault here were everybody except her, that she hadn't done anything wrong and had nothing to be ashamed about—just upset and angry—but before I could say anything, she pulled away.

"This is why I talked up your innocence and purity to our whole community. That was a gift to you, one I painstakingly created over many, many years. How could you throw it away just like that, Jing-Jing? You should've been smarter! Didn't I raise you to protect your image, our family name?"

"I'm sorry." I hated myself. Whenever I had these kinds of discussions with my parents—about Hongbo, about my decisions, about our goddamn family name—I floated up out of my body and judged the Jing-Jing who swallowed her true thoughts and apologized like a pathetic loser. *Except you do it to protect their feelings, to make everything easier on them, which could be considered noble,* I heard Drew say in my head, but to me it felt cowardly. I hated what I became with them—so small everyone walked all over me. Soon I'd be so squished into the sidewalk I'd disappear.

"I know Hongbo messes around," she continued, "and it does bother me that he goes to strip clubs so often, and so openly. But I thought maybe that was good, and you wouldn't feel like you had to do . . . woman duties with him. That you could just use his money and enjoy your life."

What could I say to that? Where to even start? The sexist, violent, completely fucked-up idea of "woman duties"? Or the other ten messed-up things she'd just said?

She cleared her throat. "Well, that ship is bye-bye, so"—she waved her hands at metaphorical Hongbo sailing off—"I'm happy to hear Andrew isn't pressuring you."

And for a moment I felt the window opening, and I practiced a few ways to tell her.

No, he doesn't—he's a good guy. He may not be exactly who he said he was, but he's not all that different.

Yes, he's great, and just because he's an artist doesn't change that part of him.

Except, in order to tell her about him, I had to first reveal how I had lied and schemed to get Hongbo out of my life. Which would make her explode. And then I'd have to answer her barrage of questions about the real Drew—artist, operative, estranged-from-his-family Drew—which would make her exploded pieces explode.

Sweat pooled in all my bodily crevices and I had to breathe deeply to keep from passing out.

My mother didn't notice and stood.

"No doing the sex, okay, Jing-Jing? I'll trust you for now, but I'm also not above making an appointment for you with Dr. Tsai to check your hymee."

"Jesus Christ," I managed to exclaim just before she turned the corner into the kitchen.

Chloe

CHAPTER 54

PICKLE

M y mother made herself scarce the rest of the afternoon, staying upstairs with my father, and they only emerged, I presumed, because they grew too hungry.

For our New Year's Eve dinner, we went to one of our favorite Chinese restaurants, where we knew the servers and the owner, which was helpful in that there were plenty of interruptions from them as well as from other restaurant patrons since this was a go-to for most of our friends. Not many restaurants had stinky tofu on the menu, let alone the really smelly steamed kind this place specialized in, the kind that permeated the entire space.

After a purposefully loud family prayer, which we only did when church people were nearby, enough acquaintances approached our table to signal that Mrs. Kuo's lift of our ban had started to get around. But it wasn't quite as many as normal. I sweated through my shirt hoping my mother wasn't thinking about how they all believed me to be pregnant, the same thrown-out water she had been, her worst nightmare come true. If I had to apologize to her again, I might throw up into my beef noodle soup, which would then only further convince the community of my pregnancy. I swear, if I'd been old enough, my parents would have ordered me a glass of wine to prove to everyone I wasn't with child, but honestly? My mom and Mrs. Kuo were, sadly, right: the damage was already done. Even with the wine, people would've either whispered I was the worst mother-to-be or that I'd gotten an abortion. No matter what happened from this point forth, the rumor had already spread along the grapevine, and only the juiciest grapes would make it to market. But I was at peace with it. Getting rid of Hongbo would always trump my miànzi in a community I had never belonged in anyway.

Once the foot traffic to our table stopped, I waited for the silence to descend, but—surprise times ten—my mother chattered away.

"You know, Jing-Jing, Hongbo is a pig." For a moment I thought she had finally seen his puke-green colors, but then I realized she was talking about Chinese zodiac signs when she said, "And pig isn't the perfect match for a snake like you. That was always my one concern with him."

Yes, that was the right concern to have, I thought sarcastically.

She continued, "Andrew is a rabbit, which is a better fit, but there are still some potential issues I'm worried about. Like difficulty communicating, tendency to pick at each other, and an inability to overcome financial problems. But since his family is well off, I feel better about that last one."

I didn't believe in zodiac logic—Chinese *or* astrological, so my mother couldn't complain I was "rejecting my culture" in this instance—but I still found myself panicking a little. Probably because I was drowning in lies. And maybe because there were already too many external forces keeping Drew and me apart, and I couldn't handle another one, even one I didn't believe in.

My mother gestured to herself and my father. "We're a perfect match!" she declared with her chest puffed out. "Mouse and ox—

we're faithful, understanding, and . . ." She leaned over to whisper the last word. "Intimate."

Dear Lord, please make it stop.

My father harrumphed, low in his throat, a little phlegmy and a lot loud, and I prayed for a subject change. "Are you sure you don't want to transfer to Stanford, Jing-Jing? They have a great economics department." It was a topic I normally hated, but welcome in this moment. That is, until he said, "I'd feel better if you didn't live near Andrew and have to deal with . . . temptations." And oh, the irony: Drew lived *here*. "I know you got rejected, but maybe their standards for transfers are different? And you've gotten good grades at the University of Chicago—that must mean at least a little something, even to Stanford, right?"

"Is there another reason you want me closer to home, Bǎbá?" I ventured. "Because I can take a quarter off."

He shook his head rapidly. "No, no, that's not what I'm saying. I just—"

My mother put a hand on my father's. "I talked to Jing-Jing this afternoon. We can trust her with the sex. She may have lied to our friends the other day, but she hasn't lied to us, not when it's important. She was just so excited about her relationship with Andrew that she didn't know how else to show us Hongbo wasn't for her. Right, Jing-Jing?"

I nodded vigorously. "Yup, we can definitely move on from this topic now."

"Don't worry," she murmured to my dad. "She didn't even want sec-uh-see underwear."

For parents who still called it "the sex" and "sec-uh-see," we were talking about intimacy and whale tails a shocking amount.

But maybe this was their way of showing me they were coming around. This was the (dragon) fruit of my labor, a brief snapshot in time when my parents and I were okay, and I tried to make myself enjoy it even though I knew that if I turned around, I'd see we were on the precipice of a catastrophic fall. Because history showed that my parents and I could never be happy at the same time. The sand was shooting through the hourglass, seemingly quicker now that we were approaching the end.

The rest of dinner had been—gasp—pretty pleasant, leaving me in a dancing-and-humming mood as I showered and dressed for my night with Drew.

From the depths of my closet I dug out a silver halter top and a boring black skirt—a combination quite fitting for me. I finished the look off with a poppy-colored cross-body purse just big enough for the essentials.

I was excited, but I had also gotten myself into a pickle while making this evening's plans. For a good reason, but still. That pickle had taken on a life of its own, which I now realized was a common problem for me.

So it started because I needed a lie to tell my parents about where I was going tonight. Since they didn't know we'd lost touch and she was the one 'rent-approved friend who didn't attend our church, I told my parents I was seeing Genevieve from high school. But then, after I told that lie, I remembered that Genevieve's mother had a weekly mahjong game with Sienna's mother, who was one of my mom's patients, and she had a lot of dental issues. *Like Swiss cheese,* my mother had once said of her X-rays. And after making the three-degree connection, I worried that the information of where Genevieve spent her New Year's Eve would get back to my mother, in which case, holy guacamole. So I texted Genevieve for the first time in a year and a half to see where she'd be ringing in the new year. Then obviously that got really awkward and I had to act like I wanted to know because I was hoping to meet up. I did consider asking her to cover for me like old times, but that left behind hard evidence of my lies in the form of a text that could be used against me. So I instead reasoned, *It's easier to just make plans, then take a page out of her book and flake out at the last second.* But then my mother happened. She asked me a million questions about Genevieve and Genevieve's mother and made so many comments about wanting to see photos of what Gen looked like now that I felt backed into a corner. No matter how I tried to spin it, I couldn't win.

Me: You're horrible, and you just want to see "whether her baby fat was just fat."

Her: I said that one time! Why can't you just get a picture for me? Are you hiding something?

She made me promise to get at least one photo and to find out which plastic surgeon her mother had used because, after bumping into her at the grocery store a few months ago, my mother was sure Genevieve's mom had gotten some work done to her face, though it "wasn't Botox" and my mother needed to know the secret. "Why didn't you just ask her?" I'd said, to which she'd rolled her eyes and responded in a *duh* tone, "Because I can't let her know I know, and I can't admit I need work too."

So I had decided, okay, Drew and I would meet up with Gen and her friends, hang out long enough to get a few selfies, and then he and I would break off and do our own thing. I'd used Gen as my cover countless times before, but this time, I felt queasy.

I ignored the pit in my stomach and texted Drew, asking him if we could meet my high school friend at a Palo Alto nightclub. *There will still be dancing,* I promised. He texted back a smiley emoji and said he couldn't wait to meet Genevieve. I felt like a moldy piece of Swiss cheese thinking about how it wasn't a step forward for us, where I was introducing him to a close friend, but just another brand-new web my lies had tangled us into. And because I felt so guilty, I decided I'd introduce him to Gen as Drew, not Andrew, so we'd at least have that first step.

But then, the pickle grew. Past life-size. Just a few moments before our meet time, Genevieve texted me that Luke, Harry, and Christa— all of whom she hadn't hung around much in high school, but, doy, they were all at UCLA together—were also meeting us tonight. As in Christa with the big hair full of secrets who had been most known for collecting enamel pins and gossip. Which meant . . . I needed Andrew tonight, not Drew.

My stomach was now roiling like I was free-falling without sheep Cháng'é's antigravity boots. I was used to hating who I was with my parents, but someone else was involved this time—someone I really cared about. I didn't know how to reconcile the two.

My Uber pulled up to the nightclub, and, thank God, Drew was already waiting up front. I ran to him and begged, "Are you okay being Andrew tonight? There's a chance stuff could get back to my parents through the grapevine or whatever, and, you know."

Instead of smiling with ease and telling me *whatever you wish*, his face completely fell. But before he could say what was on his mind, Genevieve ran up to us and we dove into introductions and *oh-God-it's-been-so-long*s and blah blah blah. But I remembered to introduce Drew as "Andrew," and his stiff handshake was not lost on me.

Luke, Harry, and Christa joined us soon after, and that was that: a somber Andrew was officially my date tonight instead of excited Drew.

We showed our IDs to the bouncer—with all of us but Drew getting marked with two giant black *X*s on our hands to show we were under the drinking age—and then we weaved our way through bodies as a single-file group.

Surrounded by tiaras, top hats, and light-up glasses, we huddled in a messy circle on the dance floor and bopped to the beat. Christa and Harry were joined at the hip, Luke was a brittle, swaying tree, and Genevieve moved with complete freedom, somehow looking both cool and quirky at the same time.

Drew and I shared a smile and did the awkward where-should-we-put-our-hands and which-direction-are-we-leaning pre-dance dance. Just as we were about to find our groove, a familiar beat came on and Genevieve grabbed my hand and whirled me to her. "Ah, doesn't this take you back, Cece?" I hadn't heard that nickname in so long.

She was grinding against me in an attempt to make me squirm. She'd always been perplexed by my innocence. In high school I had played along because it had felt like my role, but now I remembered why I hadn't made an effort with her once I left for Chicago—I had wanted to shed my goody-goody skin. Was it just me, or was high school all about everyone's need to label you as one thing, with the four years revolving around you trying to either break free or live up to that label? I enthusiastically rubbed up against Genevieve to try the option I hadn't attempted in high school—to break free—but that felt wrong too.

"Whooo!" she whistled. "College loosened you up!" Which felt even worse.

At least I had my opportunity. I pulled my phone out and snapped a few photos of us, learning very quickly that there's some skill involved in finding flattering angles, and that even flattering angles were useless when trying to take flash photos in a dim nightclub where everyone was covered in buckets of sweat. But the pictures accomplished the goal of throwing my sniffing mom off the scent.

Genevieve grabbed Christa's tiara and put it on my head, then yelled, "One more!" way too loudly in my ear. Because Drew was in the background of my shot, I made Gen move to one side before snapping the photo. When I stowed my phone, Drew was looking at me, intense and enigmatic. He'd definitely noticed, but I wasn't sure if he knew what was going on. With an easy smile pasted on my face, I grabbed his hand and spun him to me.

I tried to enjoy myself. The lights thrown around the room were invigorating; the DJ was playing my favorite hits from today and from high school, the latter of which was especially fun with Genevieve here; and, finally, Drew was starting to melt into both the music and me.

We'd found our rhythm. His body moved smoothly and, yes, quite sexily to not just the beat, but also the intricacies beneath. Definitely trained. The way his shoulders moved one way but his hips and head another proved he'd had more practice than just dancing in front of a bathroom mirror like me. Damn, was it hot, and I found myself pressing my pelvis to his, then kissing him like I wanted to swallow his essence.

Except . . . his mouth wasn't as inviting as usual.

I pulled back. "Everything okay?" I yelled.

But then a camera flashed to my right and I turned in time to see Genevieve's devilish grin. Just as the song happened to decrease in volume, Genevieve shouted for all to hear, "For proof that your pussy isn't shriveled." I'd forgotten I had previously told her Hongbo's comments—in private, for a shoulder to lean on.

I stopped cold, too stunned by what she'd said. Everyone near us laughed.

"What? I said it's *not* shriveled," Gen yelled, but her words were drowned out by the laughter and crescendoing bassline.

I was still frozen with embarrassment, but Gen didn't notice because she'd turned back to her phone, thumbs flying. And then the panic set in. Because that picture was damning.

"Can you not post that?" I asked, and Drew's hands left my hips.

"Why not?" Gen asked, giving me her *I don't understand you* look, which hadn't changed with time. "If I were you, I'd be plastering this one's face everywhere," she joked, jabbing a stubby thumb in Drew's direction. Then her face changed. "Wait, do your parents not know about him?"

"No, they do," I said truthfully. "It's just . . . complicated." Like, he's supposed to be in Chicago right now. My eyes flicked over to Christa, and Gen came to my rescue.

"No worries," she said with a smile. She gave me a wide-eyed look, asking me to tell her the details later, in private. I reluctantly nodded.

Christa stared at me with one eyebrow raised, but then, with a shrug, she seemingly decided to let it go. With her butt still firmly pushed into Harry's crotch—as it had been since high school—Christa gestured to Drew, then yelled to me over the music, "I didn't peg you for one to like older men, though I guess none of us really knew *what* you liked."

He's twenty-one, not seventy, I thought but didn't say.

Harry pumped his eyebrows. "Hey, bro, think you can get us a couple drinks?"

"Nah, we don't need that," Drew said, nonchalant, but even though his body was completely relaxed, I knew he was on edge.

Harry mumbled a curse that was swallowed by the music, and Drew pretended not to notice.

Harry's eyes met mine, which—shudder—reminded me that there had always been something about him that made me keep my distance.

"Andrew looks a little out of your league," he said to me with a toothy grin that clashed with his tone. "How'd you bag him?"

"I strung up some Sichuan food as bait and waited a few days," I yelled back. Drew laughed, but no one else did, obviously. I shared a giant, in-joke smile with him.

"Wait, what?" asked Luke, his bopping slowing.

"We met in class," I told them with a wave of a hand. Drew's smile disappeared.

"Ohhh, another UChicago nerd—now it makes sense," Luke said with a laugh, even his barely-there sways coming to a halt. He turned to Drew, telling him, "She had quite the prudish reputation in school, though that's obviously changed with you given what y'all were doing a minute ago. My man!"

Luke lifted his hand for a high five but Drew left him hanging, excusing himself and then weaving his way to the closest exit. I hurried after him, but my shorter legs slowed me down. By the time I pushed my way outside, Drew was on his phone, the Uber app open but no ride requested yet.

The door shut behind me, and the blaring music suddenly became a background buzz.

"What're you doing?" I asked.

His arms dropped to his sides and he looked at me with sad eyes. "Why are we here with them, Chloe?"

"What do you mean?" I asked, feigning innocence. But everything down to my churning stomach already knew what he was talking about.

He exhaled forcefully, then gave me a pleading *come on* look.

"It all happened so fast!" I burst out. "I lied and told my parents I was seeing Gen tonight, and then I remembered that her mother knows someone who's my mother's patient, and so, you get it, I had to make sure we covered our tracks—"

"Chloe, Chloe, just stop for a second." He raked a hand through his hair. "There are so many lies I can't even keep them straight."

"Me either. That's why this all happened."

He said nothing. But he didn't have to. I knew this was my fault.

A sinking feeling came over me—shame, guilt, and so much dread.

He took a step away. "I can't be your real boyfriend and still have to pull Andrew out at a moment's notice. If I didn't care about you as much as I do, I might be okay hiding in the shadows. But I want to be with you, actually *be* with you." He looked at me, his eyes searching my face for a reaction. "I'm just—Chloe, I'm so into you that I don't know how to be Andrew for you anymore. I can only give you Drew, and maybe that's not enough. . . ." He trailed off.

My heart constricted. What was I supposed to do with that? "Drew—" I started.

"Chloe, you're asking me to lie too," he interrupted. "I can play someone else to pay the rent, but I gave up my relationship with my parents so I could be myself with the people I care about."

"You're right," I realized. When he had a choice, he fought. Sacrificed everything to stay true to himself. Then I came along and dragged him so far into my mess neither of us could see the sun anymore.

He sighed. "I get it. Really. Your parents aren't going to approve of me for the same reason my parents cut me out." After a heavy beat, he said, "It's true that I don't fit in your world. I don't have any degree, let alone from Harvard or Stanford or whatever. Just fake ones, backed up by a closet full of logoed shirts."

"That's nothing to be ashamed of."

"I didn't say I was ashamed, but clearly you think I should be."

"I . . ." The defensive words that had been on the tip of my tongue dissolved. "I'm sorry. I'm being all kinds of shitty. I'm sorry," I said again. "Really. I—I don't even know what to—I just want—" I took a breath. "You deserve better than me. Better than what I'm giving you." I hated myself for hurting him.

The hourglass was on the last few grains of sand, our borrowed time running out and the universe coming to collect.

"I think we should walk away before it gets even harder," I said. "Before I hurt you more." The words were so painful I almost choked on them, but the realization that I should've done this sooner, before I hurt him at all, forced them out.

He looked away from me, away from the club, and into the dark, engulfing night. "Maybe that's for the best."

It was what I'd suggested, but his words gutted me. Stuck a knife in my abdomen and dragged it across. Because his agreement confirmed how much pain I'd caused him.

"I'm so sorry." My words came out in a shaky exhale, as if someone had just punched me in the chest.

He still wasn't looking at me when he said, "Me too."

There were so many other things I wanted to say, but it hurt too much.

I'm so ashamed of how I treated you I want to throw up.
I don't know how to say good-bye.
I don't know how to be myself without you.

Instead I took my phone out and called an Uber. When I saw the car was only two minutes away, I felt both relief and panic.

He finally turned back toward me. "At least let me take you home."

My nose burned. Tears formed and pooled, blurring my vision. "You've already done too much for me."

I wanted to hug him, kiss him, pull him to me and never let go. So as soon as my Honda Civic was in sight, I chased it down and jumped in. Because otherwise I wouldn't have been able to leave.

He didn't stop me.

Drew

Fix this! a voice screamed in my head as Chloe and her warmth, her scent, her everything disappeared, leaving me alone in the parking lot.

But I was too beaten down. I could only take so many hits, and I had reached my limit.

I understood why we were in this mess. How impossible her situation was.

I also knew I deserved more.

So much frigging irony. She was the one who'd helped me see my worth, and because of that, we were now parting ways.

Well, all I did was tell her how I feel. She was the one who chose to walk away instead of fight. So I let her.

It hurt to breathe.

Would anyone I cared about ever choose me back?

Chloe

CHAPTER 55
FAREWELL FRANKENBREAKFAST

December 31–January 1

arrived home well before midnight, but I stayed awake long after, tossing and turning in bed.

I wanted to jump out of my own skin. Everything felt too fucking much and I needed to scream or punch my rage into the wall or tear the room apart.

I had hurt him. The one who had put me first. The *only* one.

I was so desperate I texted Gen, secretly hoping she'd want to chat, maybe offer me some clarity, but when I messaged her thanks for not posting the photo, sorry I had to run, my night really blew up, all I'd gotten back was np. All for the best, I guess.

That night, in my dreams, I ran and ran and ran from a monster, only to realize that the monster was me.

New Year's Day, I had a farewell breakfast with my parents. I always flew out January first because flights were cheaper, UChicago's winter quarter started soon after, and I was usually itching to leave by this point. But this year, I wished I had a couple more days in Palo Alto.

"Make us proud," my father said to me over raisin toast and

honey-drizzled sriracha beef. Non-Frankenbreakfast had been too much to hope for on my last day.

"Um-hmm," I mumbled with my mouth full, only because I hadn't been able to swallow this bite yet.

"This is always the toughest part, you know," he said. "Sending you back off to school. I wish you were closer to home."

The guilt over my Stanford lie was worse than Frankentoast, which I forced down with a gulp of bitter tea.

"It's tough for me, too," I answered honestly.

AFTER NEW YEAR'S

Voicemail from Chloe's mother

January 7

Eh? Wéi? Jing-Jing? You there? I guess not. I hope it's recording. What's Andrew's parents' names? I told the girls at Bible study today about his parents—oh, and don't worry, I've been telling everyone behind Kuo Ǎyí's back that you lied about the pregnancy because you knew you were too good for Hongbo but were so selfless you wanted to protect the Kuos, and it's spreading. And of course I'm also telling them how much better Andrew is than Hongbo. Oh! And, my new Bible is the envy of *everyone*!

Anyway, what was I saying? Oh, yes. I told people about Andrew's parents being top-notch surgeons at the University of Chicago, and Tsai An said she has a friend there, but it can't be Andrew's parents because her friend has two daughters. But they probably know each other! She's going to ask her friend if she knows any surgeon couples there, but tell me their names to make it easier.

Oh, and of course, how is his grandmother? You sent them a good gift from us, right? Not pears? [laugh] Call me back tonight so I can stop worrying myself silly about the gift.

Chloe

CHAPTER 56

REIMMERSION

January 1–8

n Chicago, I didn't feel fully myself because a piece of me had been left behind with Drew. And, in a different way, with my father.

I tried to shift my focus. Now that Hongbo was gone, how simple would it be for me to reimmerse myself in my schoolwork—the way it was meant to be?

Answer: not simple *at all*.

I tried—really, I did—so freaking hard. I skipped like a carefree child to my classes, listened to every word my professors said, introduced myself to my new winter-quarter classmates, and made study plans and non-study plans.

But between the forced happiness and meaningless small talk, my spaces were empty. I was missing Drew. It also didn't help that my Rent for Your 'Rents app suddenly went wild with random ba-boop-boop notifications, as if it were trying to remind me how much I'd fucked up.

After a few days of faking, I gave in to my impulses. I reread our texts, opened the Rent for Your 'Rents app to look through the limited Drew data on there, ran my fingers along the edges of the sheep ornaments I'd brought with me because I hadn't been able to leave them behind. And then, last night, I unfurled the painting that so far in my possession had only seen the underside of my Palo Alto bed and my suitcase. The rip in the corner was a tear in my heart but also a reminder of what my presence did to him.

You can't hurt him now that you're out of his life, I told myself.

But why did that feel like a lie?

Voicemails from Chloe's mother

January 10

You know, Jing-Jing, I've been thinking. It really doesn't sit right with me that we haven't met Andrew's parents yet. Do you think we could talk about arranging something in the future, maybe the next time we come visit you at school? I just . . . you know me. I need to make sure he comes from good people. I know they're surgeons, but that's not a *guarantee*. I want to see their home, their church. How can I fully know Andrew until I see those things?

I'll look at the calendar. Bye-bye!

January 13

Jing-Jing? Eh, did you know not to pick up this call because it would be a tough conversation? Well, good instincts. Don't get mad, okay?

I've been thinking, and I just want to make sure you keep Andrew. See? That's a good thing. I'm on your side now about him. So with that in mind . . . you were looking a bit chunky last time I saw you. Are you getting enough exercise? Now that you're in a relationship, it's even more important you maintain yourself. Putting on foundation, eyeliner, mascara—that's a politeness normally, but even more important to do for your boyfriend. I only pushed it a little before, but now it's time, Jing-Jing. You need to become more of a woman. Makeup is your friend. It helps plain girls look pretty—glamorous, even! I know I already gave you the tuition check, but maybe you can take some of it to pay for some makeup classes? And once you lose the weight, we'll talk about some new clothes and underwear—underwear for show only, for when you bend over and your pants accidentally fall too low! No hanky-panky!

Okay, that's plenty for now! I'll save the rest for another time when you're actually there! Maybe we can video-call soon.

Don't be mad! It's all for you! And Andrew! I'm just trying to help! You know me, always putting you first, Jing-Jing!

Chloe

CHAPTER 57

PURGATORY

January 13

My mother was right in her voicemail. I did know her. And in all this time, she hadn't changed one bit. Months ago, when Hongbo first became a problem, I still held out hope that I could make her see the puke green. When I hired Andrew, I'd tempered the hope accordingly but still believed she would at least be able to accept someone else—a better someone— over ol' Dreamboat. Now, after all this, she was as clear as a Waterford champagne flute.

And for the first time, the truth started to sink in: my parents weren't going to change. If they couldn't come around during the Hongbo mess for the sake of my happiness, they wouldn't with anything—or anyone—else.

And I would never be enough. Not my looks or any of my choices.

I'd sacrificed so much for my parents' sake, yet we were still landing in this purgatory where no one was happy. Maybe the problem was trying to please both of us, having my (moon)cake and eating it too.

Since they weren't going to change, the question I now had to ask myself was: Them or me? Was I able to fully accept them and their expectations of me? Could I be the Jing-Jing they wanted for the rest of my life? Or would I choose to live the life *I* wanted, even with the possibility that they wouldn't be able to accept the real me?

January 13 unsent texts to Drew

<Chloe>
I'm sorry
Do you regret choosing art?
How did you know what you wanted?
I miss you
I choose you
I can't choose you
Why is this so hard?
I miss you

January 13, 8:16 p.m. CST

<Chloe>
Are you happy?

<Mǎmá Wang>
Is something wrong? You're not having dark thoughts are you?

I just want to know if you're happy

Of course I'm happy.

Do you want to know if I'm happy?

Why would you not be?

Do you care if I'm happy?

Aiyah Jing Jing why you need to ask that?

Everything I do is for you. To make you happy. It's my biggest care in life.

What's going on? Why all these questions? You're scaring me.

> Nothing to worry about
> Just a class assignment
> We're supposed to ask our parents a
> few questions

Oh. OK.
You tell them how good I am! No helicopter mom!
Just an airplane heehee.

> Okay I will
> Great joke
> I love you

Work hard. No hanky panky. Put on some makeup.
I will send more money when I can.

> Thanks, Mama

Chloe

CHAPTER 58
THE CLIFF
January 14

Something had changed over the past few months, slowly, first with Hongbo and then with my parents' betrayals. Then because of my time with Drew. Something had changed in me. The first few buds had sprouted when I'd hired Drew, and a few leaves had grown at the Christmas Eve party, but now, with some time-induced clarity, I *felt* different, like I was on the verge of blooming.

I could no longer have the same relationship with my parents. I couldn't be the version of myself I hated, not anymore. Not even if it was limited to my infrequent California visits. And especially not with the one person who truly cared about me.

I had to do better. I couldn't live with myself if I chose my parents and full-blown Jing-Jing. As much as it made my stomach revolt, as much as it made me want to hide under the covers with a string-cheese-shaped xiǎo zhěntóu, I had to choose me. How could I expect anyone else to if I didn't do it first?

I was finally ready to jump off the cliff.

I choose the life I want, not the one my parents want.

My palms pooled with sweat as I called him. To prevent the phone from slipping out of my grasp, I switched to speakerphone.

"Chloe, hi."

The sound of his voice filled the hole he'd left in his absence.

"Drew . . ." I forgot all my words. "Hi."

I wished I could see him.

"Hi," he said again.

The awkwardness shouldn't have been surprising, given how we'd left things, but it still caught me off guard. I'd worked through so much in the past two weeks I felt like a different person, but now I remembered that I still had to explain it all to him. And that he might not want to hear it.

Shit.

"Hi," I repeated. The *fourth* one. "Um . . ."

I glanced at the notes I'd jotted down beforehand. It was dorky, but without them I had nothing.

"I'm calling because I wanted to tell you just how incredibly sorry I am, to my core, and also that I've had some revelations since we last spoke—"

"Oh shoot, I must've missed the script you sent. Is it okay if I don't know my lines yet?"

My laugh was much higher-pitched than I would've liked, but I was also relieved he'd made a joke. But then the awkward silence returned.

I dropped the paper and started again, no prepared lines: "I'm really sorry I hurt you. It's been killing me that I caused you pain, and all because I couldn't be honest with myself or my parents. I—I don't like who I've become. I'm ashamed I wasn't there for you when that's all you've done for me."

His breathing deepened. Without being able to see his face, I had no idea what he was thinking.

"Thank you for saying that," he said, his voice even.

"I hope you can forgive me." *Especially when I don't know how to forgive myself.* "And if you can, I want to try again. I mean, only if you want to too, of course. Except this time, I'm all in. I choose you. You come first, the way it always should have been. Like you've always done for me. When we decide we're ready to tell my parents, I will. And I'm going to accept whatever comes, even if it means cutting ties."

Complete silence. Seriously? Was this boy trying to make me pee myself from stress? Because I was close.

Finally he said, "I can't ask you to do that, Chloe."

"You didn't ask me to do anything. I'm telling you this is what I want."

I knew it was my turn to fight for us—really fight for us—but I was also disappointed my big moment hadn't gone as planned.

Some shuffling on his end—maybe he was adjusting the phone? Then: "Don't get me wrong, I'm so happy to hear that, but it doesn't change what you'd be sacrificing. Or that I still don't belong in your world."

I insisted, "You do belong. You—"

"I'm scared it bothers you that I dropped out of college," he blurted out.

Oh, my heart.

Slowly, so it would sink in, I said, "That does not bother me. I don't judge you. I don't think of you any differently. But I *am* ashamed at how I reacted at first. And I do acknowledge that even though it doesn't bother me, it's still unfair that you have to deal with my parents' future judgment. I wish I could shield you from that, but realistically, I know it'll hurt regardless. It's already hurting you. And sometimes I feel so horrible about that I think I should stay away from you for your own good. If that's what you want, I more than understand. It feels selfish of me to ask you for another chance, but I also couldn't not ask."

"Oh, Chloe." Tendrils of sympathy reached for me from of his syllables. After another beat he repeated, "I can't live myself if I'm the reason you'd be sacrificing your relationship your parents."

"It's not a sacrifice. And I'm not doing this just because of y

It had taken me too long and too much pain—both to m and others—to finally see what I was about to say. "I can't hav relationship I want with my parents until I give us a fresh slat start from. I've been too afraid of there being *no* slate after I tell tl the truth—which is still a possibility—but I can't live in betw anymore. I know you get that."

"I do," he said quietly.

"And I can't let you go. Not unless that's what you want." I nose burned and tears pooled—happy tears this time. "I choose yc Drew. And me. I want to fight for us. If you're willing, I want try this, just us, and see where it goes. The long distance won't l easy, but I'll visit when I can, and we can text and call. When we' both ready, I'm going to tell my parents about us. Not right nov only because I think we owe it to ourselves to give the relationship chance to grow without that kind of pressure. But one day, mayb even soon. Bottom line, we're in this together. If you want."

I heard a muffled sniff, which made me sniff.

I almost dropped the phone when Drew suddenly raised his voice to exclaim, "So we're really fucking doing this?"

"We're really fucking doing this!" I yelled back, laughing with him.

The happy tears were falling falling falling. I caught them myself.

<Chloe>

I just deleted my Rent for Your 'Rents app!

<Drew>
Woohoo!
Well it served its intended purpose
Good riddance, Hongbo!

Ding dong!

Why didn't you delete it sooner?
They just did an update and I think there's a bug in there
The nonstop ba-boop-boops have been worse than talking to Hongbo
Oh wait did you figure out a way to shut it off? Please share!

No

I hadn't deleted it yet because it was the one place I had a connection to you and some of your info

That's so sweet!

Hey, are you going to tell the company about us?

Because they can advertise that too. Like, hey, rent a boyfriend for your parents, and maybe even you too, if you're lucky 😏

Ha! That's not a bad idea

I've got a million of them
Rent for Your 'Rents has a lot of untapped potential

Well good thing you know someone who can put you in touch with someone

Yeah?

If you want
They might want to hire you

😗
Yeah, all right
I think there's a lot of good to be done
For the clients

👍

Goodnight
Sleep loose

Sleep loose like a golden goose

I think you mean duck

Huh? That doesn't rhyme

I'll explain next time we talk

Can't wait

Drew

CHAPTER 59

ABOUT TIME

January 15

had spent the past two Chloe-less weeks covering the apartment with dark moons, teaching myself to do Zhōngguó jié in an attempt to feel closer to my grandfather, and watching old *Schitt's Creek* episodes. But to Jason and Marshall's relief (I was pretty sure if they heard "ew, David" one more time, my laptop was going out the window), I was now giggling on the couch, texting Chloe.

I'd just asked her What kind of car does Chang'e the sheep drive? when my phone buzzed with an email.

Screeeeaming. Literally. I jumped up from the couch and started screaming. Jason and Marshall almost shit themselves, I'm pretty sure, because I almost shit myself and I was the one making the noise.

"I got innnnnn!" I screeched, then immediately called Chloe. Jason and Marshall were jumping up and down when she picked up.

"A *Lamb*orghini!" she answered with a laugh. "That's so many inside jokes rolled into one."

"What? Oh shit, right." I'd forgotten I hadn't sent the punch line of the what-does-Cháng'é-the-sheep-drive joke, but of course she didn't need me to. "I have something to tell you," I burst out. "I got accepted into an art fellowship."

She yelled so loud I would've needed to pull the phone away if I hadn't been yelling right along with her (and Jason and Marshall). I pumped a fist in the air even though she couldn't see.

"I'm so happy for you!" she exclaimed. But then she paused and her voice lowered. "I mean, if you want me to be. You don't need more schooling. Unless you want it. I really meant it when I said that doesn't matter and you should do what's best for you. I hope you applied because you wanted to, not because of . . . anything else."

I wished she hadn't soured the moment, but I also maybe sort of appreciated the sentiment? Or not. Maybe it sucked that it was still such a big deal.

We were back, but not without a few scars. Probably all for the better in the long run, but a bit painful right now.

"I wanted to try this opportunity because it's a good fit for me—contemporary art featuring two artists I admire and draw inspiration from. I don't know if this is the specific track I'll keep pursuing, but I need to try things to figure out how I want to do this, right?" My nerves were showing more than I'd hoped, but it also felt good to air out my thoughts. My parents had made me believe my art was a dirty secret, and I was just starting to move past that.

"Of course, of course," Chloe said, still a little on edge.

"Wait, I haven't told you the best part."

"How can there be something better?"

"*Two* somethings," I clarified.

"Oh my God, *tell me!*"

My legs flailed, Irish jig–style, because I was so excited I couldn't stand it (literally, ha). "It's at the Art Institute of Chicago. All expenses paid, for a week. I arrive on January twenty-ninth."

This time I did have to jerk the phone away.

A second later I interrupted her whooping. "Wait, wait, the second thing is even better!"

"You also get a pet unicorn?"

"Better. Chloe, I took this step because of you. I really meant it when I told you before that seeing you go after what you want inspired me. Thank you."

It was quiet for a second. "You did this yourself. I'm really proud of you." Her familiar sweet voice wrapped around me like a hug.

I did another flaily-leg jig. "Hey, I'm going to see you in two weeks."

She squealed. "Two weeks! Ah! I can't believe it!"

Neither could I. Things didn't usually fall into place for me, but that just meant it was about time, right?

Chloe

CHAPTER 60

HELL OF A GREETING

January 16–29

The next two weeks d r a g g e d on, even though Drew and I texted in our free time . . . and maybe also in my not-so-free-time, like during class, whoops.

Some were lighter:

> \<Chloe\>
>
> I know they're putting you up in a hotel, but you're also welcome to stay in my dorm
>
> You can borrow pajamas

> \<Drew\>
>
> I only wear satin, and they have to be something worthy for my flock of sheep

> Satin tuxedo it is

Then I will match James Baaand
Too much?

No, not baaad

Some were more serious:

<Drew>
I'm scared I won't be good enough

<Chloe>
You got in!
You earned your place!

What if I was the fluke?
The one who was admitted when the admissions person
was drunk?

Drunk people's opinions matter too
They go to art museums

True

Though . . . I wouldn't know
I don't like to drink
Not that I've tried, of course, being
underage 😉

I don't really drink either
I can't afford to buy Pepcid AC AND alcohol 😏

Does that really work?

Supposedly?
Or you can just embrace the Asian glow
Who said redness is uncool?
Maybe I think people who have all the alcohol metabolizing genes are the sad ones
Except for the admissions guy who let me in
He rules

You will be GREAT
I promise
Chang'e believes in you

The goddess or the sheep?

Both

Phew
Ok
As long as the sheep was included
Then I can do this

Okay, so even our serious ones turned lighthearted.

During those two weeks, I became obsessed with sitting as still as a scarecrow in class so I could feel whether my phone was vibrating with a text. I mistook every slight sound and muscle tic for a notification and played emotional roulette instead of paying attention to the lecture.

And then I felt so guilty for squandering this opportunity and my parents' hard-earned money—I even calculated how much each lecture cost, and it wasn't for the faint of heart—that a few days before Drew's arrival, I started leaving my phone at home.

I felt naked walking out the door without it. At least I wasn't missing much—just my music—since I wasn't looking at my phone while outside, not in Chicago in January. It was currently the freeze-your-face-off kind of weather, which made me hurry home after class to warn pampered California-born Drew.

\<Chloe\>

You have a winter coat, right?

\<Drew\>

I'm borrowing Jason's

He's a skier

You need accessories too

Like what?

Like whatever you can find
Scarves, heavy-duty gloves, earmuffs, wool socks, boots
And I have little hand warmer hot packs you can borrow

You're being funny, right?

From one Californian to another, trust me

Shit ok

I guess I need to cross boating and lakeside picnic off our list of possible dates

Snuggling with hot chocolate in front of a fire is just as romantic

I'll bring the marshmallows!

And finally, after what felt like an eternity, the last Friday in January was upon me. The day of Drew's arrival. I was about to see him *this afternoon*. In *Chicago*. My real home. I was so excited my head was spinning.

An hour before his plane was supposed to land, I'd cleaned my dorm room, showered, put on two layers of deodorant, and paced my room only about a thousand times.

I focused on the time we would have together, not the fact that this was likely the last stretch during which I could have my mooncake and eat it too. I wanted to see this visit as a privilege, not the final, lonely grain of sand passing through the hourglass.

I reread the list of date ideas I'd written up. I sniffed my sheets for the thirtieth time just to make absolute sure, even though I'd used an entire cup of detergent and, for the first time, fabric softener.

I wanted to know what Drew was thinking right now. Would he be able to focus on the present, or would he be preoccupied with what was inevitably coming? Would we be staying here in my dorm—hence the fresh sheets—or at his hotel, where the bed was likely bigger? Or not together at all? Was it presumptuous to have an overnight bag packed? What was the etiquette for this type of thing?

Yes, I had to change into a fresh shirt right before he arrived.

Drew texted when his Uber was close. I bundled up, clomped down the stairs to the entrance, then flew straight into his arms, knocking his suitcase over.

I didn't even care. I didn't glance at the other students giving me looks, didn't preoccupy myself with how Drew was going to respond, and just squeezed him as tight as I could.

"I missed you, too," he said, hugging me back but with less force, probably because he was scared of hurting me. I loosened my arms but continued to hold on.

Then I pulled back so I could kiss him. And holy smokes did I kiss him. Hands on either side of his face, one leg looped around him.

When I finally pulled back, he panted a few breaths before saying, "Hell of a greeting."

"Come on," I said. I righted his luggage, then grabbed his hand and pulled him into my dorm.

Drew

CHAPTER 61

I'M GOOD RIGHT HERE

ven Chicago weather couldn't have kept me away (though I did cry inside when I saw the temperature would be below zero).

Chloe's dorm room was so very her: photos of her family were tacked to the wall (I particularly liked the one of her and her mother sticking their tongues out at the camera); a large stash of jasmine oolong tea lay beside the electric kettle on her dresser; and her bedding was a mishmash of bright and bold colors.

I pointed to a poster of Barcelona hanging above her bed. "You been?"

She shook her head. "No, but I'm planning on studying abroad there in a future quarter."

My heart soared at the life she was living. She felt different here. More clearly her.

And then I saw it. My painting. Right above her desk. It looked different among Chloe's things, mounted with love. The tear in the corner now reminded me how far we'd come.

I may have gasped. My heart may have burst. And I definitely did wrap her in a bear hug. She leaned against me until we fell backward onto the bed.

She kissed me. Soft, sweet, and sure. The only thing better than being here with her was how familiar her lips and taste were becoming.

The next couple of hours were Ah-mazing with a capital *A* and added *h*.

At one point, with a laugh, she pulled her lips from mine and asked if I wanted to actually see some of Chicago.

"I'm good right here," I said, looping my arm around her hips and bringing us back together.

But we did eventually grow hungry, and because we were half-dressed and it was frozen-boogers cold outside, we ordered Neapolitan-style pizza from the place next door to eat in bed. I felt bad about crumbs on her very clean sheets, but she didn't seem to mind as she grabbed a slice and curled up beside me.

We munched, kissed, and talked until the wee hours of the morning, asking each other questions ranging from playful (*If you could live in any time period, what would it be?*) to serious (me inquiring about college life, her wanting to know about my past jobs and how Rent for Your 'Rents worked behind the scenes). She was uber-adorable when shyly asking whether I'd had to kiss any clients on jobs, and when I told her I'd only kissed one client, willingly, and not for the job, the relief and joy on her face made my heart soar.

"Most parents, especially Asian parents who necessitate a rental, don't have a huge desire to see their daughter kissing someone, even if it's a person they approve of," I pointed out as she laughed, probably remembering when she fell off my back just because her father had appeared. "In fact, a kiss on the head is more endearing anyway, and I'm comfortable doing that when needed." She didn't react as positively to that, which made me feel guilty, but she moved on swiftly. Our conversation shifted to sharing funny, sad, and embarrassing personal stories.

When she asked whether I regretted picking art over my parents, I surprised myself by answering, "No. I wasn't picking it over them. They were the ones who didn't pick me. While it used to make me sad, and at the beginning I considered begging them, changing my path, whatever, to fix it, I'm now just really disappointed in them. And maybe still a little angry."

Then I found myself pouring out so many emotions I'd bottled up in the past. I thought I'd set them out to sea, but apparently they were floating back. "Parents are supposed to believe in us—or at least that's what society claims. So when they didn't think I could do it, when they decided to stop loving me . . ." I trailed off. There weren't words to describe what it was like.

"I get it," Chloe said quietly. "I . . . may not have told you all the details with the whole Hongbo thing." She paused. "The real reason I panicked and turned to Rent for Your 'Rents is because when I refused the proposal . . . when I tried to explain to my mom why I didn't want to be with Hongbo . . . her response was . . ." She swallowed. "She told me I wouldn't be able to find someone else. That I was too flat-chested, my face too ordinary, and my personality too anxious to attract anyone." Her voice changed to eerily resemble her mother's: "'Who will want you?'" she mimicked. "Which was also the reason she was fine with Hongbo using me as a cover-up." Her face and tone shifted again. "'Why else would Hongbo—would the *Kuos*—want *you*?'"

"Shit, Chloe." How could her own mother not see how much she shines, both inside and out?

"So I told her I already had a boyfriend, one who was rich and handsome and smart and loved me for me, because it hurt too much to tell her that she'd just voiced my own fears." She took a breath. I wanted to hug her and never let go. "And it's just like what you said: your parents are the ones who are supposed to think you're the best, so when they think the opposite . . ." She also couldn't seem to find words to describe it.

I turned my palm up and squeezed. "I can't believe your mom said that pile of crap to you. What the hell."

Her head drooped. "I know," she groaned. "It's terrible. But it's also just one side of her, and . . . I don't know! She's not all bad, but yeah, she says some really horrible things sometimes—things that make me want to scream and hurl stuff."

This shouldn't be a conflict for her. It pained me emotionally and physically. Yet if anyone could understand what it was like to still crave a relationship with parents who didn't fully deserve it, it was me. I didn't act on it, but the ghost of them haunted me daily.

So much churned beneath her shadowed expression as she said, "Sometimes I'm ashamed at how I've clung to them with bloody, torn-apart hands, trying to make it work even after they show me again and again it's not worth it. But I'm somehow also ashamed of choosing myself now." She hunched over, and her voice grew as small as her balled-up body. "Why am I forever doomed to be unhappy?"

I wrapped my arms around her, big spoon to her little ball. "Chloe." She looked at me. "I don't think anyone treats you as well as you deserve, including me. Because how can anyone give enough to the girl who loves so unconditionally and puts others before herself? Your love for your parents doesn't make you weak; it's why you're so special, and why you deserve everything. Including happiness. They're the ones who didn't choose you, not the other way around. You feel guilty because you're you. I wish I could take it away but I can't."

"Right," she whispered, hearing me but perhaps not quite feeling it yet.

I continued to squeeze ball-Chloe, hoping I could at least replace some of the pain with love.

She adjusted and exhaled into the crook of my elbow. I laughed at how much it tickled. She did it again, on purpose this time, and I tackled her to the mattress. She was wearing a loose pajama shirt with a neckline wide enough to expose her collarbone and shoulder, and I couldn't focus as it danced in front of my face while she play wrestled with me. She tried to grab my arm to tickle me again, but I escaped her grasp and wrapped her in a hug so her fingers couldn't reach me. A fire flashed in her eyes and she kissed me hungrily, and, shit, I was going to lose it on the spot.

That night (er, morning), right before we fell asleep in each other's arms, Chloe whispered, "Thank you for wanting me."

I hugged her tight and didn't let go.

Voicemail from Chloe's mother

January 30

Jing-Jing? You there? Eh, if you keep this up, Bǎbá and I will come to Chicago very soon to make sure you're okay! Hmm, actually, that's a great idea! Then we can have dinner with Andrew's parents and meet his pastor. That would put a lot of my worries to rest.

[into the distance] Eh! Lǎo Gōng! Do you want to take a trip to Chicago soon?

Jing-Jing, call me back!

Chloe

CHAPTER 62

FLYING

January 30–February 5

My week with Drew in Chicago was somehow both fireworks and comfy sweats in rocking chairs. Being near him made my nerve endings sizzle, but talking to him also felt like putting on your favorite fuzzy, broken-in socks that make you say *ahhh* and feel like everything is going to be okay even though the world is shit.

Yet with every message from my mother, even fuzzy-sock time was tainted with a dash of dread. The thought of my parents—and the threat of what was to come—sent chills down my otherwise well-insulated toes. I decided to shut off my phone while Drew and I were together so I could compartmentalize, at least for now.

Depending on our schedules, we spent some nights at his hotel, some at my dorm. Even though we never explicitly said so, our plans mostly revolved around who would be able to get to the other one sooner so we could maximize our time together. And while the king bed at the hotel was roll-around-making-out, starfish-when-you-sleep awesome, there was also something so cozy about curling tightly in Drew's arms in my twin bed.

Even though we were physical, it didn't feel like the main thing. It complemented our conversations, another way to show affection. I was neither expecting nor opposed to sex, but it just didn't feel necessary right now, not for us in this moment.

In between our laughing, kissing, and soul-searching on the bed—my favorite moments thus far—we put on our tourist hats. Literally: a UChicago winter hat with a poof ball for me and a fur-lined ski one for Drew. And for the first time since I'd moved here more than a year ago, I did touristy things like take shivering selfies at the Bean and observe the otters at Shedd Aquarium—things I hadn't done before because I'd been too focused on school, too shěng qián, too self-conscious, too past-me.

And when Drew told me he wanted a tour of campus so he could have an image in his head when I told him in the future I was in class or walking to the library or getting boba, I took him to all my favorite UChicago spots: Rockefeller Chapel, the Quad, and Saieh Hall, the last of which resulted in a lot of unintended laughs.

"Is this a church?" Drew had asked me. And I'd responded, "Sort of. This is the economics building. But it's fitting it looks like a church given how the economics department is treated around here."

As we walked through Saieh, I had whispered to him about Becker and Friedman—the godfathers of UChicago economics—and how it was an honor to study at a place with so many economics Nobel Prize winners but also a little creepy how close it was to a religion here.

Drew took in the Gothic architecture—"Looks like Hogwarts," he had said—with awe and wistfulness, and my heart ached for the college experience he had missed.

But based on the way his eyes lit up like the moon when he talked about his Art Institute experiences, he was on the right path. Visiting him there and walking around the museum as he told me about his day was another highlight of our time together, and I couldn't help imagining his paintings on those walls one day. I knew how near impossible that was, but I also believed in him so much I couldn't *not* dream it.

Drew made me dream. For him, for myself, for us. I'd been so focused on what I didn't want for so long that I'd forgotten how to fly among the stars and the moon—where the sun belonged.

Drew

CHAPTER 63

SOARING

'd always thought that finding your partner was equal to finding the person who pushed your buttons the least, but I was wrong. Finding your person was finding a piece of yourself. Finding your best friend.

Finding Chloe.

I knew there were more serious times to come, but because it was inevitable, I tried to focus on the now. How lucky were we to have this little window of sunshine—three suns' worth?

Meanwhile, my fellowship further convinced me that art was to be celebrated, not hidden away in secret. I was introduced to others (entire rooms full of them) who cherished what I loved. Some had even achieved my dream. My classes took feelings and instincts I'd had and defined them in clear lines and strokes and gradients.

I drank it all in like Cháng'é drank her longevity potion, and for the first time I believed that I could do this. That I was where I was meant to be. Even if I failed, I would be okay. Because at least I would have tried something that coursed in my veins. Even if my family didn't come back, I would walk forward. *Because I tried to choose this* and *them,* I reminded myself for the millionth time. But now I felt it.

Voicemail from Chloe's mother

February 5

[cut off because Chloe's mother started talking before the beep] can't just leave me a message saying you're alive and think that's enough! I'm glad you're alive, but that's not enough! And stop calling me when you know I'm at work!

I'm putting a package in the mail to you today: it's a cream you rub on your belly, and then you bind it up real tight with Ace bandages soaked in this special mud taken from a volcano, and it just poof! Melts your fat away. We'll video-chat as you do it so I can help you. It's a present for you *and* Andrew.

Chloe

CHAPTER 64

MY KIND OF FISH BALL
February 6

I woke before Drew on our last full day together. We were at the hotel, snuggled up haphazardly with one of his arms slung over my hips and my forearm nestled beneath his neck. Worried he'd wake up sore, I considered reclaiming my limb, but when I took in the peaceful look on his very familiar face, I instead wrapped both arms around him.

A tear rolled down my cheek. This week had flown by too fast. I wasn't ready to pop our bubble yet.

But it was already popped. All the decisions I'd been putting off rushed in, demanding my attention. Was I going to tell my parents about him in a week when I returned home for Chinese New Year? My God, it was *a week*. That was too soon, wasn't it?

Except . . . talking to Drew about his family the past few days had given me hope. I had the privilege of seeing someone who was already on the other side, and even though his situation was bleak, he was also whole. Scarred, but whole.

I could do scarred.

I drifted back to sleep hugging my scarred, beautiful man to my chest. I wouldn't be letting go.

When Drew woke me in the early afternoon with a shower of kisses on my head, face, and arms, I felt so light I could've floated right up out of bed even without antigravity boots. The reality that he would be flying back to California the next morning hung over us, but I also had so much clarity I couldn't stop grinning at him with all my teeth on display—the way my mother hated, since "classy girls only show six teeth." That same smile always made Drew's eyes light up, which they did now.

"Hey," he said, matching my giant grin.

"Hey."

My cheeks hurt.

"If you're okay with it," I said, "I want to tell my parents about us. About everything. Next week. When I come home for Chinese New Year." I was flying into Palo Alto next Friday evening, Chinese New Year's Day.

His eyes widened. "Yeah?"

I nodded.

"I'm ready whenever you are," he said, tapping my knee with a finger. "Are you okay with the fact that they will definitely be upset?"

I sighed. "I'm going to lose them one day with or without you. It's inevitable. My relationship with them is already cracked, and it's been waiting to fully break for a long time. At some point I'm going to have to be myself with them. I'm ready now, with you."

His eyes glistened. "Yeah?"

I nodded. "Because you're my kind of fish ball."

He chuckled through his tears, then laced his fingers through mine and brought my hand up to kiss it. "Infinite mooncake points to House of Chloe. And . . . you're my kind of fish ball too. A meat-ball. Wait, I didn't mean it that way—"

"I know," I said with a laugh. "This isn't my first interaction with you."

When his lips met mine, I somehow managed to hit pause in my brain, putting off the storm on the horizon and focusing on the positives of the huge decision we'd just made. I was trying. Moving forward. The end result might not be what I wanted, but I was fighting.

He gently sucked my lower lip, then broke away to nibble his way from my neck to my earlobe. And I forgot not only what was coming but my own name.

Voicemail from Chloe's mother

February 6

Jing-Jing, you can't ignore me forever! If you keep this up, I really will fly out there! Tomorrow! Surprise you at your dorm! And as punishment, I will bring you three pairs of those underwear you hate! [laugh]

Call me back. I . . . I just want to talk to you. I'm . . . thinking of you is all. Okay?

Chloe

CHAPTER 65

COLD

February 7

started to get cold feet about telling my parents once Drew left Chicago and my previously warm bed turned cold. And my mother's voicemails weren't helping.

If I had been on the verge of peeing my sweat-soaked undies introducing my parents to fake Drew, well, now I was going to need some Pepto-Bismol.

I wanted to both delay the conversation *and* rip off the soggy, smelly Band-Aid immediately. The anticipation was almost worse than what was to come. Only almost—because I was ninety-six percent sure the hundreds of scenarios I imagined at night lying in bed were plausible. Hence the Pepto-Bismol. And the other four percent? Was me imagining my parents embracing Drew with open arms and telling me they were thrilled I was happy. That was even more painful than imagining—predicting?—their anger and ultimatums.

I was dreading Chinese New Year more than my mom dreaded menopause. And I was slowly running out of my defense-mechanism humor.

CHINESE NEW YEAR

Drew

CHAPTER 66

BUNS

February 12

Chinese New Year fell on a Friday this year, which meant the most lucrative rental night with the highest demand was Thursday, Chinese New Year's Eve, for the big family reunion dinner. My New Year's Eve client was a kind, quiet, twenty-nine-year-old girl who wasn't interested in being in a relationship but was tired of all the comments from family. She had asked me not to have physical contact, but to simply "be present and nice," which was so easy compared to some jobs that I felt bad about the rate she was paying.

And because that job had been a single-nighter, I had a different client the night of Chinese New Year, one who hadn't been able to afford peak New Year's Eve pricing. So far, things were going smoothly. Well, save for the fact that I couldn't stop thinking about how Chloe's plane was landing around this time, Chloe was now calling an Uber, and, oh, probably about home, and then, sweet Mother of God, telling her parents about me.

Luckily, the Rent for Your 'Rents mission was straightforward: stop the parents and nosy aunt from bugging the client, Jeannie, about dating (more specifically, to stop them from telling her to dress more hip or learn how to flirt before she became "a leftover woman," yikes). Jeannie was open to dating and had been in a few relationships this year, but none she was ready to "subject to the torture that is my family. Maybe when I'm engaged."

Tonight I was a "future lawyer and art enthusiast" currently studying political science at Stanford, by the client's request. (Since I was the first boy she was bringing home and she wasn't sure what her family was looking for, she'd requested a Renaissance man to cover all the bases.) As I chatted about art history (yay), the Du family and I enjoyed a lovely dinner at a fancy Chinese fusion restaurant that served foie gras dumplings, Peking duck, and whole steamed fish, as well as the fancier loose-leaf tea that made me want to wrap my hands around my mug. Then, because Mr. Du claimed that the dessert at the restaurant was "just dreadful—all show and no taste," we decided to drive across town to get dessert boba. This hadn't been a planned part of our itinerary, but apparently Mr. Du's disdain for fancy dessert was a recent development that his daughter didn't know about.

I got the all clear just as we were parking. Because the evening was crisp and calm, we took a leisurely stroll around the lit-up shopping square before making our way to the best boba café in Palo Alto, and also one of the few that was open late.

As we neared the café, I was laughing at one of Mr. Du's jokes when I heard, "Oh shit," from a distance. I'd know that voice anywhere.

Don't look. It wasn't too late yet. I tried to pick up my pace, leading the Dus toward a fountain and away from the voice and café. It was almost an out-of-body experience as I pulled something out of my ass about the fountain's historical significance.

As I yammered away, I glanced behind my shoulder to assess the situation, and Chloe's frantic eyes met mine.

Chloe

Holy cannoli baloney guacamole. I swear, my mind fuzzed out for a moment, my vision blurring and my brain shutting off from overheating.

I knew Drew was on a job tonight, but they were supposed to be having dinner far from here, at a place we would never set foot in because it was "like flushing money down the toilet," as my mother liked to say.

I tried to steer my parents into the closest shop, which was . . . a baby store, shit. And it was closed. *Joke's on me today, Universe—hope you're getting a good laugh.*

My mother pointed toward the café we'd trekked here for. "I need more buns, remember?" she said. "Kuo Ăyí told me this place is the best."

"You have so many buns already!" I motioned to her backside to try to get her to face away from Drew and his client. "See? Buns of steel!"

She chuckled and swatted my hand with hers. "Definitely not!" my mother joked back. "I've always been embarrassed by how small my buns are!"

But I barely heard her. Because I was panicking, sweating, about to yell "Fire!" if not for the fact that it was illegal.

Yes, obviously I was going to tell my parents the truth tonight anyway, but on my own terms, not with an epic explosion to rival Christmas Eve.

And to think, when I'd arrived home just an hour ago, my parents had been aglow asking me about Andrew and his family. We'd finally reached a peaceful, happy, albeit fake place, and I couldn't even have that for one second.

Jing-Jing, we are happy for you and Andrew, my mother had said to me in the car on the way here. *We wish we had behaved differently in the beginning, though I stand by my motivation of watching out for you.*

But ... maybe I have some regrets too. Well, not regrets. But, just, well, I hope Andrew is not mad. Maybe I even wish he were here right now.

It had both warmed my heart and sunk it to my pelvic floor. How much of her fondness for him was based on his made-up history? How much was because of the real him? And in that moment, for a split second, I had wavered on my decision to tell them the truth, a teeny-tiny voice in my head whispering, *Is it that bad to ride the wave I paid Rent for Your 'Rents for, just a little while longer?*

But because of my mother's love of buns, everything was a moment away from crashing into each other, quite literally. It hadn't happened already only because my father was playing Sudoku on his phone and my mother was fumbling with her purse, trying to find the reusable plastic bags she kept in there. I had about three seconds to decide what to do. Before they looked up. Before they saw Drew. Couldn't he just feign diarrhea and run away? To be fair, he had managed to divert his client's family in the other direction briefly, but they were clearly antsy to get to the café now.

Without thinking and without knowing what else to do, I yelled, "Stop!" to my parents.

They indeed did stop, but then my mother said, "Andrew?"

Because Drew and his client's family were close enough to have also heard me yell, they had stopped in their tracks too, looking over to see what the commotion was about. And even though Drew had his back to us, my mother apparently knew what his backside looked like. Maybe he had too many buns, although that hadn't been a bad thing until now.

"Hunh?" my father said, still not looking up from his phone.

"Eh, are these friends of yours, Andrew?" the client's mother asked.

My mother looked from Drew to me, confused. "Jing-Jing, you said he was spending today with his parents and flying out tomorrow!"

The client suddenly understood, panic taking over her face.

"These are the Wangs," Drew said quickly. "And these are the Dus. Sorry, we're in a rush, but it was so lovely to see you!"

He started to leave, but Mrs. Du said, "Honey, we can chat for a minute if you like. We're not in a rush at all!"

My father finally looked up. "Who's this? Oh! Andrew, why are you here? And why are you wearing a Stanford shirt?"

"Nice to meet you," I said to the Dus as I pulled on both my parents' arms in the direction of our car. "We have to get going."

"The buns, Jing-Jing!" My mother yanked her arm from mine. "What's going on here . . ." She trailed off, and now Drew, the client, and I were all trying to push the parents along.

Then, suddenly, my mom pointed a finger at Drew. "Tiān āh!" She looked back at me, frantic. "He's cheating on you!"

"No, no," I said quickly as Drew and the girl joined in. "No one's cheating," she said as Drew garbled, "You've got it all wrong."

But that was all drowned out by the girl's aunt—well, I was guessing it was her aunt, based on age and looks, et cetera—who was saying, very loudly, "I knew it was too good to be true!" Then, to the girl's mother: "I told you Jeannie was too naive! This is what happens to good girls like her! They get played!"

My mother jumped in and snapped back, "No, being innocent is a *good* thing!" because that was what was most important right now.

There was no easy solution here, but in the hopes of saving Drew's job and the client's mission, I offered up, "I'm the ex—I just haven't told my parents yet." Since I was about to spill all anyway, what was one more lie? I could take the hit for now and reverse in a minute, once it was just my parents and me.

My mother exploded. "You let him get away? Zěnme gǎo de, Jing-Jing!" she yelled just as my father, surprisingly, demanded an explanation: "Shénme huí shì?"

"And he moved on this quickly?" My mother shook a finger at Drew. "Shame on you!"

My father's expression was more dejected than angry. "What happened?" he asked again, in English this time.

I shot the girl's family a pained expression, hoping they would take the cue and give us some privacy, but the aunt took a step closer and the parents rooted their feet.

The aunt crossed her arms over her chest and asked suspiciously, "When did you break up?"

But her question was buried by my mother's Mandarin exclamations. When the aunt tried to ask again, my mother yelled out, "Wait, then why is Andrew coming over tomorrow?"

Even though the odds were low, I had told her he would be joining us for a belated New Year's dinner on the off chance that my parents would be interested in getting to know the real him after the truth came out tonight.

"He's not," I lied quickly. "I didn't know how to tell you yet."

"Then why did I buy so much beef, Jing-Jing? You need to tell me these things! And you let me go on and on about him in the car like a fool! Oh, my face is so red. And, my goodness"—she threw a hand over her forehead dramatically—"we tossed away Hongbo for this!" She was spiraling fast.

"When did you break up," the aunt demanded, through her teeth, more forceful this time. The girl's parents looked embarrassed but also curious for the answer.

"We have to go," I said, just as the girl answered, "Thanksgiving, right before Andrew and I met."

Oh no.

My parents started yelling at the same time. I was ready to drop to my knees and beg the Dus for some privacy, but they were already backing away. Well, except for the aunt, who tried to stay behind, but, thank God, the parents ushered her along. Drew hung back for a second, unsure whether or not to leave me, but I hissed at him to go; his loitering only made him look more suspicious.

He had a mess to clean up, and right now, I had to mop up my own.

I dragged my parents over to a bench and sat them down. "I need to tell you something."

"Yes, you bet your pìgu you have to tell us things!" my mother yelled as my father said, more calmly, "Start talking."

"Okay, but just listen. To the end. Please."

They listened to the end, but even though I didn't know what to expect, their reaction was *not* one of the many scenarios that had played out in my head earlier this week.

As soon as I finished telling them I had rented Andrew, then fallen for him, and that he was currently on another assignment, my father asked, "When did you become such a liar?" at the same time my mother said, "So many lies, Jing-Jing! How are we supposed to know what's real?"

"This. Right now. What I'm telling you now is real."

My mother threw her arms in the air. "But this is the most preposterous thing you've told us yet!"

Yes, I slowly realized. Jesus, how had I gotten here?

This is why you're coming clean now, I reminded myself. To do better.

My parents were staring at me like they didn't know who I was, which was accurate.

I explained, "I did all this because you weren't listening to me, and I didn't know how to make you see. But I cared about you and our relationship, and I wanted to find a way to escape Hongbo without fighting. It wasn't right, but I hired Andrew out of love. Just like you two set me up with Hongbo out of"—I couldn't quite say "love"—"your concern for me. But it wasn't right. Just like how I shouldn't have lied to you."

"Lies, out of love?" my mother threw back. "Those contradict each other."

"You guys haven't told me about Băbá's prostate cancer, supposedly out of love," I said quietly.

Neither of them said anything.

"Bā, are you okay?" I blurted. I'd bottled up my feelings for too long, and they were spilling out now. "You know I love you, right? I'm here—I want to support you through this. You don't have to hide things like this from me. In fact, you shouldn't; it makes me worry *more* because I don't know any of the details."

"You wouldn't understand, not until you have kids," my father replied.

There was an uncomfortable pause.

My mother was looking at me like she couldn't swallow my past lies and was silently choking on them.

The knife in my heart twisted.

Then, for the first time, I ignored that my heart was injured and bleeding, and I spoke from it anyway.

"Mămá, Băbá, I love you both. So much. Which is why I'm here, trying. I'm sorry for the lies in the past. I promise I'm going to be honest with you from now on, even when it's painful. I hope . . ." I exhaled. "I hope you can one day do the same."

Their faces were a mix of shock and anger at what I'd done. As those emotions worked themselves out, I left before they could say anything. I knew they would need time, and I didn't want to hear words that would be said in the heat of the moment and impossible to forget.

Clean slate. Take one.

February 13, 12:23 p.m. PST

<Chloe>

Is everything okay with your client?

I'm so sorry

<Drew>

Yes, yes, you played the jilted ex perfectly

More importantly, how are your parents?

They still want you to come over for dinner tonight

Seriously???

That's a good sign, right?

Well tbh I'm not sure what their motivations are

They're not talking all that much

Could be they want to get to know you

Could be to confront you (sorry I hope not 🥀)

Um could be we really just have too much beef

Ok so prepare for anything?

Yeah

Maybe don't bring any pears

That I can do

Come at 6

This will suck and I'm very sorry in advance but . . .

I can't wait to see you

I can't wait to see YOU!

Drew

CHAPTER 67

DREW CHAN

February 13

have been to many Chinese New Year dinners, all of them awkward, but compared to tonight, the others were a 1950s-television-family gathering.

Today I was dressed in a red button-up and slacks, with a fun Pollock-like tie I'd painted myself, and no glasses: a.k.a. full Drew. And Drew had brought non-company-sanctioned Chinese New Year gifts: a Zhōngguó jié wall hanging I'd knotted myself and red envelopes filled with some of my creations (paper stars, moons, and a sheep for Chloe).

My heartbeat was in my ears as I rang the doorbell—the first time I was arriving without Chloe by my side. *Maybe try to think of tonight as the first night,* I told myself in an effort to keep my brain from toggling between Drew and Andrew. I didn't have that problem with Chloe, but I didn't know what it would be like back in this house again, where I'd grown accustomed to being someone else.

Chloe opened the door with a weary smile. I gave her an *everything okay?* look and she sighed dramatically. *Stubborn as an ox and a mouse,* she mouthed to me, which made me stifle a laugh because it was the perfect use of her parents' zodiac animals.

I pulled her into a hug, careful not to drop the gifts in my hands, and she surprised me by kissing me on the mouth, assuredly, before helping me with what I was carrying. Despite the weariness, she seemed to be moving more freely than before, a weight lifted.

Her parents did not come out to greet me.

"Are you sure it's okay I'm here?" I whispered as we made our way to the kitchen.

"Like I said, they haven't said much. But that also means I was able to tell them all about you."

I raised a questioning eyebrow. She gave me a tight-lipped smile. Shit. (How could they not be excited about their brilliant, beautiful daughter dating a college dropout who painted moons between fake-boyfriend jobs?)

"I got you," she whispered in my ear before giving my side a squeeze. "You got this. We've got this."

The kitchen smelled like home, with beef broth simmering on the stove, kōng xīn cài sizzling in a wok, and made-from-scratch dumplings lining the table. It looked like home too, with red decorations hung from every crevice.

The Wangs smiled and waved, but no hugs and no break from bustling around the kitchen. I hopped in and lent a hand, trying not to let their reaction (or lack thereof) bring me down. If Mr. and Mrs. Wang appreciated my help or noticed my dumpling skills (yes, there had been a class), they didn't express it in any way.

When the food was ready, I gave them the Zhōngguó jié and put the red envelopes on the table for after dinner. They gave me a curt thank-you before setting the Zhōngguó jié behind a pile of religious books so it couldn't be seen.

Chloe shrugged at me. I guessed she was saving her strength for what was to come, and she proved me right not two minutes later.

We had just sat down and started passing food around when Mrs. Wang said, "So how many Chinese New Year dinners have you crashed, Andrew? Or, I guess it's Drew."

At least they're here and this dinner is happening, I reminded myself. (Except I was digging through three layers of crap to find that silver lining.)

"He didn't crash them, Mămá; he was invited," Chloe said, exasperated.

"Under false pretenses," Mr. Wang argued.

Maybe they were here just so they could berate me.

"We had you in our home! When you were a stranger!" Mrs. Wang exclaimed.

"The company does very extensive background checks," Chloe supplied.

"That's not enough!"

"It's more than what you get with other people you date," Chloe pointed out.

That made Mrs. Wang stop, but she turned down one of the many alternative paths in front of her. "What kind of person does this job?"

Chloe's head dropped to her hands. "Someone who wants to help people." She looked back up at them. "He's here as my boyfriend, to get to know you better."

"Which we're doing," her father said coldly. "This is part of his real life, isn't it? Lying to others?"

"He supports himself," Chloe retorted. "Do you know how hard that is?"

"Yes, Jing-Jing, of course we know," her father said calmly.

"He supports himself doing *that*," her mother added, spitting out the last word.

I felt as small as their words were meant to shrink me.

"If you want us to stop talking about his job, fine," Mrs. Wang said with an undercurrent of spite. "Drew, do you go to strip clubs?"

355

What? "No, Ǎyí. I don't." *Not even for the steak.*

Mrs. Wang pointed an accusatory finger at me. "Aha! He's a liar! I knew a professional liar wouldn't be able to help himself. Jing-Jing, we can't trust him!"

I looked to Chloe for an explanation, but her eyes were rolled to the ceiling.

Mrs. Wang continued her onslaught. "Tell us how you plan on supporting yourself and our daughter on an artist's salary. Are you going to sell those Christmas ornaments you made?"

My face flushed. This was one of my nightmares come to life. She might as well have mentioned doodling tourists at the beach.

"You haven't earned the right to ask him about that!" Chloe exclaimed.

"Then what *can* we ask about?" her mother said, a smug look on her face.

"Stop," I said quietly. Then again, louder: "Please stop." They all turned to look at me.

And, without thinking, I embarrassingly but sincerely launched into this:

"My name is Drew Chan, I'm the son of Taiwanese immigrants, I love Chinese culture but I am also bitter because I blame it—maybe a little unfairly—for why my parents decided to disown me when I pursued art. I turned to being a rental boyfriend because it offered me the opportunity to be paid, with benefits, while I helped others in familiar, heartbreaking situations. I don't regret my decisions, but I do hate how everything turned out with my family, and even though it hurts, I'm still hopeful for a reunion with my parents, though I don't think it'll happen until I have some success as an artist, which is terrible that it has to be that way, but I think that's what my parents need. I'm trying to be patient. I'm very sorry to you both for how this all started, but I'm also not sorry, because it brought me to your daughter, who you named perfectly, because to me she's the sun and moon and stars.

Also, I'm a cheesy romantic, but it only started when she came into my life. Nice to meet you, Wang Āyí, Shūshú. Thank you for having me in your lovely home; the food looks fantastic."

Dead. Ass. Silence.

Then a year—I mean, ten seconds—later, her mother pushed back from the table.

"I'm sorry, I can't do this," she said, her eyes downcast.

Shit. Had my speech been too much? I pressed my lips together, vowing not to talk anymore.

"Please, Māmá," Chloe begged with her words and her expression.

Mrs. Wang shook her head. "Jing-Jing, I can't. I need some time. I don't know this girl in front of me who lied about so many things. My heart is broken."

And Chloe fell apart. I waffled between wanting to pick up her pieces and wanting to let them work this out without me here. Ultimately, I decided to fade into the background for now, keeping track of where each piece landed so I could hand them back to her when this was over.

Chloe

"I don't know how to make it so we can both be happy at the same time," I exclaimed to my parents, the tears pooling. "Half of me wants to beg you for forgiveness so we can move on, and the other half is just so angry and exasperated and tired."

"Maybe . . ." My father swallowed. "Maybe I know what that's like."

My mother turned and glared at him.

"Jing-Jing, I still think it was the right decision to keep my diagnosis from you. But I didn't mean to hurt you."

The tears flowed down my face. "I didn't mean to hurt you, either."

"But you're both still hurt," my mother said harshly. "As am I."

"I'm sorry," I whispered for what felt like the thousandth time.

"I'm . . . I wish things had gone differently, Jing-Jing, I really do," my father said. He cleared his throat. "I . . . I don't know how to talk to you. I don't know how to do better."

I wiped my cheek. "That . . . is already doing better."

He couldn't look at me as he said, "Dr. Lin told me a couple of weeks ago that you knew I was sick."

That explained why he hadn't been more shocked when I'd brought it up yesterday. "Were you going to talk to me about it this weekend?"

He hesitated. "I didn't know how to bring it up."

That was so upsetting I had to sit and bite my lip for a second while my insides roiled. I knew it was a step forward that he was telling me this now, when he didn't have to, but still . . .

Then he said two unexpected words: "I'm sorry."

I released my lip from my teeth and looked at him.

"I'm sorry," he repeated.

I was still processing, trying to move past the hurt so we could take a step forward together, but before I could get there, my mother stood.

"I've lost my appetite," she said, then left.

"You should go after her," my father said quietly. Then, tenderly, he told me, "I'll be here when you get back."

I only managed a nod.

Before I'd even entered her bedroom, I heard my mother say through the half-open door, "I think you should break up with him."

"Why?" I pushed past the nerves and into the room to see her lying in bed, a forearm over her eyes. I sat on the empty half, near her head.

"Jing-Jing, you gave up a wealthy, respected suitor who would've provided for your entire life. And for what? A struggling artist estranged from his low-class family! And you live in different states, lǎo tiān yé! How do you expect to make this work?"

"I don't know yet," I answered honestly. "I just know I care about him and I want to try. Is that so terrible? I'm nineteen and I just want to continue dating my boyfriend."

She didn't move a muscle.

I took a breath. "Mǎmá, I'm not . . . myself with you. But I'm working on it. I want to show you the real me."

She removed her arm, finally looking at me. "Then who was the girl I loved and laughed with?"

I tried not to fall apart at the past tense. "That was me too."

She sat up, frustrated. "Then what are you saying?"

"I don't know! I just—I want us to move forward from this. I want all of us to do better. I want to feel *enough* for you and for you to stop—"

"Aiyah, Jing-Jing, I pick at you because you're my daughter," my mother interrupted. "That's how I show I care. I want you to be the best."

"Why isn't me just being me good enough?"

"That's not the point. No one is perfect, and I'm showing you that I think you can be even better. I believe in you."

We were speaking different languages. "I will . . . try to keep that in mind, if you can try to do it less."

She lay back down and rolled over so her back was to me. "My head hurts, Jing-Jing. Please let me rest."

I started to leave, but then I remembered something and paused. "Someone wise once told me that all relationships have problems. It's how you solve them that matters. I hope you can forgive me for the mistakes I've made. When you're ready, I really do want to start fresh. I believe we can."

She said nothing. I waited a minute longer than was comfortable in this stifling silence. Then I couldn't take it anymore and fled.

When I returned downstairs, my father and Drew were sitting frozen and silent. Both their faces flooded with relief at the sight of me.

As soon as I sat down, my father started talking.

"Jing-Jing . . ." He looked down at his hands, not at me, as he spoke. "I'm sorry our relationship became so broken you felt you had to go to such extremes. I've been paying more attention and I've noticed . . . things . . . about Hongbo I didn't notice earlier. They've been lying about their company—did you know that? The stocks I bought have tanked, and when I tried to ask what happened, he yelled at me. Anyway, the point is, I should have trusted you to decide for yourself. I may . . ." He trailed off, a little winded—from emotion I hope, and nothing else. "I may have been scared of my illness. I wanted to know you'd be financially secure just . . . in case. But Andrew—I mean, Drew—reminded me a few months ago that you're quite capable yourself. I wasn't ready to hear it then, because you'll always be a little girl to me, but . . ." He sighed. "Maybe things aren't as black-and-white as I once believed. I used to think life was so straightforward, but then . . . you can do everything right—exercise, take vitamins, go to acupuncture—and still get sick."

"Oh, Bǎbá," I said softly, leaning over and reaching a hand across the table toward him.

He finally looked at me. "I didn't tell you I was sick, even after you already knew, because I haven't been able to truly face it myself." He placed his hand on the table, angled toward mine but not touching. "I don't want you to feel like you can't tell me things, okay? And I'll try to be more open with you."

I nodded, attempting to hold the oncoming wave of emotions in check. "You know vitamins and acupuncture don't do anything, right?" I joked, and he *laughed*.

"Maybe you can come with me to my next doctor's appointment," he said, then added, "So you can tell Dr. Lin that."

I smiled. "I would love that."

We didn't hug or cry or say I love you; we simply dug into our food. But for us, this was monumental. I tried to force my mother out of my mind so I could focus on how my father and I had just taken a long-overdue step forward. Together.

Chloe

CHAPTER 68

VALENTINE'S DAY

February 14

"Are you sure you don't want to spend the day with your parents?" Drew asked the following afternoon as we journeyed our way to San Francisco in the back seat of a so-far private UberPool. I was flying out of the San Francisco airport later today, and I'd asked him if he wanted to come with me and make a day of it. I only had a backpack, so luggage wasn't a problem.

I poked his side. "It's Valentine's Day."

"Every day feels like Valentine's Day with you, not just the rando day some Catholic priest died."

I smiled, but the moment was laced with poignancy. "I wish it had gone differently yesterday. But I'm not surprised? Maybe I'm even a little relieved it didn't go worse?"

"I would not have guessed your dad would handle it better than your mom."

I chuckled. "They're both roller coasters. Different ones, both unpredictable." I rested my hand in the middle seat, and he reached over to clutch it. "My dad told me to give my mom some space. I think he might need some too, just to process. But . . . I'll email him in a few days. Ask for a health update. I think it'll be okay with him."

Drew nodded in support and agreement. "I'm sorry I didn't prepare more for today," he said with a sad smile. "I would've made you something! I assume you feel differently about origami roses than real ones?"

I beamed. "Maybe we can find a pack of paper somewhere and you can teach me."

We spent the day laughing, half talking in our own language made up of inside jokes, and gallivanting around a beautiful city I'd never really spent time in despite living adjacent to it my whole life.

Our first stop was the Ferry Building Marketplace, where I showed Drew very quickly how not shy I was around samples, especially cheese samples. We ate and giggled our way through some very fun and very tasty chocolate, ice cream, and olive oil stands.

At the ceramic shop, Drew hovered outside nervously, so I boldly walked in, introduced myself to the owner, and asked about her creative process and journey to this point. I also introduced her to my favorite artist, who was adorably shy but also talkative and passionate once pressed.

Somewhere in the middle of the indoor street, we clinked West Coast oysters, and the briny, salty deliciousness that filled my mouth made me feel guilty for preferring them over oyster pancakes.

Toward the end of the marketplace, Drew and I bought a chocolate croissant to share. But right as I was sitting down at a table by the water, he pecked me on the cheek, shot me a mischievous smile, and darted away, no explanation. A minute later he returned with a pack of origami paper. I raised one arm in excitement while using the other to hide the fact that I'd already eaten half of the croissant.

Our red, pink, and blue origami roses ended up smeared with little streaks of chocolate and even more love. Mine didn't look anywhere near as luminous or in bloom as his, but he cradled them like they were treasures, making me turn as red as the first rose I'd made. I scooped up the handful he'd folded and carefully tried to position them at the top of my backpack so they wouldn't get crushed.

After grabbing a second croissant to go, we Ubered to the Asian Art Museum, which we explored languidly. Drew showed me some of his favorites, but since it had been a while since he'd visited, he was discovering a lot of the pieces with me.

As I walked among images of cranes and Buddha inked in Chinese calligraphy brushstrokes, I felt connected to them even though the works were so purely Asian. I used to think those pieces of my life were removable, but now I realized they were so ingrained, such an integral part of me, that they were mixed throughout, evenly. Like my blood vessels or connective tissue or nerves. They were not just a part of me, but *me*.

Before, I'd associated my Chinese side with judgments about my body, clothes, grades, and romantic life, but my eyes were opening to how far it went beyond that superficial interpretation. Parents wanting more for their kids than they themselves had, the emphasis on hard work, Dr. Lin helping Drew and me out with a courtesy visit, my mother making free Essix retainers—these were small examples of the better parts that had been lost beneath the toxic waste. But now I was ready to see. Being honest with myself and my parents helped me realize that Jing-Jing was a side of me that I should be embracing, not pushing out. My drive, my loyalty, my selflessness—they were fostered by the community too. And I could love those pieces without embracing the negative parts. I was allowed to find the joy in sharing a second language, a deeper connection, and Cháng'é jokes with Drew. Maybe one day with my parents, too.

As I looked at a porcelain vase painted with images of children playing, it dawned on me that the name Jing-Jing bothered me because the repetition was a practice done with little kids, and I wanted to outgrow it and how my parents treated me. When they were ready, I'd ask them to drop one Jing.

I had my own moments with the art, but I also couldn't stop watching Drew as he took everything in with a reverent silence. I gestured to the hanging scroll in front of us, a stunning landscape of trees, mountains, and clouds inked with thin, rounded strokes thousands of years ago. Then I pointed toward the contemporary section we'd just come from. "Your work is so unique, blending Chinese techniques with American landscapes, but I think what makes it the most special is the je ne sais quoi you bring to it. Your perspective, your creativity, your—"

"Pain," he finished, and I stopped, waiting to hear more. A second later he said, "Sometimes I wonder if there was a silver lining in my wayward journey. I tapped into myself and had complete freedom with my work and found my voice, my style first." His lips curved up in a small, reflective smile. Then he added, "Though it's not a journey I'd recommend if there are any other alternative paths," and we laughed together.

A few hours later, when it was time to head for the airport, parting from Drew felt both difficult and easy—difficult because I didn't want to be away from the person who brought so much light and comfort into my life, and easy because I knew where we stood. Where I stood both with and without him.

For the first time, I didn't feel like I was changing skins as I left California and returned to Chicago. There was just one skin now: a Chinese-American one that deserved to be wanted and *was* wanted. By herself. As is.

<Drew>

Watching you fight for what you want, trying to find balance and not just give up . . .

You inspire me

<Chloe>

♥

I've been thinking about Jordan a lot
I wrote him a really long email
But I haven't sent it yet

He may have been young when everything happened but he's old enough to make his own decisions now
Send it when you're ready

I think I'm ready now
I just . . . needed you to know first

I'm in your corner

I've got the stool and water bottle ready to go

Now I just need my Rocky montage

I'm not running up all those steps with you but I'll cheer you on

Haha ok
Thanks for having my back

Always

SPRING BREAK

Chloe

CHAPTER 69

SCAMPERING MOUSE

March 21

My mother didn't talk to me for a month.

To be fair, I didn't talk to her for a month either. I think she was still too upset at how I had thrown our miànzi in the toilet over and over again, and I was too angry that our reputation was all she cared about.

But, as usual, I was going to be the bigger person. So the week before my late-March spring break, I started calling, leaving voicemails, sending a few texts. She didn't return any of them, but I knew they were chipping away at her defenses, because by the day I left Chicago, she'd stopped sending my phone calls straight to voicemail.

When I arrived home, Drew and my father were waiting for me in the living room, my father on the couch and Drew on the armchair. I dropped my bag and ran and hugged my dad, then kissed Drew. My father didn't smile, but he didn't look upset, either.

"Welcome home, Jing," my dad said, and I beamed at the single-syllable sound of my name, which was still fairly new. Then he joked, "And to think I was so worried about Drew living in the dorms with you when you've been thousands of miles apart."

I didn't tell him about all the canoodling we did when Drew visited Chicago, which he'd done again in the past month. I also didn't tell him that Drew was looking into moving out there to be closer to me. The plan was for him to transition into training new operatives at the Chicago branch. And the two of us were also working together with Rent for Your 'Rents to expand their operations. A month ago Drew had put me in touch with someone at corporate, as promised, and after a few conference calls, they'd offered us a chance to spearhead an expansion team together. They were excited about my ideas to increase the number of algorithms run, to present multiple options and probable outcomes to potential clients, and to hire company therapists for client counseling or, if all parties were willing, family counseling.

"Have you been playing nice?" I asked my father, wondering how long Drew had been there. I took a seat on the couch beside my dad.

Drew gave me a one-second, wide-eyed look, and I simultaneously wanted to laugh, shield him, and run away.

My father and I had kept in intermittent touch, mainly through email, and mainly about his health—which was obviously *huge* progress, but our curt two-liners left much to be desired. I was guilty too, but I couldn't bring myself to write essays back to his minimalist updates.

"I was just asking Drew if he can actually make money with the art thing," my father said with a shrug.

"Bǎbá," I chastised. My poor Drew. "What happened to believing I could take care of myself?" *Or being less of a jerk?*

"Ah, everything is more complicated than I used to think!" my father exclaimed. He was still coming to terms with his illness and apparently other things.

"That's obviously the goal, to make money from the art," Drew answered calmly. And kindly. "There are a lot of different ways to do that, and I'm happy to explore a wide range of them, including freelancing, teaching, and doing commercial work to support the more personal projects."

"And the two of us have something in the works," I added in an attempt to share more. "It combines our skills."

Out of the corner of my eye, I registered movement from the kitchen. A little whale-tail-loving mouse scampering about eavesdropping, perhaps?

"What are you working on?" my father asked.

"We're helping Rent for Your 'Rents make some changes," Drew said. "I'm using my experience with the company and my art; Chloe is using her economics—"

"Yeah, and one of the ideas I came up with all on my own is to use a mahjong game as a ruse to interrogate people. They said it was the best idea they've ever heard in the whole history of the company," I improvised.

My mother ran into the room. "That's my idea, not yours!"

"Aha, I knew that would work!" I exclaimed, pointing a finger at her.

She was frozen for a second, then burst into laughter.

We were not in a healthy, communicative place, and we were dysfunctional AF, *but* we were going to move forward. I could already feel it. It was pretty messed up that we never *really* talked about everything we should, and no one seemed to fully understand the other's side, but maybe we didn't need it to be perfect for it to be good. I'd never known what "family" meant, because that word didn't represent the same thing to me as it seemed to for others, but in that moment I finally understood that inexplicable underlying bond. That desire to move forward out of love, even when it wasn't perfect. Even when there was still anger underneath. Anger that, I hoped, would fade in time.

TODAY

Drew

CHAPTER 70

EPILOGUE

can't remember what life was like before Chloe. She's been so momentous in my life that everything started over with her: the big bang. Oops. Pun *not* intended. Really.

After moving to Chicago, my days are now filled with laughter, love, and so many kisses I'm convinced the universe is trying to tell me sorry for what it put me through previously. When the weather cooperates, Chloe and I grab red-bean Popsicles and walk to the lake to watch the moon come up. Sometimes I bring my sketch pad. I miss Jason and Marshall, but I'm thrilled they're officially living together without this third wheel. (And how cool is it that my old room is now an art studio for Jason?)

I'm slowly building a personal community of local artists as well as a small fan base through social media. I decided that pursuing more school wasn't the right move for me at this time, and Chloe was wonderfully supportive and made it the small deal that it was.

As I chase my dream, I support myself by working for the corporate side of Rent for Your 'Rents. The newest offshoot, Our Two Cents on Your 'Rents, is thriving, most likely because it's the brainchild of the most hardworking, passionate, and intelligent person I know. In addition to spearheading that, I'm also training new operatives. I tell them some rules are worth bending, especially ones that sort of rhyme (but only for the right kind of fish ball, of course).

Jordan and I are back on speaking terms, and before moving to the Midwest, I took a trip out to Berkeley to see him. It was a lot of him asking me about Chloe (and Rent for Your 'Rents), but we also had time to fill in the other blanks, reminisce, and joke about our parents in that way only siblings can. It had been so long I'd forgotten that was a thing.

And . . . I reached out to my parents. In a cowardly way, with a letter, but Chloe assures me it was the best choice given their preferences and our history. It was a way to make a move while respecting their space. A month later I'm still waiting for a response, but that's okay. I have faith that one day it'll be okay again, then good.

Chloe

CHAPTER 71

EPILOGUE

The more days that pass, the more ridiculous I feel about how much time and money and energy I spent protecting my parents' feelings at the expense of my own. Like, I hired a fake boyfriend? Who does that? And I needed that experience to learn the bumper-sticker slogan BE YOURSELF? Jesus, Chloe! Except that when I talk to potential Rent for Your 'Rents clients in my capacity as part-time director of Our Two Cents on Your 'Rents, it's still like, *Yup, yup, I totally get it.* The first time I video-chatted with another client, we both ended up bawling on-screen. Now I at least hold it together somewhat—enough to offer some thoughts and give my testimonial, which does reopen a wound, but it's becoming less painful each time.

My parents and I are . . . fine. They're freaking out that Drew moved to Chicago, and I hear questions about "the sex" way too much, but I gave them the choice of what role to play in the life I chose, and they want to be involved. Maybe too involved, if we're being honest, but that's not the worst option.

My father is in remission, and he updates me on his health in phone calls and emails. My mother is still figuring out how many toes to dip in the water, but I know that her cringeworthy questions and mailings of whale tails stuck with *No hanky panky!* notes are her way of saying she cares. About the wrong things, but I want her to be herself too. She recently commented that she was relieved Drew's family was actually in California and not Chicago so she could stop worrying about us staying in the Midwest after I graduate. Even though I'm not sure I want to move back in the future, I count it a temporary win that she wants me around.

I don't spiral while falling asleep as often anymore—I'm usually busy co-designing sheep pajamas—but the few times I do and whimper out loud, a loving arm will reach out and embrace me, and I fall asleep immediately, hugging my string-cheese-shaped xiǎo zhěntóu.

Snippets from
Chloe's application

Q: Does your family have any superstitions?
A: Not that I know of.

Q: What would be the ideal gift to get your parents?
A: Anything, really. I guess something Chinese would
be ideal? They love mooncakes, Taiwanese pineapple
cakes, Asian fruits, that type of thing.

Q: What are some traditions they follow?
A: The Chinese zodiac and Eastern medicine are important
to my mother. Not so much my father. Their house is feng-
shuied, but they view that more as an interior-decorator
kind of thing; they're not religious about it. What they are
religious about is religion, ha. See religion section for way
too much info about our community.

My parents believe strongly in filial piety and in
traditional roles like the eldest son taking care of the
family. They're big on upholding the family name and
saving face.

They're strict, so physical stuff shouldn't go past like
a hand graze or kiss on the head. My mom is especially
big on "purity," as she grossly says.

And we're big on food. Everything revolves around
food for us. Bring a big appetite! Oh, and warning: my
mom's cooking can sometimes be a little inventive. Okay,

a lot inventive. It may not be the easiest to stomach. Her Chinese food is great, but hold your breath for the fusion food. You'll know when you see it because it won't look like anything else you've ever eaten.

Q: Anything else we should know?
A: If you can find a way to work in how economics is actually a prestigious, difficult major that my parents shouldn't be complaining about, I'd be forever grateful. If you feel like you're laying it on too thick, I promise you're not; they are experts at not letting in nice comments about me or UChicago.

Sample of
Rent for Your 'Rents Classification Chart

	Greeting to parents	Showing affection to client in "private" moments	Showing affection to client in most settings	Showing affection to client in sad moment
Type A	Start with handshake; move to hug if the situation allows	Caresses to face, arm, hand Kiss to the forehead or head in appropriate circumstances (see appendix for more)	Physical contact to hand, arm, face, small of back	Hug Holding them close Stroking their hair
Type B	Start with handshake, touch their elbow with other hand if situation allows	Hand grazes Holding hands Kiss to the hand or head when appropriate	Light physical contact to hand, arm, face, small of back in select moments	Hand squeeze Quick hug in appropriate circumstances (see appendix for more)
Type C	Handshake, address as Āyí and Shūshú	Meaningful eye contact Shared smiles Hand grazes when appropriate	Limit to very infrequent light physical contact, eye contact, smiles, and polite gestures like pulling out chair, dishing food out, etc.	Lean in Place hand in close proximity Show them using eye contact that you're supporting them

Glossary

aiyah: An expression of dismay, exasperation, or surprise, positive or negative. No accent marks are used since this is common enough that it has found its way into some English dictionaries.

ǎyí: Translates to "aunt" or "auntie" and is used to address family friends.

bā: Shorthand for "bǎbá."

bǎbá: Dad.

bài tuō: Sometimes written as "bài tuō le," it's a phrase of exasperation meaning, roughly, "Please stop," with a pleading, fed-up connotation.

bāo: A soft, fluffy, white steamed bun.

Cháng'é: This Chinese goddess drank a longevity potion and now lives in the moon with Moon Rabbit.

chāshāo bāo: A Cantonese bun filled with barbecue pork, often found at dim sum and in Chinese bakeries.

chī: Literally "to eat." You say it in mahjong when you pick up a tile discarded by the player directly before you to form a run.

dòuhuā: A silky, sweet tofu dessert that has many different regional varieties. The one I grew up with is soft tofu in a sugary syrup that melts in your mouth. Just thinking about it makes my mouth water!

èrhú: A two-stringed, bowed musical instrument sometimes known as the Chinese violin.

farmer's calendar: The Chinese farmers' calendar is analogous to astrological horoscopes, using Chinese zodiac animals instead of astrological signs.

fēnlí: "To separate," or "to split a pear," depending on which Chinese characters are used. The two phrases are homophones.

giǎ xiláng: A Taiwanese phrase meaning "scared to death."

gōng kuài: A pair of chopsticks used solely for serving.

gōngxí: Congratulations.

guāi: "Good" or "obedient," usually used in reference to children.

Gudetama: An egg yolk Sanrio character known for its laziness (and for being an egg yolk with a butt crack).

hǎo: Another word for "good," it serves as a polite greeting when used after "Āyí" or "Shǔshú."

hú: What you say when you win in mahjong.

huàidàn: "Rotten egg," often used to refer to naughty children either playfully or seriously.

jìn lái: Come in.

Jing-Jing: The "Jing" character in Chloe's name is 晶, which is composed of the character for "sun," 日, written three times. Her legal first name is "Jing," but her parents and family friends call her "Jing-Jing," the repetition being a common Chinese tradition of endearment usually done with children.

kě'ài: Cute.

kōng xīn cài: The "hollow-heart vegetable," so named because of its hollow stems, is also known as water spinach.

lāo: To scoop or fish something out of water.

lǎo gōng: "Old man," the companion to "lǎo pó."

lǎo pó: "Old woman," sometimes used by a husband for his wife.

lǎo tiān yé: Also said as "wǒ de lǎo tiān yé," it's similar to "Good heavens!" with an undertone of "How could you do this?"

lèsè: Garbage.

lí: Pear.

liǎn: "Face," as in the front part of a person's head, or as used in the concept of saving face.

Little Emperor syndrome: This term originated to describe the sons in mainland China during the one-child policy. Because the son was the sole heir to carry on the family name, he was often overindulged.

mā: Shorthand for "mǎmá."

mǎmá: Mom.

máobǐ: Literally a "brush made of hair." It's a paintbrush used for Chinese calligraphy and painting. A unique technique is used with this type of brush: it's held perpendicular to the paper, with the index finger and thumb pinching the bamboo handle and the other three fingers curved beneath.

miànzi: Oh, this phrase. It is discussed in detail in the book, but for the sake of brevity, it is "saving face" times a thousand. It refers to a person or family's social status, reputation, and dignity.

nǎinai: Paternal grandmother.

nǐ hǎo: "Hello," to someone you see in person.

pípa: A four-stringed musical instrument sometimes known as the Chinese lute.

pō chūqù de shuǐ: Poured-out water. This phrase is part of a longer Chinese saying about how daughters who are married off are like poured-out water to their old family, leaving them behind to join her husband's family. This tradition is becoming less and less common.

pòng: What you say in mahjong when you pick up a tile discarded by any player to form a triple.

pìgu: Butt.

printed name seal: Analogous to a signature in the West, and is often used on official paperwork, contracts, etc.

qǐng jìn: Please enter.

qípáo: A tight-fitting Chinese dress with a high cut that dates back to the nineteenth century and has modernized over time.

Red Thread of Fate: A Chinese legend. It is believed that the god Yuè Xià Lǎorén uses an invisible red thread to connect two individuals destined to be together.

shāchá: A savory, slightly spicy sauce or paste made from soybean oil, garlic, shallots, chilies, brill fish, and dried shrimp. Often used with hot pot.

shěng qián: This phrase simply means "to save money," but because of the frequency and severity with which it is used by some Chinese parents, it has come to evoke a whole world of emotions and duty to some Chinese Americans.

shénjīng: Nerve or nerves.

Shénme huí shì?: "What happened?" or "What's going on?"

shítóu: Rock.

shūjuàn jiǎng: An honor given at Táidà University in Taipei to the top student in each department in each class each year.

shǔshú: Translates to "uncle" and is used to address family friends as well as any uncle who is younger than your father.

sī bǐng: Strip cake. Turnip sī bǐng is a flaky pastry with strips of turnip and often some seasoned meat and spring onion.

Táidà: National Taiwan University.

tiān āh: Similar to exclaiming, "Heavens!" *Tiān* means "sky."

tiánmiàn: Thick, smooth, sweet bean sauce.

wàigōng: Maternal grandfather.

wàipó: Maternal grandmother.

wéi: "Hello," used on the phone.

wǔxiá: A genre of Chinese fiction that usually follows a martial-artist protagonist.

xiàoshùn: Demonstrating filial piety. And so much more. My parents grew up learning about Confucius's Twenty-Four Filial Exemplars, which gives examples of what you should be willing to do for your parents, including warming an icy lake with your naked body to catch fish for your mother and feeding yourself to the mosquitoes to spare your parents' blood. While I was not taught the Exemplars as a child, obeying my parents was an expectation, not a request.

xiǎo zhěntóu: Little pillow.

xīnshǎng: To enjoy, appreciate, admire. This phrase somehow feels less like bragging and more sophisticated in Mandarin.

yéye: Paternal grandfather.

Zěnme gǎo de?: "What happened?" with an undertone of "What did you do wrong?"

zhàjiàng noodles: Noodles with soybean paste.

Zhōngguó jié: "Chinese knotting," sometimes called "decorative knots," is a craft dating back to the Tang and Song dynasty that is still practiced today. Long pieces of string are knotted and layered into elaborate designs to be used as wall hangings, jewelry, key chains, and more.

Acknowledgments

If you had told 2013 dentist me to pursue the writing path because I'd have three published books by 2020, I wouldn't have believed you. The journey thus far has been filled with wonderful, supportive people without whom none of this would be possible.

First, thank you to my readers. I write for you.

Kathleen Rushall: You are the best cheerleader, advisor, friend, and agent. Thank you for being you. Working with you is a privilege and comfort.

Jen Ung: There is something so special about our connection, and I'm grateful to have worked on this story with you. Even after three books, I still can't believe how deeply you understand my characters, and working with you on this one especially was an honor. Thank you for your enthusiasm for this story.

Kim Yau: Thank you for your passion and hard work. I'm grateful to have a film agent who understands my characters as much as you do.

Simon Pulse: Thank you for being my publishing home and for trusting me with my out-of-the-box ideas, e.g., my college-age characters in this book and *American Panda*, my weaving a historical story into a contemporary narrative in *Our Wayward Fate*, et cetera. BFYR: I'm thrilled to join your family!

Laura Eckes: Thank you for the stunning cover! I still can't get over how you managed to capture Chloe, Drew, and the feel of this book so perfectly! I love it so much I had it open on my computer as I edited.

Cassie Malmo: Thank you for being so on top of things and for all your hard work!

Special thanks to Mara Anastas, Liesa Abrams, Chriscynethia Floyd, Christina Pecorale, Lauren Hoffman, Caitlin Sweeny, Michelle Leo, Chelsea Morgan, Sara Berko, Karen Sherman, Tom Daly, Stacey Sakal, and Alison Velea.

Rachel Lynn Solomon: Thank you for cheering me on from the baby idea stage, for reading early pages, and for your friendship.

Thank you to my Chicago writing community: Stephanie Kate Strohm, Susan Blumberg-Kason, Samira Ahmed, Maddy Colis, Lizzie Cooke, Rena Barron, Kat Cho, Ronni Davis, Anna Waggener, Amelia Brunskill, Kimberly Gabriel, Michelle Falkoff, and Franny Billingsley.

Thank you to my friends and family who've supported me in this journey: Dan, Matt, Diana Fowler, Lexi Klimchak, Minnie Yang, and many more. Thank you, Abe Bueno de Mesquita, for always being my first teen reader! Brianna Wahl: Sorry for all the horrible Christmas cookies we made at my house in high school.

Thank you to booksellers, librarians, teachers, and bloggers for all that you do. I'm so grateful for the wonderful support you've so kindly shown me in my career.

Mom and Dad: I love you. Thank you for your love and support. And thank you for answering my endless questions and verifying so many things in my books. Dad, I loved laughing with you about the translations in this one. Mom, calling you to talk about Chinese culture, your stories, random Mandarin idioms (and other things not book-related) is a highlight of my day. I'm grateful for how close we've become thanks to these books.

Anthony: I dedicate each book to you because you're my biggest supporter. I don't know any other spouse willing to read every draft like you do, and you brainstorm with me so much I can't remember which ideas are whose. Thank you for living and breathing my books with me. Thank you for this life that's better than I could have dreamed. I love you more than three suns' worth.